AFTER
THE
ECLIPSE

AFTER THE ECLIPSE

FRAN DORRICOTT

TITAN BOOKS

After the Eclipse
US print edition ISBN: 9781785657887
E-book edition ISBN: 9781785657894

Published by Titan Books
A division of Titan Publishing Group Ltd
144 Southwark Street, London SE1 0UP

First edition: March 2019
2 4 6 8 10 9 7 5 3 1

A CIP catalogue record for this title is available from the British Library.

Printed in the USA.

What did you think of this book?
We love to hear from our readers. Please email us at:
readerfeedback@titanemail.com, or write to us at the above address.

To receive advance information, news, competitions, and exclusive offers online, please sign up for the Titan newsletter on our website:

TITAN BOOKS.COM

For Shadow, without whom this novel
would have been written two years earlier.

...and the sun has perished out of heaven and an evil mist hovers over all.

Homer's Odyssey XX. 345

Prologue
11 August 1999

THE DAY SHE BECAME a local legend, Olive Warren did not do as she was told.

Normally a well-behaved child, and as unlike her sister as it was possible to be, Olive hated to be told off. She liked quiet things: libraries, dinosaur bones in museums, her model of the solar system. People told her it was odd, but she figured if she wanted to be a curator, or even an astronaut, then liking rules and silence was probably a good thing.

Still, staying with Gran in the summer was never the same as being back at home in Derby. Here at Gran's, rules were bendy and punishments were non-existent, especially when her older sister was in charge. And anyway, this was an extra special day.

She'd been looking forward to the solar eclipse for weeks and she wasn't going to miss it because her big sister was too busy with her new "friend". She'd counted down on her calendar, ticking off the days until the event, even when Cassie made fun of her. When the day arrived, they went to Chestnut Circle, the centre of Bishop's Green's universe.

There was a big party; the town seemed more alive than

Olive had ever seen it, thrumming with the sense of possibility. Olive had been excited at the thought of all the people in town coming together to watch the eclipse – but the reality was overwhelming. The crowd was too thick, and although there was a stage and children playing party games she couldn't see any of what was happening. Some kid won a large cuddly unicorn and all Olive saw was the rainbow mane and a spindly golden horn.

The music was too loud. Olive longed to be back at Gran and Grandad's house, perhaps sitting on the roof outside the bedroom she shared with Cassie. She wished people would quieten down and just wait. Olive followed the minute hand on her watch. The main part of the eclipse was supposed to happen at ten past eleven but what if she couldn't see it?

Cassie and her friend Marion were hanging back in the little alley next to the corner shop, their heads bent together, totally oblivious to everything. They were whispering, their noses almost touching, completely ignoring Olive. It had been like this between them for days now, but today was worse because Marion was meant to be going on holiday soon and neither of them wanted her to go. Olive decided she didn't mind if Marion went. At least then she wouldn't have to share Cassie.

Olive's frustration boiled in her stomach as she watched them. She couldn't decide whether to do it – to stretch Cassie's one rule. Stay in sight. Her body was tense with the idea that she didn't have to do what Cassie said all the time.

"Olive, stand still, will you? Gran said you're meant to stay near me," Cassie called.

Olive sighed. She'd only been trying to get a better view. She couldn't see anything, least of all the sky, through the awning above the shop. They weren't here for Cassie to get all moony with the policeman's daughter. Cassie had even been grumpy when Olive went into the shop for a can of Coke even though she was only gone a minute and Gran had given her the money for it. It wasn't fair.

In that moment, Olive decided. She was going to break the rules, not just bend them. It was only going to be the once, and it wasn't going to be for very long. The crowd was pressing in on her, making her palms sweaty; even though nobody touched her she felt breathless. She just needed to see better. She needed what Gran called a "vantage point".

Olive knew Folly Hill from the picnic her gran and grandad had taken them on the summer before. It wasn't far, maybe a mile. Olive was good at walking, she enjoyed it, and Olive knew that from the hill she'd have a view to die for as the sun shimmered into darkness. She'd be able to see much of Bishop's Green in its little dip between the green hills, would be able to watch as the shadows chased across the streets near her gran's house. She could write her summer paper about it when she got back to school.

Plus she could probably get back before Cassie even noticed she was gone.

So she waited until Cassie and Marion were whispering again, hidden in the mouth of the alley. The candy-striped awning stretched around the side of the shop and they were huddled in the growing shade. They were so busy, so full of each other. Olive sort of wished she had a friend like Marion – somebody who just soaked up all of the badness and the arguments. Cassie never had to listen to Gran and Grandad talking about Mum and Dad and their problems; she was always on the phone with Marion, thinking about Marion. Talking about Marion.

Olive took the plunge. She sneaked out of the alleyway, skirting along the edge of the crowd and towards the road. There were a few cars parked beside the corner shop, stragglers coming late to the party in the Circle, but nobody paid any attention to Olive. The noise was growing from the people crowded around the fountain in the middle as the DJ on the stage gave a countdown. Half an hour to go until it was dark. Until the eclipse. Olive mouthed the word and felt the magic of it tickle her with excitement.

She'd been waiting for ages for this. She wasn't sure if it would get totally dark here – Gran said it would be the best down in Cornwall – but they stood a decent chance since it wasn't too cloudy. Bishop's Green was the perfect place to watch it, really. A town soaked in its own magic. It even had the Triplet Stones – sort of Druid stones up on the hillside – which Olive loved. Visiting her grandparents here was like going on holiday back in time, to a world where people still believed in omens and spells and lucky charms.

The eclipse was the event of the year. Of the decade. Olive could already feel the moon on her skin as the shadows lengthened. Gran had told her that crescent moons were meant to be the most powerful lucky symbols, but Olive figured eclipses probably beat them since they happened so much less often. It would be years and years before there was another one.

As she headed away from the noise there was an eerie quality to the sound fading away, as though that too was being eaten alive. She felt like she was running out of time. Willow Lane, the road out towards Folly Hill was dusty and uneven. It was deserted, Olive realised, because everybody who had thought of going to the hill to watch the eclipse was already there. The lane was longer than she remembered, too. Olive's chest was tight from the dryness of the air as she walked faster.

It must be gone eleven o'clock now. The dark was growing. She should have left sooner, should have been braver. Cassie was never going to chase after her. What had she been so afraid of?

She started to run. Slowly at first, a jog, but soon she was panting and running so hard her legs were going like jelly. She caught her foot in a dip, her knee crashing down and scraping the ground. She didn't make a noise. She hated to cry.

Her knee stung like it had a thousand tiny scratches – and her palms hurt too. They were gritty with the gravelly white dust from the path, not helped by the Coke she had spilled earlier, or the segment of orange she had eaten in the shop, the juice still tacky on her fingers. She wanted to wipe her palms on her shorts, but that would only sting worse. A little hiss escaped from her mouth.

She got back to her feet, her ankle complaining and the skin on her knee stretching and creasing in all the wrong places. She wiped her forehead with her arm, glancing up at the sky. Not yet, she thought. Not yet, please. I don't want to miss it.

Just then, somewhere behind her, she heard a rumbling sound. Willow Lane didn't look like the kind of place that saw many cars. Or many people, Olive thought, except dog walkers.

She turned as a van approached up the long, steep lane, the hedge on the left rising up high above her and making the sound seem like it was coming right at her. She stopped walking, squinting to see if she could see the driver.

She couldn't. Not at first.

The van slowed to a walking speed when it came closer. The driver waved. That's when she recognised him. Now he came to a stop, wound down the passenger window and leaned across to speak to her.

"I saw you leave the party," he said. "You heading for Folly?" He was wearing sunglasses hooked onto the neck of his shirt and a baseball cap like one her dad owned.

She nodded. The darkness was growing, like it was chasing them. She wanted to look upwards, to see the silhouette of the moon start to creep across the sun, but she didn't want her eyeballs to burn because her special glasses were still in her pocket. It felt rude to get them out now. The shadows were getting longer though, and Olive wished she'd brought a jacket. The birds had gone quiet, and all she could hear was the rumbling of the van and the far-off sounds of celebration from the Circle.

"You'll miss it if you don't get a move on," he said.

"I know."

"I can give you a ride, if you want. Just up the hill."

Olive thought about this, but only for a moment. She'd been

told to never take a car ride with a stranger, but everybody knew everybody in Bishop's Green. It was just that sort of place. Gran and Grandad gave Cassie and Olive the run of the town when they were here; Bishop's Green felt like the seaside, everybody smiling and friendly. And she knew him well enough by now, didn't she? It wasn't like at home, where Mum was always telling them to be careful and not to talk to strangers.

So she nodded again.

He opened the door from his side of the van and she clambered inside. It was surprisingly chilly inside, a breeze blowing through the open windows. She shivered, the sweat cooling rapidly on the back of her neck. She was thirsty, despite the Coke she'd had earlier, which just made her tongue feel fuzzy in the heat of the day.

The man noticed and handed her a bottle of water. She took it gratefully; the coolness of the bottle on the grazed skin of her hands was soothing even if it stung a bit. She drank greedily from the bottle.

"Why did you leave the party?" he asked as they moved off. The van felt like it was crawling up the hill and smelled faintly of antiseptic. "You looked like you were having a good time earlier."

"It was okay," Olive said hesitantly.

"But then Cassie ruined it. She's not really very nice to you, is she?"

Something about the man's voice made Olive stop. Her heart fluttered nervously, although she didn't know why. He was watching her as they drove up the hill, his gaze no longer fatherly.

"I…"

He'd been nice to her all summer – but now it didn't feel like he was protecting her. The way he said her sister's name made her shiver. The wrongness of it settled in Olive's stomach along with the stale water and she squirmed uncomfortably. It was like something had changed, right here in the van. The air was too cold, the sky outside too dark. Olive was belted in and she didn't like how the man seemed too close to her, how he smelled like antiseptic and somebody else's clean clothes.

She realised she didn't even remember his name.

Suddenly the silence was unnerving, the quiet she'd craved was too much. Olive wanted to stop the van. She wanted to get out. But she found that her mouth wasn't working properly; her tongue felt heavy and she was pretty tired. Panic started to worm about inside her. He'd rolled the windows up. The van kept moving. Further away from Cassie, from Gran and Grandad. From everything.

The man kept looking at her. He drove faster.

And as the road grew darker, as the sun was eaten by the moon, Olive Warren began to wish she had just done as she was told.

1

Monday, 16 March, 2015

THE SUN WAS JUST rising as I headed out for my run but I had been awake for hours. My eyes were gritty. I could feel the long sleepless night behind me like a spectre and my whole body ached with it – but I focused on the relief instead of the tiredness. I listened to the steady pounding of my feet on the pavement, and then on compact dirt as I pushed away from the residential streets of Bishop's Green and into the woods south of town.

I tried not to think at all, focusing on my breathing, my heartbeat, the ache in my legs. At least it wasn't the job that was going to kill me these days. That could only be a good thing.

When I'd traded city life and the battle for a decent journalism gig in London for my grandmother in Bishop's Green, I'd had visions of family dinners, of me playing the doting granddaughter who managed her grandmother's dementia with ease. Instead I felt like a prison warden – and that was on the days when Gran remembered who I was. The days when she didn't were harder still, having to explain who I was and why I always felt like such a failure.

I felt the itch even as I ran. The itch to call it quits, to hold my hands up and claim defeat. When I'd made the decision to leave London it had been on the back of a six-month rough patch. Losing my job had been hard enough – but that had been my own fault. The three-year relationship and the cushy London flat that I'd lost with it, however, still stung. But I shook the thoughts from my mind as I ran; it didn't matter why I'd left, I was here now.

I let my feet guide me as the thud-thud of my trainers drowned out my worries. I cut away from the trail, brambles scratching my legs as I widened into a loping, unsteady pace and let my breathing go wild. This was my first run in over a week and I relished the damp air on my hot cheeks, sucking in the sweet scent of evergreens on the March wind.

The woods began to thin, and I passed a gnarled old tree with a rope swing on a low branch. It was the sort of thing Olive and I would have spent hours playing on during our summers here, although she'd probably have spent a good fifteen minutes trying to determine its stability first. I smiled at the memory.

I'd been thinking of Olive a lot recently. She was always there, a soft phantom at the back of my mind, but it had been worse in the last months. Moving back to the town where we'd last been together had seemed cathartic over a drink in a distant London pub. Now it felt misguided. Morbid, even. And I knew that the looming solar eclipse was only upping the frequency of the nightmares.

I didn't want to think of my sister this morning. I was too

tired, too emotional. Gran had managed to escape in the night, wandering the fields for hours before I tracked her down. Her midnight escapades were getting more frequent, harder to prevent. I just wanted to run, to get sweaty and think about nothing except my aching body.

I stumbled back onto the trail and followed it out of the trees, panting now with the effort. A grassy bank came into view, and I slowed for a minute, blinded by a sudden brightness. Hands on my knees, I came to a complete stop at the edge of the lake.

It was how I remembered it. Big, dark, stretched taut like blown glass. The sun, fully risen now, was a distorted disc among reflected clouds. There weren't many people around yet but the weather wasn't entirely to blame. The whole town had lost the bustle I remembered from my childhood summers here. Still, by August the tourists would be back, drawn by Bishop's Green's reputation as a magical hotspot, blessed by the Triplet Stones or Druids, or whatever nonsense they'd been peddled to reel them in.

I was about to turn for home when something further down the bank caught my eye. I angled back, spying a group of people gathered beside a crop of small trees. They were rapt, staring across the lake. Two women with pushchairs, a man with a dog, a young couple. All of them focused on the same thing, which I saw for myself as I drew closer.

A boat in the water. And, judging by the official-looking people inside it, I'd bet my last cigarette that they weren't there for sport. I headed for the woman closest to me, my curiosity like an addiction. I never could shake it; it's what had led me into journalism in the first place – that, and the victims.

"What's going on?" I asked.

She half turned to me but kept her eyes fixed on the boat as it moved at glacial speed. I could hear its humming now, the wind pulling the sound towards us.

"That girl – the one that went missing on Friday. Nothing good ever happens on Friday the thirteenth, does it? God, I think they're looking in the water. Her poor family."

I felt my heartbeat stutter. I knew I'd been wrapped up with Gran, but how had I not noticed a child disappearing? The woman's superstition wasn't lost on me but I shrugged it off as the same kind of silliness the whole of Bishop's Green thrived on. I noticed that there were more people on the other side of the lake now. A few policemen. Dogs.

"She's only, like, eleven." The woman made a noise in the back of her throat. "This shouldn't happen here. Nothing like this has ever happened here."

I stopped listening, the blood roaring in my ears. A missing girl. Here, in Bishop's Green. The sun was suddenly blinding, a hot white circle in my eyes. When I blinked, black spots eclipsed my vision just like in my dreams. An eleven-year-old girl – missing.

I didn't correct her. Couldn't bring myself to speak. Instead I ran away, back towards town and home. The home that I'd hoped would be a fresh start.

The woman on the bank was wrong. Something like this had happened here before. Sixteen years ago it happened to my sister.

* * *

At home I made myself busy. Coffee on, laundry in the machine, and breakfast on the table in record time. I did the jobs I'd been avoiding, too. I made Gran's check-up appointment with her GP and even willingly spent ten minutes on hold to the adult day centre to rearrange a taster session. Adult jobs completed, I'd just settled down at the dining-room table with my mobile when the landline rang.

"Cassie, darling. How's it going?" My frayed nerves were soothed by Henry's familiar voice, gravelly from years of cigarettes and still betraying his Cornish roots despite three decades in London. It was good to hear from him. "How's northern living?"

"Still only in the Midlands," I replied. The same answer I'd given every time he'd called since I moved here two months ago. To Henry, anything north of the Watford Gap was northern enough. He still couldn't believe I'd gone through with it.

I could tell he half expected me to give up and head back to the anonymity of the city. And if I didn't come home of my own accord, he was determined to convince me. As if going back there, with no home and no job, would still be better than this.

"You sound shattered," he said. "Are you sleeping?"

"I wish." I rubbed my hand over my face and sighed. "I was out all night looking for Gran again. I don't know how she keeps doing it. I hid the key last night and she still managed to get out. I found her wandering about in a bloody field at just gone five this morning. She was frozen."

"Christ." Henry paused, a tapping sound on the receiver warning me that he was about to say something he thought I wouldn't like to hear. "I know you're not close to your dad, but can't he help you? It seems like a lot for one person to deal with, even with carers popping in during the day. This always seems to happen at night. I know you said they've assessed her and she's okay to be at home but—"

"Dad wants to put her in a home, Heno. He's no help. She's not his mother so I don't expect him to be. I just don't want that for her – not yet. She was always such a rock, you know? Especially after my mum died. I can't lock her up in one of those places without exploring our options first." I didn't say that living here with me as her jailer was hardly much different, but Henry seemed to sense it.

"Is she all right now, anyway? After last night."

"She's fine. Asleep again. Like I should be."

"Go to sleep then, darling. I'll call you later."

I didn't want Henry to go. After this morning, seeing the police on the water like that, I was rattled and I needed to hear his voice for a while longer. He had been an excellent mentor when I'd moved to London a decade earlier to begin my career in journalism, but over the years since he'd made an even better friend. He'd retired last year and still read all of my articles before I submitted them.

"Can't sleep now. Too much caffeine in me," I said. "Too little booze. Don't know why I thought moving here would be a good way to learn to be an adult."

I started to laugh but stopped myself.

"Spoken like a true millennial," Henry said.

There was a tense silence. Something unspoken in the air between us that sounded like, "At least you're not using the sleeping pills any more." Henry knew I had a tendency to self-medicate when I got stressed, but I hadn't told even him how bad it had become when I'd first moved back to Bishop's Green. It turned out that sleeping pills, which had always been my go-to way of switching off from the world, were a terrible choice when pitted against Gran's Houdini act. They made me groggy when I needed to be able to keep up with her disappearances. Now I didn't like to have them in the house.

But considering how little I'd been sleeping before my grandad died two months ago, and how the loss of my job might have had something to do with the three double brandies I'd consumed before decking the sexist bastard I was meant to be interviewing, it was probably better not to joke about the fact that I'd switched back to the booze. Honestly, it was lucky I'd only lost my job. If the guy had pressed charges I'd have been much worse off and a drink here and there would have been the least of my worries.

"You've got to get out of that house more, Cass," Henry admonished me finally, his voice deliberately light. "You sound like you're going stir-crazy. I knew you would. You're not meant to live in a cage."

"I've been out all morning."

"You know what I mean. You're a hack. No good hiding from it. You live for the story. Keeping yourself all cooped up in that house won't make you feel any better about the situation with your gran. Get yourself a job and things will seem brighter."

"No. You're right." I watched through the dining-room window as a flock of birds flew overhead. The sun seemed too big in the sky. Too bright. I thought again of the upcoming eclipse and then shook my head.

"Did you hear about the missing girl up your neck of the woods?" Henry asked, obviously realising he'd upset me. This was his peace offering. "Seems like your sort of story. You'd have dived at it if it were down here. I know you haven't been writing since you left London but this might be good for you. I'll read over anything you send me."

I'd had the news story open on my mobile even before Henry mentioned it. Like a scab I couldn't stop picking at, it had been calling to me all morning. And the more I tried not to think about it, the worse it was. But I wasn't sure I was ready to start writing again yet, ready to put myself back into that world.

"Not interested," I said. But I kept the article up, and I couldn't banish the curiosity from my voice. This girl – her name was Grace – was the same age Olive had been. The coincidence made me nervous.

"Liar," Henry said. "Doesn't look like the family have been interviewed yet. You should get in there. Try to get an exclusive with the mother—"

"Not. Interested."

"You're so bloody stubborn."

"No I'm not," I said. But I couldn't help smiling. Henry

was right. It was the sort of story I'd have leapt at before now. When my own sister was taken I'd hated the reporters who swarmed my family, but as I got older I'd become determined to be a voice for the victims, not a sensationalist. It was an attitude that had made me as many friends in the business as it had enemies. Most hacks didn't like that I referred to them – to us – as vultures. And meant it.

The missing girl, according to the article on my phone, had left school at half past three on Friday and hadn't made it home. No note, no indication that she was going anywhere. None of her friends knew anything. I scrolled down the article with the tip of my finger, itching for more information, when Henry's gravelly chuckle brought me back to my senses.

"All right, you're not stubborn," Henry said. "But I do think it would do you good. Give you a bit of focus. And anyway, it's an excuse to go and see—"

"Don't say it," I grumbled. "I haven't seen her since her dad's funeral, Henry. That was two years ago. Why would she want to see me now? It would be too…"

"Awkward? Come on, darling. I've heard the way you two talk on the phone. She can't get you to shut up. She's your Juliet."

"Oh God. Don't start that again. Just because you're super into gay marriage doesn't mean I have to be. Besides, it didn't exactly work out for the best for Romeo did it? I'd rather stick with Rosaline."

Henry let out a barking laugh but didn't press me any further. We chatted for another few minutes and I could almost pretend that I had everything under control.

Then Henry said, "Helen asked about you, you know. I told her you were okay. She seemed glad."

The pit in the bottom of my stomach opened right up and I thought my heart might fall in. I swallowed. Truthfully, it didn't hurt that she'd dumped me as much as it hurt that she didn't think we could stay friends. That, and the flat I'd lost when she said it. Moving to Bishop's Green had seemed like a good way to start over, to move forward, to stop wallowing and do something different, but I'd forgotten how isolating it could be here. How lonely. I hadn't even told Henry that my only friend in town was the guy who sold me coffee, and he was a good twenty years older than me.

"Thanks," I said softly. "Yeah, I'm okay. Talk later."

I hung up, pushing down the frustration. My gaze fell on my phone again, and I caught sight of the photograph in the article. Grace Butler's face was round and pink and scrubbed clean for a school picture. Blonde hair, blue eyes. She was positively angelic.

MISSING.

Pictured: eleven-year-old Grace Butler, who disappeared
on her way home from school on Friday, 13 March.

A growing sense of unease filled me as I read the article for the third time. Her stepdad, Roger Upton, was pictured as well, looking dishevelled and distraught.

She'd been missing two days and they were already dragging

the lake. Christ. I shook my head and pushed back the awful memory of that other time, sixteen years ago. Men on the lake, boats, a crowd gathered at the edge of the water.

I'd watched it unfold on Gran's television set, shaking and unable to believe that it was real. That it was happening. That Olive wasn't going to walk into the bedroom any moment and complain that I'd hidden her library book, and our summer holiday with Gran and Grandad wasn't going to go right back to being boringboring*boring*.

The memory gripped me tight. I saw the relentlessly blue sky – not even the decency of rain. The wind barely stirring the trees around the lake. The woman on the screen tolled a number that was growing and growing. A hundred and forty-six hours since the eclipse. A hundred and forty-six hours since she'd vanished. A hundred and forty-six hours since I'd made the worst mistake of my life.

And now it was happening again.

2

THE ROOM THAT WAS now my bedroom had once been my grandad's art studio. The walls were still decorated with the little four-leaf clovers he had believed to be so lucky. I still sometimes caught a whiff of acrylic paint, or turpentine and dusty brushes, although I'd cleared most of his stuff into the attic when I moved in after the funeral two months earlier. It was a comforting smell, one that reminded me of him and his warmth.

The spare bedroom was bigger than this one. Twice as big, actually, with a better view of the garden. But I hadn't touched it. It had been the room Olive and I used to share – and although it had been redecorated at some point I still saw the bunk beds and lava lamp. And a small part of me still feared the ghosts of Olive and myself that might haunt it.

I settled down at the desk in my poky little room with a fresh cup of tea. I couldn't stop thinking about the missing girl, Grace. And about Olive. What were the chances of two little girls the same age vanishing sixteen years apart in the same town? Probably quite high. Bishop's Green was bigger than it looked on first glance. It was a warren of residential streets around a central hive, a town that still believed it was a village, the fact remained that it could easily be a coincidence.

But we were due another solar eclipse and that set my teeth on edge, my journalist brain making all sorts of phantom connections. The timing was too much of a coincidence – more of a coincidence than anything else.

They're not connected, I told myself. *They can't be.* Olive was taken during a public event. A chance abduction during the minutes of murky twilight, everybody too busy counting omens or waiting for the do-over the eclipse had promised them. I tried to think clinically. This Grace kid, she just hadn't come home from school. She might even be a runaway, although eleven was a bit on the young side. Perhaps she had fallen out with her friends, her parents; perhaps she had simply been in the wrong place at the wrong time.

I bit my lip. The box in front of me on Grandad's old desk was battered, the Dr. Martens logo on the side badly faded. Its corners were crushed from years of being shoved about inside my wardrobe and the lid was caked with a layer of dust.

I always took it with me when I moved. It had followed me from Bishop's Green to Derby, and then to Sheffield and York and then London. And now back again, full circle. I rarely opened it, and when I did it was usually to shove some other painful Olive-related memory inside.

Now I wanted to look. Needed to, even. Maybe it was like Henry said – I needed a distraction. Or validation. I wasn't sure.

I took a shaky breath and lifted the lid. Inside, it was exactly as I remembered, filled with photos and stickers, writing on napkins and even a couple of newspaper articles, folded into yellowing squares. There was a birthday card Olive had made me. One I'd told her I'd ditched.

I sifted through pictures of Mum, me and Olive. Dad, always behind the lens, had captured us on the beach, at Christmas, at the park. The photos were familiar, worn by my teenage fingers. The ones of Mum were the most faded, all of them taken in the years before Olive was abducted. Back when Mum was still her strong, occasionally smiling self.

I picked up one of Olive on a roundabout, and beneath it was one I'd found on Grandad's noticeboard of me and my sister in the garden right here in Bishop's Green. It must have been taken the summer she was abducted. We were on the verge of hysterical laughter as Olive accidentally swore at the camera as she tried to make Ginger Spice's peace sign. I looked away, the image of Olive frozen in the nineties with her Buzz Lightyear T-shirt, friendship necklaces and platform trainers making my eyes begin to itch.

This was stupid. I was only going to upset myself. I started to put the things away, organising them carefully, until my fingers brushed the journal at the bottom of the box. I felt a shudder of something. Anticipation? Fear? I didn't even know why I'd started looking but now I couldn't stop.

This was my "Olive Diary".

The psychiatrist I saw after Olive disappeared suggested I keep a journal. She didn't know that I already had one. I was sure if she'd known the sorts of things I'd filled it with she'd have changed her mind about it being good for me. It was filled with my loopy fourteen-year-old scrawl, stuck throughout with newspaper clippings and other bits of paper. It had been an obsession.

I flicked through and my fingers came to rest on a page almost of their own accord.

I read in the library that most child abductions happen because of family. The police aren't looking for a stranger for Olive. Why?? Mum was at work. Gran was getting her hair done. Grandad was at the vet's with Molly. That leaves me and Dad.

And then there was a question. Biro scrawl, shaky and smudged out of shape.

DAD. Where was he?

I sat back, my heartbeat in my throat and my hands starting to sweat. I remembered the damp hotness that preceded the writing of this note. Too many people crammed into my grandparents' house – too much crying. I was sitting on the floor outside the kitchen, knees to my chest. Mum and Dad were out of sight but I could still hear them.

"You have to tell me where you were. You owe me that much at least."

"I don't owe you anything, Kathy." My dad's voice was taut, tired, the secret eating him up. "How can you think I had anything to do with this? How can you think I'd hurt her?"

"How can I not? You won't tell me anything." A pause. *"Did* you hurt her?"

"No." Not an exclamation. A weary statement of fact. The same answer to the same question.

"Tell the police, then. They know you're lying. Cassie knows. I know. At least tell somebody."

"It's not that simple."

"So you are lying, then."

"Fucking hell, Kath. This isn't my fault. Cassie was meant to be watching her."

I hadn't been able to stop myself. The kitchen was hot and the windows fogged with the endless heat Mum kept blasting because she was cold all the time. I marched into the room, whole body shaking.

Before I could stop myself I was howling.

"I didn't mean to. I didn't mean to! I told her to stay where she was—"

"Don't you blame her. Don't you *dare* blame her!" Mum was shouting too. She moved to put her hand on my shoulder but I couldn't bear it. Couldn't stand the thought of being touched because it seemed like the grief had pierced every inch of me and even my skin ached.

Dad didn't move, frozen in the corner, arms straining against the counter behind him as though he was having to hold himself back.

"Where were you?" I screamed at him.

He didn't speak.

"It wasn't her fault," Mum repeated. Over and over. "Not her fault. She's all we've got."

Dad and I stared at each other. My breath heaved and with every movement I thought I would be sick. Because it *was* my fault. Even Dad thought so. And although Mum hadn't said it, I knew the only reason she didn't blame me, couldn't blame me, was because then she would have to agree with him.

I'd felt myself get hollower and somehow heavier too as I stormed out and then slunk up to my bedroom, sickness churning in my belly.

Dad hadn't answered the question. Where had he been? *Could* he have hurt Olive? He hadn't been at work like he'd said. The police had told us.

By the time I'd written Dad's name in my diary I knew things would never be the same again. He'd known it, too. He had seen the doubt in my face. There were no words that could change what had happened between us, that fracturing, splintering – even after the police cleared him. It wasn't about truth, it was about guilt. I felt guilty for losing Olive, and he felt guilty for it too.

Then he moved out. And that was the last time Mum ever stood up for me – or did anything that might have been considered warm or passionate, or anything much at all.

My mouth had grown dry. I swilled cold tea around my teeth with a grimace, realising with a jolt that I'd been looking in the box for a sort of confirmation – about my own instincts. I'd known something was up with my dad long before my mum had. I'd known Dad hadn't been telling the truth about where he'd been, what he'd been doing on days when he was meant to be working even before Olive was taken, but I'd never listened to my gut. In fact, I'd gone out of my way to pretend that I hadn't noticed.

Even if he hadn't hurt Olive, Dad was guilty of lying. And the feeling I'd had about my own dad was the same sort of feeling I got when I looked at the picture of Grace Butler's stepfather.

He had a secret.

I knew, suddenly, that Henry was right. It was too late to pretend that I wasn't interested in Grace's disappearance. Because I was interested. I couldn't let a good story go without at least a quick look, especially a story like this one. And I couldn't live off the money Grandad had left me for ever.

And, *dammit*, that meant that there was somebody I needed to speak to about a job.

Marion's house was almost identical to the one I shared with Gran, right down to the dry-stone wall out front and the lace curtains in the window. She'd inherited it when her father died and it didn't look like she'd changed much.

I sat in my car for several minutes working up the courage to go and knock on her door. Just like I'd been putting off driving over here all day. I felt like a teenager again, my palms sweaty and my heart racing. It had been two years since I'd seen Marion – actually physically *seen* her – and now I didn't know why I'd let it go this long.

Just as I was about to suck up the courage to get out of

my car, I saw Marion's front door open. Out stepped a dark-skinned man in a suit, smart white shirt and a red tie that flapped in the wind. I saw a hand reach out – Marion's – to squeeze his shoulder. Then he cut across the drive and passed my parked car on the way to his.

I told myself that it didn't matter – that he was probably a colleague and anyway I didn't have the right to be upset when I hadn't seen her in ages – but the sight of Marion touching somebody in such a familiar way made my stomach lurch. And she hadn't told me about him when we last spoke. Did she want to hide him from me? Was she embarrassed – or concerned I'd ruin it for her?

When I finally made it to the front door, I was so wound up that I'd forgotten everything I wanted to say. And I had no time to compose myself because suddenly, there she was, door open wide and a small smile on her face.

She looked good. Really good. Her dark hair was pulled back into a messy bun and her fringe was just that little bit too long. She'd probably only been home from work for an hour or so, probably having a drink with *him*, and she was dressed in a creased white shirt and black trousers. I noticed that she still wore the necklace I had bought her. A little golden acorn – an amulet that in Norse folklore had symbolised luck and protection, the oak tree immune to the lightning and wrath of Thor. I didn't believe in that sort of rubbish, but Marion had spent too long in Bishop's Green and the town's superstitious nonsense had well and truly claimed her.

The last time I'd seen Marion had been at her father's

funeral. I'd come to town just for that. We were both emotional. Marion's dad was her only family. I'd just had my first massive fight with Helen and I wasn't good for anybody, much less somebody who was grieving.

We hadn't had words as such but I had too much to drink at the bar after the service and ending up puking in her kitchen sink, which was probably the low point of my year – although it wasn't the first or the last time during that year that I drank too much. After that we stayed in touch by email and still had regular phone conversations, but I was more careful. She at least couldn't *see* me doing anything that stupid again.

Now I was surprised to see the lines that had crept in around the corners of her eyes. They made her look more sophisticated – more grave, somehow – than before.

"Hi, Cassie," Marion said simply.

I was overwhelmed by a rush of warmth, and then embarrassment. I was still a mess – a sober mess this time, granted – but Marion looked impeccable. High cheekbones, strong jawline, brows perfectly groomed; she was sleek, almost cat-like; her eyes, bright blue ringed with steely grey, sparkled with kindness.

"Your fringe is too long."

It was the first thing I could think of to say. I saw Marion reach up self-consciously, but she smiled anyway.

Two years. For two years we'd been dancing around the subject of me coming back to town to visit. And I never had. Yet here I was, without warning, living only a few streets away just like when we were kids. Marion didn't look surprised.

"Do you want to come in?" she asked. I didn't want to. My heart was thudding and I felt like I might puke. But I also did want to – very badly. So I nodded and followed her inside, trying not to think about the man I'd just seen leaving. I couldn't imagine Marion with a boyfriend. I knew that time changed people but she'd never been particularly interested in men. Especially not the clean-cut type. And she never dated colleagues or Suits.

"I did wonder when you'd finally screw up the courage." I saw her lips twitch as she led me into the dimness of her lounge. "I've only been waiting six weeks. I saw you at the police fundraiser last month with your gran."

I avoided meeting her gaze. I hadn't realised she'd seen me. I'd done my best to duck for cover, heart hammering in the way of a nervous teenager. I tried not to look sheepish now, but the warmth in my cheeks belied my embarrassment.

"Sorry," I said.

Marion shrugged.

"I'm sorry I missed your grandad's funeral," she said. "I know he meant a lot to you. I just didn't think it was my place to show up out of the blue."

It was my turn to shrug. I hadn't expected her to be there. I hadn't told her it was happening, and although she could have found out the date I wasn't surprised when she hadn't shown up. Now I didn't know why I'd shut her out.

"It's okay," I said.

The lounge was crowded with travel knick-knacks that had belonged to her dad. On the mantelpiece there was the Statue of Liberty in miniature, her torch alight with a colour-changing rainbow flame. Next to her was a snow globe from Cornwall with two busty ladies on a beach. And on every surface there were elephants: statues, cushions with elephant embroidery, artistic photographs of elephants bathing, even a little plaque above the door. Elephants. More elephants than you would think could fit in one room, symbolising wisdom, power, loyalty – and overcoming death. These didn't belong to Marion's father.

Marion noticed my gaze.

"For the Hindu god Ganesha," she said. "The remover of obstacles." She gestured to the sofa. "The kettle's actually just boiled. Sit and I'll get you a cup of tea."

I sank onto the sofa, hands between my knees, frustrated by how awkward I felt. It wasn't like we didn't know each other. I had often thought that I knew Marion better than I knew myself. But our friendship had been virtual for a long time; emails, text messages, phone calls – no substitute for the real thing.

I thought back to the summers I'd spent here, the long weeks with Marion out in the fields or hanging around Earl's café for cheap hot chocolates or sundaes. It had been our yearly ritual – Olive and me. Summer in Bishop's Green with the grandparents while Mum and Dad stayed at home so they could work. We'd loved it; the freedom, the seaside feeling of this landlocked town with its amusement arcades and ice-cream shops right down the middle. Its obsession with symbols of luck and prosperity. The fact that you could walk pretty much anywhere in less than an hour.

And Marion, the policeman's daughter, who knew all the

short-cuts, the best places to get two-penny sweets in great big paper bags, and which arcades had the best win-lose ratios. She always knew which department stores were having closing down sales, which boutique was flavour of the month, and which film screenings we could sneak into without being caught.

She was the prettiest girl I'd ever seen.

When Marion came back into the room, I jumped. She was carrying two cups, and she handed one to me. I wanted it to be like no time had passed, wanted for us to be able to talk easily, but the years stretched between us.

"I knew you'd come if I waited long enough. You've been ignoring my emails."

I had. Since moving to town, I'd put off answering anything that wasn't urgent. I'd pretended it was Gran, that I was busy, but it wasn't true. I actually had a lot of free time.

"I'm going green," I said. "Less tech. More… Zen."

Marion laughed. "I get it. I'm terrifying." She narrowed her gaze. "You look tired. Is it – stuff with Helen? I know you were feeling a bit down when we last spoke…"

I shrugged but I knew she wasn't being mean. She was reminding me that it had been weeks. That I'd been avoiding her since I told her I was thinking about moving to town. It meant she'd been waiting for me.

"No," I said firmly. "I haven't spoken to Helen since I moved out. That's all over. More than over, actually. It's just Gran. I'm trying to get a better care situation in place. Grandad was doing so much for her and it's just exhausting."

Marion put her cup of tea down and my heart stuttered as

it looked like she might reach over and touch me. But she only straightened some magazines on the coffee table. I exhaled.

"I'm sorry," Marion said. "If you'd told me I could have given you a hand or something. I don't know. Still, I'm glad you've finally come."

"Did you miss me?"

"I missed having an excuse to check my emails at work." She smiled again. "But anyway, I get the feeling that you're not here just to see me. What brought you out of the Cass-cave?"

I was about to deny it, but I couldn't. Even after all this time, she'd know. I never was a very convincing liar.

"Grace Butler," I said. Marion didn't flinch exactly, but something about her body language changed. Banter aside, I could see that my being here had affected her, and so had the missing kid. But I'd already said it, so I continued, "She's been missing for a couple of days, hasn't she? I wasn't going to bother you – but then I saw that she's the same age that Olive was... Anyway, I got interested."

"You know I shouldn't discuss it, Cassie, even with you. I could get in trouble."

"I'm just intrigued. I don't know. I was thinking about writing something. It's just with Gran, and the eclipse coming up in a few days... I'm a bit antsy. I mean, they're dragging the lake. That's kind of a big deal."

I thought of the poor girl's parents, having to watch it all happen, powerless to stop it or to help. I felt my insides clench, as they always did when I thought of the families.

"Do you have any leads?" I asked.

Marion sighed. Shook her head. "She's been gone two days and we're not getting anywhere. Plenty of leads but nothing is panning out. A lot of people are trying to help, organising searches and things, but we have to consider the worst while hoping for the best. You've spoken to enough families in the aftermath of things like this. You know how it goes."

Marion exhaled again, and I saw that her knuckles were white when she picked up her cup. I started to get up.

"Sorry. I'll go. I didn't want to pry. I realise it's early days."

"No, Cassie. Wait." Marion didn't move to stop me, but I heard an urgency in her voice and when I looked I saw a flash of indecision in her face. "I know it's rough for you. I've been thinking about Olive a lot lately, too. Especially with the eclipse. But do you think this is for the best? Grace Butler isn't your sister – I don't know if it's a good idea for you to connect—"

I tried to fight my growing frustration.

"Come on, Marion," I said. "You know me. The personal touch is what people want. They want to feel like they know them – the family, the police. Those people out there, helping you search, they want to know who they're helping. All I'm asking is for a bit of info. And I'm a bloody good journalist."

The more I talked to Marion, the more I realised that I wanted to do this. To get my life back. To claw back my reputation, make a living. To help find that little girl and bring her home.

"If I don't agree, you're still going to do this, aren't you?" she asked.

I faked a grin. "Yes."

"Look… I can probably put in a good word for you with the family. Strictly a suggestion. They're not speaking with a lot of the press – but I know they've been looking for somebody to write something. I wasn't going to get involved with that side of things, but maybe I can make an exception for a bloody good journalist."

This time my smile was real. I took in Marion's wiry strength, trying not to let my gaze linger. It would be good to have an excuse to see her again, too.

"Just be careful though, will you? This is sensitive. I don't know if you remember what it's like here, but… it's not like London. People are softer. They won't want an outsider digging around. Just wait for me to set this interview up, okay?"

I nodded, but didn't agree. Marion was half right: this wasn't like London, but people here weren't soft. I remembered that much from Olive's disappearance. They might be more subtle than city people, but they would fight tooth and nail to protect their own. To keep their secrets. Perhaps even if it meant that another little girl never came home.

3

Tuesday, 17 March 2015

THE NEXT MORNING I headed to Ady's corner shop on the Circle. It wasn't far from Gran's, and despite the prices being a little higher I never had to queue inside and Ady was a real stickler for keeping the shop pristine. Besides, it reminded me of my grandad, who swore there was something better about the cigarettes behind the counter than any supermarket in a ten-mile radius.

Ady had only just opened as I entered and he still looked half asleep. His grey-brown curls were wild, his warm eyes crinkling at the corners. He was fixing flyers to the noticeboard behind the till, where his daughter was sitting with a colouring book. Ady didn't allow her to have a phone yet because she was only just out of primary school, and there was something refreshing about her old-fashioned creativity instead of mindless scrolling.

I scanned the wall and saw a flyer for a fun run Ady was hosting in a couple of weeks for the local RSPCA, and another for a jumble sale at the church. Today was St Patrick's Day and there were several posters adorned with four-leaf clovers and cartoon leprechauns. Then one that made me shudder:

an invitation for people to enjoy tea and cakes in the garden at Earl's café while watching the eclipse on Friday.

Suddenly I could taste heat and sweat, the scent of fruit in the air as I remembered the darkness, the silent birds, the silvery sky. Blinking, I swore I could still see the crescent burn pattern behind my eyelids.

"Morning." Ady's daughter, Tilly, was dressed in school clothes, her white shirt so wide on the shoulders it looked like a tent. Her short blonde-streaked hair was pinned back with a brass clip in the shape of an owl.

"Hi. Nice hair clip," I said, wiping my slick palms on my jeans. I was terrible with kids, but I actually tried with Ady's daughter because he was probably the nicest person in town – the only one to date to make me feel welcome in Bishop's Green. Most people seemed to have a sixth sense for Londoners in their midst and acted accordingly. "Those were all the rage when I was a kid. You look pretty."

"Thanks," she said awkwardly, reaching up to touch it, knocking her glasses with the tip of her thumb so they sat crookedly. A green four-leaf clover ring on her finger caught the light. "It was my mum's. Dad's really into them. Owls, I mean. For like… wisdom and that."

Ady's wife had died when Tilly was a baby. I didn't know what to say so I grabbed the newspaper I had come for, Grace's face smiling up at me.

"I'm going out to look for her after I close up," Ady said when he noticed my gaze. He stopped to straighten Tilly's crooked glasses and she waved him away. "There are a few

44

of us going to walk the path behind her school – Arboretum Secondary. You should come. We need all the manpower we can get."

"That's nice of you," I said.

"I'm always nice."

I laughed weakly. "Sure you are. I'm just not sure I'll be much use. I've been thinking a lot about my sister lately. Trying to remember. Grace being missing is bringing up a lot of stuff. A lot of questions about Olive and what happened to her. Do you… remember anything?"

"I'm sorry," Ady said awkwardly. "It was a long time ago."

I avoided his gaze, not wanting to see the pity in his eyes. "Yeah. Okay. Anyway, are we still up for that coffee morning at the end of the month?" I was hoping that getting Gran out and about more might help her to feel a little bit less like a prisoner at home. Ady did so much for charity that he had become the central point of my sad little social calendar. Never mind that he was the only point.

"Sure," he said. I could see he had questions about what I'd said. About Olive. He started to say something and then changed his mind. "Remind me next week. I can't really think about it right now. Organising these searches is frying my brain."

I paid for my newspaper and a coffee from Ady's little instant machine, not trusting myself to speak. I'd spent all morning telling myself that I mustn't keep thinking about Grace as though she was like Olive. Especially after what Marion had said. *She isn't your sister.* But I couldn't help it. That flyer for the eclipse viewing at Earl's almost felt like a sign. Of what, though, I wasn't sure.

In the car I spread the newspaper out across my knees so that the front page lay before me, a new photo of Grace Butler beside the old one. This one looked like a more recent picture from somebody's phone, the quality grainier but more up-close, the colours dark and muted. She was very blonde, dressed in jeans and a plain T-shirt, no jewellery except for the silver and black mood ring in the shape of a mermaid on her finger as she gave a thumbs-up to the camera. The ring – it reminded me of something, but I couldn't place it.

Below it there was a smaller image, a man with dark hair cropped short and day-old stubble darkening his jaw. He was tall, but a little podgy, dressed in a too-tight polo shirt. The caption read: Eleven-year-old Grace's stepfather says, "Don't hurt my daughter."

The mother still hadn't agreed to be interviewed. I thought about Henry's suggestion. Marion's offer to recommend me. It was the sort of story I could sell. I looked at the photograph of the stepfather for a long time, unable to shake the oily squirming in my stomach – the same feeling I'd had yesterday. Something wasn't right.

Marion had asked me to wait but I knew from experience that once one interview was granted, others were likely to follow. I wanted to get a feel for Grace's mother, see what she might tell me about her husband.

I didn't like the look of him and, frankly, I wanted to know why.

4

BISHOP'S GREEN WAS LAID out in much the same way as many similar towns in Derbyshire. It had grown up around a tiny village-like hub of gift shops, restaurants and tacky boutiques, drawing tourists in with the surrounding lush fields and the Triplet Stones and keeping them with the promise of more overpriced cafés than they could visit in a day. The fountain in Chestnut Circle sat at the heart of town, and the main shopping streets with the arcades and art galleries branched off from there, the houses getting bigger and grander the further from the middle you went.

The street I wanted was lined with cherry blossoms, a fifteen-minute walk from Grace's school, and right on the other side of the Circle from where I lived with Gran. I took a photo of the trees and made a mental note to show it to her later, when the carer had gone. She'd always loved cherry blossoms.

There were only two secondary schools in town, both almost interchangeable to me but probably less so to the parents and students who fought for the places at Arboretum, which was the smaller of the two. Figured.

I parked my Fiesta under one of the blossom trees and sat

for a minute. The street was speckled with pastel pink petals, as were several of the cars that were parked along it. I wondered how many of these belonged to journalists, camping out and waiting for a chance interview.

I was going to go one better.

This area of Bishop's Green was all Tudor houses and neat front gardens, lace curtains in the windows and freshly painted front doors. It felt almost old-fashioned, but wealthy, the houses decently sized but outside of the maze of more central streets surrounding mine and Marion's little houses.

One house stood out from the rest here, not because of the building itself but because of the flowers and messages of hope that lay against the garden fence. Well-wishers had left teddy bears and pictures of angels, which, I thought, were more than a little premature.

The garage to the house was open, and as I approached I heard a clatter. An errant basketball rolled out into the daylight. It was followed by a woman. Skinny and dressed in a white T-shirt and dark tracksuit bottoms. I inched closer, not wanting to startle her as she picked it up.

"Excuse me," I called gently. "Mrs Upton?"

The mother of the missing girl spun around. She looked older than I had expected. Haggard, almost. I strode forward and stuck out my hand.

"Mrs Upton, my name is Cassie Warren," I said. "You don't know me but I was hoping we could have a chat."

The woman froze, her expression shifting from startled to suspicious. Her hair was blonde but dark roots showed, the curls limp and a little greasy. She folded one arm across herself, tucked underneath her small chest, while the other dangled at her side and she nervously spun her wedding ring round and round her finger with her thumb. The circle made me think of the eclipse, that white-gold band in the darkness.

"Are you with the newspapers?" she asked. "You're not police. I'm not talking to the papers."

"I'm not a detective," I agreed. "But I would like to have a chat with you – about your daughter. I'm not like those other vultures."

I watched her for a second, taking in her posture, the way she wasn't watching me, not really. The way she was looking behind me, even as we spoke, even as her brows dipped and she started to leave.

"I know what you're going through." This halted her in her tracks. I saw a flicker of anger in her face, a *how dare you* bubbling on her lips. But I ploughed on. "I've been there. I know how this feels. You're out here waiting for her, aren't you?"

I'd seen it before, the look of defeat that had come when she saw it was me in her driveway and not her missing child. I'd seen it in my mother a hundred times. Each time her eyes were duller, her lips thinner. I'd seen it in my own face, too, in the years that followed.

"You want to be here when she comes home. To be the first person she sees."

Mrs Upton's blue eyes started to water and she blinked hard. A cold wind whipped down the street and she wrapped both arms around herself.

"Listen, Mrs Upton, I want to help. If you want me out there on the streets that's fine, but I can do more than that. Can we please just go inside? You're no good to Grace out here in the cold."

Her gaze was fixed on my face, as though she was seeing me for the first time since hearing my name. She pointed at me, her finger hovering just below my collarbone.

"I know you," she said. "I recognise your name. Don't I? Oh God. You're that girl's sister…" She stopped, sucked in a mouthful of the cool air, her whole body trembling. "I think you'd better come inside."

The Upton home was tastefully decorated in shades of cream and brown. Vases filled with fake flowers and sprays of twigs filled all available surfaces, illuminated with what looked like Christmas lights. We went through the open garage straight into the downstairs hall, the polished wooden floors echoing our footsteps back at us.

Mrs *Call-Me-Adelaide* Upton led me into a large open-plan kitchen-diner with patio doors looking out over a neatly pruned garden. On the kitchen windowsill were a few photographs in silver frames. A wedding photo of Mr and Mrs Upton, faded from the sun; a picture of two blonde girls in bikinis eating ice cream on a beach. Another photo was propped up without a frame, a group of girls all crowded together, wearing almost identical outfits, and another taken on the same day, of Grace posing and pointing at the camera. I noticed that she was wearing the same ring she had been in the other photograph. Something about it tugged at my thoughts as it had done earlier, but I couldn't think what it was. The ring seemed familiar, maybe, but I wasn't sure why.

All of the girls in the group photo were laughing. I couldn't suppress the pang of sadness that washed through me. I studied them, knowing I might need to remember their faces.

"Are these two recent?" I asked.

Adelaide nodded.

"Last week. I printed them both off. I like that she's happy in them." She stopped. Shrugged, helplessly.

We sat down at the small dining table overlooking the grass and trees outside. I noticed an empty swing set out there, and an old Wendy house that was covered in a patina of moss.

She sat opposite me, facing away from the empty garden. Waiting for me to speak.

"I read about Grace in the newspaper," I said. "I want to help... My... My ending wasn't a happy one, but yours can be."

My tongue felt heavy but I knew I had to press on. Mrs Upton might decide any moment that she didn't want me here.

"I'm a journalist," I said. "I know that's a dirty word right now, but I'm not like the others. I practically grew up here. And I know from personal experience how scary this all is – how you don't know who to trust. But you can trust me."

"You're the one who lost a sister," Adelaide asserted again. "Aren't you? All those years ago? People have mentioned her because she went missing too. They think Gracie was – *abducted*. Oh God, they never found your sister and people think..."

She started to cry.

Hearing it laid out like that I felt a numbness begin to seep into me again, that same old feeling that I'd almost, but not quite, forgotten. But the numbness was better than the sadness so I let it wash over me and then sat up a little straighter.

"That's why I can't just sit here and do nothing," I said firmly. "Sometimes people tell me things they don't tell the police – because of my sister." Also because I don't look threatening, and I don't always follow the rules, but I didn't say that part. "I'd like to ask questions for you, Mrs Upton. I know the area relatively well and I know how things work."

Adelaide didn't say anything for a moment, chewing on her lip as she began to twist her wedding ring around again. I watched the metal band as it spun and spun.

"Do *you* think there's a connection between Gracie and your—"

"I don't think anything," I said firmly. "And the police won't jump to any conclusions either. The chances are that Grace just went somewhere without telling anybody. Kids these days, they're so independent with their phones and tablets."

"But Gracie knows she's not allowed to talk to people she doesn't know. And she's a good girl, she doesn't break the rules."

She started to cry again, this time giving in to whole-body sobs that wracked her until her shoulders were hunched and she'd almost doubled up on herself. I found a box of tissues on the counter and brought a couple to her, waiting by her side until she could speak again. I didn't say that that's what people had said about Olive, too.

"What do you need from me?" she asked.

"Just tell me everything you can. Tell me what sort of person Grace is. Does she like school? Does she have a favourite subject?" This was for Mrs Upton's benefit as much as my own; if I was going to help, in any sort of way, I needed to know who Grace was, but telling me about the mundane things might help to calm her down, too. With the information she gave me I'd decide where to go next.

"She's quiet. Sort of shy, I guess." Adelaide fought back a hiccup. "But she likes school. Or she did, until recently. You know how kids are, changing their minds every few minutes. She likes history, though, the teacher is really helping her to come out of her shell." Mrs Upton smiled sadly. "Last week she told me they were doing a family tree, but Grace didn't want to do it – you know, because of John – her dad – leaving and the fact that I married Roger.

"She said that some of the kids teased her. Said her dad didn't love her and that's why he left. I told her it wasn't like that – you know how it is. We just fell out of love. Things got a bit nasty between us but she never saw any of that, she was only a baby, and we're okay now – well, not *okay*, but we keep out of each other's way. Gracie's too young to understand that's what happens sometimes. It happens all the time now, but some of the kids at Arboretum are – well, a bit stuck up, honestly."

I took out a notebook and began to make notes. Once again I found myself thinking of Olive, of our own parents' crumbling marriage when we were kids, and how sensitive she always was about it. I remembered Olive asking a question, only a few weeks before she was taken: "Will Dad still love us the same if he has to go away?" At the time I'd told her she was being silly, that Dad wasn't going anywhere. I even half believed it. But looking at Dad now, with his new wife and his new daughter… Maybe Olive had been right to ask.

I tried to clear my head. Olive's ghost was making me itch, her cold, eleven-year-old hands tracing my spine like they hadn't in years. I had to focus.

"I don't know how this is of any use," Mrs Upton said. "I told the police everything, about the kids and the teachers. They asked if she had any special routines, and if she has any friends outside of school, but she doesn't, really. Not that I know of. Just those girls in her class."

"Anybody she's particularly close to?" I prodded.

Adelaide shook her head. "I think there's one girl mainly, but I don't know her that well. Her name is Bella. They've not been friends for very long, only since October, November-time."

Another onslaught of tears distracted Adelaide from her train of thought and I had to wait for her to stop crying again before I could ask any more questions. We spoke some more, about Grace and school and her habits, but mostly I made notes on Adelaide. On her posture, the obsessive spinning of her wedding ring, the glazed look on her face. If Henry wanted me to get writing again, this was the jackpot of human emotions. And yet I couldn't help feeling like I was taking advantage of her, so eventually I put my notebook away and just listened.

I wanted to ask about her husband, but I had a strong

feeling that Adelaide would clam up if I did. She hunched her shoulders when she said his name, as though she'd already been asked uncomfortable questions about Grace's relationship with her stepfather.

I tried to smile in what I hoped was an encouraging way. I wasn't going to ask her any more of those questions. Not right now, anyway. It was all about trust, building it a layer at a time.

"I'm sorry," she said. "I'm such a mess. That's why I didn't want to talk to anybody. I just keep thinking that it was something I did. That there was something I could have done…"

"You're doing everything you can. Grace's case is in good hands. The police are a good team. I know the DI. She's incredibly capable and very good at her job."

I reached out. Mrs Upton seemed like a hugger. Some women I interviewed craved physical contact, the gentle reassurance that they were still there, that they still existed. These women were the opposite of my mother, who in those early days of Olive's disappearance became cool and aloof. A woman made of stone. Too afraid to speak in case her emotions got the better of her again.

I pressed my warm hand to Mrs Upton's cold one and felt it relax in my grip.

"So, Grace was walking home from school on Friday. And she never arrived?"

Adelaide nodded. "I thought she'd just gone back with one of her friends. She's done that before, but usually she'll call to let me know whether she'll be home for dinner. But you know what kids are like: they forget; time isn't important. I called her a couple of times and got voicemail, but she leaves her phone on silent or it runs out of battery. All the time. So I waited until about 9 p.m. – that's near enough her bedtime, but I didn't want to interrupt her if she was with her friends, it's just so nice to see her happy – and then I called a few of the girls' parents. I don't like to do that unless it's important. I want her to know that she – that she can trust me."

"These friends, can I have their names? I'd like to see if they remember anything, if Grace said anything to them."

Mrs Upton looked exhausted, as though she'd done three rounds in the ring with a woman twice her size; she deflated.

"I gave a list to the police already."

"I know," I said. "But it's important we don't miss anything so I want you to write one for me as well. You'd be surprised how much people forget when they talk to the police. And the girls might be more willing to talk to me. Less intimidated."

This wasn't the only reason. I didn't want to have to beg for Marion's scraps of information. I didn't want to have to admit to her that the more I spoke to this girl's mother the more similarities I started to see – similarities between Grace and Olive. A connection between the girls that I couldn't pretend I hadn't made, despite Marion telling me not to.

It was the eclipse. The eclipse loomed over it all like a dark shadow, inky tendrils reaching to draw them together. People didn't just leave Bishop's Green. It was the sort of place where people were born, lived and died on the same street, sometimes even in the same house. People came into town; they didn't usually run out of it.

Adelaide pulled the paper and pen towards her and began to write. Then stopped as if she'd heard something. She looked up. Like a storm cloud moving across the sun, her expression changed. She flinched, retracting her limbs and shrinking inwards, shoulders curved as though she could become invisible. I half-turned in my seat.

"Oh," Adelaide said.

"What the fuck do you think you're doing? How did she get in, Addie?"

Mrs Upton got to her feet.

"I – let her in."

"Ah," I said, pushing my chair back. "Mr Upton. A pleasure to meet you—"

Mr Upton didn't stop. Not when his wife laid a hand on his arm, which he shrugged off with a practised roll of his shoulder. Not even when he grabbed my jacket, pinched it tight between his hands, and frog-marched me all the way to the door.

He didn't stop moving until he drove me right out of the front door.

5

OLIVE OPENED HER EYES slowly. So slowly that the world came into focus in a golden-grey blur, and for a second she thought that she must have fallen asleep under one of the trees on Folly Hill and missed the eclipse.

Soon she realised: she was right about the eclipse. She had missed it. But this wasn't Folly Hill.

As her eyes opened wider, there was more grey and less gold. The walls were grey concrete, plain and rough. The ceiling was quite low, but the single window above her still seemed impossibly high. Two long, thin bars separated the thick glass from the world outside. Like a prison.

She was on a bed. It wasn't comfortable like the one at home. More like the one at Gran's, with a spring that dug right into her back. She shimmied up, her brain taking a second to respond. But she wished she'd just stayed where she was, where it still felt like a bad dream. Where she couldn't see four walls, and very little else.

Oh no.

She felt her throat start to itch with tears, but she wouldn't cry. She looked around, trying to figure it out, like a puzzle. The bed was beneath the window, and on the opposite wall there was a door. Olive climbed unsteadily to her feet, swinging her legs over the edge of the bed – and noticed that something wasn't right. Wronger, if possible, than this funny room and the funny smell of paint and damp.

These weren't her shoes.

She wriggled her toes, momentarily stunned by the discovery that, suddenly, in place of her old white trainers, she now wore a pair of the shiniest shoes she'd ever seen. Patent leather, like her old Dr. Martens, but black and so new they weren't even creased yet.

They were too big. Her toes fought for grip as her feet hit the floor and she swayed slightly, foreign material slithering against her bare legs as she gripped her thighs. That wasn't right, either. A *dress*? Olive hadn't worn a dress since she was nine. She hated them. Everybody knew she did. You couldn't do things in a dress, like climb trees or dig for fossils in the mud. And this one was hideous, with a big bow on the back that dug in when she tugged at it.

Where were her shorts? Her T-shirt was gone too. She snapped her head back and forth as she stood in place, searching the empty room. The only thing left, she realised, was her jewellery. Her ring, and her stupid Mickey Mouse watch that was too young for her, that was a baby's watch really, but it had been a present from Cassie for her eighth birthday.

She stumbled towards the only door in the room, now unable to contain her panic. Her heart was skipping about inside her, so much that she felt dizzy. She hit the opposite wall in less than fifteen steps.

The door was cold. Made from metal, not wood. She tried the handle but nothing happened. She pressed both palms against it and pushed.

Nothing.

"Hello?" she called. She waited, but all she heard was the tearing sound of her own breaths and the stamp-stamp-stamp of her heart. "Excuse me! Is anybody there?"

Still nothing.

She felt the tears stinging her eyes before she even realised she was crying. She wiped her hands over her face, feeling the grazes on her palms from earlier. Was that even earlier? Was it still today? Olive spun around and tried to look out of the window. All she could see now was a greyish patch of sky. Was it sky? It might be tarmac. She couldn't even tell. She tried to stop crying for a minute, to listen, but it sounded all empty and hollow and nothing.

Just nothing.

Now the tears wouldn't stop. She sat down in the middle of the room, cradling her face in her hands. She couldn't help it. She might be a baby if she cried, but she wanted to go home. She wanted Gran and her mum – and even Cassie. What if she never saw them again? Why would the door be locked if she could just go home? She couldn't remember anything. Except the road and the sun and the moon…

And *him*.

Olive looked up. Her heartbeat quickening, she looked

again around the room. But there wasn't anything she'd missed. Not another person. Although there was a fridge by the door. And a sink and a microwave. She hadn't noticed those before.

Was this somebody's kitchen?

But there was the bed and those bars on the window... And then she noticed the toilet, a small one like in the primary school she'd just left behind. Too small for her. It was partially hidden by a low wall that looked half-finished. A tin bath sat in the corner. A kitchen and a bedroom and a bathroom all in one?

Olive's brain was hopping and jumping about all over the place, but at least she'd managed to stop crying. She sat on the floor for a while longer, noticing that there was a carpet. It was grey and thin, its cheap speckled appearance illuminated by the weak evening sunlight coming through the window. The floor underneath the carpet was hard and bumpy in places. There was a lamp on the floor by the bed, plugged in like when they'd moved house and got some stuff from the moving van before the big furniture. They had put the lamps on the floor in the new house too, but this didn't feel exactly like that. The light fitting hanging from a wire over her head didn't even have a bulb in it.

The whole room felt like somebody's garage. Like the time she'd gone to Angela's house after school in year three. Her dad had a garage with loads of games in it, and a little kitchen. Angela had called it his "den". But he also had a pool table and a TV and there was nothing like that in here.

Olive climbed to her feet. Already her bum hurt from sitting, and she wandered back over to the bed. She took the shoes off, setting them carefully on the floor. Maybe whoever owned them would come back for them. She wanted to take the dress off too but she knew she would be cold without it. Then she sat down on the lumpy bed.

She thought about the man and the van. She felt an oily sickness in her stomach and wondered if she'd passed out. Maybe she'd got heatstroke like Cassie had last summer. It had been warm enough, and she hadn't been wearing a hat… Maybe the man had brought her here to wait for Gran.

Olive pushed back the other thoughts. The ones about another reality. One where she wasn't going home. One where she should have jumped out of the van. One where she hadn't been tricked by the sandman in disguise, where she hadn't been put to sleep by strange-tasting water. She pushed those thoughts so deep that her head hurt and she wanted to close her eyes.

Instead she sat on the bed and watched as the light faded from yellow to grey to nothing much at all. The eclipse she had been waiting for was long gone. Olive knew from practising that she was good at waiting. Like the time Mum had promised they could have a dog for Christmas if they stopped asking. Olive had buttoned her lips right away, counting down the days in her head so that Mum didn't get annoyed. So they could have their puppy. In the end Cassie had ruined it by asking again. Like she always did.

A little sob bubbled up inside her. Cassie would know what to do. But she didn't want to cry again, so Olive bit her lip and turned her eyes back to the window. To the sky or the tarmac, or whatever it was. And as the shadows grew and grew inside the room, and eventually it got too dark to see, Olive decided she would wait. Maybe if she was good she could go home before morning.

6

"GET YOUR FOOT OUT of my bloody door."

I glanced down.

"This foot? Oh, I'm sorry. I wasn't aware that your wife and I had finished talking."

I tried to keep the wince hidden as Mr Upton shoved the door again, hard. I could already feel my skin throbbing from the impact of the wood through my worn old boots.

He let out a growl.

"Get out now or I'm going to call the police. I don't care what my wife said – she's not ready to talk to anybody. She's too upset." He bared his teeth, his whole face going beet red.

I started to speak and then changed my mind as he shoved the door again. This time I couldn't control my face as my foot twinged and I yanked it back. The slam of the door set my teeth rattling.

Well, that hadn't gone exactly to plan. I tried to avoid swearing as I walked back to my car, fists clenched tight. Roger Upton hadn't done anything at all to alleviate the suspicion that was bubbling away inside me, although I couldn't deny that the adrenaline singing in my veins made a nice change from the stupor I'd been in for the last couple of months.

Even the throbbing in my foot was almost welcome. I'd forgotten what it could be like. Being *alive*. Working. Digging. Getting the truth – or something like that.

I slid into the driver's seat and pulled out my phone. I was just about to make a call when a knock at the window surprised me. I wound it down quickly. Mrs Upton's face was hovering outside.

"The list," she said. "Of Grace's friends. Not sure it'll help, but there you go."

I was stunned, just for a moment. Thankfully, my autopilot kicked in. "Thank you." I took the paper. "Mrs Upton – Adelaide. Can I ask you something?"

She narrowed her eyes at me but didn't back away.

"Your husband – if he's so against you talking to me, why did he do that interview?"

Adelaide's brows furrowed. She shifted from foot to foot.

"He's just protective," she said quietly. "It's not that he doesn't want me talking to you. It's that… he's worried about me. He's not sure I can handle it. I – I suppose I can't really. It seems like everywhere I look there's more darkness."

A fat tear wobbled down her cheek.

Anger threatened to rise inside me, the memory of my own father saying something similar about my mother. She had been inconsolable when Olive was taken, wild and angry and unapproachable for days; then she became silent, her fears stark in her eyes, and we were all terrified she was going to do something drastic. Like hurt herself.

But Mrs Upton wasn't my mother.

"Protectiveness shouldn't ever manifest as violence," I said firmly. "No matter whether he thinks he's helping or not."

Adelaide shook her head, as though she was about to argue.

"But…" I added, "maybe it's for the best that you don't speak to anybody else. At least not yet."

Mrs Upton looked at me for a long few seconds. Then she nodded.

Little worms of guilt started to wriggle in my chest. The word "exclusive" rattled around my skull, making me feel hot and cold at the same time.

It was better for Adelaide this way. Why submit herself to unnecessary probing, to questions that would make any mother flinch? I shook the thoughts off and watched as she walked away.

Once she was gone, I glanced back down at my phone, still in my hand. If I made this phone call, admitted to Henry that I might write something, it felt like there was no going back. I'd be invested in Grace Butler. In the job. In trying to get my life back.

Henry was right. I couldn't just keep coasting aimlessly. And I knew that now I had started, I wouldn't be able to stop. It was more than just an interview; for the first time since moving back to town I felt *alive*. For the first time since things ended with Helen and I left my job, I had a purpose. It wasn't about the writing, it was about finding the truth.

I made the call and Henry picked up on the second ring.

"Hello, Miss Investigator. I wondered how long it'd be before you caved." His voice was hoarse, as though he'd been on the phone all morning.

"How do you know that's what I'm calling about?"

"Save it." The words were warm with the smile I knew would be on his lips. At this point Henry probably knew me better than my own father did. In fact, he'd been more of a father to me over my ten years in London than my own dad had been. It was Henry who'd got me my first freelance gig, who'd shown me the ropes, who'd taught me the professional benefits of alcohol, how to mingle and ask the right questions. And since he retired he'd provided me with more support than ever.

"You were right," I said. "I wasn't going to. But I spoke to... I spoke to Marion." Even as I admitted this I felt a flush in my cheeks and I swallowed to hide the thickness of my voice at the thought of Marion in her white shirt, tired and gorgeous.

"And?" Henry prompted. "Is there a story there? Do you think you'll give it a shot?"

"The kid has been missing for three days, Heno. Of course there's a story here. I can put something together on the mother pretty quickly. But, thing is, I think there's more to it than a character piece. I think I could have a real crack at this." I didn't mention my sister. The eclipse. Not yet. "I probably need another pair of hands, though. I can do the inside stuff, but..."

"You want me to do some digging for you?"

"If you haven't got anything better to do. You've always been better than me."

It wasn't flattery. Despite being nearly sixty Henry was better with computers than I could ever hope to be. It was his super power. I didn't know where he found half his information. And frankly I didn't want to know.

"Anything specific you want me to look at? I assume you've got the basics covered."

"There's just something fishy about the stepdad," I said. "I don't know. I don't have any proof, just this… feeling. I was at the house and he was not happy when he came home and saw me there. He was very controlling. It's probably nothing, but I could do with a bit of background."

"Sure, sure." I heard a faint tapping sound, and knew that Henry was knocking his pen against his teeth as he often did when he was thinking. Then he coughed. "So… the situation with Marion—"

"Shut up, Heno," I said. "Don't get cocky. We just talked about work. Christ, you're worse than most teenagers I've met."

Henry let out a bark of laughter. "Well I have to do something to pass the time, Cass. It'll be good for you to have a distraction. You've seemed a bit down lately. Unsurprising with the ecli—"

"Heno, I'm fine." A spark of anger flared in me but I smothered it quickly. "I know you're worried, but I'm okay. Just because it's the first proper eclipse since Olive was – since she was taken – doesn't mean I'm not okay. Please can we just drop it?"

"I was just saying." Henry cleared his throat and I could tell that I'd upset him. The anger died in me. I knew he was only trying to help. "I know how you get sometimes, that's all. I don't want you to feel like you haven't got anybody to talk to."

"I'm trying not to think about it," I said. "But you're right. If I focus on this then I'll be fine. Just find me some dirt on Roger Upton."

I heard the smile in Henry's voice. "You got it, darling."

The walk to Grace's school was almost pleasant. I had time to kill before the kids were let out so I parked near the Circle, which was busier than I'd seen it in a while, and then walked up the long, gently sloping hill. I shaded my eyes with my hand, taking in the green and brown patchwork fields that rolled in the distance as Bishop's Green began to spread out behind me. From up here, if I turned around I could make out the smudge of the Triplet Stones on the northern hillside, their shadows cast long and rangy across the emerald grass. I breathed deep, sucking in the clean air. The sun was warm on my back but I couldn't suppress a shudder at the sight of them.

They stood like sentries keeping watch over the town. Or, rather, like goddesses, gazing from a distance and not doing a damn thing to help us. Each of the three stones was over fifteen feet tall, carved with swirling patterns and inlaid with creeping moss. Old stories said that the Triplets were the remains of three ancient beings who had made a home for themselves here, enchanted as they were by the lush, green landscape. Some said they were guardians, watchtowers, blessing the area with fertile farmland and plentiful crops.

Others said they were a warning. A reminder that whatever energy you put into the earth you received back threefold, whether that was positive energy, or negative. And the world had a lot of negative energy to give.

Perhaps they were right, those people who went searching for luck or fertility. Perhaps it all came down to what you asked of the stones.

I came to a stop just opposite the gates of Arboretum Secondary. The school sat nestled in the hillside like a fat hen, feathers fluffed, amidst playing fields and, further out, the houses of the wealthiest people in town. I pulled out my phone, leaving it dark but giving myself the look of a bored nanny waiting for her charge. My plan was to just watch, see what kind of mood the children were in.

In other words, I didn't have a plan.

I didn't have to wait long before I saw children I recognised. A gaggle of younger kids came out of the gates. A redhead, at least, I was sure I'd seen in Mrs Upton's photograph. One of the girls hung back a moment, deep in conversation with a curly-haired teacher. He put his hand on her shoulder and then gave her a gentle nudge towards her friends.

"Hi," I said to the kids closest to me. "Hi, Tiffany? Sarah?" I rattled off the names from Mrs Upton's list at random. "Bella? Hannah?"

They all spun en masse as the last girl reached her friends, five girls and a boy looking at me with open faces.

"Sarah's not here," one of them said. "She didn't come to school today."

"Who are you?" asked the boy. He stepped forward, scowling enough that the girls didn't bother to. They just stood behind him and waited for something to happen.

"Sorry," I apologised. "My name's Cassie. I'm helping Grace's family figure out where she's gone. We're trying to work out who she's with, you know, that she might not realise how worried they are. Mrs Upton said you guys are Grace's friends…?"

I thought open questions would be the way forward, but all I got was a wall of silence.

"I dunno," the boy said, his scowl deepening. "I don't think we should talk to you."

"Well, you don't have to," I told him. "But I'm not going to hurt anybody. I'm a friend of Grace's mum. A journalist."

The boy examined me thoroughly before nodding. I thanked God that whoever had told him about stranger danger hadn't extended the lesson to petite, scruffy journalists with glasses.

"I'm Alex," he said. "I'm Grace's friend too. Sarah didn't come to school today. She's off sick."

"My mum said it was because *her* mum is afraid she'll go missing too," cut in the smallest girl in the group, a blonde who was so fine-boned she looked like a pixie.

"Oh that's rubbish." This came from a girl who until now had hung back behind her friends. She had dark brown hair, bright hazel eyes, and sun-kissed skin despite the drab March weather. She looked right at me, her stance and expression surprisingly adult for an eleven-year-old. She was the one who had been talking to the teacher just a minute ago. I wondered if this was the history teacher who Mrs Upton had mentioned, the one helping Grace to come out of her shell.

"What's rubbish?" I asked. They said nothing at first, so I groped in my pocket for an old business card and pulled it out as though it was proof I could be trusted. I passed it to the pixie girl, who looked at it with disdain before passing it along.

"It's rubbish that Grace was abducted," the hazel-eyed girl said then, very matter-of-factly. "People keep saying she was probably abducted but Grace isn't stupid."

"Shut up, Bella." Pixie-girl rolled her eyes.

"She'd have told one of us if she was meeting somebody," Bella persisted.

"Even if it was a secret?"

Bella opened her mouth to speak, but then stopped. She shrugged. Then she leaned in conspiratorially, her brown hair moving like a curtain to keep her words hidden as though they were just for me.

"That's the thing," she said slowly. "Grace doesn't keep secrets from me."

7

SECRETS. THAT WAS THE thing, wasn't it? At eleven I didn't have many secrets, but by thirteen I was brimming with them. I loved them. Hated them, too. The summer we lost Olive I had a lot of things to keep to myself; I gorged on my secrets, on the stories I was writing and on my expanding emotions as if they were sweets and chocolate that I'd never had before. For once I had something I didn't have to share.

I had Marion; I had feelings that nobody else had.

The thrill of the secrets was greater still because Marion and I knew our parents wouldn't approve. Girls didn't like other girls. Not like that. Mum had told me as much herself. It was a different world, then, and I was trapped by its customs and rules.

Holding hands in the back seat of Gran's car on the way to the Bishop's Green fête had given us such a rush that the evening before the eclipse we could hardly keep our hands off each other. The jasmine scent of the air mixed with the trembling excitement in the hot summer night. The fear of getting caught was almost as fun as knowing that only *we* felt this way.

I realised later that Olive had secrets, too, but she didn't flaunt them like I did. She kept them close to her chest, guarding her hand relentlessly. And I was so wrapped up in myself that I didn't see it. I almost wanted to be found out so I didn't have to tell my parents how I felt. About myself and about Marion.

Olive was different. When she was small she'd shared everything with me, but the prospect of moving to Big School at the end of the summer had closed her off. It was almost as though she felt she had to hide things in order to grow up.

The week we arrived in Bishop's Green, I'd found Olive writing in a diary. She'd never kept one before that I knew of and I wondered what had prompted the change. She'd left it under her pillow, and I found it while looking for a hair clip of mine she'd borrowed. The diary was blue, covered with stickers of Pokémon and dinosaurs and planets, a mixture that I thought summed up my nerdy sister perfectly.

I wanted to read it.

I was burning to rip it open and devour the contents – but something stopped me. Not guilt as much as a fear of retribution. I hovered at the edge of the bed, holding her pillow in a tight grip, indecision rendering me completely immobile.

If Olive found me reading it she'd never forgive me and I still had the summer to endure with her. I hated being punished by her because Olive was so insufferable: she never rubbed it in my face, never gloated that I was in trouble, and that quiet calmness was always so damn infuriating.

So I put the pillow back and left it alone.

When I went back for it after Olive was taken, it was gone. I always assumed she'd hidden it somewhere but I never found it. In the months and years that followed I often wondered what might have happened if I'd read it. Would it have taught me anything about her that I should have known? I was her sister. It wasn't supposed to be like that, all locked-up feelings. Sisters were supposed to share things. Maybe it would have told me other things about Olive's life that would have saved her.

She might have written about Dad, too, about *his* secrets. She knew more about him than I did – because she paid attention. She was the quiet kid who people forgot about when they had adult conversations. Maybe reading her diary would have told me about Dad's affair and where he might have been when she was taken. Maybe I wouldn't have hated him so much if I'd known about Carol from the start, instead of finding out weeks later when everything had already been ruined by our mutual doubt and suspicion anyway. Maybe the police would have found Olive – if they hadn't been so preoccupied with our father and his damn lies. If they'd had more leads they might have known where to look.

She might have even written about *him* in her diary. The man who took her. Even now I was tormented by the thought that she might have known who he was.

When it came to dinnertime, all we had was a tin of beans and some bread because I hadn't been shopping. Being a functioning adult never had been my speciality. Beans on toast would have to do. As I served it up, Gran came to the table and I made small talk that was unlikely to upset her. She paid me no heed.

"You know, it's my granddaughter's birthday next month." This came out of the blue. There was a spot of bean juice on Gran's shirt.

I felt my body get heavy. She didn't mean me. Today she was in her favourite reality, the one where Olive and I were still children, still safe and secure and living in Derby with both parents.

"Yes," I said. "The thirteenth."

"That's right. I'm not sure what she would like. I don't know what she's into any more." Gran shovelled a forkful of beans into her mouth. "I was thinking I could get her something from that shopping centre they just built. My daughter and her husband – they work a lot. She's a high-flyer, works in sales. You know, he's a lecturer in English? He writes all these papers and things. So when the children stay with me I make it fun. I thought I could get the girls something to share, but of course I want to get Olive something special too."

I could guess what year Gran thought it was. They'd built a shopping centre years ago just outside town, one of those monstrous things that sucks local businesses dry. I hadn't visited it since I was here for Marion's dad's funeral two years ago but I doubted it had changed much. If anything I figured there would be more empty shops, space forfeited because of the astronomical ground rent.

"I don't know." I shrugged. How could I answer? Olive had been gone sixteen years and here was Gran trying to work out what to buy her for her birthday. I felt a hotness welling up behind my eyelids as I always did when Gran spoke about Olive as though she was still here.

I knew I had to make the effort, though, as Gran watched me expectantly.

"Books," I said. "She liked books. Book tokens."

Gran didn't catch the past tense. She nodded, scraping her plate noisily. "Not some jewellery? That might be nice, too. My Cassie loves jewellery."

I shivered. Hearing myself being spoken about like that, as if I wasn't right here – it made me feel like a ghost. But I couldn't bring myself to correct her. Sometimes it was best to just become somebody else and let her live in the reality of the moment.

I thought back to my childhood summers in Bishop's Green instead, trying to imagine the world Gran thought she was still living in. There were little gift shops all the way around Chestnut Circle that sold beautiful hand-crafted silver jewellery and incense sticks and precious gems. Every summer I would bring my savings with me and waste countless pounds on bracelets made of rose quartz to aid me in finding love, tiger's eye pendants to bring me luck. I would beg to go to the Triplet Stones, to rub them or kiss them, or whatever it was that people did. Mum always laughed when I told her. It was all just old superstitious nonsense.

But the eclipse's power was meant to be nonsense too. It was just science, Gran said. Something that happened almost by accident. I hadn't believed in its power to take, to steal. To make new. And then Olive was gone, and our lives were different. New. Just not in a good way.

"I think she'd prefer a book," I said quietly.

Olive had always scoffed at me when we were children; she thought precious stones and mood jewellery were daft. Or at least that's what she'd led me to believe. With a funny twist in my gut, I suddenly remembered the mood ring Olive had come home wearing after a day out in town with Gran the summer she disappeared.

Now I knew why Grace Butler's mood ring had seemed so familiar when I'd seen it in her photo.

"Do you remember Olive's ring?" I asked suddenly, the question jumping out before I could stop to consider it. "She got it that summer?"

My heart raced and I swallowed hard. I felt stupid for not having noticed before. What were the chances of that? Both girls going missing right near a solar eclipse, both the same age, both wearing a mood ring with a mermaid on it? The mood ring seemed final, somehow, a tangible connection between them both.

"I don't…" Gran frowned, her lip puckering. "I'm not sure. I…"

Stop it, I told myself furiously. *Now you* are *being stupid.* Yes, Bishop's Green might be in decline – yes, a lot of the shops closed and people moved away – but this was still a town that drew its income from tourism. Was it really a surprise that two little girls had been drawn in by the promise of mildly magical jewellery?

Magic was what this town sold, after all, with its Triplet

Stones and New Age shops. The eclipse in 1999 was supposed to be a new beginning for all of us. That's why everybody had been so obsessed with it, counted down to it, waited for the sensation of newness and freshness to cleanse them. The shops had been buzzing, and so had we, despite the warnings that it was all nonsense.

The summer after Olive disappeared, I found a book in the library in Derby where I lived with my mum. It was after Dad started renting his first house with Carol, after Mum and I moved into the dingy flat we'd lived in for six months, where everything was smaller and made for two instead of four.

The library book was about superstition and myths. In many cultures, solar eclipses were seen as evil, as bad omens. Pregnant women and children were warned to stay indoors. The ancient Greeks believed that a solar eclipse was a sign of angry gods, that it was the beginning of disasters and destruction. That seemed more accurate to me than all of the fresh start crap. It was an ending of the world as I had known it.

This eclipse, the one I could now feel brewing like a storm, this was how it should have been before. People were wary, now. Even the viewing at Earl's was tempered by the memory of what had happened last time. Olive's name was on their lips and they were nervous, especially with Grace missing as well. This time people knew to be careful.

I was not a superstitious person – not any more – but even I could see that it was dangerous. The darkness, the excitement. The buzz. It led to bad decisions.

After Olive was taken, there was a spike in tourists visiting the town. But they were the morbid kind. The ones who wanted to stand where she was last seen and imagine what might have happened. The ones who couldn't hide their curiosity, who didn't care that she was a real person. My sister: just another unsolved mystery.

Gran stared at me blankly, no memory of Olive's ring and no clue why I'd be asking about it. My stomach dipped.

"You really ought to finish your dinner," I said. Gran's silence should have made me feel sorry – for confusing her, for asking a question she couldn't answer, but I only felt frustrated. "You'll be hungry."

When the doorbell rang I let out an exasperated sigh but I was glad to leave Gran to her imaginary birthday planning. I yanked it open and found a familiar face.

"Marion," I said.

She was dressed in tailored trousers and a pale blue shirt that matched the cornflower hue of her eyes. She smiled at me awkwardly and shifted from one foot to the other. Her eyes had lost their sparkle, tiredness making them dimmer, but the smile was genuine.

"Hi Cass. Can I come in?"

"Only if you save me from dinner duty," I joked.

I wondered how word had reached her so fast that I'd been to see the Uptons. I would put money on it being the stepfather, he seemed like the vengeful type. I backed away and let Marion into the hall.

"Who's that?" Gran called.

"Hi, Peggy." Marion wandered into the lounge and poked her head into the small dining room where Gran was still sitting with her cold beans. "It's me, Marion."

"Marion." Gran thought about this for a second, and then burst into a beaming smile. "Marion Adams," she said. "My goodness I haven't seen you in years and years! You're all grown up now."

"Oh sure, she remembers you." I rolled my eyes, but was secretly pleased that Gran was smiling.

"Do you mind if I borrow your granddaughter for a little while? I need to talk to her."

"Granddaughter?" Gran's eyes misted over. I saw it even from across the room and felt my stomach lurch as Gran shook her head. "Well, you can talk to her, but I'm not sure she's around to listen."

Marion turned back to me, met my gaze, and I just shrugged.

"Come on," I said. "I'll put the kettle on."

I ushered Marion through to the kitchen and shut the door behind me, flicking the kettle on so Gran wouldn't overhear our conversation.

"So—"

"She's so much worse than when I last saw her," Marion spoke over me. Then she looked sheepish. "Sorry, I didn't mean to interrupt."

"It's okay." I grabbed three mugs from the cupboard and put a teabag into each. "Look, I'm sorry—"

"No, *I'm* sorry." Marion stepped towards me, her arms

slightly outstretched as though she was reaching for me. But she stopped, the years still a wall between us.

"The great Marion Adams, apologising," I said with a wry smile. "But why are _you_ sorry?"

"About before," Marion said. "I don't know. I'm sorry if I made you feel uncomfortable or anything. This whole Grace Butler thing is just really pissing me off. A girl disappears on her way home from school and somehow nobody knows anything. I was just a bit afraid you'd... I don't know. It was stupid to think you couldn't be objective."

I swallowed, feeling hot embarrassment in my cheeks. I thought about my panic when I'd remembered Olive's ring – about the way I'd felt when I looked through my Olive Diary. That I'd even looked through it at all was probably evidence enough about my lack of objectivity. And how did I explain that my awkwardness wasn't something she had to apologise for?

"It's lucky I'm the forgiving type."

"You don't have to say anything. I just wanted to come round and apologise. And, I know you're just trying to help find her, so I don't want to chase you off. I know you're a good journalist, and if you can help us in any way..." Marion paused and seemed to let her brain catch up with her mouth. She was breathless.

In that moment I wanted to kiss her. No matter how long it had been since I'd seen her, she was still the person I'd texted and called and emailed – the person I'd turned to when I didn't have anybody else. And she'd never pushed me, never demanded an intimacy I couldn't give her. She knew my secrets because they were hers too.

I wanted to tell her about speaking to Grace's friends, about my bad vibes from Roger Upton. I wanted to talk about Olive, and what happened with Mum, and Gran; the whole lot. But I was afraid. So instead I turned around and busied myself with the tea.

"Tell me again what an amazing journalist I am?" I said.

Marion smiled. "I know you're in a rough place right now. It's got to be shit, moving to Bishop's Green after what happened here. It must have been a hard decision…"

I half-turned but couldn't trust myself to say anything.

"So anyway," Marion continued. "I just wanted to say that I chatted with the Uptons. I told them I'm friends with a 'sensitive' journalist and they're going to think about whether they want to do any interview together—"

Marion saw the look on my face, which was a mixture of embarrassment and guilt, and she stopped.

"What?" she asked.

"Nothing," I said quickly. "I appreciate the offer but right now I'm just looking after Gran and that's kind of a full-time thing and—"

"Oh my god, Cassie. You already bloody went to talk to them, didn't you? I told you to wait."

"I couldn't wait," I said. "Not after the stepdad did that full-length interview. And he acted very strangely when I was there – and now I keep thinking about this mood ring I saw in a picture of Grace. She was wearing it, and I swore I'd seen it somewhere before – and I realised it's just like one that Olive had—"

I knew immediately that I shouldn't have mentioned the ring. Marion's frown deepened. This wasn't banter now. She shook her head and I knew I'd overstepped. I sounded crazy.

"Christ, I didn't mean to plant that idea in your head, Cass. I was warning you *not* to connect Olive and Grace."

"It's not just the ring though," I said. Too late to back down now. "It's the timing. Two solar eclipses sixteen years apart and both times a girl goes missing? And you obviously must have thought about it, otherwise you wouldn't have warned me."

"It's a *coincidence*, Cassie. It was Friday the thirteenth when Grace went missing but you don't see me linking it to some sort of cult, do you? Just because people might make a connection doesn't mean there is one, like there being similarities doesn't mean they're the same."

I could tell I'd touched a nerve, and this time I backed off. I hadn't meant that Grace and Olive had been taken by the *same person*.

Had I?

Marion didn't wait for me to say anything else, just turned on her heel to leave. I chased her out of the kitchen, but she was already at the front door.

"Marion, wait!"

She didn't stop. I stumbled out onto the driveway as she got into her car.

"Marion! Hang on—"

She backed her car out onto the road before rolling down her window a few inches.

"Cassie, you shouldn't get involved. We have to be objective

– because a little girl's life is on the line. This isn't just a *story*."

She put the car into gear and was gone before my body could unfreeze, before I could say or do anything at all. I hadn't gone looking for a connection between Olive and Grace – but I had found one.

Grace Butler's disappearance happening a week before a solar eclipse in the same town where Olive was taken couldn't be a coincidence. They were the same age. The location was too close to be an accident. Bishop's Green might be full of people who had been denied their fresh start in 1999, who felt like the universe owed them more…

Perhaps whoever took Olive *was* trying again.

8

THE WAITING ROOM AT the doctor's was quiet tonight. They were trialling late opening hours, and I didn't think it would last long, although I liked how empty the new health centre was at this time. Our only company was a sniffling old man with watering, beady eyes and a frazzled-looking young mother and her grizzling baby. I held Gran's arm and guided her to a free spot by a little water cooler, which she eyed with suspicion while I registered her arrival on a machine by the door. Gran was used to the old building, and on every visit she found something new to dislike. A receptionist looked on with a bored expression, glasses riding low on her nose as she stabbed at something with a pen.

This was the last place I wanted to be right now. I was still smarting from my confrontation with Marion, antsy and snappy, but I also knew that I'd reached the end of my tether with Gran and her night-time antics and I couldn't put it off any longer.

I felt like I had failed Gran. Disappointment in myself made me want to curl up and avoid eye contact, but I tried to keep my features schooled to neutrality when we were called into the last of the twelve appointment rooms.

The room smelled faintly of antiseptic, like hand sanitiser tinged with cologne, but the walls were far from the sterile ones I'd seen in other doctors' surgeries over the years. These were plastered with posters, most of which were decidedly non-medical – a cat Photoshopped into a yoga pose, a peaceful landscape. All, I supposed, meant to put his patients at ease.

Doctor White was in his fifties, smartly dressed and with a sort of well-groomed friendliness. He always greeted my gran as though he hadn't seen her in years. It was no wonder his appointments ran late.

"Peggy! How are you? And Cassie. What can I do for you both today?"

Gran smiled and looked straight to me, sure that at least *I* knew what we were doing here. I didn't know how else to say it, so I bit the bullet and faced the issue straight on.

"She's not sleeping," I said quietly, explaining that what had started as just the odd occurrence was now happening twice or even three times a week. "She's out all night sometimes. I don't know how she manages it, but it's happening frequently enough that even with locked doors neither of us are getting much sleep."

Doctor White raised a dark eyebrow, pursed his lips and made a sympathetic little noise in the back of his throat. It wasn't judgement that I sensed, not quite, but it reminded me of a time I'd been to visit him as a kid, Olive with some bang or sprain from climbing trees or falling over, and me dragged in just because Gran didn't know what else to do with me. He'd done the same eyebrow thing back then, almost a question, as though prompting Olive to say more. To explain herself.

I clamped my lips shut and waited.

"Well, it's not entirely unexpected," he conceded eventually. "Most people with Alzheimer's do experience changes in their sleep patterns. It sounds like what you're describing is 'sundowning'."

He explained to both of us about the studies he had read, skimming over the details but expressing the importance of regular meal times and sleep patterns. I shifted uncomfortably in my chair. I had been trying to maintain a sense of order, but when you weren't used to having to care for somebody else it was easy to lose track. The only thing I had managed so far was to keep her blood pressure medication regular.

I stared at the doctor's desk while he spoke, taking in the lunchbox that was filled with discarded orange peel and a chocolate wrapper, and the beautifully carved wooden bowl he kept for the children who visited him. I knew it was filled with an assortment of trinkets, little pieces of jewellery and pin badges, and occasionally a fifty pence piece. He'd told me once that it was better for the children than lollipops and he liked the fact that it meant the kids never wanted a different doctor as they got older.

"Have you thought about sleeping aids?" Doctor White's tone changed and I snapped back to attention guiltily.

"I was reluctant to—"

"I appreciate that it's not necessarily something you'll want, but Peggy will feel the benefit after a few uninterrupted nights of sleep. And so, my dear, will you." He stared at me pointedly, that damn eyebrow raised again, a coil of his brown hair coming free of the oil that usually kept it pushed back.

"I…"

"Both of you look tired. I'm going to prescribe something for you, Peggy, to help you sleep. There are a few options, but we'll try the tablets first since you seem to be managing the other medication okay, right?" He nodded in my direction. "You'll need to make sure you keep them somewhere safe – a locked cabinet, really – and I suggest given the circumstances that it might be best if you're in charge of making sure she takes them so she doesn't have too many. If the tablets don't work out there is something you can mix with water." He scribbled something on a pad of paper at his elbow and then turned to his computer screen.

"Now, Cassie, are you making sure that you take care of yourself as well as your grandmother?"

Gran nodded emphatically, her expression sad and a little confused. I reached out to her, patting her knee gently.

"I'm trying," I said honestly, surprised by the question. "I've been thinking about my sister a lot recently. Having dreams. Wondering if there was stuff I didn't understand back when she was taken. But I'm getting back into the swing of things. I've just started working again, freelance."

The doctor finished making a note on his computer screen and then turned to take Gran's blood pressure.

"Writing again?" he asked. I was surprised he had remembered, but I supposed being a doctor he probably had to have a good memory. And I was happy to talk about anything that wasn't sleeping pills.

"Yeah," I said. Then a thought struck me. Doctor White had always been known for the fact that he saw a lot of children – something about his treat bowl and warm smile. "I'm working on a piece about Grace Butler, actually. The little girl who's missing. Do you know her?"

Doctor White frowned, glancing up from his task. "I know a lot of the children in town," he said, "they generally come to me for one thing or another. But I can't talk about them. Don't get any ideas." He smiled, but awkwardly, as though he had just made a joke.

"Sorry," I said, my cheeks warming. "Seemed like it was worth a shot. I just wanted to know what sort of kid she is…?" I allowed the blush to play to my advantage, a small innocent smile on my face. Doctor White let my grandmother's arm dip back into her lap and then shook his head.

"She's lovely. Shy, quiet. Clever, though. I'm surprised by the whole situation, to be honest. She doesn't seem like the kind of girl to get herself into trouble, or who wouldn't ask for help if she needed it." He fixed me with another knowing look, and I realised that he was only half talking about Grace. "That's all I'll say on the matter. Now, I've prescribed these for your gran. They're your basic sleeping tablet…"

He explained the dosage to Gran and then handed the prescription to me. He ran me through a list of precautions and side-effects, but it was almost as though he knew I was already familiar with it. As though he had understood my reluctance to discuss the sleeping pills as an option. As though I was *that* transparent about my own misuse. So much for keeping a low profile.

He knew I had taken them before, and he had just offered me a chance to talk about it. I felt shame slither inside me and avoided his gaze as we left his office. But I filled the prescription on the way home.

I held my breath as the phone rang and rang, scrubbing the corner of my thumbnail hard against a groove in the dining-room table. I'd not long finished writing a piece about my interview with Adelaide Upton and had just sent it to Henry for his opinion, but for some reason I didn't feel the usual sense of completion. Perhaps I'd feel better after I'd sold it. I was wound up, my chest tight and my palms sweaty. Dad answered the phone on the tenth ring, not that I was counting.

"Dad," I cut off the voice at the other end of the phone. "Dad, it's me."

There was a moment of static quiet as my dad took in a long breath, and then I heard him exhale. The sound was muffled, as though he had his hand over the receiver, and another few seconds passed of rearranging, something moving over the surface of the phone, before I heard his voice properly.

"Hello. How's it going?"

"Oh, Dad…" Now that I had him, I didn't know what to say. I'd run through a hundred different scenarios in my head while waiting for him to answer the phone, and now not a single one seemed right. I thought of my Olive Diary, sitting just across the room, and I got a squirmy feeling in my chest. I didn't even know why I'd called.

"Are you all right?" he asked.

"No, I'm…" I thought about telling him about Gran, about her escape and the doctor's appointment, but decided against it. He didn't need another reason to say, 'I told you so'. "I'm all right. Just a bit tired. I'm writing again, though."

It was nice to tell people I was working again. Somehow telling people made it official. I needed a banner proclaiming *Cassie is getting her shit together*. Although that might have been too much faith.

"Oh, that's nice." Dad made a noise in the back of his throat. "Anything good?" It was clear he didn't want an argument but I knew he'd never really approved of my career. Even if I was writing for the victims, he had always felt it was somehow disingenuous.

"No. Well − no. Have you heard about − about the stuff happening in Bishop's Green?" I didn't care if we argued.

Dad lived in Chesterfield and had done ever since my mother's suicide when I was seventeen. After what happened with the police during the investigation he'd grown distant from me. Mum's death was the final nail in the coffin, a severing of the ties between us. Now he had another family, another life. One that, despite his best attempts, I'd never felt part of.

"Yes. It's tragic," Dad said, his voice detached. Although I knew this was his way of dealing with his emotions, it still flamed the frustration and anger that seemed to be simmering in me all the time lately.

"Dad, there's something not right about it. That's why I called. The kid's exactly the same age as Olive. There's the solar eclipse on Friday. It's not exactly the same, but it's making me feel like there might be something worth—"

"Cassie." Dad's voice was a warning. "We're all thinking of Olive right now, but it's probably just that. Don't let it affect your judgement."

"I'm not making it up."

I heard Dad close a door, a muffled voice calling him on the other end of the line. Probably his other daughter. Hailey. The one who wasn't "highly-strung". I let out a long sigh and massaged the bridge of my nose in a gesture similar to the one I knew he was probably making.

"Sorry sweetheart," Dad said. "I didn't mean that. It just rubs me wrong. We shouldn't get involved in other people's lives."

"I know. Sorry. I just wanted to talk. They're the same age. It's just weird."

"She's not your sister." This could have sounded harsh, but somehow it didn't. Just sad. I realised that I'd been insensitive to think Dad would want to talk about this. He was probably having a rough time just like I was.

"Okay," I said quietly. So I counted to ten, and then I dropped it. We talked about Bishop's Green, about the weather, about things that Dad thought didn't matter. He asked if I'd made any new friends yet. I told him I might progress to shopping at the Tesco just so I had more cashiers to befriend. We both laughed – only Dad's laugh was tinged with pity.

When we said goodnight, Dad didn't mention Olive again. Neither did I.

Lying in bed that night I couldn't stop thinking. About my family, about Gran and Grandad and how they must have felt when Olive disappeared. The fear. The guilt. I thought about Dad, too, and how much I had hated his lies. He couldn't even tell the truth when the police thought he might be guilty of hurting Olive – all because he was afraid he'd get fired because of Carol. Because she was a student at the university and he was her teacher.

I avoided thinking about Mum. These days, I felt more like her than ever. Tired, frustrated all the time. At least that's how she was after Olive was taken. She had always been strong before. Too strong, sometimes, but warm and passionate. Afterwards she never wanted to talk about things. She didn't talk about Olive or her feelings; she was too proud to appear weak. She locked everything up so tight that none of us even realised she needed help until it was too late.

I saw a lot of myself in her – the stress to make things perfect, the inability to back down. The downward slope, too: the turn towards the numbing bliss of alcohol, or drugs; the anger, the refusal to talk. I didn't want to be like that. Mum had always been busy, always thrown herself into her work, but it got worse after Olive. A decline so gradual I don't think any of us really noticed. And once Dad was gone it was easier to ignore because it was just the two of us.

When she ended her life, I'd acted surprised. Said all the things that people say about family members who choose to end their lives. But really it was only the same thing I'd thought about doing and I was angry that she got there first.

That was about when I'd discovered sleeping pills, how just one was enough to curb the panic attacks that left me shaking. It was like smoking weed, only completely legal and cheaper too. And the pills didn't smell nearly so bad. Alcohol worked at a push but the hangovers were monstrous.

I thought about my job in London. It hadn't been perfect, and things getting rocky with Helen hadn't helped, but it was my own recklessness that had been the final straw; I'd punched an interviewee and expected righteous anger to help me get away with it. Helen had had enough. I didn't blame her.

Dad and Marion were probably right – I was taking this too seriously. Too *personally*. I might be drawing connections between Grace and Olive where there were none. But over the years I had written features on several families who'd lost children – always with the desire to help, to fix what was broken – and I hadn't felt this way about any of them.

Marion's warning for me not to connect Olive and Grace only told me that she had had the same thoughts. That the solar eclipse had left us both teetering on the edge of what was logical and what was fantasy.

As the clock rolled over to 2 a.m., a text lit the screen of my phone, followed by a buzz that made me jump. I felt a shiver of unease ripple through me. Nobody ever texted this late. Not even Henry, who hardly ever slept. My blood zinged and I wondered if it was from Marion.

It wasn't. The number was unknown. My skin grew clammy as I opened it. Two words, no punctuation. No preamble. Nothing, except:

back off

My heart slammed an uneven rhythm. I copied the number and pasted it into Google. This had to be some sort of joke. The search results yielded nothing. I felt too hot. It had to be another journalist – I was stepping on somebody's toes. But how did any of them know I was writing? Had they seen me coming out of the Upton house?

I took a deep breath and massaged my forehead until my chest stopped heaving. Who knew I was asking questions? My mind drew a blank, fear creating a fuzzy confusion.

Somebody thought I was making a nuisance of myself, that much was clear. It had to be because of Grace. It had to be. Or was it Olive? I couldn't shake the questions that haunted me. I couldn't distinguish my thoughts about Grace from the dreams that had been plaguing me, the ones of Olive. Of the eclipse.

It couldn't be a coincidence that I was back in town now. That Grace had gone missing near a solar eclipse, just like my sister. It had been a long time since I'd thought about fate. Unlike Marion, who had been sucked into Bishop's Green's love of superstition, I'd happily shed that part of myself when I left. But now I could feel in my bones that I was meant to try to help that little girl. And this text message only made me more convinced that I had to do something.

I was going to wait for anything Henry could find out about

Roger Upton, and in the meantime I'd focus on other stuff. Connections. If Grace *did* have something to do with Olive, then I'd find out.

I got up, checked on Gran who was, thankfully, sleeping peacefully, and then slunk down to the dining room. The sleeping tablets were locked away in the creaky upstairs bathroom cabinet with the key tied around my neck. I wasn't taking any chances. But downstairs there was a bottle of bourbon on the side. Not something I normally touched, but I needed it. I grabbed a glass. Poured a finger. Poured two more. And I drank it all down just to help me sleep.

I tossed and turned all night. I fell into a deep sleep around dawn, punctuated by vivid dreams. They started as they always did. With Olive. She always haunted me at night. Sometimes she was the focus. I dreamed that I was in an airport and she stepped off a plane, or that she was in a school play and I was late. Sometimes she was just an extra face in a crowd, but my heart always stuttered when I spotted her. Always the same as the last time I saw her, eleven years old for ever.

Tonight was different, though. Tonight I dreamt that I was walking through the fields, looking for somebody. For Gran? No, it wasn't Gran. I marched on, the wet ground sucking at my feet, pulling me down. Still I forged ahead, palms slick with sweat. I had to find her. Had to see…

Was that her?

By the trees I saw a wooden den like one Olive and I had

once built. Green wood and nails, empty pallets fitted to look like walls. The girl disappeared inside, her body still partially visible. Not Olive, but—

"Grace!" I shouted.

I caught sight of a hand. The hand waved, and then started to beckon. I began to run, breath puffing hard in the cool twilight air. My whole body screamed in protest, aching all over. The hand continued to beckon, the distance between us closing slowly. Impossibly slowly.

There was a ring on the finger. A silver ring, its mermaid tail twitching, a murky, blackened stone in the centre catching the light. *Grace.* I tried to call out to her, but the closer I got, the further away she seemed to be. Her hand started to morph. The ring, dissolving, reforming. The stone in the middle flashed bright – red. Nervous. Stress. The hand was different. Now they were not Grace's slender fingers but…

Olive's.

Just out of reach. A hand I could have been holding. If only I'd been watching. *Keep an eye on her.*

back off

I woke with a start, sweat dripping down my forehead and stinging my eyes. I swiped at it angrily. Reached for the bedside table. Poured myself another finger of Gran's bourbon and swallowed it down.

9

WHEN I FINALLY WOKE up my mouth was dry like sandpaper and my tongue felt heavy. Actually, my whole body felt like lead. The bedside table clock read almost eleven. I groaned and pushed the heels of my hands into my eyes to try and dislodge the sleep. My head was throbbing, and when I rolled over I felt sick. Why did I think a hangover would be a good idea? The alcohol had just turned the bad thoughts into bad dreams, and I still felt like I did after every panic attack: stiff, sore, and very fragile.

I lay in bed for several minutes, trying to clear my mind. I could hear somebody moving around downstairs, and hoped that it was just Gran and not some thieves come to take what little we had left. I hauled myself out of bed and poked my head over the top of the bannister. There was some music floating upwards, sultry like jazz.

Jazz had been Grandad's favourite kind of music and he'd had all sorts of albums, vinyl and CD versions of his favourites scattered about the house. When I'd come back for the funeral, I'd spent two days just trying to sort through them all.

This music had the faint crackle to it that I associated with our badly tuned kitchen radio. I let the sound wash over me as I popped down to check on Gran. I poked my head around the door. She'd managed to dress herself and had settled in her favourite armchair with a cup of tea. I let out a relieved sigh and headed back up to the bathroom. She'd be okay while I got ready and then I'd sort breakfast. We had a dementia nurse due to pop round later on and I really, *really* needed a good shower.

By the time I'd washed my hair I was starting to feel better. I even surprised myself when I saw I'd had a text from Helen and I didn't feel much of anything at all.

I dragged my fingers through my mousy hair, pulling the damp curls into a loose plait. When I stood in front of the mirror, I was shocked to see how normal I looked. In control, almost. I met the gaze of my reflection, thinking about Olive. We had the same sort of eyes, gold rather than just hazel. Although Olive's were incredibly beautiful – and mine always seemed duller, not bright and shining like my sister's. The morning sun broke through a patch of clouds, making my reflection seem to shimmer, and I shivered. Sometimes I wished I'd inherited Gran's blue eyes; then I wouldn't think of Olive whenever I looked in a mirror.

Downstairs Gran was still sitting with the two cups of tea she had made, a book balanced in her lap as she listened to the music coming from the kitchen. This was one of the small things that reminded me of the past, called up the woman who had spent so many months trying to pull me back from the brink of darkness when my mother died. She made me tea. Always. I was the only person she'd make it for, and she made it just like I loved it – tooth-achingly sweet.

I'd stayed in town with my grandparents for only a few months after Mum died. I made my plans and was eager to move on, too exhausted to ask questions about Olive, and what had happened. Now it was too late and I wished I'd asked anyway.

The tea Gran had made for us both this morning was, it turned out, just hot water. The spell was broken, and gone was the Gran I remembered. I knew she was in there somewhere but she was buried so deep by the dementia that sometimes I couldn't see her any more.

"Who are you?"

I resisted the urge to make something up, knowing that wouldn't help either of us.

"It's Cassie," I said calmly. "Kathy's eldest. D'you remember? I'm living here with you at the moment."

The frown lines around her lips deepened as she pursed them. Her cup of water, balanced precariously on the arm of the chair, wobbled and I tried to catch it. The cup bounced on the carpet and the liquid splashed across the floor.

"Oh, dear. Let me – let me get that…"

"No, no. It's okay." I held up my hands. "My fault."

She watched as I bent to mop up the mess. Then she shrugged, clasping her hands in her lap.

"Do you want some breakfast?" she asked. "I always make breakfast. Pancakes, or eggs. I make the best pancakes this side of the United States! My granddaughters love them. Joe can't cook to save his life, but I always say that's why it's lucky that he married me. You know, we had pancakes at our wedding, although they called them crêpes and they served them with *ice cream*! Can you imagine…"

Gran trailed off as she followed me into the kitchen. When I turned to her, the look on her face was like nothing I'd ever seen before. Her eyes were wide, her mouth open, as though moving into different lighting had triggered something.

"Wait," she whispered.

I half-turned, confusion making my movements sloppy. Gran lifted her arms slowly, and when she walked towards me she opened them wide and pulled me into a hug. I was too surprised to move, our contact recently having been fairly limited. This was like the old days.

I held her close, breathing in the smells of baby powder and old, musky perfume. Her hair was scratchy as it brushed my cheek. I felt her body start to convulse, and I realised that she was crying.

"What is it, Gran? What's the matter?"

"Oh my Lord, oh my Lord," Gran repeated over and over.

"What? What happened?"

"Oh, my Lord. You've brought my sweetheart home!"

I felt my whole body clench. I was never – had never been – Gran's sweetheart. Not once. I was monkey, or honey, or love. Never sweetheart. I tried to pull back, disconnect from the hug, but Gran held me with surprising strength, her chest heaving as she cradled me to her body.

"Sweetheart, sweetheart," she said. "Where have you been?

Did you get away? I knew it wasn't that man they said. I knew they were wrong. Oh I wished you would come home."

"Gran, I'm not her." I tried to stay calm, but my heart was skipping and my throat felt so tight I couldn't breathe. Our eyes and face shapes had been similar, but Olive's hair was always darker. "I'm not her, I'm not Olive."

Gran finally let go. She held me at arm's length and stared right into my face. "Then who are you?"

"I'm *Cassie*," I said.

She stopped. Took another step backwards, regarding me with a more critical gaze. She looked at my forehead, for the mole that was mine and not Olive's. Her eyes traced the line of the scar on my neck – the one I got the summer I fell out of the tree in the garden of this very house. Not Olive's scar. *Mine.* She glanced down at my hands, saw the nails that had been bitten so much they no longer grew back evenly.

"Oh," she whispered. Her whole voice seemed to disappear on that one word. She started to collapse, to fold in on herself, and I had to reach for her. She steadied herself, stumbling slightly on the kitchen tiles. And then she looked at me with eyes filled with tears, and said it again. "Oh…"

"Why don't you – why don't you go through there? I'll make you a cup of tea and a sandwich," I said, trying to calm my voice. Trying to control the skipping rhythm of my heart. "Go on. I'll bring it through."

She did as I asked.

* * *

Did you get away? Gran's words were rattling around inside my head like a pinball. *I knew it wasn't that man they said.* I went up to my bedroom with a cup of tea and sat on my bed, laptop across my knees.

I'd never asked Gran who she thought had taken Olive. The police suspect pool in 1999 was limited, and fleeting. The list, in the end, had boiled down to my father and one other man.

I knew who Gran was thinking of. It was all over the news at the time. *Local man arrested in connection with missing girl case.* And then, later, *local man released.* But the police didn't involve us. At least, they didn't involve me.

Cordy Jones.

I clenched my teeth as I opened my laptop and navigated to the search page. If Grace and Olive were connected, this was the place to start. In my Olive Diary – on the pages I had specifically avoided yesterday – I had written everything I knew about him.

Cordy, or Jonesy as we'd known him, had run the Bishop's Green youth group between 1992 and the summer of 1999. I remembered little of him now, apart from the blurred and grainy images I'd seen in newspapers. I didn't recall that he'd been particularly nice to us. Or particularly not nice.

He'd been a Nothing Man. One of those adults that I had never paid attention to. Olive and I had been to the youth group only a handful of times that summer, once for a barbecue, and to a couple of other smaller events where the children would play party games or have water fights. I didn't think Olive had ever been alone with him. Was that enough?

The Google results weren't anything new. Although there weren't any of the original articles, here I found several web pages dedicated to unsolved missing child cases. I'd always avoided them before.

Somebody had taken the time to write about Cordy, though. To find old news headlines and compile them into one streamlined story. The story of a man, first condemned and then, suddenly, freed. "Cordy Jones questioned in missing Olive Warren case" read one headline. The next said merely: "Cordy Jones cleared of involvement".

I tried to recall how Mum and Dad had reacted at the time, but all I could see was Gran's expression as she shook her head and said, "I don't think so. He's been running that club for years. I knew his uncle, Barry"

Cordy Jones had played a role in many of my fantasies about what had happened to Olive. On my darkest days he had played the role of captor, keeping my sister from the world. But most days I preferred the fantasies where Olive turned up one day like Jaycee Lee Dugard or Elizabeth Smart; in those fantasies I didn't like to think of who had taken Olive, or what had happened to her since, only that they had somehow, for some reason, let her go again.

I scrolled through the web page, desperate for new information. For evidence that he could have taken Olive, that the police might have been wrong when they dismissed him. That he might still be around now. I wondered if we might have missed something, if somehow the bastard who took Olive had been living out the rest of his life in anonymity while we had the crucial evidence needed to put him away.

But the information here was still inconclusive. As far as I could tell, it was all circumstance. Cordy Jones had been in Chestnut Circle during the eclipse, but nobody remembered seeing him after the event was over. Last I'd heard, people in town were harassing him so much that Grandad thought he might leave Derbyshire altogether.

The day Olive was taken Jones had arranged a youth group photo session in the Circle that he never showed up to. He had no alibi, could only tell the police that he had been "around town" when Olive disappeared. I started to feel the old familiar anger well up inside me, fear creeping close behind it.

As I stared at his photograph now, I felt my insides start to cramp, the fear growing. Could this be him? Was he still in Bishop's Green? What would he look like after all these years? Was he with Grace even as I typed? Even if Grace's disappearance was unrelated, could this be the man who had kidnapped my sister?

I fixed my eyes on his face: he had chubby cheeks and bright green eyes, and a dark mop of hair. I couldn't imagine he would look much different now. But the longer I stared, the more his expression morphed into something fiendish, something unworldly.

I realised I was shaking, as cold tea dripped down my fingers. I hastily wiped my laptop keyboard. It took half an hour of steadily typing up nonsense notes to myself before my hands stopped trembling.

10

August 1999

TIME SEEMED TO HAVE this sort of shifting feel to it. Like Olive couldn't trust it. She had only a vague idea of what day it was because of the turning of night into day and then into night again. An endless cycle, already. It didn't help that she had spent most of the first few days beating her fists against things, scrambling about with her hair in her eyes and her whole body clenched taut with panic.

She hadn't seen Sandman since the day of the eclipse. Was that three days ago? Five? Seven? She tried to count them but got a different number each time. She had been too focused, in the time since, on not going crazy, on playing games inside her head and singing "Ten Green Bottles" backwards and forwards.

She still didn't know why she was here or when she could go home. Gran still hadn't come. Olive knew now that she wasn't going to.

Sandman. She had stopped thinking of him as anything else, now. Whoever he had been before, whatever part he might have played in her old life, now he was nothing more than a nightmare. Like her bad dreams, she discovered that he only came at night. After she was asleep. He would slip into the room and leave her things; food, clothes, and often toiletries, too, would be in their rightful places on shelves and in the fridge when she woke up. The first morning she woke up and there was suddenly a bulb in the fixture overhead. Once, she had taken her ring off before sleep and when she woke up it was back on her finger.

Sometimes he left nothing, but she didn't doubt he had still been to visit. She never heard him come into the room, never heard him leave. But she felt that he'd been there – felt his icy presence each morning like a ghostly hand on the back of her neck.

What she thought was the seventh night was different.

It wasn't yet dark. What little she could see of the sky was smudged a sort of charcoal blue and tinged at the edges with orange.

She had developed a sort of routine since those first couple of days, when she had dozed and woken in a crazy cycle. After what she thought was probably the third day, she had tried harder to keep things normal, waking as the sun fell on her face in the morning and staring at walls until she got hungry. Already, she knew, she was thinner than before. The clothes he had brought her originally were too big now. The dresses that were tight before had become baggier around the middle.

A week.

And now, sitting on the bed and waiting for the light to filter out of the room – she didn't like to use the lamp because of the brightness, because of the way it made the room feel hollow – she heard him.

She knew it was him. There was something about the weight of footsteps outside the room, perhaps coming down some stairs… Getting louder all the time. She felt herself shrink instinctively, her knees going up towards her chest. Her breath came thick and fast as a million horrible thoughts rushed through her mind. She didn't have time to do anything else.

The door opened. He stepped inside, his arms full of bags. Plastic bags, mostly. Some from Tesco and others from clothes shops like Next and Gap. He was wearing similar clothes to before: jeans, faded T-shirt, trainers. His hair was pushed back from his forehead and a little greasy, the curls lank.

He closed the door, locking it carefully with a set of keys, which he hung around his neck, and then he dumped the bags on the floor. Olive didn't move. She was frozen. Her blood felt like ice in her veins and her stomach cramped in panic.

"How are you, Olive?"

His voice was calm, but gravelly. Like he hadn't had enough sleep. Olive didn't know what to say. What answer could she have given to that? Instead she just shook her head, mute.

"Well, come on now," he said. "There's no need to be scared. I haven't hurt you, have I?"

Olive thought about this, a weird mix of feelings fizzing in her stomach. She lowered her knees slightly so she could see him better. He was right. He hadn't hurt her. Did that mean there was something she was missing? Some fact she didn't know about why she was here? Could it be that he was trying to... protect her? Like Cassie did sometimes when Mum and Dad argued? But Cassie had been oblivious to what the arguing meant, that Mum and Dad were getting divorced. So what good was that sort of protection?

Anyway, the look on Sandman's face told her that this wasn't true. She wasn't missing anything. He wasn't going to let her go. He frowned a little bit, his lips pouting and his eyebrows dipping – but his eyes were hawk-like and fixed on her face. She shivered.

"No," she said, very quietly. "You haven't hurt me."

This was what he wanted to hear. Her voice sounded funny to her ears, rusty after days of only crying. She licked her dry lips.

"Good." He stood awkwardly by the door, as though he didn't really know what to do with himself. This frightened Olive more than anything else. He was in control, he was the grown-up here. And he didn't know what he was doing.

"Are you... here to bring me some things?" she asked.

Sandman glanced down at the bags, and then looked at Olive again.

"Do you like your bedroom?" he asked, ignoring her question. It was like he'd found what he wanted to talk about now, and Olive felt giddy with fear and hope and everything in between.

"I want to go home."

This was the wrong thing to say. His face darkened and it was like the eclipse all over again as his expression morphed into something else.

"You can't," he said.

"Why not?"

Olive was surprised at herself. As though the words weren't hers. She slapped her hand over her mouth straight away, but Sandman seemed amused rather than angry.

"Because your gran is ill. She asked me to watch you until she's better."

Olive felt any hope she had shrivel inside her, like her whole body had become wooden. She wasn't stupid. Gran was fine. This was a lie. All of it. He wasn't safe, he wasn't kind just because he brought her things. He wasn't her friend and Gran was fine.

Olive was going to tell him so, but she remembered the darkness in his face when she'd said she wanted to go home. She didn't want the darkness to spread, to catch her too. So she nodded.

"*When* can I go home?" she asked, quieter. Trying to look like Cassie did when she knew she was in trouble and wanted somebody to forgive her. Maybe – just maybe – he would see that she wasn't going to cause a problem and he'd let her go.

"Soon." He gestured at the bags. "More clothes. Food. Take off what you've been wearing. You're disgusting. Get me your other clothes, too. I'll wash them for you. And you need to wash yourself better, too. But for now, get those dirty things off."

Olive paused.

"Take my clothes off now?"

"Well I'm not coming back for them."

Sandman stared at her. Olive felt her insides trembling, like her whole body was TV static. Another wave of dread washed over her.

"Don't just sit there gawping," he snapped. He moved towards her, jerkily as though he wasn't in control of his body. But neither was Olive, and she jumped away, holding in a yelp.

"Oh, for Christ's sake I'm not going to hurt you." He stopped. "I won't need to if you do what I'm asking like a good girl."

Olive moved robotically. Inched to the edge of the bed. Turned away to pull the dress over her head. She held her hands over her chest, feeling the tepid air brush her sweaty skin. She was shivering again.

"Here."

He thrust something at her, and she realised it was the Gap bag. A skirt and top, this time. Still old-fashioned, still like clothes you'd give to a younger child. She hurriedly snapped the tags off and slid the foreign material over her head. The top had a collar that caught in her hair and smelled like a shopping centre, like somebody else's life. She wanted to cry but tried to swallow the tears behind her sore eyes.

"Better," he said approvingly once she turned back to him. "Much better. Next time I'll bring you clean sheets, too."

He started to gather the dirty clothes into the empty plastic bag. Olive held her breath. She wanted him to go. To leave her. Him being in the room was like a suck on the air, like she couldn't breathe. She stood trembling in the same place while he put the food in the fridge and cleared out the things she hadn't eaten. He tutted once, but said nothing else.

And then he was heading back to the door.

"Can you tell my family I'm okay?" she asked, the words bursting out of her. "Please? Just tell them I'm okay?"

He didn't answer her.

The lock clunking back into place on the other side was a sound like the shutting of a coffin lid. Because that was it. She might as well be dead. And if she couldn't make him let her go, eventually she might be.

11

AFTER MY FAILURE TO get anywhere in my research on Cordy
Jones, what had felt like determination to succeed this morning
now felt like sheer stupidity. Perhaps Marion was right when
she told me not to connect Grace and Olive. But even as I said
this to myself, I knew I wouldn't stop.

I dropped in to Ady's shop to grab a coffee from the instant
machine. He was behind the till with a thin smile on his face.
He waved when he saw me. I paid for my coffee and we chatted
as the machine clicked and whirred to life, hot water spurting.

I glanced at the newspapers at the till. Grace's face was
still splashed all over them. I'd sold the piece I'd written on
Adelaide Upton and filed it with a local online news outlet, but
rather than pride I felt simply uncomfortable at the thought
that I was once again part of the circus. I was deep in thought
when Ady cleared his throat.

"Huh?" I asked.

"I said that it's awful. That nobody's found her yet." He
gestured at the papers. "And all these vultures, snooping
around the place." He stared at me pointedly and I felt

embarrassment clog my throat, though I wasn't sure if he'd read my article. "I had two in here earlier. I'm not having Tilly walking to or from school. She's been pushing me about it and I'd said I might consider it but I think I've changed my mind." He shook his head.

"It's just a job for some people," I said quietly.

"Yeah, well." He shrugged. "I didn't see you searching with the others last night…?"

"No. Sorry. I was with my gran. And like I said, my head's all over the place thinking about my sister and work." I felt guilty. Perhaps everybody was right: I'd be more use out there searching for the poor girl than writing about it.

"You're definitely working again, then?"

So he hadn't seen it yet. For some reason the feeling filled me with dread.

"Yeah," I said, grabbing my coffee and getting ready to head out. "Just one piece so far." It was good to have a purpose. But why didn't I feel the satisfaction that I had always felt before?

By the time I left Ady's it was just about time for the kids to be coming out of school, and although I had no real intention of doing so I found myself once again pulling up outside the gates and sitting quietly, watching as the children started to filter out.

I'd booked a call with Doctor White that morning and he rang while I was waiting. Gran's last outburst had scared me more than I liked to admit, and I wanted to make sure the sleeping pills wouldn't exacerbate her symptoms, but our conversation was muted and I couldn't focus.

"Well, they shouldn't," the doctor said after I explained my concerns. "But you can monitor it for yourself and we can find an alternative if you're not happy with the results. Just give it a few more days and see how she gets on."

There were more children in Grace's friend group today, and I figured that the others who hadn't been there before were now back at school. I half-listened as the doctor listed several other options for Gran, thinking of the bills I'd have to pay for the carers and wondering how else I could help her, marvelling at how normal the world seemed, how collected the kids were, even in spite of the craziness that was kicking off around them.

"I'm sorry I asked you about Grace Butler," I said, once the doctor had finished. "I know that was rude. I just wanted to make sure I had all the information I could get."

Doctor White snorted, but accepted my apology. "Listen," he said. "I'm sorry, I've got to go, I've got another patient waiting. If you have any concerns going forward make another appointment and we'll talk. Okay?"

I watched as the boy in Grace's group – Alex – made a joke, and the girls burst into false laughter. All except one of the girls, who saw my car. She was the brunette, the ballsy one who'd challenged me. Grace's best friend, Bella.

"That would be great," I said. But now my focus was shifting. The doctor hung up with another promise. I watched the crowd across the street more closely.

The girl stopped a second, pausing to let her friends get ahead of her. She met my eyes, her gaze piercing. And then she waved her hand a little and dipped her head in a smile. I didn't know what to do, shocked by her friendliness. I half lifted my hand to wave back, but by that time she'd already run after her friends.

The parents were out in force again today. Like Ady, they seemed afraid to let their children walk even the shortest distance home. I saw Tilly with a woman I didn't know – perhaps a babysitter. Even before all of this, her father hadn't allowed her to walk home alone. I'd wanted to tell Ady that controlling Tilly wasn't likely to help – there were dangers everywhere – but it didn't seem my place to say anything.

There were also several other people outside the gates today. Journalists. I'd seen a few in town, and more outside the police station when I'd driven past. I even recognised one from my London days, a woman who I didn't know well enough to speak to but whose face was annoyingly familiar. I had been tempted to go to the official police updates, but I couldn't stomach it. The station in Bishop's Green made me think too much of Olive. I was better off doing this on my own. And I hadn't written anything beyond the piece on Grace's mother.

Grace had been missing for five days – almost a week now. By a week, the evidence would be gone, wouldn't it? A week into Olive's case the police were already calling the leads "cold", hopping from one thought to the next, fixating on innocent people because they had nothing else to go on.

If, of course, Cordy Jones *was* innocent.

I leaned back, itching for a cigarette.

I was just about to pull my car back out onto the road when I noticed the van. It was white, the paint chipped and rusting around the bumper. The roof was covered in pink blossoms from the cherry trees, and it looked like it had been sitting around for a while. I craned my neck, trying to see inside.

The windows were dark, obscured by the moving clouds and the light drizzle that had started to fall. I flicked my wipers on and sat perfectly still for another minute, watching for movement. The flow of children had dried up now. The rain got heavier. One of the teachers was lingering outside the school, his tie flapping in the wind. Still the van didn't move. The owner probably wasn't a parent.

Before I could work out whether it was a good idea, I was out of the car. My body moved on autopilot as I marched over to the van, feeling the rain begin to soak me through, coating my glasses in a spray of wetness. The driver became more tangible, a more concrete shape. The shape of a man. And as I got closer, I heard his engine turn on.

"Nope."

Without thinking I stepped in front of the van and placed my palm on the bonnet. I made a rolling gesture with my other hand, suggesting that he wind down his window. The man seemed to struggle, sitting completely still for a good few seconds.

I saw his expression flicker between fear and anger. Anger succeeded, and he revved the accelerator. I fought the urge to jump back, knowing that would mean he'd won. Instead, I kept one hand on the van and moved around so I could bang my hand against the driver's window.

"I just want to talk to you!" I yelled.

And then, finally, he let the window down. I tried to calm my breathing as he stared at me. Up close, he was less intimidating. But he still had a car that was capable of running me over if I wasn't careful.

The bloke was small, skinny like a weed, and dressed in an *Adventure Time* T-shirt. He had several days of beard growth, crooked teeth, and he smelled faintly of Lynx body spray.

"What d'you want?" he asked.

"I could ask you the same question." I gave him my best authoritarian stare. At first he didn't budge, but then I saw his resolve begin to waver as he shifted in his seat.

"What are you doing sitting outside a *school?*" I tried to cling to the moral high ground, praying that he didn't ask me the same question.

"I'm allowed to be here," he said.

Somehow I doubted it.

"Yeah, right. Come on, mate. Don't give me that. You're being a creep."

This got him. It was probably a bit rough off the cuff, but I was still pissed off that he'd threatened to run me down. He opened and closed his mouth like a fish out of water.

"N-no," he stammered. "No! I just... Gracie—"

I slammed my hand down on his car again, making him jump.

"Stop," I said. "*Gracie.* Only her family call her that. You know her?"

"Ye-yeah," he admitted. "She's a friend, like. Nothing weird, I promise. We talk sometimes."

I failed to see how that could be the truth. This guy was, what, at least as old as I was? Late twenties maybe, but more likely in his mid-thirties. What on earth would an eleven-year-old want with a guy like him?

Before he could say anything else I pulled out my phone.

"What are you gonna do?" the guy asked. "Please don't get me in trouble. I know it's not the right day—"

"Why shouldn't I?" I demanded. "You're sitting in your car outside a *school*. What are you doing here?"

"I'm allowed to be here," he whimpered again.

I stared at him. "Really?"

"I swear. I come every week."

"And you talk to Grace. What about? How do you know her?" I still had my phone in my hand, but I didn't hit the dial button. For one, because Marion would skin me alive if she knew I was down here hanging around the school and making a nuisance of myself. And, I thought, I might get more out of him by myself.

"What do you do at the school?" I prompted again. "Do you know where she is?"

"No! I just…" The guy rubbed his hands over his face and let out a long sigh as though trying to calm himself down. "We're sort of friends. I used to know her dad, like. Before he moved out of town. Gracie's nice. Sometimes she sees me after school when I do the car boot. You can ask the lady I run it with sometimes. Gracie says hi. That's all."

I thought again of Cordy Jones, of how he'd been friendly with children too. I went cold, shaking my head. What kind of idiot was this guy? But then, it was so ludicrous it might be true. *Like Cordy might have been telling the truth when he said he was innocent*, my brain suggested, somewhat unhelpfully.

"Why are you here *today*?"

"I wanted to… I just thought I'd look for her. See if I could figure it out…"

"You could be out there searching for her," I said. I was aware of my hypocrisy – I could also be out there searching for her. Walking the streets, going through the woods and down by the lake. But that felt too much like searching for a body – not a person. And maybe this guy just felt the same way.

"I tried looking," he said quietly. "I was out last night with a bunch of people, teachers and police, like. But I just hoped she'd turn up here… I just thought maybe…"

My phone was beginning to get wet with rain and felt slick in my hand. I stepped back a little and glanced down the road. There was nobody there. Nobody to have seen us – or to back up his story. Now what?

"What's your name?" I asked.

"Darren," the guy said without missing a beat. "Walker. Please don't call the police. I swear I wasn't here to cause trouble. I don't – I didn't—"

"Shut up." I cut him off with a wave of my hand. "Let me think, will you?"

But the more I thought the more confusing it got.

"I want your address," I said. "And your phone number."

And every other damn thing about you. "I'm *not* going to ring the police right now, but I'm going to confirm what you told me. All right?"

Darren Walker stared at me, confusion evident on his face. "Uh, okay."

I handed my phone through the window on the notes app, indicating that he should type the details there. He hesitated, and then did as I'd asked. When he handed my phone back, I realised that his hands were shaking. I stood for a second before saying anything else.

"If you mess me around, you'll regret it," I said. He nodded. "And I'd better not catch you around here again anytime soon."

With that, I went back to my car. I made a note of the number plate of the van and watched until it drove away. I didn't know whether I'd done the right thing. Just because I wasn't going to tell Marion right away didn't mean he wasn't odd. And it certainly didn't mean I wasn't going to do some digging.

I looked at my phone, realising too late I could have asked Walker to let me see his phone and he'd probably have obliged. He could have been lying about his name – about everything. I should have asked him more questions. But I wasn't thinking straight.

I went back to Cordy Jones. There was something that made me think of him after seeing this guy skulking around the school. A reminder of the past, maybe? The obvious suspect? I'd given up guessing why my mind worked the way it did. But now Cordy was in my head, and I needed to do something about it.

I texted Marion. Just to be sure they were following old leads too.

The minutes waiting for a reply were agony. And when I got one it was unsatisfactory to say the least.

We checked it. It's not relevant.

What did that mean? Annoyance building, I scrolled down to Henry's name and dialled his number.

"You work me hard, darling," Henry said immediately on answering. He sounded like he was smoking, his breaths irregular and punctuating his sentence in the wrong place.

"Sorry, I don't want to interrupt." I ran my hand through my hair, watching as rain began to fall even more heavily and splatter on my windscreen. I really wanted a cigarette, but I tucked my hand between my knees and that helped a bit. Smoking wasn't my biggest vice, at least.

"Well, you've done it now," Henry joked. "What's up?"

"Can I ask you for a favour?"

"Another one?" Henry made out like he was thinking about it. "I guess I can manage that. Listen, if I come to Derbyshire this week for a holiday, you owe me dinner. Okay?"

"It's about a different case," I said, ignoring him. "Sort of off-topic. I want an outside perspective on it – but I also don't want you to dig around too much. Just on what I tell you. It's... sensitive."

Something in my tone must have given me away, because I heard Henry make a sniffing sound. I knew he'd do as I asked. Whatever Henry's flaws, generally he had a decent understanding of boundaries. Especially mine.

"So, what is it?" he prompted.

"Well, first off, can you see if you can trace a phone number for me?" I read him the number from the anonymous text message.

"Any reason?" Henry asked.

"No. No reason. And, something else, too. There's a guy – I'm not sure if he has anything to do with Grace – but I can't find any evidence of him after the late nineties. I don't want to waste too much time on it if it's not relevant, and I already asked Marion to look into it but she says they've ruled it out. But I know how you love a good mystery and I want to know for myself."

"What information do you have?"

"Just his name," I said. "But that's all you'll need."

Henry sounded like he was reaching around for a pen, and then he went quiet.

"It's Cordy Jones," I said.

"Shit."

Henry knew who he was, then. He'd probably googled him when I finally opened up about Olive. In fact, he probably knew more about the man than I did.

"Yeah. Like I said, I'm not sure it's relevant, but given the media circus that exploded at the time I'm having trouble finding out any current information on him. Do you think you can work your magic for me?"

Henry didn't even pause to think about it.

"Okay," he said. "Give me twenty-four hours. There's something else, too. Might be important. I found something on Grace's stepdad."

12

ROGER UPTON'S WHITE AUDI nosed into a small pub car park about fifteen miles outside of Bishop's Green and I guided my own car to a stop just beyond. Had he driven all this way just for a drink? I waited until Roger went inside, and then I followed him. This was a bad idea but I couldn't stop myself.

It was warm in the pub and my glasses steamed up after the cold night air. I scanned the room for Roger, alert for his stocky build, but I still jumped when he appeared directly to my left, two glasses in hand.

"I thought it was you."

I spun around quickly, morphing the alarm on my face into what I hoped might look like steely resolve. We stood facing each other for a moment in silence. I didn't know what to say. At least we were in public.

"Here," he said, thrusting one of the glasses at me. I could smell the gin, and it made me cringe. Cheap vodka was one thing, a horrendous taste I'd slowly learned to deal with, but gin? Nope.

Taking the glass gingerly, I half-nodded my head. This wasn't what I'd expected; I'd thought he might be angry, or suspicious, but instead he seemed thoughtful.

Roger gestured to the table nearest us. When I didn't immediately take a seat he did it again, this time with more emphasis. I saw his eyes flash and suddenly became aware how big he was. His muscles bulged under his shirt and I felt like a child in comparison. So I sat down, grateful at least that I wouldn't have to smell the gin if I put it on the table.

"I'm not sure—"

"You're wrong about me—"

We had both spoken at once. I stopped myself so he could continue.

"Go on," I said. "Why?"

"I saw you following me," Roger said. "You wouldn't follow me unless you thought I'd done something wrong."

"If you didn't do anything wrong, why have you driven all the way out here when there are plenty of pubs nearer your house?" I scowled at him. "That smacks of a guilty conscience to me. Aren't you worried?"

"Of course I'm worried about Gracie," he snapped. "But I don't see why that means I've gotta have strangers breathing down my neck every minute of every day. You're not the bloody police, are you? Why did you follow me?"

"Mr Up—"

"No, hang on. I just want to tell you that I'm not this bastard you think I am, all right? I know what everybody is saying. Oh, the stepdad did it. But I'm just as scared as anybody else. I've been out there with the others for hours and hours looking for her. But at the end of the day what good's gonna be done by me sitting at home moping about? We'll never get anywhere like that. We had this family liaison officer come round and he was all, 'It's important that you spend some time together as a family,' but we haven't got one any more. Without Gracie we're just two people. That ain't a family, is it?"

"You could be supporting each other," I tried. "And yet you're out here."

"Of course I am!"

I glanced around furtively as Roger's voice rose another notch, but nobody even looked our way. It was already too noisy in here. God, if ever a drink would take the edge off and stop me overthinking everything it would be *right now*. But I couldn't risk relaxing too much, letting my guard down. This wasn't just some interview, it was important.

"I'm not likely to go to the pub down the road after – after everything, am I? Any bloke in there could be – could be the one that's got Gracie. And if he ain't then at the very least they're all bloody staring at me and it's all, 'Sorry your kid got snatched,' or, 'Don't worry mate, they'll catch the bastard.' And what am I meant to say to that? 'Oh, course they will, Joe. No that's okay, Matt, I don't feel too shitty about it, so you can all quit apologising and enjoy your pint.' Either that or they think I hurt her."

He was breathing hard, and I felt a knot of guilt form in my stomach. But I couldn't stop now. Not after what Henry had told me.

"*Did* you hurt her?" I asked.

The words fell into the air like stones. I saw the curling of his lip, the narrowing of his nostrils, and I tried not to flinch. I wouldn't let him intimidate me.

"D'you really think I hurt Gracie?" Roger said, each word punctuated with spit. "Is that what you're saying?"

"What I'm saying is that I know about what happened – in 1992. When you were accused of having inappropriate relations with a minor—"

His face paled considerably, and I wondered if he might actually hit me.

"Does Adelaide know? Is that why she's afraid to talk to the press? Because she's worried she'll let something slip?"

"Oh you have *no right* to bring that up." Roger started to stand. "I talked to the police already and I don't have to explain myself to you. You're just a vulture. I did that interview to help Gracie. I want her home. Adelaide isn't good at talking – she's too nervous. It might have been different with you but I didn't want to take the chance. She hasn't got the strength to stand up there and have her picture taken, and somebody needed to do it. The world needs to know Gracie's out there – *I* needed to know we were doing everything we could."

"Does your family know about your past, Roger? Do the people in Bishop's Green?"

Roger's expression contorted again. He raised his hand and this time I flinched.

My reaction seemed to bring him back to the present.

His face fell and he sank back into his chair.

The barmaid moved into view from behind the bar. Her gaze locked with mine in a silent, but obvious, *Are you okay?* I fought back my fear, wrestled it under control. And then I nodded. *I'm fine.* Fine.

"You don't understand," Roger repeated, quieter now. "You've got it all wrong."

"Explain it to me then."

I felt my phone buzz in my pocket, the second time since we'd sat down. I ignored it, thinking instead of what Henry had told me earlier: *Roger Upton was accused of having sex with a teenager.* I had to play this right. "How am I confused?"

He took a deep breath, and then looked me right in the eyes.

"It was a long time ago."

"Like that excuses it?" I couldn't help myself, the anger fizzing in my gut igniting like wick paper.

"No, let me finish. It was a long time ago. I was... I was twenty-five. She was — she was younger. I'm *not* into kids," he said quickly, "but she looked — she seemed older. When I met her she told me she was nineteen. I believed her. But she was only fifteen. We dated a bit. Then when we broke up her mum found out and went ballistic, said I'd had sex with her and that it was basically rape."

"And you went to trial?"

"No, because they couldn't prove it — because it didn't happen. Okay? We just went to the cinema and hung out. Obviously I hoped people wouldn't find out because I didn't

129

want them to get stuck on me when they should be out there looking for *Grace*."

"Then why do the interviews?" I pressed.

"I told you. Adelaide wouldn't do it and somebody had to. Somebody has to make Gracie look *human* so they let her come home. Adelaide asked me to handle the press because she was worried she'd say the wrong thing; she was so guilty she couldn't make herself do it. When you came to the house I thought that she didn't want you there. But then...

"Look." He sighed. "It was never about hiding this. I've already lived through people judging me once. I just want to keep Grace's name out of it. I don't want her to... To be ashamed of me."

I felt hot, suddenly. I'd come here expecting a confrontation, or denial. Instead I felt dirty, guilty for dredging up something that had nothing to do with me. My face prickled. I pushed the glass of gin back and stood, suddenly convinced that I *needed* to leave. Had to. Before I made it any worse.

"Mr Upton, surely you expected this to come out. Your daughter is missing. I was just doing my job. Better that it was me than one of those other *vultures*. I haven't written anything – and I won't. But it may still come out."

I set my mouth in a grim line, steadying myself for the inevitable eruption. But nothing happened. He stared at me for a moment, sadness and shame burning in his eyes. I didn't wait for him to process what I was saying because he already knew. There was no fear. Those were the eyes of somebody with a lot of regrets.

And the way he cared more about Grace's embarrassment than his own, I was no longer sure that hurting his stepdaughter was one of them.

I marched back to my car, confusion consuming me from the inside. I fumbled for my phone in the half-light, breath coming thick and fast as my frustration steamed up the car windows. The reception up here in the hills was patchy, sometimes non-existent. The bars morphed from zero to three in seconds.

A text popped up. For a second I felt panic trill in my fingers, remembering the text I'd had before. *back off.* It was the same number.

Still, I swiped the message open, curiosity getting the better of me.

i told you to back off. let it lie. stop sniffing around

I was a different kind of agitated now. I should tell Marion, ask her to follow up, to trace the number like I'd asked Henry. It was probably just some hack taking the piss but I couldn't shake the feeling that something wasn't right. But if I told Marion, I'd have to admit that I was afraid and I wasn't ready for that.

I hardly had time to digest this thought when my phone buzzed again, this time in a frenzied vibrating ring.

"Cassie, thank God. I've been trying to call you." It was Marion.

"Sorry, I was just – I was going to get in touch." I stopped dead, dread curdling in my stomach. "Wait. What's the matter?"

"It's – your gran, Cass. Are you near your car? Can you meet me at the Babington Hospital?"

"Hospital? Marion, what the hell's going on?"

"I just got a call," Marion said. "Apparently your phone was going to voicemail and they tried you at home – and… Look, I think she's okay but she got out and she was wandering down the street and somebody – somebody hit her, in the road… I can't tell you any more because I don't know. I think she's okay. Cass, can you just meet me there?"

I dropped my phone. My whole body felt numb. All thoughts disappeared except Marion's words and suddenly I was driving. I forced the car out onto the road without checking my mirrors and raced the miles to the hospital.

I pushed my foot down on the accelerator, my heart hammering so loud that I hardly heard the honked horn of a fellow motorist as I skidded at a junction. What on earth had Gran been doing? Where was she? Why would somebody have hit her? Could she have broken bones? Or worse…?

I reached the hospital in record time, my tyres screeching as I slammed to a stop outside the emergency entrance. I hadn't even asked Marion where she would be, but thankfully I saw her car in the car park just outside, a blue light visible where she'd left it sitting on her seat.

I jogged through the entrance. And there was Marion, standing awkwardly by herself on one side of the waiting room, which was half full of people with sprained limbs and broken fingers.

"Marion!" I said breathlessly. "What's happening? She

wasn't meant to be on her own. The carer..."

Marion pulled me into a hug, her whole body taut with unspoken words. She held me for a second, and I could smell the police station on her, a familiar smell that was offices and printer toner, coffee and cigarettes. I wanted to cry, but I couldn't. The lump in my throat was too big, and I could hardly breathe. I pulled back, and looked right into her face.

"*Tell me what happened,*" I said.

"She was in the street," Marion said. "Somebody hit her with their car. Thankfully they weren't going very fast. One of your neighbours found her and called an ambulance."

I took a moment to collect myself, trying to force down the panic that was still rising. Had I got the days mixed up? Was it my fault she was alone? I tried not to panic. That's what it meant, looking after Gran; I had to learn to control my emotions. Never mind the sick, shaking feeling that was threatening to engulf me. Never mind the text message on my phone.

The threat.

i told you to back off.

But I couldn't think about that now. If I did... I would lose it. So I took another moment, and another, until I realised I was just staring into Marion's face and I didn't have anything to say.

"She's okay, Cassie," she said. "It's okay. It's not your fault."

But it *was* my fault. I needed to make it right.

13

GRAN'S INJURIES WERE FAIRLY minor. A broken arm from the way she fell against the kerb and some nasty bruises on her face where she'd landed. The hospital wanted to keep her in for a couple of days just to keep an eye on her. I wanted to stay but the nurse sent me home when it got late, assuring me they would call if there was any change.

Marion offered to make me a late dinner. By the time I pulled up outside her house I was exhausted, my head pounding and mouth dry. I wasn't sure I wanted to be there but the thought of going home to an empty house had made me agree. I couldn't shake the feeling that Gran had been hurt because of me. She was out on the street because I hadn't made sure she was safe. I thought of the text messages. Had they had anything to do with her accident? Was it deliberate? I'd deleted both texts after I'd read them but now I regretted it.

I should have shown them to Marion. She would know what to do. Yet I couldn't bring myself to tell her about them, even now. What if she got hurt, too? What if, by telling her, I put her in danger? And a guilty part of me couldn't bear the thought that she'd tell me to stop digging, too.

The guilt squirmed inside of me. It was my fault. The timing of Gran's accident, of the last text message… It was too close to be anything else and I was left with the trembling certainty that somebody thought I knew something. Something I shouldn't know. Or they were afraid that if I didn't already, then I would soon.

Marion greeted me with a cup of tea. She pressed it into my hands and I sank into her sofa gratefully. For a blissful few seconds my mind felt emptied by my exhaustion, and I could think of nothing but the warm steam rising and the familiar childhood smell of sweet milky tea.

I thought of my dad. How when I was very little he would fetch me home from school and the house would always smell like warm tea. He forever had a brew on, the kettle going or the teapot beneath a cosy on the kitchen table. I remembered the way he'd smooth our hair back, pop our school jumpers on the backs of our chairs. Little things he stopped doing after a while.

He used to practically force-feed Olive and me shortbread biscuits during those afternoons when Mum was working and he was watching us. His own mother had spent many years living in Edinburgh before she passed away, and shortbread had been her favourite afternoon snack. It was something he never failed to tell us.

I cupped the tea Marion had made to my chest, soaking up the warmth of the mug. It was times like this I missed my dad. Missed what we had been before things started to fall apart. It hadn't been good between him and Mum before Olive was taken, but it might have resolved itself... I shook the thought from my mind.

"Are you okay?" Marion asked, sitting on the coffee table opposite me. She looked tired, too. Her hair was a mess, dark circles forming under her eyes.

"Not really," I said quietly. "It's been a long few days."

Marion sighed, drinking from her own cup and then resting her elbows on her knees.

"Cassie, I really think you need to cut yourself some slack. Take a break. After what's happened you ought to be with your gran instead of running around trying to do my job for me." She winced, realising even as she said it that she was being harsh. "That's not what I mean... But do you understand where I'm coming from?"

"Grace Butler is still out there," I said, suddenly more awake. Gran's accident didn't have to be for nothing. "She's still out there and I can still help her. And when I was at the school there was—"

"Cassie..."

"And I talked to Roger Upton—"

"*Cassie*," Marion cut me off again. "I know that you want to help, but I just... I think you're putting a lot of effort into something that isn't going to pay off."

"What do you mean?"

"I just mean that... With Grace, I think you're barking up the wrong tree. Okay? There're a lot of leads we're following right now, and I do think we're getting somewhere. It's not worth you putting your life – your gran – on hold."

"Marion, you're speaking in riddles."

"Cassie, in cases like this – we start with the family."

"That's why Roger—"

"Roger and Adelaide Upton aren't Grace's only family. She has a biological father, and her dad's in the – look, promise you won't write any of this? I can't go on record yet."

"He's in the *what*, Marion?"

"In the wind," she said. "He's self-employed, works from home a lot which explains why nobody batted an eyelid when they didn't hear from him for a couple of days over the weekend. We left messages and heard nothing back so we sent a team round to check out his house. He wasn't there. He's got an assistant and she's not heard from him since last week, and apparently there's been some contention about him jetting off on holiday in the past without letting anybody know, especially when he has a low workload. We've checked and he's not left the country but he's got his car…"

I gripped my trembling cup tighter. I thought of the way my dad had been treated when Olive was taken. It couldn't be Grace's father. Could it?

I remembered my dad's face when he told me he was leaving. His eyes had been bloodshot, his brow creased. Stubble on his chin. He was truly heartbroken – but whether it was because Olive was gone, or whether it was because he knew he was about to walk away from the family he'd spent so long building, I hadn't known.

"It won't be for long," he'd said. Lied. "I'm just going to stay in a hotel until all of this blows over."

The morning light had lit up his wrinkles like scars and I'd known, right then, that he wasn't coming back. I also knew it wasn't because of the police inquiry. It would have happened anyway. He hugged me, bone-deep and long, and I breathed in the scent of books and aftershave, knowing that soon it would all be different.

"Why?" I'd asked. Tears made everything blurry.

"You and Mum are better off without me."

"No we're not. You can't have a family with just two people."

Dad held me at arm's length, looking at me so intently it hurt. All the while it felt like my heart was breaking, the world collapsing under its own weight.

"We're still a family, Cass. I'm still your dad."

He was wrong. Dads didn't just leave when it got hard. Dads didn't move in with other women. They didn't pretend that everything was okay when it wasn't. The eclipse still hung over us, even then, the darkness invading everything – every look, every conversation.

I pictured the eclipse as I said what I'd wanted to say since I found out about her. About Carol. I bared my teeth at him in a disgusted snarl.

"You stopped being my dad the day you chose screwing her over looking after us."

He hadn't even argued.

"I…" I pulled myself back to the present. Marion was watching me carefully. "Do you really think Grace's father has something to do with it?" I asked.

Marion ignored the question.

"I think you need to take some time and get yourself together," she said. "I can see how you're linking this to Olive and I know you've been asking questions, and that's all fine if it's for your writing or whatever, but I really don't think…" She took a deep breath. "I think you're taking it too far, Cass. You're too invested. And I know what you're like."

Although Marion's voice was filled with warmth, I couldn't shake the feeling that I was being reprimanded. Told off like a stupid kid. This wasn't me just being reckless or making stuff up. I wasn't taking it too far.

I wasn't taking it far enough.

"You can't tell me it isn't a connection you made yourself," I said. "Grace. Olive. The eclipse."

Marion shook her head. "I won't deny that the eclipse had me spooked. I still can't shake it, like every time I blink it's right there, in my eyes…" She rubbed her face, as though trying to scrub away the image. "But timing isn't everything – and Olive was taken *during* the eclipse. So it doesn't even match up. I have new leads to follow so can you give me some time to prove it to you?"

I could see how hard Marion was trying. Especially when she didn't believe herself a hundred per cent. I looked at her and tried to nod. Really tried. But I couldn't get my body to lie.

I was in too deep already. There was Darren Walker outside the school, Roger Upton's history, and I couldn't stop wondering about Cordy Jones. And then there was the mood ring, the one Grace was wearing that looked so much like Olive's, and the anonymous text messages on top of all that…

I had too many open leads, too much inside my head to just drop it. I knew that made me awful, plotting and scheming and thinking while Gran was in hospital, but I couldn't stop it. I couldn't have her hurting for nothing.

I had been unable to stop since I'd opened the Olive Diary. Like Pandora with her box, I couldn't close it now. Olive's ghost was back, insistent; I needed to ask the questions, no matter what answers I might find.

"Okay," I promised. My tongue didn't betray my lie. "I'll try. Now can we just watch some shit TV until I'm ready to go home and fall asleep?"

I typed up some of my thoughts about my meeting with Roger Upton before bed in the hopes I might be able to sleep better without my mind whirring. I couldn't face turning any of this into a proper article. Something just didn't sit right with me although I knew, as I'd told him, that it would probably come out eventually. But I hoped that by sifting through my thoughts I might be able to push back the dreams for one night. I thought of the pills Doctor White had prescribed, sitting in the cabinet just down the hall, but I made myself ignore them. They weren't mine to take.

I hoped I would be too exhausted to dream.

I was wrong.

The darkness was heavy, smothering me like a blanket. It pulled tight around my skin, making it hard to breathe. I was sweating, tossing and turning and fighting. The walls were silver-grey, hostile and sterile. Mum gripped my hand as we walked. My blood thrummed in my ears, memories haunting me. I'd had variations on this dream before.

"I don't want to do this," I said, voice hoarse.

Mum tightened her grip on my hand and marched on. I had no choice but to follow. Gone were any of the soft edges I remembered in her face; now she was all hard lines, her strong grip making me wince.

Eventually we came to a room. We didn't go in. A man hovered at the edge of my vision, his clothes dark. I realised where we were and felt my whole body go numb with terror. My heart beat loud in my ears; my face was already wet with tears. Mum gripped my hand harder. I felt my knuckles crack.

"Mum, it hurts—"

"Are you ready?"

There was a voice. Disembodied. And then the dark wall in front of us came to life; not a wall, but a window. A sheet of glass bigger than the span of my arms. I could feel my heartbeat double in speed. Triple. I thought I might die. I held my breath until my lungs screamed for air, and gripped my mother's hand right back.

"Do you see? Is it her?" Mum's voice shook.

I realised my eyes were closed. I forced them open.

In the room there was a table. On the table was a girl. I felt the bile rising inside me before I could stop it, but I swallowed it down. I wouldn't let this beat me. It couldn't be true. Wasn't true. The body was too long. Too pale. The hair too bright, the eyes – *all wrong.*

Mum started to cry. Horrible, vicious sobs that ripped through her. Through me. She pulled away, took her hand from mine. I clung to her sleeve but she pushed me off. The darkness started to swallow her, as if in slow motion. *Mum, wait.* She didn't wait. Distance between us growing, she began to blur through my tears.

Then she was gone and I could still smell the sharp, expensive tang of her perfume. It was the last time I saw her alive, the last time I touched her while she was warm and strong.

The next memory came no matter how hard I tried to wake up.

The house muted and still. The door unlocked. I trailed down the empty hall.

"Mum?" In my hand I clutched the papers, the ones that said I'd provisionally been accepted to university. I thought if I could show her – that there still might be a chance for us to have a future, that I wasn't as stupid or reckless as it always seemed. There might be a life for us – for me – away from the body in the morgue, the teenage body that was more like mine than Olive's. Away from all the hurt there might be something fresh to look forward to.

The house was cold. I'd been drinking – just a bit, just to gather the nerve to tell Mum about the uni place that was waiting for me if I got the right grades. But it would mean leaving her alone if I wanted to go. I'd spent the evening with friends in the safe, anonymous shadow of an empty park; I'd almost calmed myself into believing that things might be okay. I could taste cheap vodka and expensively bad weed on my tongue as I flicked on light after light, spilling yellow across the black in the house.

"Mum?"

In the kitchen there were candles burning. Burning so low they were almost out. They were on the table, red and green Christmas candles decorated with wax wreaths at the base. The wreaths were melting too.

It wasn't Christmas. It was late spring. The table was set with our fine china, the knives blindingly silver. I blinked in confusion.

Only then I saw her, and I knew. She wore her best dress and her smart shoes, polished to a high shine. Her feet were twelve inches off the ground.

I screamed. Screamed and screamed. The darkness invaded as the candles extinguished. One… Two… *Three…* Black air hit me as I stumbled out, and then I was back in the hallway – in that sterile place that wasn't home, staring at a wall of dark, mirrored glass.

I dried my tears, swallowed to ease my sore throat.

"No," I said to the darkness. "That isn't Olive."

14

Thursday, 19 March 2015

ONE DAY UNTIL THE eclipse.

I woke up with the thought burning inside me. I struggled upright in bed, suddenly seized by the feeling that if I didn't find her before the eclipse, then we never would. I knew it was stupid but the eclipse and Olive had become so connected in my mind that I couldn't separate them.

I caught sight of the few framed articles that lived on the wall opposite the bed. They'd been there when I moved in, relics from Grandad's studio. My face beamed out from next to the bylines, the text of the features as familiar as my own thoughts from the time I'd spent writing them.

I had built my career on the grief and confusion of families like my own. Those who had lost children – even those who had found them again – still couldn't hide their new scars. The experience had changed them. Like it had changed my dad, who was now emotionally distant – and Mum, who hadn't been able to beat her grief into submission. Who had eventually chosen death over sadness and alcohol and a lifetime of regret.

It had changed me, too.

But I knew, staring at those articles, that I wasn't going crazy. If there was a connection here then I was going to find it.

I dragged myself out of bed, a new determination washing through me. I rang the hospital to check in, then showered and made a quick coffee, which I drank in scalding gulps. I grabbed my hoodie from the hook on the wall where I'd hung it the night before. As I pulled it on I noticed a scrap of paper in the pocket. *I'll speak to you later x.* At first I didn't recognise the handwriting, but the little kiss in the bottom corner made my heart gallop and a flush creep across my cheeks. Marion must have slipped it in before I left her house.

They were only just serving breakfast as I arrived at the hospital – eggs on toast, more than a little limp. Gran didn't seem to notice. Eggs were her favourite.

"Hello," she said brightly. She smiled. Even if she wasn't lucid, I'd take happy any day. I smiled back, glad that she was okay. It could have been much worse.

I thought of the text messages again and a familiar trill of guilt made my smile falter. But I pushed it down. At least Gran would be safer here than at home. I wanted her home but I was grateful that it meant she would be out of harm's way, at least for a little while.

"Morning," I said.

I settled down on the small chair that was beside Gran's bed, and I helped to cut up her breakfast so she could dig in. There was a television mounted on one wall that I'd sorted for her last night, subtitled into silence. I couldn't help watching it. A banner circling the bottom of the screen admitted that the police had still given no new updates in the Grace Butler case.

In several shots there were people out on the streets, in the fields, searching for her. I thought I recognised a few of them, Earl from the café, that curly-haired teacher I'd seen outside the school, Ady, even Doctor White in one of the shots with his back to the camera. Bishop's Green had somehow never felt so small and yet so full of unknowns.

I felt a sudden, overwhelming loss. I missed my mum. Or, I missed her as she'd been in the early days, not the distant work-obsessed alcoholic she'd become.

It was funny, I supposed, how I'd probably turned out just like her. My one saving grace, I'd often joked with Henry, was that I wasn't homophobic.

The next news story was about the eclipse. I glanced away quickly, but still managed to find the black and white crescent burning into my vision even when I stared at the lino on the floor.

When I looked back up they were playing repeat footage from the press conference that had been held yesterday. Adelaide and Roger up on a podium, their faces wrinkled with concern. My exclusive interview was gone. I focused on Roger's face but found that I couldn't get a gut feeling on him any more. Was it possible that he'd just made a mistake all those years ago? The thought made me sick but his concern for his stepdaughter certainly didn't seem fake.

I was startled out of my reverie when Gran reached out and touched my hand.

"She won't come home like that," she said, so quietly I thought I'd misheard her. But I could see from her face that I hadn't. I'd heard her perfectly.

I swallowed hard, blinking away the tears that formed. I thought of my dreams, of Olive's face as she shouted my name. Crying wouldn't do any good. I poured Gran a cup of water and refused to look at her.

"No," I admitted, "she won't."

When I got home there was a car I didn't recognise parked outside the house. It looked out of place, its shiny white bonnet and elegant black wheels making my Fiesta look like a hipster's dream.

As I got out of my car, I realised that I recognised the driver, and I was filled with unexpected excitement. A rush of warmth and good feeling filled the void that had settled in my heart when I'd left Gran in that hospital. I hadn't thought he'd make good on his promise – and not in a shiny new set of wheels.

"Heno!"

He looked the same as he always did. Lean body hidden in jeans and a tweed jacket that was slightly too big for him, his white hair cropped tight at the sides and longer on top.

"Morning, darling," he said.

"What are you doing here? I know you said you'd come but I didn't think you would."

"That's really no way to greet your knight in shining armour," he said, smirking. I couldn't believe he'd driven all this way, to holiday *here*.

"Sorry," I said, my own lips curling into a grin.

"I *told* you I was coming to visit. You owe me dinner, remember? Anyway, it's all right, this town is making heathens of the both of us. You know I saw five posters on my way here, that ghastly eclipse staring at me wherever I go." He narrowed his gaze. "Are you holding up okay? I got your text about your gran. How's she doing?"

I didn't want to lie, so I just shrugged. I wasn't going to tell him that I saw eclipses every time I blinked, that sickle-slice of moon cutting the darkness whenever I closed my eyes, that I was terrified about when Gran came home in case she was in danger again.

"That number you asked me to trace," Henry said when he saw I wasn't going to answer. "It's a burner. Pay-as-you-go type thing. Sorry." He tilted his head, watching me. Waiting.

I shrugged off his curiosity. "Do you want to come in for a cup of tea?" I asked.

Awkwardly I glanced towards my home. Henry followed my gaze, taking in the small house with its old-fashioned lace curtains and unkempt garden. It was a million miles away from the flat I'd shared with Helen in central London, all decked out in chrome polish and brand-new appliances. I could see the amusement dripping off him, but he didn't say anything.

Henry shook his head in answer. He gestured vaguely and lit a cigarette. I swallowed, trying to contain the craving and thinking pointedly of the nicotine patch on my arm.

"No can do, darling," he said, breaking into my thoughts. "I'm not just here for a holiday. I have some answers and time's a-ticking. But…" He took in my hospital outfit – tracksuit bottoms and the old hoodie. "Well, you might want to change first. Smart-casual is fine."

15

August 1999

THE SECOND WEEK IN Olive's prison was the same as the one before it. Six nights of secret visits while Olive slept. Sandman was always silent, and no matter how hard she tried to stay awake Olive couldn't do it. She couldn't keep her eyes open long enough to catch him. Not that she knew what she would do if she did. She could hardly beg him to let her go again, and as long as she slept he seemed to be happy enough.

But part of her needed to do it. To catch him sneaking in. To prove her growing feeling that he was doing more than being a "parent" and bringing her the things he thought she needed. He reminded her of the boy at Olive's primary school who the teachers had told off for bugging the girls. He hovered near them, all day. Quietly. And most of the girls had just ignored him. He'd given Olive the creeps.

Sandman was the same. Olive was sure he was watching her at night. Her skin squirmed at the thought that he was doing more than that.

On the seventh day he came to the room in the evening again. This time Olive was eating, a cheese sandwich clutched between two hands. She tried to swallow the dry bread, but her throat was all clogged up and cheese wedged in her cheek so she had to cough.

Sandman's steps on the stairs outside the room were heavier this time. More threatening. Or at least they seemed that way to Olive's sensitive ears. His face was like a storm as soon as he came through the door and for a second Olive felt panic burbling inside of her. But she'd been waiting for this, and she couldn't chicken out now.

Boredom, she thought, was almost as bad as fear. She wasn't afraid now as much as she was crazy and tired and angry and everything else as well. What use was doing what she was told if she was going to die of boredom anyway?

Before Sandman could say anything, before the butterflies in her stomach could make her explode, she screwed up her face and tried her best Sensible Voice.

"Could I have a book? Or a newspaper?"

Although she knew she'd been polite enough, Olive realised that she'd judged it wrong. All wrong. The words themselves were sharp like little knives and she saw Sandman's body change. He flew across the room before Olive could claw her words back. He slapped the sandwich from her hands and grabbed her by the shoulders.

His grip was red hot. His thumbs dug into her skin and she yelped. Sandman's face was centimetres from hers and she could feel his anger as well as see it – in the heat of him, that crazy hotness.

"How dare you." The calmness of his voice made Olive's

body feel like jelly. "A newspaper? Christ, girl. You're still *news*. I knew you'd be like this if I wasn't careful."

Olive's voice was stolen from her throat. *Like what?*

As if he saw the horror in her face, he stopped. Let go of her. Stepped back as though she'd burned him and not the other way around.

"You kids these days are so rude. It really drives me crazy. Would it kill you to have some manners?"

Olive didn't miss the way he said kill. As though it was something foreign. Something that didn't apply to him. Death was not part of the equation. And although Olive thought this should make her feel better, it didn't. Her body went cold as sweat cooled on her neck.

Sandman went back to the bags he'd dropped by the door and began sorting through the contents. Olive didn't move. Couldn't move. She could still feel his thumbprints in her shoulders, like they might be there for ever.

"Okay," he said eventually. "Laundry time. Strip."

Oh no. She'd been hoping that was just a one-off. She knew what men did to girls when they took them. She'd heard stories. She wasn't stupid. When she was nine her mum had told her that if a man tried to hurt her she could kick him in the goolies. But Olive couldn't do that to *him*. To Sandman. He wasn't like other men. He was a monster inside a man.

Olive glanced at the pile of clothes in the corner, her eyes prickling. If she'd known, she might have worn fewer outfits. Made the clothes last. Maybe then he wouldn't have had to do more washing.

"*Now.*"

She dragged herself to her feet, turned away from him as she had last time while she unfastened her skirt. He cleared his throat. Wriggling fear and a hot wave of embarrassment flooded her brain.

No...

She half-turned back to him, her fingers shaking so much she could hardly move them. He watched her with his hawk-eyes, and handed her new clothes slowly. With relish. Olive closed her eyes against his glittering stare and tried to think of home. Of summers by the pool back when they'd gone to Spain for holidays. Sun on bare skin, salt-knotted hair... Anything but this.

When she was dressed, he left without another word. A pile of clean bedsheets and clothes and food waiting by the door the evidence of his visit. And she realised that there were worse things than boredom.

16

"I DON'T SEE WHY you always get to drive," I muttered as Henry drove his car down another unfamiliar – yet identical – country road.

"Because you're a bloody maniac behind the wheel." Henry rolled his eyes, and I knew he was only barely restraining himself from mentioning the time in London I'd smashed the back of his car up on a bollard. "Anyway, you don't know where we're going."

"So, are you going to *tell* me where we're going?" I pressed. Identical roads aside, I had no idea where we were, and Henry didn't believe in satnavs.

"I thought you probably wouldn't want me poking my nose in up here unless I had something to offer," Henry joked. "So consider this a sort of trade."

"Go on."

"I tracked down Cordy Jones's wife. I called her yesterday, told her you were doing a story on her husband – and I didn't think it would work, I was just trying to confirm a few things – but she agreed to see us. I think she wants to meet you."

"You… You found him?" I asked.

"No," Henry said, regret thickening his voice. "It's complicated. As far as I can tell, nobody has seen Mr Jones since the end of 1999, not least his wife. He went out for a drink after having a row with the missus, and he never came back."

"Right."

I tried to digest this, pushing down the swelling disappointment that threatened to overwhelm me. I gripped my open notebook in one hand, my notes sprawling across the page as I tried to read what I'd written about Cordy Jones.

"So why are we going to see her?"

"Mrs Jones has a theory about what happened – but she wants to tell you in person. I think she wants to *talk* to somebody."

We drove the rest of the way in silence. It was unusual, being in a car with Henry. We'd hardly ever driven together when we lived in London. We'd travelled out of the city a few times, but the last time was years ago. This trip was nothing like the one we'd shared to Brighton for a mutual editor's birthday three or so years before.

"Here we are."

We pulled out of a small lane and into an open area that was split from the lane by a big wooden gate. Henry parked just outside after a little fussing about his car being so close to the road, and then we got out.

It was like something out of a movie. A small farmhouse, whitewashed and crooked with little windows. We didn't have far to go before a woman emerged from the front door, wiping her hands on her jeans.

"Mrs Jones?" Henry asked. "I'm Henry Francis. We spoke on the phone?"

"Yes. Come in, come in." She ushered us inside quickly, her cheeks raw from the cold air of the day and her greying hair straggling out of her bun.

We followed Mrs Jones into a small sitting room that was crowded with mismatched furniture, and Henry had to move his head quickly downwards to avoid being brained on a low-hanging beam.

"Tea?"

"Sure."

Mrs Jones ducked out of the room and I turned to Henry. He just shook his head and muttered, "Give her a minute. She seemed all right on the phone."

Mrs Jones returned with two cups of tea so strong they would have frightened a builder. She handed the drinks over and then immediately began to wring her hands.

Perhaps she was regretting her decision to be forthcoming. After the media circus she must have been exposed to years earlier, I really couldn't blame her. All I had overheard about Cordy back then could be summed up in my Olive Diary in two sentences: *They thought he was guilty. Then everybody stopped speaking about him.*

I wondered what Mrs Jones had heard about her husband – and how much of it she had believed. I knew from personal experience that rumours could be devastating.

"We'll keep it short," Henry said. "I know you wanted to chat in person, so… This is Cassie. Cassiopeia Warren."

Mrs Jones twitched at my name.

"I… It was nice of you to come," she said. "I just wanted to tell you that – that Cordy would have never… I knew your – look, I know you're looking for him now because of that missing girl. I wondered how long it would be before somebody came here. She's from Bishop's Green, so it must have something to do with Cordy because of his history. That's why you're here, isn't it?"

Her forwardness surprised me and I didn't have time to think up a lie. So I half nodded, half shrugged.

"I wanted to tell you in person that he's not – he wasn't like that. Cordy. We had our problems, but he never…" She stopped. Took a deep breath. "It doesn't matter anyway, because the reason I asked you to come is I think Cordy – I think my husband is dead."

"What?"

Henry's eyes widened in genuine shock. So he hadn't known about this.

"I don't have any real proof," Mrs Jones went on, "which is why I never followed it up. I told the police the other day, but I doubt they'll find any evidence. A reporter in the nineties asked my daughter and me about it – but we'd had enough back then. Do you understand? I don't want to seem callous. But it was a rough time." She massaged her neck. "The police said he'd probably run off because of the guilt. I guess that could be true, too, but I don't know. When he didn't come home, I started to get suspicious. I asked around.

"And then I started to get these dodgy phone calls, where

there wouldn't be anybody there. They were like threats. Never the same phone number. People in town hounded him, but he seemed afraid of one person in particular – I don't know who. And then, about six weeks after he left, I found his hat outside my door. Just the hat, no note or anything."

She paused, as though waiting for the penny to drop. When it didn't she continued, "I think somebody killed him and left the hat for me to find as a message. I think they thought he hurt – that little girl. They couldn't run him out of town. Don't get me wrong, they tried. He wouldn't leave. So somebody killed him. They thought they were getting justice – for your sister..."

"But why—"

"Why didn't I go to the police at the time?" Mrs Jones shrugged but without conviction; she had clearly wrestled with this question for a long time. "I guess I kind of hated him then. I was glad he was gone at first. All of that shit with the press. People were much nicer to me after he disappeared. At first I tried to convince myself that I was wrong, that he'd just run away. Later, it was easier this way. People left me and Katie alone."

To contain the growing feelings of frustration I glanced around the room. Anywhere but at Cordy's wife. On the crooked mantelpiece there was a photograph that drew my eye. It was a group shot, fairly old and in a faded wooden frame. In the centre stood Cordy Jones. He was wearing a hat, a distinctive baseball cap with a stag on it; presumably this was the hat his wife had mentioned, shading his face from the summer sun. I tried to imagine him leading Olive away, his face dark under the cap. It made my hands shake.

On either side of Cordy in the photograph were several teenagers and younger children. Almost exclusively boys, but there were a couple of young girls there too. All of them were grinning at the camera, their arms linked together. I was about to look away when I noticed a face I thought was familiar.

"Who's that?" I asked, stepping closer.

"Cordy's youth group," she said. Her expression closed off as she spoke. "I don't know why I keep that photo, but I can't get rid of it. You know, he did so much good for those kids. And it all went so wrong."

"Who's that one, there?" I asked, my voice cracking. "Who's he?"

But I didn't have to ask. I already knew. It was a face I'd only seen recently – although he was older now. I knew it was him. It was the man I'd seen outside the school.

Darren Walker.

17

LATER THAT EVENING, BACK at home, I rang Dad. Gran's accident and seeing that photo of the youth group had shaken me but I didn't think Marion would like the connections I was drawing between Olive and Grace. Dad was the only person left.

"They're going to keep her in another night," I explained once I'd given him the run-down of Gran's injuries, "but it's actually a lot less terrible than it looked – thank God."

I rubbed the bridge of my nose and sank into the empty sofa. The room seemed so bare without Gran, without her rattling around somewhere or humming to herself.

"Did she say what happened?" I could hear Dad fiddling about with something on the other end of the phone – as usual he wasn't paying full attention to me. I tried to ignore the annoyance that was prickling under my skin, telling myself that Gran wasn't *his* mother. The same thing I'd told myself ever since Grandad died and Dad had essentially washed his hands of her.

"No," I said. "She didn't have a clue. It was a hit and run, but whoever it was couldn't have been driving very quickly or else they'd have done more damage."

I felt my pulse quicken at the thought. I shouldn't be talking about it. I didn't want to endanger anybody else. It was paranoid, maybe, but it felt like every move I made was twisting some unseen thread tighter.

"It's my fault," I said, so quietly I hoped Dad might not have heard it.

But he did. "Oh, Cass," he said. "It's hard. I know you're trying to make it work with the nurses and the day centre and stuff but maybe it's time we moved her somewhere a little more secure."

I heard more rustling, and then I realised what it was. He was eating crisps. I pushed the anger outwards, letting myself lash out.

"Are you *eating*?" I demanded.

"Well… Yeah." Was that embarrassment? "I still have to eat, Cassie."

"Not while you're on the phone!"

Dad sighed and all I heard was a crackle of air. "Look, you said she's okay. It could have been worse. You've done all you can until they let her come home."

He didn't understand. Coming home wasn't going to be any safer for her. I'd done this to her.

"Gran might be okay – but I'm not." It came out scarily close to a sob. I clenched my fists trying to calm my racing pulse.

"You know I've always been there for you, Cass. Even when you don't believe it. We're always here."

This was just like Dad, to drag up my lack of trust in him.

And I'd never liked Carol, especially given that she was a good fifteen years younger than him. Besides, Hailey didn't need a sister like me.

When I was fifteen I threatened to kill myself if he didn't leave Carol. She was only seven years older than me – it was disgusting. He'd chosen some student, with no job and rich parents, over me and Mum. I expected Dad to get angry – I wanted him to. I wanted him to yell at me so I had the excuse to yell back. But he didn't. Instead, he told me that he was disappointed that I would joke about something like that.

Less than three years later Mum ended her life.

The silence now was charged and I couldn't bear it. I swallowed hard and I heard Dad do the same.

"I'm going to go," I said before he could speak. "I'll text you about Gran when I know a bit more."

"All right," Dad said.

I put the phone down and silenced it.

After a few minutes I realised that what I'd wanted from Dad wasn't something he could easily give me. Even before Olive was taken we hadn't been that sort of family. We didn't talk a lot – especially about our problems. He was the sort of dad who solved things by hugging, something which was hard to do after he moved out.

"I'm not this monster you seem to think I am," Dad had snapped when I'd once challenged him for leaving. He'd been living in his "hotel" for six weeks, and this was the first time I'd seen him. Mum was pissed out of her head half the time, sleeping on the sofa at Gran's so she didn't wake us up when she broke down in fits of tears at two in the morning. But I could hear her, and each sob broke off another piece of me.

"You're exactly the monster I think you are," I said coldly, righteous with teenage anger. I wanted somebody to talk to, and all Dad cared about was protesting his innocence. But I'd reached the point where I didn't give a shit if he thought he was innocent – he'd done enough.

"I didn't hurt your sister."

"You hurt *me*."

Now, I shook the memory of the grief in Dad's eyes from my mind. I couldn't blame him for everything. He was trying his best.

After Henry had dropped me off, and gone to check in at his hotel, I'd spent hours trying to find out everything I could about Darren Walker. But the man was a ghost. He had only the barest social media profiles – a Facebook page with only one photo, a Twitter account I wasn't even sure was his, the little egg profile picture staring at me and driving me mad. There were about twenty-three million search results for his name and none of them produced anything close to what I was looking for apart from one note on the Arboretum school website that mentioned his so-called "vintage car-boot".

I'd given up around dinnertime and driven to Ady's for a few essentials. He'd surprised me by still being in the shop – normally he only worked mornings, but he'd muttered something about staff holiday and working all hours and rolled his eyes while I tried to be sympathetic.

Posters about the eclipse had been everywhere: warnings

not to watch without special glasses; offers of half-priced cake and tea at the church and for the viewing at Earl's café. Even Ady, after the initial worry about my Gran, had stated his excitement for the eclipse, his superstitious nonsense about "new beginnings" setting my teeth on edge. He sounded like my grandad, with his four-leaf clovers painted in his studio, the copper band he wore around his wrist because he claimed it connected him to the earth.

Now, sitting on the sideboard along with a new loaf of bread, was a bottle of vodka. And there was a bottle of incredibly cheap rosé in the fridge, as well. I knew I shouldn't, knew that this was a slippery slope – but there was nothing to stop me. No reason not to without Gran to keep an eye on, and the jelly feeling in my limbs seemed like every reason to go ahead and just forget the rest of the world existed.

I sat in silence for what seemed like for ever. The sky began to darken, and I didn't move. I didn't get up to turn the lights on as I would have if Gran had been here. I didn't make myself dinner or set up a TV show on my laptop.

I just sat, completely still, and stared out of the window at the road. One by one the street lamps came on. A flickering orange light filtered through the blinds and striped everything in a ghostly gold.

When I did get up, I used the bathroom and then went straight back to my spot with a glass of vodka. I smiled just to see if I still could, the small movement making my cheeks hurt because they'd been still and tense for so long. I sniffed the vodka, let a tiny taste of it sit on my tongue. I hated it, but the hangovers from sugary cocktails were much worse. Plus, the corner shop had cheap bottles that cost less than I'd ever paid for booze – or sleeping pills – in London.

I wrinkled my nose in disgust. And then I drank the whole glass in two swallows.

I was five drinks deep when my phone buzzed. I swiped at it ineffectually, getting into the message on the third try.

It said:

Hi. We met before. I have some things I want to tell u abt Grace, but I dont want to txt it. Can u meet me after school tomoz? I'll wait outside the gates. Bx

I paused, my brain going into overdrive. I started to type a reply, stopped. Fumbled with my phone and started again. Relief mingled with excitement and concern. Perhaps here, finally, was a solid lead. But it was late. Who was texting now? Was it the girl who had said Grace didn't keep secrets, Bella somebody? In the end, I managed to type, "*Sure.*" My brain was unable to formulate clearly the many questions I had.

As the night went by, and the moon started to rise, I took my glass out into the garden, my thoughts spinning. There was a wooden swing out there along with an old fire pit. I set it up, and then sat in front of the glow with the bottle of vodka. It was liberating, like I'd been able to drop the worry and the guilt and now I was *free*. I didn't have to clean up, or make sure Gran was in bed. I didn't have to cook for her or make her a cup of tea. I didn't have to do *anything*.

I didn't have to do those things but I found that I missed them. Gran's absence was like a sliver of glass in my heart and every action made it ache that much worse. I hunched on the wooden bench, feeling the fire warming my face as the cool night air caressed my back. I leaned into it, drank some more, and let the fuzzy warmth envelop me. Wrap me up and keep me safe.

As I sat, I realised that I'd left my phone inside. But I didn't bother to get up and find it. I'd instructed the hospital to call the landline if they ever couldn't reach me, which I could hear from out here, and I didn't want to talk to anybody else anyway.

I just poured myself another drink and nursed it quietly, the buzz of the alcohol sitting low across my brow, obscuring the heart of my thoughts about tomorrow. The eclipse. I was a failure now, just like before. I wasn't any closer to finding Grace than I had been days ago. I thought vaguely about the text message, and promised meeting, but now struggled to believe Grace's friend would be able to tell me anything useful.

I missed Olive with a keenness I hadn't felt in years, and I felt the threat of the twilight-like darkness hovering over me like a spectre. I tried to push it away.

When I closed my eyes, I saw Marion. Her smile. The warmth in her eyes and the way she leaned towards me when she spoke. I tried to remind myself of the man I'd seen leaving her house – but instead I saw the curve of her jaw, the jut of her collarbone beneath her shirt.

I remembered the first brush of her lips against mine, the feeling of the moon cooling my skin as she sun disappeared during the eclipse. The way my heart thudded. The way I could see her pulse in her throat as she licked her lips...

I hadn't ever stopped thinking about Marion. Even when I'd been with Helen, even when things had been good, Marion was always there. Always in my mind, in my heart. But with a detached sense of shock I realised that loving her from a distance wasn't enough any more.

I wanted her hands in my hair, her mouth on mine. I wanted to feel her skin at my fingertips, wanted her support and help with my gran… I didn't just want Marion; I needed her.

Sleep came reluctantly. At some point I'd moved back inside. The lounge was cold and the world shifted and spun, images shooting past my eyes so fast I couldn't tell whether they were memories or fabrications.

In my dream it was hot. I stared at the bruise that was blossoming on Olive's pale arm. It was purple and green and had the very definitive shape of fingers. Angry fingers.

"She didn't mean to," Dream Olive said, rubbing at it gently. "I almost got hit by that car. She pulled me back. She freaked out."

"She pulled you bloody hard," I said. Did I say that? I said it in my dream.

"You shouldn't swear."

"Yeah, well, Mum shouldn't have hurt you. You need to tell somebody when she gets stressed." I scowled, and Olive smiled. A big dream smile. In the waking world I wasn't sure I remembered what her smile looked like.

"I know. But it was an accident. She was so sorry afterwards, even got me an ice cream from the little shop. She just doesn't realise how strong she is."

I remembered that it was days before the bruise started to fade, even though it wasn't big. As I tried to get comfortable in the waking world, in my dream Olive told everybody about the car, about how she wasn't looking where she was going. How somebody had yanked her to safety, hard enough to bruise the skin.

Olive was slipping away. All I could see was the back of her head.

"Olive, wait!" I shouted. "Wait for me!"

But she was going. Slipping further, gliding now. The darkness closing in, just like it had done during the eclipse.

And then she was gone.

I screamed to consciousness, my mouth desert-dry. Wiping my forehead, I felt the sweat that trickled down my neck. I paused, listening for Gran, but of course she wasn't there. I thought of the car that had hit her. How it hadn't been going fast. There was no doubt in my mind that the driver was the person who had sent me those texts.

Could it be Darren Walker, the weirdo with the van, who'd sent them? The missing-and-presumed-dead Cordy Jones? But the texts had been strangely typed, punctuation non-existent. Nobody who had my mobile number would text like a teenager under normal circumstances.

I had a jolt, then, wondering if it could have been. A *teenager*. One of Grace's friends. That would make sense, wouldn't it? Except that didn't explain Gran's accident or the text from the other friend. So could it be somebody familiar with children? A parent? A teacher? Or anybody for that matter. I was going round in circles.

I resettled, trying to even out my breathing. I could see the bruise on Olive's arm, stamped across my vision like sun spots. I hadn't remembered it until now. It had happened the week we came to Bishop's Green for the summer. Mum had been frustrated. Stressed. Angry with Dad. They fought that morning and she was still angry when Olive stepped into the road outside the corner shop. It was an accident, Olive's arm getting twisted like that, and Mum was distraught afterwards. People had seen the bruise and the judgement in their eyes had made me feel hot with shame. Even Doctor White had asked the question, "Did your mother do this?" and we had both been mortified.

I didn't want to think about my mother. So I half-lay, half-sat, perfectly still, until I finally drifted back to sleep.

18

Friday, 20 March 2015

ECLIPSE DAY.

When I woke the house was empty and the fire in the garden was long dead, the ashes blown about on the grass. I looked down and saw no evidence of the vodka, neither bottle nor glass, and I couldn't remember what I'd done with them. I winced as the world swayed and I felt the familiar heavy sickness unsettle itself in my stomach. Slowly, and with little grace, I staggered back inside to put the kettle on.

It was a minute before I felt a dropping sensation in my stomach, and I glanced at the clock. It was almost nine thirty. *The eclipse.* A shudder raced through me like a shock of electricity and I darted outside to throw up in the bushes.

I could feel the morning already cooling, the sky getting darker even as I resolutely avoided looking at it. If only I could have stayed asleep I would have missed the whole thing.

Half of me wanted to bolt upstairs, turn the shower on and sit under a stream of hot water all morning so I wouldn't have to see it. The other half of me knew that I couldn't do that. As much as I wanted to avoid it, I knew what was going to happen.

I was going to watch it.

As it began, a knot of fear, excitement, dread, all roiled in one in the pit of my stomach. It was nothing like the feeling I'd had sixteen years ago, with Marion at my side, her hands in mine – the first touch of her lips and the fear and adrenaline rushing through me at the thought of being caught by somebody who'd tell our parents…

This time there was no wonder. No magic. I felt despair threaten to swallow me whole – but I forced myself back inside, finished making the tea I'd started. And then in the garden once more I clutched the burning mug in my hands, relishing the pain that blossomed in my fingers as I held it tight.

I turned my face towards the sky, taking in the greyness, and in contrast the bright blue that was currently surrounding the sun. I had no glasses to watch with, but I couldn't bring myself to care. What was the worst that could happen? A bubble of sickness was still in my stomach, even as I sipped at my tea, and I realised it had nothing to do with my hangover or the alcohol still in my system.

I couldn't shake the memories. So many memories. The feeling of Marion's hand in mine, tense and cool despite the August heat. The wind blew and the ghost of Marion's lips brushed the hair out from behind my ear. I shivered, the zinging feeling running up and down my spine. Even now I couldn't separate the glory and pleasure of that morning from the pain and the grief that had come afterwards.

I remembered the pressure of Marion's skin against mine,

the feeling of her shoulder, her hip, the way we moulded together almost seamlessly.

Sitting in the garden now, completely alone, I had to hold back another wave of sickness tasting like bile and alcohol and guilt. Because even now, even after all these years, I could still remember what she whispered to me. *I think I love you.* And I could barely remember the last words I shared with my sister.

But it was Olive's face I had seen every day since, in passing strangers or caught in the corner of strange mirrors. Her golden eyes. Her crooked smile. I massaged the small circular tattoo on the inside of my left elbow. It had faded in the fifteen years since I'd snuck out and had it done without Mum realising. I often forgot it was there, and whenever I saw it I remembered Olive, and that was good. Such a small thing, a little circle no bigger than my thumbnail. An "O". For Olive. For the eclipse. For everything.

When Helen had first asked what it meant, I'd told her it was a full moon. She probably figured out I had lied about it later, but she never said. I was sure she hadn't understood. It was a symbol, a symbol of the shitty ending of a story in which I was the villain. It was a reminder of everything I had lost.

The sun began to slip away behind a crescent of darkness, and I realised that I must have been sitting out here for half an hour already. Half an hour of ghostly thoughts and images.

I remembered the distinct moment that my excitement had become horror on that day. A sick hollow feeling that exploded into anger when we couldn't find her, like somebody putting a trapdoor beneath us. Marion said she couldn't have gone far. But she had. And the darkness was too much, sucking and pulling us into a world where the people of this friendly town could be capable of hurting an eleven-year-old girl.

How could it have gone so wrong?

Dad said it was my fault. And although Mum had denied it when he was around, I'd noticed that she looked at me differently after that. It *was* my fault. But even now I couldn't pretend that I hadn't wanted to kiss Marion, hadn't wanted her more than anything. That she was the source of the warmth that coiled deep inside me, that magical, tingling heat like no other.

I tried to force the thoughts from my brain but they remained imprinted behind my eyelids like sunspots. My tea was cold, and I started to shiver.

I was frozen. I couldn't move even if I wanted to. Something about this moment pinned me to the bench. I was unable to reclaim my limbs. I shivered uncontrollably, this time the tea in my hand sloshing over the edge of the cup. But I didn't move. Because although I tried to deny it before, there was something there – some feeling of wonder amid the horror.

As I watched the moon devour the sun, as the garden was plunged into greyness, I realised that the shivering was not fear. Or cold. But excitement. A zinging excitement that rocketed through me, making my fingers and toes tingle and my tongue feel heavy in my mouth.

I drank it in. As the day grew darker and darker still, and I began to feel the cold more than ever before, tears welled in my eyes. This was it, what I'd been waiting for. I held my body tightly coiled, as if something terrible might leap out at any moment.

But nothing happened. Nothing bad. Nothing good, either. Just... nothing.

When it was over, I let the feeling wash over me. Relief. It must have been relief, that warm, fuzzy feeling, only brushing the inner core of coldness. I shivered again, and got to my feet. My whole body hurt. I could feel the tension rolling off me – in the stiffness in my neck and back, and the way my legs felt wooden, like somebody else's – and I knew I needed to get myself sorted.

I had to be an adult. That was what this was all about, wasn't it? Growing up. Facing the things I'd been running from my whole life. Coming to Bishop's Green, taking care of Gran... Moving back so I could go forwards.

It was more than that. It was almost like I was pushing away my childhood – by coming back here, I was refusing to accept the way things had worked out. It was more than just a fresh start, it was a new life.

I risked one more glance upwards, towards the sun and the few clouds now covering the glowing circle in the sky. I pictured that crescent again, the one that was so like the one I remembered. It was as if by staring too much at the sun I'd burned the image into the backs of my eyelids. And now it was all I could see whenever I closed my eyes.

I started to feel better as the minutes after the eclipse slipped away. I washed my face, determined to make it to the hospital for Gran's visiting hours. The house was still a mess, and I couldn't find my phone, but I ignored the stab of frustration and grabbed my keys. It was hardly a big deal. I just prayed that I was sober enough to drive.

At the hospital I repeated my instruction for them to call my landline if they needed me – not having my phone felt like I was missing a limb – and then I headed straight to Gran's room, which she shared with two other patients. The whole ward smelled of antiseptic and, somewhere, the faint trace of urine. I grimaced, crinkling my nose as I stepped inside.

The atmosphere was hushed, with the other patients sleeping or reading quietly. Gran was asleep, and I found that I was almost glad – because today I couldn't face any of it. The buzz I had felt this morning was gone and here was the reality. I was bone tired, sick, and disgusted with myself for the feelings I'd had during the eclipse. I couldn't handle this as well.

Gran looked so small with the covers drawn up to her chest, her arms straight down by her sides. She looked so thin and frail. I wondered, with a shock, when Gran had become so *other*. It was like she'd become somebody else overnight. Her face was veined with bruises from the accident, and as her chest rose and fell I could see the hint of the damage under the blankets. The doctors said she must have used her arm to catch herself and the weight of her fall had broken it.

I remembered the solid presence of my childhood, feet always firmly planted as though she expected a fight, shoulders squared. She was formidable, even as much as she was fun and carefree. What a grandma was supposed to be.

"Are you her?"

I spun around at the sound of an unfamiliar voice, reedy with old age. I realised it had come from the bed next to Gran's, where an elderly dark-skinned lady was propped up on some pillows with a book. Gran's newest roommate looked gaunt, but her smile was warm. I smiled back, confusion and hangover making me slow.

"I'm sorry, what?"

"Are you the girl?" The woman gestured with gnarled fingers at my gran, and then smiled at me showing a row of unnaturally straight dentures.

"Am I…"

I felt the dread, but before I could say anything to stop her the words were out of her mouth and they hit me like a truck. It didn't matter how many times anybody said her name, I never got over hearing it from foreign lips.

"Olive," the woman said. "Olive. She keeps saying that name in her sleep, and I thought…" She trailed off, a frown creasing her brow. "Oh, I'm sorry. I never meant to upset you."

"It's – it's all right," I said. "It doesn't matter. I'm not her."

The older lady looked embarrassed. I tried to shrug, but the action came across half-hearted and wonky. I shuffled quietly to sit at Gran's bedside, but the beads of sweat along my spine were making me itch with discomfort, and I suddenly felt clammy and sicker than before.

I sat for a couple of minutes, feeling my heartbeat rattle inside me like a dying bird's – but then I couldn't take it any more. Not today of all days. I couldn't face waking her up, having to pretend I was fine. I shifted in my seat. Once. Twice.

She didn't wake up. So I swallowed hard, and got to my feet.

"Excuse me," I said to the lady, who glanced up from her book and pushed her glasses down her nose so she could look over them. "Can you tell her — that I stopped by? Please tell her Cassie — her granddaughter — stopped by."

I didn't wait for a response. I just gathered my jacket from the chair, and before I knew it I was racing down the hallways, endless identical hallways, and panting so hard that I barely realised I'd made it out onto the street before a rush of cold air hit me. I sucked it in, trying not to hyperventilate. It was okay. I was going to be okay. *Gran* would be okay.

I stopped abruptly when I got to my car and fumbled for my keys although I already had them in my hand. There was something about driving away that felt sort of like crossing a line. I felt like I was betraying Gran by leaving. But I also knew I'd be no good to her in the state I was in. I felt like a hot mess, I could still smell the booze, sickly and sweet and cloying inside my nostrils. Not for the first time I missed the old days, sleeping pills before bed and I could pretend whole days didn't happen without the bloody hangover.

After what seemed like for ever, I broke out of my indecisive fumbling and got into the car. It was cool inside, the air smelling faintly of old cigarettes. I breathed deeply, allowing myself another moment or two before I kicked into reverse and pulled back out onto the main road towards Bishop's Green.

I drove aimlessly for a while. The fields were lush and green, the air damp and cool through my window. I thought about turning the radio on, but in the end I couldn't face listening to all the stuff about Grace again. It only made me angry that we still had nothing. Or *I* did, anyway. With a jolt I remembered last night − the text message. The meeting after school. I thought about what Marion had said about Grace's father. Could she be with him? Would he hurt his daughter? Did the mystery texter know where she was? I knew I needed to find out as much as I could about John Butler, or risk accusing an innocent man of something terrible.

I was turning into the person who I'd always despised in TV soaps − I was the crazy one, the one who went off on one at every bloody opportunity. God, how had I not realised how obsessed I was getting? And why couldn't I stop?

As I finally pulled onto my street, head stuck in thoughts of anger and frustration, and a steady bubbling of sickness still in my stomach, I saw Marion's car parked out front. I knew it was hers, even from here, because of the old bumper sticker I'd bought her and posted from London when we were still young enough to think it was cool.

I slowed my car down to a crawl as a feeling of rising dread trilled through me. Was it Grace, still stuck in that corner of my mind, that made me want to turn tail and run? Was it the acknowledgement that I was going crazy over this?

No. It was simply that I was afraid of telling Marion about my inability to talk to my own grandmother. I was afraid she'd smell the booze on me, and I was afraid that she'd write me off as a bad job. How did other people keep their brains from boiling over without pills or alcohol or drugs?

Marion had no real patience for my anxiety, or for the way

I dealt with it. She was all business – had been since Olive was taken. After that, the girl who didn't care what people thought was quickly replaced by a clone of her father: driven, serious, determined to succeed. The police suited her, but I couldn't help but think that it was Olive that pushed her into it. And away from the fiery girl who couldn't keep her temper in check. Away from me.

Marion got out of her car as I pulled onto the drive. She was dressed in a knee-length dark coat. She had the collar turned up against the bite in the air, and I could tell just by looking at her face that she was dressed for work underneath it. Her hair was pulled back in a bun that had probably been tidy this morning, but as usual little wisps of hair had escaped. She looked exhausted, her face wan with dark smudges under her eyes. I wanted to kiss her.

"Have you come to arrest me?" I joked as I clambered out of my car. No laughter. When Marion opened her mouth to speak I realised that she was holding back tears. "What's up?"

"Cassie…" Marion looked me right in the eyes, her nostrils flaring. "It happened again. I've been trying to call you, text you, from the station all day. Where have you been?"

"I was with Gran."

"What about just now? I've been here for half an hour. I tried to ring the hospital but they said you left—"

"I went for a drive." And then there was a pause as my brain caught up. "Wait," I said, "what do you mean it happened again?"

"Cassie, another girl is missing."

19

SEVEN DAYS LATER, THE same again. This time he didn't hand her the clothes right away. He held them in front of his body, just below his stomach. He watched her remove her dress with a look that he didn't even try to hide.

Afterwards, as the light began to fade in the room, Olive lay on the bed and watched the shadows creep across the ceiling. She was trying not to think of Sandman – as she did a lot of the time. But today her usual ways weren't working and she could think of nothing else. Was this all there was? Was this her life for ever now?

If Cassie were here, they might be able to banish him together. Cassie was good at stuff like that. Cassie always scared monsters away. Olive wished she'd told her big sister about Sandman when he was first nice to her. She'd thought he was just friendly. The memory made her stomach feel empty and full at the same time, and she had to roll onto her side to stop it hurting.

She wondered what they were doing. Mum and Dad, and Cassie. Whether they had any idea what had happened to her. Whether Mum would be angry, or sad. Olive thought she might be on TV. In newspapers, probably. She wondered what it might all look like.

Although she wanted to feel hopeful, Olive thought that she hadn't really felt hope since that first day. There wasn't that sort of lightness in her chest to battle with the darkness. Her head told her that if they were going to find her – well, they'd already have done it. The police would have come and helped her home by now…

The first few days she'd tried screaming. And then listening. But there wasn't anything – there were no sounds outside of the room. The only thing she ever heard was her own voice and his footsteps on the stairs. She must be in a basement, but she could still see sky. Or maybe it was a reflection… Olive didn't stare out of the window because it only made her feel sick.

She pictured her mum at Gran's, yelling at Cassie. Wondered if Dad would be doing his usual silent thing. Probably Cassie had been in trouble, which Olive tried not to think about. Her eyes prickled again and she wrapped her arms around herself. If only she'd done as Cassie had told her

A noise startled Olive. She snapped upright. It was coming from under the bed, right underneath her. Wasn't it? She strained her ears, and – yes, there it was. A scuffling, snaffling sound. She sat perfectly still, a statue with a wet face, and listened.

The sound continued. She leapt off the bed, her heart slamming about inside her. There was a gap between the bed and the floor. She'd crawled under there days ago to check the walls for any cracks. Now she peered into the semi-darkness, smelling dusty air and her own sweat.

And then she saw it. A ribbon of something like excitement shot through her before her stomach flip-flopped and the fear kicked in.

There, right at the back, next to a few breadcrumbs she'd dropped, was a mouse, all brown and white and black. But there was red everywhere, too. Gloopy, dark red that reminded Olive of the time she and Cassie had been vampires for Halloween.

Only this wasn't fake blood in a tube. This was the real thing. Olive threw herself under the bed, wrapping her hand around the small warm mass before it could shoot off. Its tiny heart was beating a million times faster than Olive's, its fur sticky with blood. She hoped it wouldn't bite her.

As she moved the tiny thing into the light – or what was left of it coming through the window – she noticed that the tail was missing. The very end gone, just snipped right off. And then she saw the faint droplets of blood on the carpet towards the door and realised what had happened.

The mouse tried to make a run for it but Olive kept hold of him tightly enough until she could pop him into the sink. The sides were high enough, and slippery enough that he couldn't get out easily.

She set about tearing off bits of tissue to wrap around the tail like a bandage. The more she looked, though, the less scary it was. There was no more blood except what came off her hands, and even that was drying fast.

Olive sucked in some breaths, holding them inside her lungs until they burned and her heart started to slow down. The mouse seemed happy to settle into his new home, cautious but calm enough. A faint *skritch-skritch* among the shredded tissue in the stainless steel sink was the only reminder of his presence as she cleaned up the little drops and smears of blood.

She wanted, immediately, to keep him. She'd never been allowed a pet at home. But then, she laughed as she realised, what else could she do? She couldn't set him free. He must have come through the door when Sandman entered; Olive knew there was no other way in or out.

What was she going to do?

Sandman would hate him. She knew this like she knew her own name. He hated things that were unclean, or untidy. Today he told her that she needed to clean up better or he'd stop buying her fresh food because it was *unhygienic*.

Olive's body felt like it had been punched a thousand times over as she sank down onto the floor. She couldn't let Sandman take him. What could she do? Could she hide him?

Maybe this was the answer to her fear. To her loneliness. To her long empty hours with nothing to do but draw pictures with the few pencils and bits of paper he'd let her have.

Olive couldn't help thinking that this confirmed something, too. Cassie said God existed because *somebody* had to answer prayers. But if somebody was listening to her prayers, then they weren't a good person. A good God. Because now, both she and the mouse were trapped in here together.

Two lives in a box.

The mouse – Mickey, she'd call him, like her watch – was proof. There was life in here, there was hope, but it wasn't a guarantee. It was a luxury.

20

"MY DAUGHTER'S NAME IS Izabela Kaluza," the Facebook post announced above a photo of a girl I knew. "Bella. She is eleven years old. A sweet girl. She was walking to school, and she didn't get there. She does not do this and I am very worried. She left our house on Randall Street at eight thirty in the morning, and she didn't make it to the school. Please, if somebody has her, just know that I want her back. I want my Bella back. Bella, if you see this, please come home to me. This post is public. Please share widely."

"Bella," I said, so quietly I wasn't sure Marion heard me. "That little girl who's friends with Grace. I was meant to — she..."

The one who had texted me. It had to be her.

The post had already been shared hundreds of times. I didn't want to see any more. I turned my face away.

"Yes," Marion said. She had heard me. And she knew that I knew who Bella was – knew that I'd probably met this girl. Spoken to her. "She was on her way to school this morning. She left home late. They delayed lessons for the eclipse and held registration outside at half ten, but a lot of kids were late and it was chaos."

Now I knew why Marion wasn't going to say anything to me about knowing Bella, or why I hadn't mentioned her before. She was here on official police business. I turned very slowly in my seat until I was looking at her, and I confirmed that she was being her official self. Eyes narrowed, brow furrowed.

"What are you saying?" I asked.

"Cassie," Marion said slowly, still standing by the door, "I have to ask you where you were this morning. During the eclipse."

"What, Marion? What on earth are you talking about?"

"I'm talking about this morning, Cassie. Where were you? Between eight thirty and ten thirty? I have to ask you. Bella left her phone at home because she was running late. We found the texts."

"What?"

"Texts. That Bella sent you. She'd deleted them but we found them. About her meeting you this afternoon?"

"What?"

I couldn't believe it. The world started to go fuzzy, a sound like droning bees humming inside my ears. I couldn't think straight. I felt like I'd stepped right into a bear trap.

"I – Marion… I talked to her in the street after school the other day. Her and a bunch of kids. One of them – Bella – texted me last night. Quite late. I was – drunk. I said I'd meet her after school."

"Cassie, you look like shit." Marion paused, her jaw working. I couldn't tell whether in anger, or whether it was because this was hard for her.

"What are you saying?"

"I'm saying I think you need to come to the station. We need to get it straightened out officially. On the record."

I opened my mouth to speak, but no words would come out. Marion had known me since I was nine years old. How could she think I had anything to do with this?

"Cassie, will you come? Just as a witness. We need to do it properly. They're already wanting to take me off the case – because I'm too involved. But I said I'd bring you in." Now I could see that it was hard for her. Hard for her colleagues to know that we had a history. Hard for her to admit this to them when we had spent years pointedly as "just friends".

The sickness in my stomach rose.

"Fine," I said. "I'll come with you. But I know it's that fucking partner of yours. Partner." I laughed, and although I could hear the hysteria I couldn't stop it, the stress of the morning was rising in me like a wave. "I know you're sleeping with him – that's what this is about, isn't it? Is he good in bed, at least?"

"Cassie," Marion warned, but her voice was tired, as though she'd already given up. "Don't."

I pushed down my rage, sucking in a breath so deep it hurt. And then I let Marion lead me out to her car, my whole body vibrating with anger like an unexploded bomb.

The police station in Bishop's Green was small, barely even worth calling it that really. Located in an older, crumbling area just outside the centre of town where it was easy to remember that most of their cases involved shoplifting and tourists making stupid, drunken decisions. It was a base for the local area, small but efficient. I'd only been there a handful of times – none of them pleasant – and I felt myself tense as we drew near.

"You're not under arrest," Marion said very calmly as we pulled into the car park. "I just need to ask you some stuff with my partner in the room. Okay?"

I didn't look at her. I saw her hand grip the steering wheel and her knuckles went white.

"Is this payback?" I asked.

"What?"

"Payback. For me. For us. For our past. Does he know about us? About you? Is that why he——"

"It's not just about us, Cass," Marion said firmly. Tiredly. But this lie fell almost as flat as her silence had before. "I told him we needed to speak to you. He said he thought he should do the interview – given our history. I agreed."

Inside, the place was buzzing with activity. There were more people than I'd ever seen here, officers in both plain clothes and uniforms marching around, giving orders, coffee cups parked on work surfaces leaving rings on pieces of paper. Marion took hold of my arm and led me down a long corridor, at the end of which she opened a door and ushered me inside.

I screwed my eyes shut, trying to keep out the images that were assaulting my brain. Images of a similar room when I was seventeen. To view the dead girl who wasn't Olive when Mum couldn't bring herself to do it.

"Cass, are you all right?" Marion's voice brought me back to the present.

I tried to nod.

Marion didn't seem convinced, but she just gestured towards the large mirror that I knew was probably mirrored glass. Moments later the door opened again and in came a man, perhaps a few years older than Marion and me. He was dark-haired and dark-skinned with warm brown eyes and the kind of posture that screamed police even if you didn't know. This was Marion's partner. The same man I had seen leaving her house.

She hadn't denied sleeping with him.

I felt sick and wasn't sure whether that was the booze, or the thought of Marion and him together, or the tang of burnt coffee and too many people pushed together in a small place.

"Cassie, this is Detective Sergeant Matthew Fox." She gestured to him as he swung the door to with his right foot, leaving it cracked so I knew I wasn't trapped. A ploy, no doubt.

"So, Cassiopeia Warren," Fox said, holding his hand out as if to shake mine. When I didn't move, he turned this into a smooth motion to pull out one of the chairs so that he was sitting down opposite me. He appeared alert, but his tie was crumpled and it looked like he'd spilled something down his shirt earlier and managed to get most of it off with a wet cloth.

"My friends call me Cassie," I said.

He smiled showing too many teeth. It was almost a grimace. "I've heard a lot about you."

I swallowed hard and made a mental note not to rise to his

bait. With an expression like that, something told me that not all of what he'd heard was good.

"So what you're telling me is that you have no one who can vouch for your whereabouts this morning," Fox said. He held his coffee mug in front of him on the table like it was holy water, stroking the handle gently. I couldn't take my eyes off his hands, which was probably a good thing because I didn't want to look at Marion right now. She stood in the corner of the room like a ghost.

"I'm sorry, I wasn't aware I would need one. I already told you what I did. I watched the eclipse at home, went to the hospital, then I went for a drive."

"Where did you drive to?"

I let out an exasperated sigh and looked to Marion. She avoided my gaze.

"I went to visit my Gran in hospital," I said pointedly. "She has dementia and she was in an accident. I was stressed. And then I drove around afterwards to calm down. I didn't go anywhere in particular."

I raised my chin and stared right at Marion. Marion, who knew what had happened to Gran. Who knew that I was a coward, an anxious mess who self-medicated with sleeping pills and cheap booze – but I wouldn't hurt anybody. She stayed silent.

"So, you watched the eclipse – alone?"

"That's what I said."

"And what about the text messages we found on Bella Kaluza's phone. Can you tell us about those?"

"Messages *plural?*"

"Yes."

I shook my head. "I had one. *One.* Last night. I didn't know it was her for sure, but I guessed as much. She said she had information about Grace Butler."

"And you were going to meet her. To get this information."

"Yes, she said after school today." I pushed down the exasperation that was making my voice sound reedy.

"What about the second text?"

"I don't know what you're talking about."

"This morning," Fox said. "Bella sent you another text from her phone just before she left home confirming that she was going to meet you. She left her phone on the kitchen table."

"I didn't... I don't..." I swallowed hard, a lump forming in my throat. My phone. "I didn't see it. I was..." I looked at Marion. "I was drinking last night. I didn't check my messages after that one I told you about. I didn't see the one from this morning. I don't even have my phone on me right now."

Fox stared at me, his eyes flashing.

"You can do a damn cavity search if you want," I snapped. "This is ridiculous. Surely you can see that I didn't text her back today. Why would I hurt her? I was trying to help find her best friend. If I was going to meet her this afternoon why would I have seen her this morning?"

"Matthew," Marion said, quiet enough that at first I thought I'd imagined it. But when I looked at her I could see concern on her face. "We talked about this. She's not a suspect."

"Isn't she? She's been seen talking to these kids outside school by a teacher; she's harassed the parents of one of the missing children; she's been making a general nuisance of herself – and she might be the last person who spoke to Bella Kaluza before she went off radar. It doesn't exactly look good."

Marion opened and closed her mouth. Her skin was pale, her eyes glassy. She hadn't intended for any of this to happen.

"I was just doing my job!" I exclaimed, throwing my hands in the air. "I'm a journalist, that's what I do. I ask questions – which is more than you seem to be doing."

"You're on thin ice, Miss Warren. Don't push me."

Fox's eyes were steely. I could see right then what he was: a career ball-buster. Tough on cases, tough on suspects. Probably good at his job – but no flexibility. The thought of Marion with this guy made me squirm.

I didn't dare open my mouth for fear of what might come out so I clamped my lips shut tight, only just resisting the urge to bare my teeth at him.

"Matthew," Marion said again. "Please don't."

The room fell into silence. Just a moment. Long enough for me to see that she'd rattled him, made him question himself.

"You're treating me like I'm a suspect," I said coldly, "when I'm just trying to help. I'm putting myself at risk, here."

Fox's gaze snapped back to me. "What do you mean by that?" he said. I stared at him in stony silence. "Miss Warren, withholding information from the police is a very serious offence."

I clenched my fists. Stupid. I shouldn't have mentioned it. I sighed and turned to Marion.

"Look, I didn't say anything before because I didn't want you to think I couldn't handle it. And then with Gran, I was worried that it was… my fault. But I've been getting these messages – texts. Telling me to back off. Threatening. Even before I knew what I was looking at.

"It's as though I'm onto something. But I don't know…" I faltered. Marion was staring at me as though I'd just stabbed her through the heart and she couldn't understand it. "But I don't know what I know," I added. "And I didn't want to worry you."

Fox frowned. "You realise this is very serious," he said. "We'll have to look at your phone. Have you any idea who might be sending these messages?"

I avoided Marion's gaze. I didn't want to be stuck in here, waiting, while they proved my story. Not with another girl missing, and the eclipse like a ghostly clock counting down the hours since her disappearance… *A hundred and forty-six hours…* I remembered the toll after Olive had been taken. A hundred and ninety-two *hours… No new leads…* I had to give them something else.

"There was a man outside the school the last time I was there," I said slowly. "He told me he was allowed to be there but it was a bit weird. He said he knows Grace – and I think he knows Bella too but I'm not sure. I let him type his name into my phone. They could be from him."

"Who is he?" Marion asked, her back rigid and her lips drawn in a thin line.

"His name is Darren Walker."

21

ON THE WAY HOME Marion was silent, but I could see her expression flickering between guilt and hurt. Her shoulders were tense and her hands gripped the steering wheel so tightly that the lucky ring she wore on her index finger dug into the skin. The streets passed by in a grey blur in the late-afternoon light and I stared out of the window so I didn't have to look at her.

I ignored the anger that burbled away inside me and tried to focus instead on her guilt. I was glad she felt bad. The way she'd treated me wasn't fair – she *knew me*. And if she felt bad, then there was hope.

"Why didn't you tell me about the threats?" she asked as we pulled into my driveway. "I could have done something."

I shook my head. "I told you. I didn't want to worry you. I didn't want you to—"

"You were worried I would have made you stop." Marion sighed, her shoulders bobbing. "I get it. We'll track down this guy and see if he can give us some answers." She didn't look away from the windshield. "It might be harmless but given what you told us I don't want to take any chances. Can we please see if we can find your phone now?"

"I want to find it too," I said. "I've probably got a hundred texts." That was a lie but it didn't matter. Both of us wanted to find it. The thought that Bella was gone, missing too, made me feel like the whole world was spinning backwards – something was going on right under my nose and I just couldn't figure it out.

"I think you need a shower," Marion said turning to me. "I can still smell it on you."

I didn't want to acknowledge this, but Marion didn't turn the car off until I looked at her.

"How much did you drink last night?" she asked, very quietly now.

I unclipped my seatbelt and started to get out of the car, but Marion reached out for me, grabbing onto my arm.

"How much?" she pressed.

"I don't know," I said.

"A few glasses? Half a bottle? Please Cassie, I'd like to know. You were driving around this morning – the way you spoke to Fox…"

"What does it matter?" I snapped. "I'm an adult, and sometimes I like to have a drink and just chill out. Gran wasn't there and I needed to wind down. I didn't think I'd be needing a bloody alibi. I was fine to drive and anyway who else have I got—"

"Why didn't you call me?"

"Why should I? You were probably with Dick Cop back there." I yanked my arm away from her and got out of the car.

I stomped up the driveway with my hands inside my jeans pockets, angry at myself for my outburst. I didn't have the patience for this. While we were here, she wasn't out there doing her job. While we were arguing, Marion wasn't ever going to find Grace or Bella and bring them home.

"It isn't like that, Cassie."

We went into my house. It was empty and cold. Without Gran the whole place felt haunted. I realised just how much I missed her.

We split up in the lounge, where Marion left me looking for my phone as she headed into the kitchen.

"If you find it, I need to see it first," Marion informed me. "Before you do anything else."

"Yeah, like chuck it at your head," I muttered under my breath.

When we finally found it, it was on the ground near the garden gate, the screen black and cracked right from top to bottom.

"I'll have to send it to our lab."

"Great. Screen's fucked anyway."

While Marion fiddled with the evidence bag and then some paperwork, I wandered back into the house and collapsed on the sofa.

"Cassie, you've got that look." I didn't move at the sound of her voice. She was in the doorway again, and I could see her out of the corner of my eye, running the necklace I'd bought her between her fingers and looking awkward as hell.

"What look?"

"That one. The look that means you're going to do

something stupid." Marion hesitated for a second and then came further into view, stepping around so that she was facing me. "Please, don't."

"Marion, you just hauled me into a police station. I'm supposed to just, what, sit here and take it? Ride it out as though my pride doesn't mean anything? Come on. You know me better than that."

Marion sucked on her teeth, anger making her jaw tight. "I'm sorry about that, okay? I didn't think he'd be quite so vicious. We just had some – inconsistencies. You know. I thought at the most you might have some information you weren't sharing. And I was right about that, wasn't I? You never told me about this Walker bloke before, or the texts."

"I didn't tell you about the texts but I tried to tell you about Walker. You wouldn't listen to me."

Marion's face softened, and she took a step towards me, indecision on her face. Then she took another step closer, bent and lifted my chin gently with her hand. Where her skin met mine it was like an electric shock.

"I'm sorry," she said quietly. "I want to make it up to you. I was a cow. I didn't mean to be but I had to do it. Fox pushed, *hard*. Will you come over later, please? I've been working for days straight and I've got a couple of hours tonight to grab dinner. We can just… sit. Watch TV. Talk – I don't know. Just spend some time together away from all of this. Or I can come to you if your gran is coming home?"

I didn't say anything immediately, because I didn't know how I felt. The offer seemed like it was more than just a suggestion;

it felt like Marion was offering me a lifeline, and I couldn't tell her whether, in a few hours, I'd be strong enough to take it.

I remembered the first time Marion had touched my jaw like that, run her finger across it as she had done just now. Our noses pressed close together, a blanket pulled over our heads so nobody could see us. Gran's sofa had felt like another world, a world of endless possibilities – at least until Olive had come in and ruined it.

That was before Fox. Before Helen. It was before the world ate us whole and spat us out; before we started to hate each other, just that little bit, and the guilt we mirrored in each other.

I thought again of Gran. The accident and the text messages. A shiver raced down my spine. What if, just by being with her, I was putting Marion in danger? I couldn't lose her again.

"All right," Marion said, stepping back as she saw the look on my face. "You don't have to if you don't want to. I just want to be there for you."

22

ONCE MARION HAD GONE I sat in my lounge, the world feeling empty. My insides were hollow, my stomach growling. But I couldn't face food.

I had done this. To Bella. If she hadn't stopped to text me would she have been late? Would she have been safe at school in time for registration at the end of the eclipse, gossiping excitedly with her friends?

I'd put her life in danger, just like I'd done with Gran. Like I was going to do with Marion if I couldn't distance myself from her. *You could have done more*, said the voice inside my head.

As I sat, I heard the landline ring. I checked the caller ID to make sure it wasn't the hospital and then I ignored it. The answerphone picked up and Henry's voice filtered out. He was checking up on me. Letting me know he'd heard about Bella. I stopped listening.

You could have done more. More. Always more. I was sick of the guilt. I ground my teeth and grabbed my laptop. This was more than just a job. I had to do more. More, more, more...

I started to research, digging up Bella Kaluza's Facebook

page, her Instagram. It seemed she had accounts on several sites despite not being old enough. I devoured every news article I could find, no longer shying away like I had done with Grace. Bella Kaluza, eleven years old from a Polish family. Her parents, it seemed, were going through a messy divorce.

Just like Olive.

The thought echoed in my mind. I scrolled through pages of well-wishing commenters, plans for searches along the south and west edges of the lake, the woodland and the fields towards the north, the suburbs and their parks. I saw the same names popping up again and again, two teachers from Arboretum Secondary School and a man who ran a karate class two streets off the Circle. I noted all of their names down. I knew that it wasn't uncommon for guilty parties to insert themselves into the police investigation and the thought made my blood boil.

The landline rang. Again I screened it, then ignored it. I went back to my laptop, my brain whirring as I devoured social media pleas for Bella's return, scanned comments from well-wishers and teenage hopefuls, grasping for something – anything – and getting nothing.

Bella's Instagram was photo after photo of books piled high, and fairy lights and artistic arrangements of flowers around Young Adult novels. So Bella, like Olive, loved to read.

The feeling made me hot, bile rising. The similarities kept on coming. Bella had been in the newspaper her last year of primary school when she won a fancy-dress competition for World Book Day. She got the highest grades. She quoted Darwin and goddamn Nietzsche on her Facebook page and shared articles about space and science too complicated for my brain to comprehend.

Just like Olive.

But how did Grace fit into all of this?

I got into my car intending to drive to Bella's house, but once I was on the road I hesitated. What good would that do? The hacks would be out in force, and if they got wind of my interview with the police then I wouldn't be able to move about unnoticed. Even if I wasn't a suspect my name would be linked to Bella's disappearance and Olive's face would be everywhere. And, if I was honest, I wasn't sure how I felt about writing about Bella. Or writing at all.

No, better to get a sense for the police investigation first. I drove aimlessly for a while, sorting through my thoughts. When I finally came to my senses, I was idling outside Marion's.

I sat in my car with the windows rolled down despite the coolness of the evening. Marion wasn't there, and I didn't have a mobile phone to call her now, but I wasn't ready to go home either. I thought about Henry in his hotel. I could go to him, have dinner, but I just didn't want to. I wanted Marion.

I turned the radio on to distract myself, hopping between stations for a good ten minutes. A song here, two more there. There were two girls missing in Bishop's Green. *Two.* If one was a coincidence, what did that make two?

As I sat I couldn't shake the sense of wrongness. Marion ought to be home already. It was nearly nine and she'd been working late all week. Surely at some point she would have to sleep? What if something was happening right now and I was sitting here without a phone or any way for her to tell me? I flicked between stations, unable to settle on any for long.

Wrong. Something is wrong.

I pushed the thought down and kept my eyes trained on the street, where Marion's car should appear at any moment. Still she didn't come.

As the clock ticked over on the hour, the music on the Bishop's Green local station stopped playing and a newscaster started to read. I wasn't really listening, only half an ear focused on the distorted chatter.

But then I heard it.

"Breaking news on missing local girl Grace Butler."

I held my breath, unable to smother the fear that shot through me.

"Police have announced this evening that missing local pre-teen Grace Butler has been found. At four o'clock this afternoon, Grace and her father – who police had been trying to locate – were spotted coming out of a campsite in Scotland.

"Her father told police that he had been unaware of Grace's so-called 'disappearance', knowing only that she came to visit him while he had some time off work. The two decided to go camping – and only today was it revealed to him that his daughter had not informed her mother of her whereabouts.

"Police spokesman Michael Ardent said this: 'We are all very happy to hear that Grace is safe. Investigations into Bella Kaluza's whereabouts have not ceased, and we only hope to find her in as good health as her friend'.

"Otherwise there is no new update in the Kaluza case. Listeners are reminded that search parties for Bella continue to…"

My brain stuttered.

"What?" I hissed.

Grace is okay.

My body felt heavy and the pounding in my head slammed out all thoughts but this. *Grace is okay. Grace is okay…*

But the thoughts weren't happy. Sick with shame, I realised that I was angry. I was wrong. I had been wrong about everything. Wasted hours – valuable hours – of Bella's life today because they weren't the same. They weren't taken by the same person. And it had nothing to do with Olive.

My chest rose and fell so heavily I thought I might pass out. The thoughts whirling inside my head were out of order, outraged and confused at the same time. *What does it mean? How could I have been so wrong?*

I was still in the same position, with my head against the steering wheel and my arms cushioning my ears from the outside world, when Marion found me. I barely heard her over the rushing in my ears. Her hand on my shoulder was warm.

"Cassie?" she asked. "Cassie, are you all right?"

"I heard the news, Marion," I said, tears making my throat tight. "Grace is okay. But what about Bella?"

23

October 1999

SOME DAYS, MICKEY WAS good company. He liked to snuggle up to her as the weather got colder. Sandman started to bring thicker clothes, more jumpers and even a pair of jeans once. Olive wore the jeans for two weeks before he noticed, and when he took them away for laundry she didn't get another pair.

At night all she had was a T-shirt unless she wanted to sleep in her dresses, and she would try to keep warm under the duvet – but it was lumpy and thin in places. She wanted desperately to sleep with Mickey near her, as though he might warm her up. But she knew she couldn't. So every night she hid him in the small bread bin, hoping that Sandman wouldn't start leaving her bread in there instead of in the fridge.

Some days, Mickey was less companionable. Once he bit her. Just a little nick, right above her left index knuckle. Sandman, ever watchful, noticed during his next visit and got very angry.

But Olive had stayed firm. She'd scratched it while trying to sharpen her pencil. Could she – please – have a book to read? For two months, nothing. He liked to toy with her, tell her he couldn't get one for her. She knew he could. He had access to books now just like he always had. He just didn't want to give her one. The thought made her sick.

"Please," she had said quietly only a few days ago, during his visit one evening. She'd learnt when was best to ask him these questions. Learnt to read his face for signs of stress, or anger. This time, he only sighed and ignored her.

"*Please*," she said again, more forcefully. "I've drawn enough pictures. Can't I have one book? I'll read anything – even one of your grown-up books—"

He hadn't liked that, though. He shook his head with conviction and Olive knew that the conversation was over. He didn't like her pointing out that he was starving her – not of food, of course, but of *life*.

Tonight, it was particularly cold. Olive, less groggy than usual, woke up several times through the night. Sandman watched her less, now. Came less regularly. And, she realised, she was less sleepy now than she had been at first. Hollowly, she thought he must have been drugging her somehow.

But tonight she wished she could sleep. The cold was persistent, and sleep would not come. She got up to check on Mickey, who was doing fine in his nest of shredded paper and tissue. And then, she heard him.

Steps on the stairs.

A feral panic overtook Olive, as it always did. She would never *ever* get used to it. She shot back to her bed, leaping onto the mattress as she heard the first lock disengage from the outside.

It was too late for this. And she was too awake. She felt

violent shivers of fear making her teeth chatter together. Or it might just have been the cold.

Sandman entered quietly but something was different than usual. Olive stayed upright, her body rigid, her mind whirring. He cut a dark shape against the pale grey of the badly painted wall.

And then he flicked the lights on. He'd finally replaced the bulb about a month earlier, although Olive still didn't like to use it.

Olive squinted, her senses flailing as the bright light and brief smell of something other than the room assaulted her.

"Oh good, you're awake," Sandman said. His eyes were bright, glittering in the harsh light. Olive's stomach flipped over.

"Ye—"

"Do you know what day it is?"

Olive did, but she didn't say anything. She didn't want Sandman to find the tally she'd been keeping on the wall under her bed. That was the only thing stopping her from going mental – that and the diary she was keeping, a stash of pages written on the cheap paper he brought her, thin and slightly grey.

"It's October eleventh."

Something was definitely wrong. Everything was wrong. He wasn't supposed to be here tonight. He always came for the Health and Hygiene checks on Thursdays. Olive's trembling was now more to do with the thought that maybe he wouldn't stick to his routine any more, and that was all she had left.

But Sandman's face was sort of happy. She hadn't seen him like this since that first day when she'd climbed into his van.

"Is that… special?"

"Two months! Eight beautiful weeks since I saved you."

Olive swallowed. She didn't dare question what he meant by "saved". Two months. Her heart started to hammer faster, louder. Would he let her go? Was this the end of some sort of trial…? Olive squashed the thought like a bug. Hope was no good.

It was then that she saw his hands. How he was holding something.

"Is that a newspaper…?"

Sandman glanced down. Smiled a little. Then he thrust it at her. It *was* a newspaper. Two of them, actually. And a beaten-up copy of a Roald Dahl book with a crease right down the front cover.

"Happy Anniversary," he said.

She took them from him, almost expecting him to yank them away. Her hands were shaking. Sandman watched as she lowered them into her lap, and then he reached out a hand. Swooped it down on top of her head, in an awkward patting motion. Like you might pet a dog.

Olive flinched. Thankfully, he didn't seem to notice.

He didn't wait for her to say anything, or do anything else. He just spun on his heel and left the room.

When he was gone, Olive waited for what seemed like an hour. Until her heartbeat had returned to normal. Until her face felt less numb, her body slowly returning to itself. The newspaper had bits missing.

Olive let out a small sob. These were her pages. He'd cut them out. That was what he thought he had *saved* her from.

Her pages. Her family were still looking for her.

Again that little balloon of hope started to float inside her. And for a minute, just a minute, she let it.

24

MARION HANDED ME A cup of tea and then moved to sit in the armchair across from me. I noticed for the first time how thin she was getting, the dark circles under her eyes more pronounced than usual, and the realisation only made me feel worse.

"Why didn't you tell me?" I demanded. "Were you trying to hide it from me?"

Marion's eyes flashed, whether with anger or hurt I couldn't tell.

"Don't be stupid, Cassie. I tried to call you but you weren't home."

I fought to keep my features neutral. My fault. Again.

"I just feel so…"

"Cheated?" She arched an eyebrow.

"*Overwhelmed*." I corrected. But Marion was right. I felt cheated. And the thought made me sick.

"It's okay, Cassie," Marion said quietly. "I get it."

"No, I don't think you do."

I wanted to hit something. I half-rose in my seat, sloshing hot tea down my hands and onto my legs. The pain brought me back, and I sank back down again.

"Cassie, stop for a second. Don't do this – don't beat yourself up."

"How can I stop? Bella Kaluza is on her own and we have nothing. What about her parents? Where were they?"

"Bella's mum went to work just after her daughter left for school and the dad's a taxi driver with fares to alibi him. We don't have *nothing*," Marion said firmly. "We still have Darren Walker. And those text messages. They started before Bella was taken, didn't they? The threats?"

"What?" I frowned.

"You said yourself that Walker knows both girls. He works at the school twice a week selling vintage clothes and old books out of the back of his van. He started this "car-boot sale" with one of the school mothers, but now she only helps out at one session. Today he lied about Bella Kaluza, said he'd never met her."

Marion's gaze was searching as she stared at me. Waiting for the penny to drop. Darren Walker might not have had anything to do with Grace but he knew Bella. He knew her and he had lied. Whoever had sent me those texts had wanted me to back off before Bella had even been taken.

"Walker does know her then?"

Marion nodded. Yet somehow this didn't make me feel any better.

"What aren't you telling me?" I asked.

Marion pursed her lips, deep in thought. She didn't answer me for a moment.

"I need to tell somebody." She looked up at me, her

midnight hair shining as she brushed it back off her face. "But this sounds crazy."

"What about your arsehole partner?" I asked. "Can't you talk to him?"

Marion shook her head. "No. I just… Okay, we have Darren Walker. A guy who is clearly unnerved by the police, who ducks official questions and lies. I'm sure he knows something he's not telling us – but I don't think that information is Bella Kaluza's location."

"Wait," I said. "What?"

"He's… He's slow and thoughtful, and *something* is stopping him from talking to us but he seems more afraid than anything. I mentioned the eclipse and he got really jittery and muttered something about 'back then'. I didn't really notice at the time because he was so worked up – but now I can't help thinking that you were right. About the eclipses and the timing."

"Come again?" I said, my tired strung-out brain fighting to keep up. "I don't follow."

"I think you were right. About there being a connection with Olive. And the eclipse. Grace was a good distraction but the eclipse, Bella, that timing – it's too much to be a coincidence."

She was staring at me. She was flushed. Sweat beaded along her hairline. Her whole body looked tense, as though she had been holding something in for too long and now it was about to come bursting out. I noticed this without really seeing, though, because suddenly all I could see was Olive, walking off because I wasn't being attentive. *Keep an eye on her, Cassie.* Old guilt rose in me, the feeling that I was to blame. That *we* were to blame – Marion and me.

"A link between Olive and… Bella?"

Not Olive and Grace.

Olive and *Bella*.

I'd been so focused on trying to link all three girls that I hadn't looked at just the two of them. Just Bella and Olive.

"And here's the other thing," Marion said, still breathless. She was sitting so close I could see her pulse in her throat.

Blood roaring in my ears I asked, "What other thing?"

"The mood ring," Marion said slowly. "The one Grace had – with the old black gem and the mermaid tail. You told me you thought it was just like Olive's? I found out this afternoon that Grace and Bella argued about it a few days before Grace went on holiday with her father."

"Why did they argue?" I asked. I felt myself getting giddy, sweat marking a trail down my spine.

"Because it wasn't Grace's ring. She only took it after it was confiscated during class – a history teacher told us what happened."

"A teacher?" I thought of the curly-haired teacher I had seen on the news. The teachers I'd seen posting on the school's official Facebook and Twitter. The texts I'd had, which sounded convincingly like they had come from a teenager…

Marion nodded. "Grace only ended up with the ring because somebody else didn't want it."

I kept my thoughts about the teachers to myself. Wild theories wouldn't get us anywhere. With a jolt I realised what this meant. I knew why Marion had told me I was right. About Olive and the eclipse.

"It was Bella's ring." Marion laid a hand on my knee, whether to keep me calm or to keep me from running I didn't know. "Somebody gave it to Bella as a gift."

"And before that," I said, fear shooting through me like a fiery arrow, "it was Olive's."

25

Saturday, 21 March 2015

THE FOLLOWING MORNING I rang the hospital first thing to check on Gran. I'd slept poorly, woken by nightmares where Gran was hurt again, this time while she was supposed to be safe on her ward.

Without my mobile phone, I had no way of knowing whether I'd had any more text messages from the unknown number, and this thought hung over me like a black cloud. Every car that drove by might be the one that knocked Gran down, the driver the man who had taken Bella. Who had taken Olive.

I steeled myself to listen to the old answerphone messages on the landline instead. Thankfully there was only one from Henry. I almost didn't call him back, worried what it might mean if somebody was watching me, monitoring what I knew, checking who I called. But paranoia wouldn't bring Bella home.

"How's the holiday? Are you having an okay time? I'm sorry I haven't been in touch more." I launched in immediately when he answered the phone, getting in first so he couldn't ask how I was. After my reaction to having seen Darren Walker in the youth group photo Henry had dropped me back home and made me promise to keep in touch. But since I didn't have my mobile any more, it was easy to put off the lecture I'd get when he found out how personal this was becoming.

"I thought you were avoiding me," Henry said. "Your mobile has been going to voicemail. After that other little girl and what happened with her... I thought you might want to talk about it. You still owe me that dinner..."

"Sorry. I broke the screen on my phone. I'll need to get a new one."

"You're distracted." Henry paused, it sounded like he was sipping a hot drink, and then he let out a sigh. "I assume you're feeling a bit rough because of the poor Kaluza girl?"

"Yeah. I know I was wrong before, about Grace obviously. Or, I wasn't *right* anyway." I rubbed my face with my free hand. Clearly the conversation was going this way whether I wanted it to or not. "But I still can't help thinking there's a connection to Olive here. Even more so now that I'm not trying to force Grace into the equation. Marion agrees."

"Oh, she does, does she?" Henry said slyly. "I see you've been busy with Maaarion."

"I'm not talking about that with you," I said, but smiled despite myself. "Look, I know you've probably got more interesting stuff to do − walking or drinking or whatever it is you do for fun on holiday, but... since you're here..."

"Oh, just ask me." Henry laughed. "I promise I won't pester you about Marion again. Just don't start with all this 'asking nicely' rubbish. You've never asked nicely for anything in your life."

I thought about feigning hurt but knew Henry would see right through it.

"Did you find anything out about Darren Walker, like I asked before? Apparently he lied about knowing Bella despite proof to the contrary. Marion seems to think he knows more than he's saying. I'm sure she'll be speaking to him again, if she hasn't already, but I need to know if I can link him to – anything."

To *Olive*. To see if Darren Walker might know something about who abducted my sister.

"Not yet, but I'm working on it."

I drove to the hospital first, wanting to see Gran before I met with Bella's teacher – the man who had confiscated Olive's mood ring from her. Gran was sleeping when I got there, but with Marion's support echoing in my head, this time I woke her.

"Morning," I said. I plopped down a bouquet of flowers. They were already wilting but the bright colours made the stark hospital room seem that little bit more bearable.

Gran smiled at me. "Cassie!" she exclaimed, in a rare moment of recognition. "What lovely flowers. Are those for me?"

"They are indeed," I said. I smiled back, surprised that the motion came easily. Was that all it took? A single greeting that was meant for me and nobody else? I pulled my other hand from behind my back and showed Gran the box of chocolates I'd brought her as well.

"Ooh," she said. "My favourites. Wherever did you get those?"

Exploitative? Maybe. One of the few perks of Gran's poor memory was that she never remembered that the "rare" chocolates she'd loved all her life were now two quid a box and even Ady sold them.

"You're welcome," I said.

"You know, I could do with a nice can of Coke." Gran took the chocolates and immediately delved into them, ripping the cellophane off like a small child at Christmas. "I never used to like it, but she leaves it lying around half finished. And it's so sweet and sticky. Waste of pocket money but still kind of tasty." Gran smacked her lips.

"It's a bit early in the morning for that," I said, although she was already eating chocolate so I wasn't sure what harm it could do.

"That's not what *she* says." Gran stuffed one of the little chocolates in her mouth and smiled, her eyes twinkling. I didn't ask who she meant because I already knew.

Olive did love Coke. Like all small children, sweets and chocolates were welcome, but Olive would always take fizzy pop over food. Probably because Mum didn't allow it in the house. I smiled sadly, the memory surprising me. I'd forgotten that. Gran was always the one who gave Olive the money to go and buy it while we stayed here – a secret from Mum, but the good kind.

I remembered one afternoon in summer a couple of years before Olive was taken. Mum had picked us up from school – a rare occurrence, and we were giddy with it. Instead of taking us straight home, she took us to the small row of shops near our house. There was a confectioner's, a local one called *Birds* that I remembered vividly for their opulently iced cream buns and home-made jammie dodgers; Mum had taken us inside and treated us to cakes and fizzy drinks. She'd only regretted it when Olive got sticky fingers all over the inside of the car. I grinned at the memory.

"How are you feeling anyway?" I asked, channelling the warmth I felt at remembering that afternoon.

"Oh, you know. Bit sore. I do tell these doctors to be careful but they're always jabbing me with things. I don't like that." She grabbed another chocolate from the box.

"That's their job. That's what they're here to do. They're looking after you. Anyway, you always tell me how gentle Doctor White is and I'm sure you'll be able to see him again soon. But how is your arm? It's broken, remember."

Gran frowned. I tried to keep my smile warm, even as Gran's frown deepened and something flashed in her eyes. Was that fear?

"Are you okay?" My stomach clenched and my throat constricted.

"I'm…" Gran looked around, taking in the room. "He slowed down…" she whispered. "He was aiming for me but I think he slowed down."

I reached out to take her good arm. It was thin but wiry with a kind of strength I'd forgotten. She'd always been strong. The women in my family – that's one thing we were all cursed with. Strength in the shape of stubbornness.

"It's okay. You've been very brave. Does it hurt much?"

"No." Gran's eyes clouded. "Well. Yes. I suppose it does. But I guess that's what happens when you ride on the back of motorbikes, isn't it?"

And like that, the moment passed. I forced a laugh, trying to make the tension ease out of me. This was more like the Gran I remembered. Growing up, Gran and Grandad had been the most cheerful people I knew. They were never afraid of mess, letting Olive and me create castles out of foam in the kitchen or use glitter paint in the lounge. Our summers were spent making as much mess as possible – Gran always said if we got it out of our systems at her house, Mum would be grateful. I think they sensed that it was what we needed, after the tension at home: unbridled fun with somebody who enjoyed it as much as we did.

We had always looked forward to the summers away from home. Even when I was older and I claimed to be bored, it was the comfortable kind of boredom. In a lot of ways Gran's house was more comfortable than our own, a place where we could be ourselves only a little more *free*.

In the years that followed, my sadness at losing Olive was exaggerated – perhaps selfishly – by the fact that summers were never the same after she was gone. I never again spent a whole summer in Bishop's Green, visiting less and less as Mum and I withdrew into our own separate world of sadness and guilt. Mum working more so that we could afford the tiny house we rented after Dad left, and me doing everything I could to help her pretend she'd never had a husband and never needed one anyway. Gran and Grandad stopped asking me to come and stay with them when I explained that if I did, Mum wouldn't eat a decent meal or have any clean clothes to wear to work.

"Motorbikes," I said ruefully to Gran, giving her arm a gentle pat. "Well, really."

In the car my good mood soured immediately. Bella Kaluza had been missing for a whole day and night. *Twenty-four hours,* my brain tolled. *Twenty-four hours gone.* The eclipse still burned behind my eyes when I closed them, a child-stealing spectre.

I made it to Earl's café in Chestnut Circle just after the breakfast rush for my hastily arranged meeting with Marion's teacher witness who had told her about the mood ring. I hoped that he was already inside; I was too caffeinated to hang around and if I got restless I might go at him harder than necessary.

I found the teacher sitting at the back of the café with a steaming latte. He'd been blessed with a full head of curly brown hair that was only now greying at the temples and what my mother would have called a beautiful pair of baby-blues. He reminded me of the teacher all my friends had had a crush on at school. He was also, I noticed, the man I'd seen on the television, and outside the school talking to Bella.

"Jake Howden," he said. He thrust his hand at me, but I was distracted. It was the first time I'd heard his full name spoken aloud and something in the back of my brain pinged in recognition.

Shakily I returned an introduction, sat across from him and pulled out my notebook. He was, I realised, one of the teachers who had been posting on social media. I remembered his name from my list, which had been sitting untouched since Grace had turned up. He was also one of a handful of teachers I'd noted who had been in town sixteen years ago when Olive was taken.

"Thank you for seeing me, Mr Howden," I said, clearing my throat in an attempt to dislodge the lump that was forming. "I appreciate your insight."

"Anything to help." He gestured amiably. When he dropped his hands to the table there was a thunking noise as his watch – a gold, heavy, expensive-looking thing – hit the Formica. He winced. "Sorry," he said. "It's a bit big. My wife bought it for me but I haven't had time to get it adjusted yet."

He said the word wife pointedly, as though he was making it as obvious as possible that he wasn't single. I thought of Marion and pushed down the amused smirk that threatened to break my professionalism. He was a good ten years too old, for starters. And the wrong gender. But I didn't say anything.

"The girls?" I prompted.

"Ah, yes. I know Grace – and Bella – fairly well, actually. You said on the phone that you were writing a piece about them? I think it's quite clear by now that Bella's disappearance isn't connected."

I shrugged. "It's more about Bella than Grace. But they're friends, so everything helps. It'll be a bit about the town, about the girls. About the way Bishop's Green has come out in force to protect these two children from different backgrounds. The heroes who've helped the authorities. That sort of thing." I tried to keep it light, but I could see Jake Howden's face brighten at the thought that he might be a "hero".

"Sure, sure," he said, nodding. "There are a lot of us trying to organise searches. What sort of thing do you want to know? I've been teaching both girls since September. Clever kids. Especially Bella."

"Yet you had to confiscate something from her last week, didn't you? Detective Adams told me you mentioned an argument the girls had."

"It wasn't really an argument. But I did remember it because Bella's normally one of the more relaxed girls in the class, but she was fidgety and snappy all morning. I wondered what had set her off, because even though things are tough for her at home, she never usually brings it into the classroom."

"Tough at home?"

"Her parents. Messy divorce. I saw it all the time when I used to volunteer for the youth group so it's nothing new." Howden shrugged but his expression was coy. He leaned in conspiratorially as I tried to picture him at the youth group. Did he know Darren Walker? Might he have known Olive? My skin crawled. I wanted to ask but I couldn't get the words out.

"The mother seems to be struggling," Howden explained. "A couple of times I've seen Bella in grubby shirts, a dirty blazer – like her mum hasn't noticed. You ought to see what she gets sent in with for lunch. Junk food, all of it. I've given her credits for the school cafeteria a few times this year just to make sure she doesn't eat rubbish." He let this sink in and then scooted back in his chair and smiled again. "But Bella's usually fine – you know, the right amount of chatty. Friendly. She seems all right most of the time. Resilient."

I remembered Olive – that summer. Chatty, same as always. Yet still aching with the knowledge she carried of our own family's crumbling foundations. I hadn't truly seen it then, but looking back I realised that Olive was more affected than any of us recognised at the time. Perhaps Bella was the same. But Jake Howden knowing these things about Bella's life hadn't stopped her from being abducted or running away, or turning to somebody for solace, and the thought made me cold.

"You talk to Bella a lot outside of school hours?" I asked.

Howden, to his credit, didn't even so much as blink. "Sometimes," he said. "A few times recently. I only work part-time but I try to make myself available if I'm on site during lunch. We've chatted during breaks, or once she came by my room after school. We don't really have much in the way of a counsellor so I guess she finds it easier to talk to teachers than her parents." He shrugged carelessly, but I saw a glint of pride in his eyes.

It wasn't the answer I wanted and it didn't allay any of my fears, but now wasn't the time to go into it. Not while he was eager to answer my other questions. And not without Marion. I was on thin ice already and I didn't want to end up in over my head for a hunch.

"This argument," I said, then. "Between Grace and Bella. It was about a ring. A mood ring, right?"

I gripped my pen tighter, smoothing my expression into one of general interest, but my heart thudded so loudly I hardly heard Mr Howden's response.

"Yeah. Just one of those colour-changing ones you can get everywhere. I've seen them often enough. Except this one was broken. Well, not so much broken as just old. The colour didn't change any more. I assume a boy gave it to Bella, but she didn't want it. She said something about it being gross. In the end it was Grace who came back after class and got it. She said she thought it was cool."

"And?" I pushed, sensing he hadn't told me everything. He rubbed at a patch of stubble on his chin that he'd missed when he shaved. I noticed it with a kind of smug satisfaction.

"She said that she thought Bella would change her mind – about not wanting it. Grace seemed… Not jealous, exactly, but…"

I swallowed hard. So Bella had been given a ring – a ring that looked an awful lot like the one Olive had been given the summer she was taken – and Grace had known about it.

"Do you remember the conversation that started it?" I asked. "Maybe what Bella said about the ring? Where she got it?"

Mr Howden shook his head. "She just said she didn't want it. Something that sounded like, 'It's too weird getting presents like that. It makes me feel gross now.'"

"You said you thought a boy gave it to her…"

It must have seemed a significant gift, for Bella to be so alarmed by it – and for Grace to find it alluring. Could this really be the ring I had seen on my sister's hand sixteen years ago? I thought of the eclipse again, that empty black circle. The timing of Bella's disappearance. And now this mood ring, a relic given as a gift that nobody really wanted.

Even if whoever had given Bella the ring *didn't* know where it had come from, everything still pointed back to Olive. I felt sick.

"I don't know who gave it to her," Jake Howden said when he saw the look on my face. "I genuinely don't. It's certainly nothing to do with me – I try not to pry too much into my students' personal lives, and I'm sure a lot of people have stuff like it lying around at home, trinkets and the like. I only told the police about it because Bella was so freaked out. Everybody in the class witnessed it. I mean, it's just a ring, right?"

"Right," I said faintly.

"And… Well, girls get themselves into these sorts of things all the time, don't they? Receiving gifts they don't want or being afraid to upset admirers. Boys *are* very irresistible."

I tried to keep the annoyance from my face as this charmer stared right at me and smiled. I wrinkled my nose – as much disgust as I would allow to show.

"Not usually when you're eleven," I said firmly.

26

"I DON'T LIKE IT." I was in my car, avoiding putting the key in the ignition. I'd picked up a new mobile after my meeting with Jake Howden, partly so I could check up on Gran easier, and partly so I could bug Marion for an update. It was nice to hear her voice, although I wouldn't have admitted that to anyone.

"I bet those were the first words out of your bloody mouth as a child," Marion said. "*I don't like it.*"

"Actually, I think they were *I want that.*" I waited for Marion's laughter to subside, glad of the distraction from the twisting in my stomach. "I don't like that teacher though, Marion. He's really smarmy. And he seemed to know a lot about Bella even though he only teaches her a few times a week. And he mentioned the youth group."

"He's one of those charitable types," Marion said, the smile leaving her voice. "It's not that uncommon. And just about everybody in town and their dad has volunteered with the youth group or the Scouts or run a raffle or a charity competition. You know what Bishop's Green is like. Anyway, he came to talk to us, not the other way around. He seems a bit invested but he's probably just one of those teachers who thinks he's God's gift."

"He might be trying to throw us off the scent by mentioning the mood ring," I said. "If he knew you'd find out about it anyway, perhaps he was just pre-empting you?"

Marion made a sound in her throat that sounded like a dismissal.

"Maybe," she said.

I knew Marion was probably right, but something about the man didn't sit well with me. He was *too* interested. Too involved. And then there was the matter of all of his posts on Facebook and Twitter... I'd learned the hard way about ignoring my gut instinct.

"Did you alibi him?"

I virtually heard Marion roll her eyes on the other end of the phone. "Cassie, come on."

"Well, did you?"

Marion let out a sigh. "Yes, Cassie. We did. He was with his wife when Bella was taken, getting ready for work. And he was there, at school, teaching his first class of the day at eleven. He doesn't have a form this year – part-time, writing a book or something the rest of the time – but he claims to have been on site from nine thirty. We're trying to confirm this now but with the eclipse everything's a mess."

I didn't say anything, but it didn't make me feel any better. Wives and lovers lie, I thought. Carol lied for my father during their affair. Helen had lied for me the first time I was accused of being rude to a deserving interviewee. I'd lied to protect Marion from the text messages. And Bella could have been taken any time from when she left her house until the register was held at the end of the eclipse – it was a two-hour window and a lot could happen in that time.

"How is your gran?" Marion asked when I didn't respond.

"She's... She's okay. Do you think somebody hurt her on purpose?"

"I don't know. Whoever was driving wasn't going very fast," Marion said thoughtfully, sadness tingeing her words. "It could have been worse, though."

That was what haunted me. Was this a promise of more violence to come? I didn't want to think about it.

"The mood ring," I said, instead. "Did you get it from Grace? Did you find... anything? Fingerprints?"

"Grace said she lost it."

I felt my stomach heave at the thought but I knew it wasn't true. Grace wouldn't have lost it. I realised Marion was still speaking.

"It could have loads of prints on it anyway, Cass, not just whoever gave it to your sister. Especially if it's been around a bit. The girls, their parents, kids at school, teachers... It could have been given to Bella by anybody... Grace said she's not sure where it came from."

"It's Olive's ring, Marion." The words lurched out of me. "It's Olive's."

"Cassie..." I heard the warning in Marion's voice but I couldn't stop.

"I know it's hers. It's old. Black. Mood rings go that colour – but not for a while. They're... Oh Christ." I blinked back the hot tears in my eyes. "It's her ring." I said again. "And I want to find out where it came from."

"Cassie, stop. You're still on thin ice with Fox…" Marion paused, presumably realising that his name wasn't going to get me to listen. She huffed a breath that might have been annoyance, could have been resignation. "Are you sure?" she asked.

"I need to see it. But… I'm sure."

Another pause. Then a sigh.

"Do you think you can get more out of Grace than we have? I can't authorise you barging in there, Cass. If anybody asks I'll deny all knowledge. And if you get into any trouble, I'm hauling you back down here whether you like it or not."

I fought a small smile, relief fluttering in my chest. "Is that a promise, Detective Inspector?"

"You got it." Marion snorted, paused. When she spoke next her voice was warm. "*I want that…*" she muttered. "Yeah, that just about sums you up."

The Upton home looked different today. There were fewer people camping outside; they were all at the Kaluza house, pawing at the poor single mother there whose broken English was no doubt all the more endearing to them.

There were two cars on the Upton drive, one of them was Roger Upton's white Audi. I parked down the street and walked the last few hundred yards.

Adelaide Upton looked much better than the last time I'd seen her but the experience of it all had aged her. Her hair was tied up in a loose bun and she was wearing a string of pearls around her neck, but she was dressed in plain, dark clothes.

"Oh, hello," she said. "I was afraid you were the press." The irony of this comment didn't go unnoticed but I didn't say anything about myself or the job. I didn't want to think about it. At this rate, there'd be no story, and no money, and I'd be back where I started: stuck in Bishop's Green with no job and no future.

"Do you want to come in?" Mrs Upton asked.

I stepped into the same hallway, lit with the same twig lights and hung with the same tasteful pictures. It felt warmer now. There were boots at the bottom of the stairs, and a child's coat flung carelessly across the bannister and now these things didn't feel so sad. I once again felt a surge of frustration that Marion hadn't shared her suspicions about Grace's father sooner. I wondered whether they would prosecute him, although to his knowledge he hadn't done anything wrong.

"Grace?" Adelaide called.

I followed her through to the kitchen, where a girl sat at the kitchen table with an iPad and a bowl of cereal in front of her, mostly untouched. She looked up, and I was overwhelmed by the uncanniness of it all. The face that had haunted my dreams – it was right *here*. And yet not quite the same.

I was often struck, when meeting people for articles and stories I was writing, how different they looked when compared to their photographs. I would interview grieving widows, having only seen a quick snapshot of them, and I was always surprised by their vigour – how *alive*, and often happy, they looked when I finally met them in person.

And missing persons – they were often the opposite. Drained of the excitement they had held in their faces and bodies when photographs were taken. Because undoubtedly their families always chose the "best" pictures, the ones they thought were the most flattering. People would be out in the streets looking for rosy-cheeked cherubs, and not for the real children out there in the world, frightened and alone.

Grace was no different. In her photographs she had seemed angelic. Smiling, always smiling, with a gap between her front teeth and her silver-blonde hair framing her childish face. But in person she seemed older. Sullen, almost. She was skinnier than she had been in her school photo, and I could see already within her the young woman she was becoming.

"Sweetheart, this is one of the ladies who was helping me look for you," Adelaide said. Her voice was soft, relieved, but the tension in her body betrayed the anger she felt at having believed her daughter had been abducted for seven long days.

"Thanks." Grace didn't look up this time, just avoided my eyes and stared at the screen in front of her without moving.

"Mrs Upton," I said, "could I bother you for a drink? I'd like to talk to Grace, if I may."

Adelaide thought about this but only for a second.

"Tea?" she asked.

I nodded and she headed over to the other side of the kitchen to switch on the kettle.

"If you're going to tell me how glad you are I'm not dead, I'm listening." Grace stared at me defiantly.

"Oh, Grace," her mother said from across the kitchen. "Manners."

"Well, really." Grace sighed. "I'm sorry, but I've had loads of people telling me that. I was never gone, okay? I'm *fine*. I had a nice holiday with my dad and—"

"I'm not here about that. Is there anywhere we can go to talk? Just for a minute? It's about Bella."

Grace stopped. She stared at me, and then looked at her mother. But Adelaide just uttered a small sigh, and I took that as agreement.

"We have a den," Grace said eventually.

She left her cereal bowl and iPad on the table and I followed her into another room off the kitchen.

"So, why are you here?" Grace turned on me, her arms folded across her chest defensively, as though she expected me to lunge at her any second. I stayed near the door.

"You're Bella's friend," I said slowly, gauging her reaction. "Her best friend."

Immediately Grace's frown deepened and I could see that she was burning with it all. With anger, and frustration, and maybe guilt too. She wouldn't look at me, but her blue eyes were focused on the bookcase behind my head and I resisted the urge to check what she was staring at.

"Do you have anything you want to talk about?" I prompted gently. "About Bella? And what happened?"

"I don't know what happened," Grace said. "I didn't know she was going anywhere. She'd have told me. Bella... She hasn't got anywhere else to go. I mean, I know I went away without telling anybody and people said, 'Oh I don't think Grace would do that.' But I was just so sick of not getting to see my dad and I knew that Mum wouldn't let me go in the holidays. And I *told* Bella that I was going. Bella wouldn't have gone anywhere without telling me."

I didn't say anything. Whatever Grace wanted to tell me was going to come out all on its own.

"Look," she said. "I'm sorry about what I did. I didn't think Mum would get so pissy with me. I just thought she'd know I was with Dad, or she wouldn't care. I didn't even think about school. Bella covered for me because I asked her to − because she's a *good friend*. We had a deal − a week. She had to give it a week before she told an adult where I was. So if Bella wanted me to say anything to you right now, then she'd have told me to."

Grace's bottom lip stuck out, and I realised what was going on here. She wasn't guilty, or sad. She was angry that Bella hadn't told her anything, and angry because that meant maybe they weren't as close as she thought. I realised now why Bella had wanted to meet me yesterday − exactly a week after Grace left for her holiday.

"Do you think Bella would want you to tell me about the ring? The one she was given and didn't want? I saw you wearing it in the photos your mum took."

"It's just a ring," Grace said defensively, her eyes still fixed somewhere behind my head. "It doesn't mean anything."

"Well, I think it does. I think Bella not coming home has made you feel weird about it. And that's the reason you're not wearing it any more."

"I lost it," Grace said quickly. "When I was camping. She didn't want it and she gave it to me but I lost it."

I waited a second. Watched Grace's expression shift, worry making her lips thin as she pressed them together.

"So it's not on the shelf behind me." I shrugged, feigning nonchalance. "And if I turn around I won't see it?"

"*Fine.*" Grace glared at me, and I glanced upwards to thank my lucky stars that the gamble had paid off.

"So, are you going to tell me what's so important about this ring that you two fought over it?" I asked. "What's so important about it that your teacher thought the police needed to know about it?"

"It's not… It's not important." The kid shrugged, her blonde hair slipping over her shoulder. "Bella just thought it was ugly and I liked it. So she said I should go back and get it if I liked it so much."

"Where did it come from?" I asked. I had to try very hard to keep my breathing even.

"She said she got it from a man." Grace wouldn't look at me. She was still staring at the ring. I imagined I could almost *feel* it behind me. The power, the darkness in that little silver band. The circle reminded me of the eclipse and when I blinked I was sure I would see it.

"A man?" I pressed.

"She wouldn't tell me who gave it to her. She wouldn't tell me *anything* about him. And then when Mr Howden took it off her – she said she was glad it was gone. That it could go back to where it came from for all she cared."

"And Mr Howden, did he… seem overly interested in it? Or in Bella?"

Grace shrugged. "Only as much as normal. She's his favourite so he probably took it because he knew she was upset and he wanted her to go back and get it later so he could ask her if she was okay."

Not because he had given it to her in the first place and he wanted to have a reason for it to be back in his possession…?

Grace's face blanched as she continued to stare at the ring, as though she knew it was wrong but she didn't know why. I wanted to ask her about the threat we could both feel, about Bella's fear and refusal to wear it and Grace's own desire to keep the ring, perhaps searching for the same attention Bella had been given by the gift-giver.

With a jolt I realised that this was the same wrongness I recognised – recognised because I remembered it from that summer. That sick feeling and the fear that something was happening but being powerless to stop it. A feeling I hadn't even realised I'd had, deep down inside me, when Olive started to keep secrets.

And I knew I couldn't say it aloud now any more than I could back then.

I turned slowly, my whole body taut and screaming. *Just leave, just walk out now and you wouldn't have to face it.* But I knew I had to. The shelf behind me was cluttered with books and hideous holiday memorabilia. And there, perched among it all… I let out a hiss of breath.

There it was.

It was so small: a thin silver band, a mermaid with a crooked tail and a clouded black gem in the centre. It was such a nothing thing – but it could mean so much. I felt my fingers itching to pick it up, to take it with me. I reached out, my skin not quite brushing the cool metal.

Olive's ring. I missed her so much it hurt.

She said she got it from a man.

And now he had her, just like he'd taken Olive.

27

31 December 1999

NEW YEAR'S EVE. OLIVE was celebrating. He'd missed her Health and Hygiene check yesterday. And she knew he wouldn't risk coming today. He'd said something about his wife. About celebrating with her.

Olive found it hard to believe that he had a wife. That he had somebody in his life aside from her. He told her that he'd met his wife when they were very young. That she understood him – understood that he was trying to *save* Olive. From life, from the horrid world outside.

Olive didn't believe that his wife knew about her. It wasn't possible. Was it? She knew Sandman chose his wife's clothes, just like he chose Olive's. She knew his wife was younger, that she made his lunches and did as she was told. Perhaps she did know, and she chose to say nothing. Perhaps she was afraid.

But tonight Olive was celebrating for another reason. He'd finally let her have a TV. It had been a gift, for Christmas – a day which otherwise had passed the same as all the others except that she sang Christmas carols to Mickey and gave him a slice of carrot as a present.

They'd got a new TV – Sandman and his wife. This one was old, fuzzy, tiny. The aerial only found one channel. Or it did inside the room, anyway.

Olive didn't care. It was a link to the outside world, wasn't it? It gave her something else to focus on. Something other than counting up and down inside her head. Something other than drawing stupid picture after stupid picture She thought of all the hours she had spent with her grandad as he taught her to draw horses and dogs and people using circles layered on top of each other. The TV let her stop thinking about grandad. And it gave her the news.

She wasn't news any more. Not compared to the big stuff. Like that guy from the Beatles getting stabbed. Like the stuff in London for the millennium.

People seemed to have forgotten about Olive.

But she wasn't going to let it upset her. Not tonight. Mum and Dad and Cassie wouldn't forget her. She wondered if they were going to watch the fireworks on TV like they always used to.

She hoped they would. She glanced down at her Mickey Mouse watch. The battery was running low, though, because it said it was already two in the morning. The TV was still counting down to midnight.

Mickey the mouse sat on her lap, tonight. He was quieter than usual. Lethargic. She couldn't work out whether he was poorly or if he was just cold. Even now, Olive had the blankets around them both and she wasn't warm.

The fireworks started. A new year. A big year, too. When Olive thought about the year 2000, it still seemed like it was so far away. Like it would never happen. But of course, that was in her other life. Before. Now it was happening and she couldn't even be outside to see it.

At least, she thought, she could pretend. So as the fireworks popped and blasted their way into a new millennium, Olive closed her eyes and pretended she was at home. In front of the fire. Arguing with Cassie about something. Anything.

She missed them.

But at least she hadn't had this week's health test. At least she had the TV. At least Mickey was here, warm in her lap. At least Sandman hadn't hurt her. At least she had electricity, paper, pens.

At least.

28

ROGER UPTON WAS IN the lounge when I walked past. I ducked in and shut the door behind me. He glanced away from his phone but didn't get up.

"Miss Warren."

"I don't want to intrude," I said, "but while I'm here – there are some things I want to say."

Roger raised an eyebrow, suspicion etched into his expression, but he nodded.

"Okay."

"I haven't told anybody – about your past. That's not my place. I haven't written anything about you, either." I waited for his reaction. Instead of anger, or frustration, or even sadness, I was met by a blank face. His eyes seemed hollow, even.

"I just wanted to say that I'm sorry," I continued. This was the first time I'd apologised about an article I *hadn't* written. "Not for the information I found, but for how I carried myself. It's my job to hold people accountable but I didn't communicate properly—"

"You were right."

I paused, stunned at his honesty. I knew I was right to question him, given what I'd learned about his past, but I hadn't expected him to admit that.

"What?"

Roger put his phone on the arm of his chair.

"About me. I... When it happened, I didn't think it was a big deal. I mean, I knew that I'd caused trouble, stirred shit up. But I never really thought it was... *that* bad? At the time I was more upset that I was in trouble. She was a nice girl, and she liked me – and she'd *assured* me she was older than she was. We never slept together so what was the big deal, right?" He paused. I waited. "Now I have Gracie... I've been thinking about it more and more. Sometimes, I look at Gracie and I just feel – so much shame. It was stupid, but more than that, it was dangerous. So dangerous. And I should have known better. Been more responsible."

Roger paused and swiped a hand across his face, dislodging what may have been tears. He sighed.

We sat in silence for a long time. I watched the way Roger's hands kept returning to his phone. It made me realise just how little I knew about the people around me; how badly people were affected by the things I couldn't see.

I thought of Ady and his dead wife, that sadness that seemed to follow him. I thought of Olive, all those secrets she'd kept.

"I'm sorry for my behaviour," I said again, although I couldn't deny I'd repeat my actions given what he had done. "I'm like a bull with a red flag sometimes."

"Yeah," Roger said. "Well. I won't say I'm glad you did it, but I'm glad we had this talk."

* * *

As I was putting my jacket on by the front door, I heard a voice. Small, quiet.

"Do you think… do you think she's okay?"

I turned around and noticed Grace sitting on the stairs. Her knees were pulled up to her chest, a baggy hoodie now covering much of her upper body in a way that made her seem younger than she was. She looked like she might have been crying, but her face was dry and pink now. She watched me as I finished getting ready to leave. I shook my head.

"I don't know," I said. "But that's why I'm doing everything I can to figure out what happened."

"Mum said you work for a newspaper. That you were writing a story about me. Is that true?"

With Bella missing I knew I had another opportunity to claw back some semblance of normalcy, to treat this as a profession again. But somehow I couldn't bring myself to think about Bella as a job. The shine had long rubbed off and I had to face the fact that maybe the job wasn't for me any more.

"Something like that," I said. "I'm not doing very well." I paused to watch Grace for a second. She was eyeing me with cautious curiosity, as though I might morph into a monster at any second. But she *was* curious. "I don't know if your mum told you," I said, "but I have sort of a personal reason to be asking you all these questions. And that's why my writing isn't working out."

Grace frowned and shook her head. "No. She didn't say."

I didn't want to scare Grace – but I also knew this was my chance. To gamble on gaining her trust.

"When I was a little bit older than you are now, my sister was abducted. During a solar eclipse." I let this sink in, watched Grace's breathing quicken as she considered what this meant. "I'm trying to make sure that nothing bad happens to Bella, just like I was trying to make sure nothing bad happened to you. I thought that by... by writing – about you – then whoever took you would realise that you were somebody's daughter. That somebody missed you and wanted you home. And that having you home was more important than being afraid or angry, so maybe they wouldn't hurt you."

"But I didn't need protecting."

"I know," I said softly. Grace's posture slumped, the fight going out of her. I continued, "But maybe Bella does need protecting. Is there anything else you want to tell me?"

I let this thought hang in the air for a moment. Grace was sniffling, her forehead dipping down to touch her knees. When she looked up again, her eyes were shiny with unshed tears.

"She didn't tell me who she got the ring from," Grace said eventually. "I'm not lying about that. I asked her and asked her, but she wouldn't tell me. She said it was... a *gift*. I asked her if she had a boyfriend, but she said no. When I asked her if it was a grown-up she said no at first. But... I could tell she was lying about that. You know? Like, I could just *tell*. So I pushed her until she told me she got it from a man. I didn't have a go at her, but I wish I had.

"She was just so... happy at first. Like, buzzing. Excited a lot. She would be late to meet me for the last bit of the walk to school sometimes. I knew she was seeing somebody but she wouldn't talk about it. The ring – when Bella didn't want it, I – I don't know. *I* wanted it. I wanted to feel how she felt, at first, when she was happy and excited and I just… She was acting weirdly for ages before I said anything, and then I just took the ring and kept it rather than having a go at her again. What if…?"

"What if, what?"

"What if she's hurt, and it's my fault? What if I could have done more to help her?" Then, a look of true horror passed across Grace's face and she started to cry. "What if she was taken because of me? Should I have told somebody? If I was here I could have protected her."

"Grace, no." I reached out and laid a hand on her knee. "Please don't blame yourself. For years I thought the same thing as you. I thought about it every day. I felt guilty and angry at myself. But Grace, listen to me, this didn't happen because of you."

"How do you know?" Grace demanded. Her blue eyes flashed with a fierceness that surprised me. An anger that was so familiar I could have been looking at my own reflection.

How did I explain to Grace that in another situation I might have thought Bella's disappearance so soon after Grace's was merely opportunistic? That I would have told Grace she wasn't to blame but deep down I might have worried that Bella's abduction had only happened because of *chance*. How did I tell her that this was different? The solar eclipse, the similarities to

Olive… This was more than opportunity. It was fate.

Somebody had intended to take Bella all along. And Grace making the news had only made it easier for them to blame somebody else.

"It isn't your fault," I said firmly. "I promise."

I couldn't quite put aside the churning in my stomach, even as I drove the short distance back to Earl's café in the Circle. I'd been unaware when I was there earlier that Jake Howden's wife – and alibi – had been working right behind the counter, since he had neglected to mention it.

Marion had only told me reluctantly, and not without my assurance that I wouldn't do anything stupid, but I needed to talk to this woman. Just to put my mind at ease. The café was quiet, now, the lull between lunch and dinner leaving the whole place with an abandoned air.

Howden's wife was behind the counter as I arrived, cleaning the coffee steamer with a damp rag. It wasn't hard to figure out it was her – she was the only female member of staff over eighteen. She half-turned as I entered, a polite but disinterested smile on her face.

"Lizzie Howden?" I asked. She was short, probably only five feet tall, with a blonde pixie cut that somehow made her look older than she was – a haircut better suited to a woman in her twenties than one closer to forty. I pictured her next to Jake Howden, with his height and the well-defined muscles under his smart shirt, and I thought they made an odd couple.

She seemed nervous. Not quite twitchy, but close enough that my hackles rose almost instantly. She was, in a lot of ways, the opposite of the smooth-talking teacher. She put down the rag and her head dipped in a nod.

"You that reporter?" she asked.

I turned on my professional smile and pulled out my notebook.

"I'm Cassie Warren, yes," I said. "I spoke to your husband earlier. I'm just looking for more of a sense of the man behind all the charity work. And it's always important to get a feeling for the broader scope when writing a piece like this—"

"Let me stop you there." Lizzie held up both of her hands in what might have looked like surrender to anybody except me; I saw it for the challenge it was. "My husband didn't hurt that kid. He was with me yesterday morning. We made love before he left for work because the eclipse meant his first class of the morning was cancelled, and you can bet we took advantage of the lie-in."

I felt a bubble of laughter rise up. Did people even say things like that? I watched Lizzie's face as it morphed from suspicion into downright anger at my reaction.

"I'm sorry," I said. "Good alibis are usually a bit more watertight."

Lizzie snorted. "As I told the *police*," she spat the word with disgust, "I have nothing to lie about and I didn't realise he'd be needing an alibi."

Oh, Christ. Now I knew why Marion had given in and let me come here. The same words had come out of my own mouth. Ordinary people didn't usually feel the need to catalogue their every move.

"Quite," I said. "Well, thank you anyway. I appreciate your… candour."

She smiled. Wives could lie, I thought again, but as much as Lizzie Howden's openness about her sex life made me cringe, it seemed to me like she was telling the truth.

29

"YOU GO FIRST, CASS. You're not going to like what I have to tell you."

I heard Marion shuffling about on the other end of the phone, followed by the soft swuffing sound of the police-station door. I glanced at my watch. It was almost 9 p.m. and Marion was still at work – probably hadn't eaten today, either. Like me she had never been a foodie, but if she wasn't careful she was going to make herself ill. And as much as I appreciated that this was rich coming from me, I was worried about her. I thought about telling her about my chat with Jake Howden's wife, but decided that might just put her off her dinner even more.

"I asked Grace about the mood ring," I said.

"You found it?"

"She has it. I didn't take it – I didn't know if I was allowed? But I don't think she'll do anything with it except give it to you if you ask again. She opened up to me a bit. She said that Bella told her an adult gave it to her. A man. I think Bella was being groomed."

I let this sink in for a second.

"Grace started to feel uncomfortable and that's why she didn't want to wear it any more. Grace… She said Bella was happy – at first – and I think she wanted some of what Bella had. I don't think she understood why she took the ring. Or why she stopped wearing it. It's like she started to realise something wasn't right about the whole situation but she didn't know what."

"Christ…" Marion was silent for a moment as we both considered the reality of what I was saying. That somebody had made the effort to get Bella exactly where they wanted her. "I'm glad you talked to her, Cassie," she said then. "I often thought if somebody had talked to you – to us – properly back in '99… things might have been different. We might have been able to talk about it with each other. You know?"

I did know because I had had the same thoughts. I didn't answer but the silence wasn't uncomfortable.

"So what news am I not going to like?" I prompted.

Marion let out a long breath and finally said, "We pulled Darren Walker in again. When we went to pick him up, the back of his van was open. Wide open."

She paused.

"*And?*"

"And we found a school blazer," she said quietly. "Just in the back. And Bella's fingerprints on one of the rear doors. Fox is on a mission. It doesn't look good."

She didn't say it, but I could tell from her voice what she meant. Fox was afraid that Bella was dead. I knew the statistics as well as anybody. The first three or four hours were the most crucial in cases of missing children – and we had spent that time floundering. Thinking about Grace. The numbers were brutal. Within those four hours, seventy-five per cent of children taken would be dead – especially in stranger abductions.

Within twenty-four hours that would increase to ninety-one per cent...

I thought of Darren Walker. He was a creep, sure, but was he capable of hurting a child? I pictured the way his hands had shook when I'd spoken to him and a chill ran through me.

Bella had been missing for over thirty-six hours. *Thirty-six hours.* But Bella wasn't just a number. She was a little girl, and she was still out there.

She had to be.

I didn't want to go home. The house was empty, creaking without Gran. Every dark corner made me itch with what might have been fear. I thought of her in the hospital, alone and confused. I hoped they were looking after her but I'd already called for an update twice this afternoon.

I couldn't shake what she had said to me – what might have been taken for confusion had I not recognised the emotion in her eyes.

He slowed down.

I turned on all of the lights in the house, unable to sleep without them, and sank into a dazed sort of rest.

In my dream, it was another hot night. So hot that Olive and I had the windows wide open. A breeze tickled the bare skin on my legs and feet. Olive hung off the top bunk, her golden-brown hair falling around her face. Was this how it had happened in real life? I didn't know. Couldn't remember exactly. Olive's arm dangled down, and I saw the bruise. Saw the distinct fingerprints our mother had left behind. Mum was gone, now, back to Derby for the summer where she could work without feeling guilty for leaving us.

Gran and Grandad were silently asleep down the hall.

"Does it hurt when you touch it?" I asked.

Olive shrugged and her arm wiggled.

"It's okay."

It's not okay, I thought. I tossed over onto my back, sheets tangling around my legs. I couldn't breathe. The breeze was gone, and I was in darkness. When had I turned out the lights? I forced my eyes shut.

"Olive? *Olive?*" I called her name and there she was. She smiled her small, secret smile. The one that said she knew something I didn't. She knew a lot I didn't.

She watched. She listened. She *cared*.

"What are you smiling at?"

"You don't have to worry about me, Cassie. There're people out there who'll look after me. Make sure my arm doesn't get hurt again."

"People?" I asked. "What people?"

"One person." Olive smiled again. "A boy. A *man*."

I noticed the ring on her finger. The mood ring. Its stone was a dark turquoise, warmed that way by the heat of her hand. I wanted to reach out, snatch it off her. It looked wrong. The same kind of wrong that I'd seen in Grace's face when

I asked her about the mood ring. She knew, just like I had known. Something horrible was happening and we didn't know what to do about it.

"What man? Who gave it to you?" I asked. Suddenly desperation overwhelmed me. I wriggled, writhed in the sheets. Olive was getting further and further away, her features made fuzzy by the dream. I knew it wasn't real, it hadn't happened. Not like that. Olive hadn't told me anything. So why did she always torture me in my dreams?

"What man?"

"Just a man…" Olive said dreamily. "He'll protect me."

"Olive, that's what I'm for. It's my job to keep you safe."

She shook her head, hair dancing over the edge of the bed.

And then, just like in every other dream I had of her, Olive was gone.

30

Sunday, 22 March 2015

"HOW ARE YOU FEELING?"

Settled in her favourite armchair with a cup of tea, Gran shrugged in answer to my question. We'd had an almost logical conversation on the way home from the hospital, although it *had* been about the solar system project I'd helped Olive with the summer she was eight and I was ten. Gran told me how proud she was, how real it looked.

I didn't remind her of the missing years between that moment and now. It made me warm to think of the days when Gran hadn't loved Olive best – had, in fact, still loved us both the same. Distance and loss had warped it all, but today I'd clung to the joy of being told I made her proud.

My head felt fuzzy with lack of sleep. I'd been awake early and I'd driven to Bella's house first thing but the whole place was swarming with journalists, and Mrs Kaluza was refusing to talk to anybody. I waited outside for half an hour, even made it to the door, but nobody answered the bell when I rang.

So I'd driven home feeling frustrated, like I could be doing more but not knowing where to start. I spent most of the rest of the morning before leaving for the hospital leafing through my Olive Diary again, going over everything. I'd combed through the notes I'd made about Dad and Cordy Jones to make me feel better about the fact that I would have to spend precious hours today taking care of my gran instead of being out there searching for Bella. And about the fact that minutes were racing by. I'd got hold of Bella's mother's phone number and tried her repeatedly, but she never answered.

The words in my Olive Diary were as familiar now as my own name but still I read and reread whole pages, hoping to find something in my memories that I'd missed. I'd written about another man back then, a mystery man who only existed in my mind, the man who would turn out to be Olive's real kidnapper. It was a fantasy I had returned to again and again; even still did, sometimes, just before drifting off to sleep at night. This kidnapper was a cross between an extravagant millionaire and a petty criminal, like something out of the musical *Annie*.

I made up fantasies in the diary about how he'd taken Olive away from us because he wanted a better life for her; he wanted to give her the things she could never have had here. He would buy her toys – more toys than Mum could afford – and he would be married to a warm, loving woman who would never have to work or leave her with somebody else during the holidays. In my diary, if only there, Olive was safe, and happy, and somewhere hot. And one day she would come home and find me.

Just reading through the pages had made me angry. If Olive were still alive, she'd be twenty-seven years old now. There would be no way she would have gone so long without contacting me. For months when she first vanished I waited eagerly for the post, just in case. For a while I became obsessed with postcards, collecting them everywhere I visited so that one day, when Olive finally wrote to me, I'd have a slew of things to send back. Sometimes, even now, the clang of the letterbox startled me and I got that familiar rush of hope followed by a swoop of disappointment.

After shoving the diary away again, I'd found the photograph that had been on Grandad's noticeboard. Unlike my photos, which were still smooth and carefully tucked in the front cover of the diary, this one was faded and creased down the middle where somebody had looked at it often.

I wondered if that had been Grandad before he'd died. I imagined him running his fingers over it just as I'd done when I found it, imagined it tucked inside his wallet so it was always with him. I pulled it out again now, from its place in the back pocket of my jeans, holding it in a shaking hand.

"Gran, I was wondering if I could show you... something that might be a bit upsetting, but if you could have a look at it – I'd be really grateful. And if you don't remember anything, that's okay."

Gran smiled at me, her attention drawn away from the TV, a round of canned laughter breaking the quiet in the lounge.

"Of course love, whatever you like. I don't know what help I'll be though, I'm afraid my memory isn't what it used to be." Her eyes crinkled.

I held out the photograph, and Gran took it in one of her gnarled hands.

Over the years since it happened, Gran and I had never

talked about Olive. It had been too raw. Too painful. And then, by the time I was ready to talk about her, Gran had forgotten. But now she stared at the photo. Rubbed at it tenderly, her fingers tracing the exact places where the paper was worn.

This wasn't Grandad's photograph, I realised. It was hers.

"I miss her," she said quietly. "Where is she?"

I had prepared an answer for this question, but at the sight of Gran's face I suddenly didn't know what to say. I shrugged, my throat closing up, and then I swallowed hard to try to loosen it.

"She's... I don't know."

Gran looked at the photograph for another moment, and then she said, "Why?"

I couldn't answer that, either.

"Gran, do you remember − can you see that ring on her finger? The silver one?"

"Of course. It was her favourite for a short while. I remember when she got it."

My heart leapt. "You do? Can you tell me about it?"

"She was ever so secretive. Blushed when I asked her if a boy gave it to her. Said, 'Of course not.' You two could never lie, though. Neither of you." Gran smiled sadly. "She said somebody gave it to her back in Derby − but I thought somebody here did because I hadn't seen it before. Maybe one of those youth group lads she spent some time with.

"They sell them everywhere, you know. Hippie town. Earl's, the corner shop, even the bingo place and the doctors have 'em. They cost less than a can of Coke." She paused, holding the photo tightly. Her eyes were shiny and small.

"I'm thirsty," she said, then. "Can I have a Coke? There's nothing better on a hot day, that's what I always tell her. Very sweet. Pocket money and that. 'You run along and get a Coke. And mind your sister.' That's it, Kathy – I'll watch them."

As quickly as that, the moment had passed and she was confused again, the words and phrases of my childhood slipping out of her like smoke.

I didn't want to pressure her, although I was dying to ask her more. Questions about Olive, about that summer, about the weeks that followed – all things I should have known years ago but I'd been afraid to hear. And now it was too late.

It was the same ring. I wasn't imagining it. I wasn't dreaming. The ring in this photograph, right down to its bent mermaid's tail, was the same one I had seen in Grace's den.

"How is she?"

Marion's voice on the other end of the phone calmed me just as much as it frustrated me that I couldn't talk to her in person today.

"She's okay," I said. "Very tired. Banged up. Glad to be home though, I think." I watched as Gran flicked between channels on the TV and settled on some old detective show.

"And how are you?"

"I'm fine." I took the house phone into the kitchen and leaned against the counter. It was hard to explain how I felt. I was glad Gran was home – of course I was – but I couldn't shake the feeling that every second was one step closer to losing

Bella. "I'd be better if I didn't feel like I had no idea what was going on."

"Cassie," Marion warned. "Why don't you try to take some time today, spend it with your gran? She needs you."

"I will. But it's — it's like wasted time." I stopped. Shame made my cheeks burn. "That's not what I meant. I know I need to be here. I know that. But Bella..."

"I know."

"I need to feel like I'm doing something useful. What do we know about Bella's family?" I asked, desperately trying to quell the panic inside me. "I've been trying to get in touch but Mrs Kaluza still won't answer the landline number I have for her."

"They're Polish," Marion said slowly. "The mother doesn't speak very good English. She's been avoiding the press like the plague. The father left about three months ago so it's just Mrs Kaluza and Bella in the house."

"What about the father?"

"You know he's a taxi driver, doesn't live in Bishop's Green. He said he was working so we're trying to track his fares from the morning now."

"And the ring?" I pressed. "Did you ask Bella's mum about the mood ring?" This was the question that was driving me crazy. I needed to understand how all of the pieces fitted together. Marion gave an exasperated sigh.

"One thing at a time, Cass. I asked but so far she seems too overwhelmed to be much help. Sometimes it happens like that. She says she doesn't remember seeing Bella wearing anything out of the ordinary, but she does collect vintage clothes and

257

jewellery – or did before Mr Kaluza left. They're a bit tight for money now."

I massaged the bridge of my nose. "What about her room? Did you find anything in there that might tell us anything?"

Marion made a disappointed noise. "No. We've taken her laptop and her phone but so far nothing out of the ordinary."

"No diary?"

"Nothing like that. Children probably think that's a bit old-fashioned now."

I flicked the kettle on. "And Darren Walker?"

"Nothing new yet. Cass, why don't you just take today – let me do my job and I'll let you know if we find anything."

I was sure she didn't mean to sound patronising but I couldn't help feeling a surge of annoyance. The kettle finished boiling and I started to make tea. Marion heard the splash of the water and she sighed.

"I'm sorry," she said. "I don't mean to take it out on you. Just – hang in there. Okay?"

"Sure," I murmured. "I'll just twiddle my thumbs until the nurse comes tomorrow. Don't worry about me."

Later that afternoon there was a knock at the door. Doctor White stood outside, his brown hair slicked back and his slacks freshly pressed.

"Hullo Cassie," he said. "Thought I'd pop round to check on you two. It is today she's home, isn't it?"

He didn't wait for me to respond, just ducked into our front room with a practised ease. I wondered if he still made many house calls these days, or whether those were things of the past.

"Hello Peggy. How are you doing?"

I followed him into the lounge and watched as he knelt before Gran, a hand on her uninjured arm. He had with him a small leather doctor's bag, old and scuffed.

Gran made a surprised exclamation, recognition brightening her face.

"She's doing okay," I said. "Not too much pain. They patched her up pretty well." *This time.* I didn't say it, but the words hung in the air anyway. What if, now she was home, it happened again?

Something in my voice must have betrayed my worry because the doctor half-turned and gave me that raised eyebrow of his again.

"Are you giving her the sleeping aid?" he asked.

"This happened to her in the evening, not the wee hours," I said wearily. I couldn't dislodge the lump in my throat. This wasn't just a late-night accident and the thought made me sick. "She worries the life out of me."

Doctor White gave Gran a once-over before answering. He checked her arm beneath its sling, her blood pressure, her breathing. Gran obliged the gentle tugging at her arm with little more than a grimace, her eyes still following the TV show.

Afterwards I made him a cup of tea and we moved into the kitchen. The light was grey in here, washing us in tired shades. I had to force myself not to wring my hands.

"She was very lucky," he said eventually. "Although I expect you know that. Where were you when it happened?"

Although I was sure it wasn't intentional, I couldn't help notice the accusation in his tone. I felt my shoulders rise, folding my arms across my chest.

"I was – I wasn't at home. I was working on that story about Grace Butler."

He didn't respond right away, choosing instead to stare out of the kitchen window into the windswept garden.

"It's awful," he said, "about little Bella. Grace was bad enough but I've known Bella since she was born." White's face was surprisingly impassive, although his voice was filled with some emotion I couldn't identify.

"Do you know her well?" I asked. "What's she like?"

"She's…" He shrugged. "Clever. She reminds me of my daughter." He paused. I hadn't known he had a daughter, but I let the silence fill the space between us until he said, "She died."

"I'm sorry."

"Yes. Well." He turned back to me and suddenly he was all business. "Anyway, your gran will need a lot of attention over the next few weeks. She needs to keep her arm mobile so she regains all the movement she can, but it'll be weak for some time. I suggest you try not to leave her alone any more than necessary."

Now the look he fixed me with was obvious. The accusation wasn't imagined.

"I didn't mean for any of this to happen. There was a miscommunication—"

I couldn't control the frustration in my voice, the guilt and the anger at myself, but the doctor only sighed.

"I suggest," he said calmly, "we have another look at her

progress in a couple of weeks. If you ring the surgery I'm sure we can squeeze you in."

Doctor White placed his unfinished tea on the counter and gathered his things. He was at the door quickly, his movements surprisingly swift. He said goodbye to my gran, then looked at me again.

"Watch out for her," he said. His gaze was piercing. "We don't want this happening again."

The darkness of the night was cloying. Hot, oppressive. I opened my eyes wide, and saw nothing but stretches of inky blackness. I blinked. Blinked harder.

Then, suddenly, brightness. A perfect crescent of white light. Hotter than the darkness. The eclipse. So hot it burned my eyes. A silver circle with a bite out of it, spinning in the dark. The middle shifted, the crescent expanding, and then it was a circle, smaller. In my palm, searing the flesh.

The ring. It was there the second I closed my eyes, imprinted there like a scar behind my eyelids. I saw Olive's expectant face.

"Why can't I come home?" she asked. "Why can't you *do something*?"

I roared to consciousness with a scream on my lips. To calm my heart, I tried to think of Marion, alone in her house after a long day at work. That only made me feel sick with worry.

I thought of Henry in his hotel room. I wondered if he'd be alone, and then I realised that despite the hour he would probably still be in the hotel bar. I would have been, too, in another life. I thought about the bar, about the sweet cocktails that tasted like candy floss, my mouth dry. I thought of Helen, back in London. The three years we'd shared together already a dream – a complicated, anxiety-fuelled dream.

And before I knew it I was seeing a girl serving drinks who looked like Olive, with big golden brown eyes that were so unique. It had to be her. What if she was out there, somewhere, waiting to be found? That was the dream that always haunted me the most.

But then the girl in my mind was Bella. And then she was Olive again. But real Olive, this time, not the Olive from my dreams who was older and happy. This Olive was eleven years old and she wore that damn silver mermaid ring with the crooked tail and rubbed at it like Gran had rubbed at the photograph.

Where are you?

She wouldn't have run away. Not Olive. Sensible, calm Olive. When I got angry I used to go up like a mushroom cloud; screaming, crying, I took everybody else along with me. But not Olive. She got sad, or quiet, sometimes. After a brief spell of writing furiously or drawing a picture, she was always okay again, as though she'd simply had enough of being upset.

I got sick of trying to sleep. Every time I closed my eyes, the eclipse was there like an omen, the silver-white crescent spinning and spinning. Counting down the hours since the darkness. I couldn't sleep for fear of dreaming; I didn't want to see Olive again tonight, only to relive the crushing memory of her being gone when I opened my eyes.

I refused to get out of bed, although I knew I wouldn't

sleep now. I thought of Marion instead. Marion, who trusted me again. I hadn't had that in so long. The warm feeling it gave me in the pit of my belly when I thought about her. She believed me, believed *in* me. I had to prove to her that I was worth it.

So I pulled my laptop onto my legs and opened it up. The screen that greeted me was a webpage I'd found and hadn't closed. Cordy Jones. I hadn't been getting anywhere with Bella so I'd turned back to Olive, only to get myself all tangled up again. This was an article that Henry had sent me, a page on a forum from the early 2000s with theories about his disappearance.

I flicked through the first page of it with my eyes half-closed. Here was a thread I couldn't stop picking at, almost wishfully. Could he have been responsible for what happened to Olive, even if he'd died afterwards? Could Bella have been taken by somebody else? A copycat, even? I didn't think so. Cordy Jones might be dead, and I was sure the same person had taken Bella and Olive.

Suddenly I remembered Marion's text message. *We checked it. It's not relevant.* It was a lead she had looked into and dismissed. A case of vigilante justice that would get its own team, its own file. But it was nothing to do with what was happening now. I felt angry at myself for the amount of time since Bella disappeared that I'd spent scrabbling around like a chicken in the dirt.

I moved to the second page of the article, which focused on Cordy's time as the leader of the Bishop's Green youth group. There was a picture of some event, a gathering of adults and children framed by crêpe bunting and balloons.

And there, staring right at me, was my father.

I bolted upright.

Dad?

Had he ever volunteered for the youth group? I remembered him hanging around for a couple of weeks at the start of the summer but he'd stayed in a hotel working on a thesis about women in Chaucer – or something like that – for a new class he was teaching.

Although, looking back, he'd probably been with Carol. She had been his student back then, before she became Wife Number Two. She had dutifully kept their affair a secret.

How well had Dad known Cordy? I couldn't believe it was my father, but the man in the photo was definitely him. I squinted my eyes, and although he had a full beard and was wearing clothes I didn't remember, I would recognise him anywhere. Perhaps he had stopped by early in the summer to check up on us and I didn't remember. Perhaps he had felt guilty, spending his days with Carol when he should have been with us.

I lay back in bed, heart thudding. If Dad knew Cordy… Did that mean he might remember Darren Walker? I thought once again of the anonymous text messages. Of my surprise after the first one. *back off*. I hadn't thought I'd known anything at all.

Could it be possible that Dad knew something without realising too?

31

14 February 2000

2000 WASN'T PROVING TO be much of a year for Olive. The TV was on the fritz again, and she was starting to realise why he'd given it to her. Half the time it wouldn't turn on, and it tended to cut out when there was bad weather. Still, she remembered those early days, the long empty hours she desperately tried to fill with any sort of game she could think of. And she tried not to complain to herself too much.

Footsteps on the stairs outside of the usual health check days were rare, but when she heard them today it wasn't a surprise. Valentine's Day. She wondered if he'd come and see her. Bring her something. It was days like these where Sandman outdid himself; he brought her chocolates, flowers sometimes, too. Ice cream, maybe. She even found herself looking forward to it. Monthly anniversaries of his "saving" her were his favourite. He brought cake. But New Year's Day, Christmas, Halloween… These, too, were an excuse for him.

Even so, her heart thudded when she heard him. That part never got normal. Neither did the deliberate sliding into place of the lock once he was inside, keys placed around his neck…

But when he came through the door today he wasn't smiling. Wasn't even just frowning. It was like the early days again, his face flat like ice.

Olive scuttled upwards from her perch on the floor in front of the TV. He didn't wait. Just chased her across the room, shocking her into letting out a scream that hurt her throat.

"What? What?" she yelled.

"You know."

Once he had her, he pinned her against the wall. The two of them were on the narrow, lumpy bed. One of his arms was against her throat and she felt her blood pounding inside her. Her stomach was oily slick, like rainbow oil on tarmac, and she wanted to puke.

"Where is it?"

She couldn't breathe, never mind talk. Panic coursed through her, and she was ashamed to realise she was crying. Sandman shoved her again in disgust, and then let her go. His face was purple. A vein throbbed in his temple. Olive sobbed.

"Where. Is. It?"

"I don't know—"

But she did know. Mickey. He was talking about Mickey. She didn't know how he knew, but the thread of panic grew and grew until she couldn't think. If he searched, all he had to do…

"*Where?*"

Olive couldn't do anything. Couldn't help. Couldn't stop him. She was helpless, sore. Her head felt full of something fluffy. Something sharp too. She watched with wide-eyed terror as Sandman tore apart the room. He searched cupboards, pulled open the microwave and slammed it so hard a dinging sound bounced in her skull. He trashed her drawings on the wall, seemingly for the hell of it, and then, finally, came to rest in front of the TV. Panting. Sweat visible through his T-shirt, soaking his back.

He half-turned to her. Locked eyes. And then he tossed the TV against the floor. The unit smashed, bits of the screen mixing with plastic on the thin carpet.

Olive couldn't scream, because already he was moving. Back towards the kitchen. And the bread bin. And Mickey, who was testing out a new three-tier bed Olive had made from cereal boxes.

"No!" she yelled.

But that only made him worse. Sandman grabbed the bread bin in both hands and spun on her.

"Are you stupid?"

Olive's voice was gone. Broken into pieces like the TV. She sobbed harder.

"I found shit on your clothes. I could *see the hair*. Haven't you listened to anything I've said to you?"

He was still holding the bread bin. That's all Olive could see. Everything else was wobbling around her. She knew that Mickey was inside it, and she really thought she might puke up her breakfast.

"*Hygiene!*" Sandman spat. "This vermin – I don't know how long it's been in here, but Christ, girl, you've really got a death wish."

With that, before Olive could do anything, or say anything,

or even blink, Sandman dashed the bread bin against the wall. Plaster cracked, what little was left over bricks raining dust across the floor. Olive became aware of a screaming so high, so long, it sounded like a ghost.

She realised it was hers. The scream was coming from her.

She could hardly see through tears, but she knew it was over. The bread bin was metal, but the impact would be enough to stun him. And there was Sandman making sure. Satisfaction on his face, the smell of disinfectant permeating the small room.

"Stupid girl," he muttered. "I'm trying to teach you. You stupid, stupid girl."

Olive didn't care what he thought of her. She sat on the bed, unmoving. Sandman gathered the bin and the sharp bits of the broken TV, and then he left her. No new food. No new clothes.

She didn't care about that, either.

She realised Sandman was right. She had been stupid. Stupid to believe that he could be kind to her. That the man who had taken her away from everybody who loved her, could be anything but a monster.

Pity he'd taken the bits of broken TV screen, she thought absently. Those might have come in handy.

32

Monday, 23 March 2015

AS THE FIRST GREY light of dawn began to trickle through the crack in my curtains, I hauled myself out of bed. The light was watery, like it had been during the eclipse – God, was that only Friday? *Three days. Seventy-two hours.*

I showered, dressed and took breakfast to Gran in bed, while waiting for the dementia nurse to arrive. The NHS had referred me to a company called Helping Hands and they'd offered to help after the accident. Not for free, of course, but Gran was in no state to be at the adult day centre and I had Doctor White's warning echoing in my head as I thought of all the things I needed to do. I didn't trust the people I'd been using before, although I still wasn't sure whether it was my error or theirs that had led to Gran's accident. I didn't like the way the doctor had looked at me yesterday, but the feeling was overridden by shame at the way I'd spoken to him in response, and I couldn't afford another day lost when I could be searching for Bella.

With Gran taken care of for a few hours, I drove the short distance to Chestnut Circle with my hands tight on the steering wheel. This morning it wasn't Olive's face I kept seeing, it was Bella's. But the two were starting to mix in my mind. I'd only met Bella properly once and, I told myself, that was probably the reason this was happening. But I was starting to get unnerved by it, scared that it would affect my already-faltering judgement.

I pulled into the Circle, twice having to slam on my brakes to avoid collisions. The driver behind honked, but he was on his phone so I simply flipped my finger in response. Children were everywhere – just out of the corner of my eye, outside my field of vision. I heard them, saw blurred shapes moving like ghosts. They were all too young to be Bella, to be Olive. They were three, four years old, some still in pushchairs. A troupe of nursery children in bright yellow vests were herded across a zebra crossing by three harried-looking teachers.

I called Henry and left a message asking for an update on Darren Walker. I couldn't stop thinking about his arrest. I hated not knowing what was happening. Walker was creepy, but could he have taken Bella? And what about Olive? I wondered where he had been on the day my sister disappeared.

This was one question I didn't think Fox or Marion would ask Walker while he was in custody. Not when Bella was still out there; she was their priority, and rightly so.

Bishop's Green was still crawling with press. There were news station vans parked up, reporters and journalists gathered in packs around the cafes and the fountain. I saw the same journalist I thought I'd recognised before but this time her familiar face made me feel out of place. This was Big News, now. Police incompetence, another girl missing, just a way to spin a story.

Looking at it from this side, I once again felt like I had as a teenager: here were animals, preying on the weak. To them, this wasn't about Bella. They would probably prefer it if she never came home – ratings and hits galore, there. To them it was about making the biggest splash, writing the article that got the most views, no matter the consequences.

I couldn't believe I'd ever been part of that. Not when there was so much to lose. Even if I had fooled myself with the belief that I was making a difference, a voice for the victims in a sea of hungry mouths. Now I realised how futile it all was.

I stopped by Ady's just as he was dragging himself into the shop. It was almost 10 a.m., which was later than usual. He looked tired, his face showing a day's worth of stubble. He slid up to the counter just as I walked in, and I made straight for the coffee machine, digging around in my pockets for spare change.

"You're a bit late today, aren't you?" I joked, desperate to pretend everything was normal. Ady shrugged, grabbing a box of newspapers and dumping it on a shelf in front of the counter without taking them out. I was glad that he wasn't going to do this right in front of me because I didn't think I could handle seeing Bella's face plastered all across the front.

"Yeah," Ady grunted. "I was out late."

"Oh yeah. How's it going running the shop by yourself while *what'shername* is on holiday?" I'd forgotten that while I was going crazy thinking about Bella Kaluza the rest of the world was still revolving.

"It's shit. But I was out looking for that missing kid last night," he said. My stomach sank. So much for the rest of the world. "I'm gonna organise some sort of vigil for Thursday with one of the teachers from the school – if Bella's not already home by then. Although, knock on wood, she will be."

Ady superstitiously rapped his knuckles against the wooden counter.

"Is the school being supportive?" I asked, mostly so I didn't feel guilty about not offering to help organise things.

"Oh yeah. Whole town is. Especially the one teacher. Jake's really great. He's rallied the kids and they're making posters and flyers and it's really helping keep their spirits up."

"Jake Howden?" I asked.

"Yeah." Ady shrugged. "You know him?"

"Sort of," I said, biting back a comment about knowing his type. "Not really. He's a bit of an odd one, isn't he? Seems like he should be teaching somewhere a bit more cosmopolitan."

"Nah, he's all right. His enthusiasm is impressive. I've known him years."

I handed over the right change for a small cup of coffee and pressed the button on the machine. "Don't worry," I said then as Ady's expression shifted back to something more melancholy, "the police *will* find her."

While I waited for the cup to fill, I headed towards what my mum had always called the 'junk aisle' – the one at the back of the shop, filled with things to keep kids entertained.

I had memories of Grandad letting us run riot in here at the beginnings of our summers. We were allowed five minutes to browse the shop while Grandad waited outside having a smoke. We usually chose two or three things each; Olive went for crayons and a puzzle book, and then spent the rest of the time browsing the few paperbacks Ady kept next to the till. I'd usually gone for the magazines straight off, skulking where I couldn't be seen with Olive.

The junk aisle in the shop now was eerily similar to how it had been back then. But where there had once been rows and rows of colouring books, now there were interspersed boxes of small, overly expensive toys. Water-snakes, mini slinkies, and – I cringed – selfie sticks. What a time it was to be a child.

And, there, just like in Earl's café, the bingo hall, the doctor's surgery, and just about everywhere else in town: *mood rings*. £1.50. They haunted me. I peered into the box, taking great care to look at each of the designs in it. There were six: a star, a crescent moon, a four-leaf clover, a heart, a plain circle, and a shell. No mermaids.

I made a note of the manufacturer.

I felt a shiver snake down my spine as the realisation hit me. In a town like Bishop's Green, built on equal parts superstition and hokum, anybody could have been responsible for giving Olive – and Bella – that ring. *Anybody*. It could have been somebody my grandparents knew, somebody my parents knew, somebody I had seen once washing their car in the street or somebody we had trusted.

The coffee machine beeped and I had to stop my hands from shaking as I wandered back and grabbed the scalding cup.

"Mood rings," I said to Ady, rudely interrupting him again. "Do you ever sell them to adults?"

Ady looked up from the calculator he was holding, a bemused look on his face.

"Not really. Now and then, I guess. Tourists, usually."

"Do you – did you ever sell one to Olive? A mermaid one?"

"Your sister?" His expression turned to a frown. "I'm sorry, Cass. I don't know. I don't remember everything I've ever sold." He shrugged, but he looked like he wanted to say more. Dread kissed my spine again, another cold shiver making me grip my cup tighter. Something about his reluctance made me suddenly wary.

"Why not?"

Ady looked like I'd slapped him and I felt shame burn my cheeks.

This is ridiculous, I told myself. *Pull yourself together.* It was just like yesterday with Doctor White. Or my conversation with Jake Howden. Like my whole body was just waiting for the spark to ignite.

"Sorry," I said. "I didn't mean to be rude. I just... My sister had one. When she was taken."

Ady smiled gently and his eyes warmed as pity made them shine.

"I gave Tilly one for her birthday last year. The four-leaf clover. You know, for good luck. I practically had to force her to wear it, though. Were you looking for a specific one? The designs we have now are different than they used to be. I think everybody sells the same ones these days."

I let this information sink in, sipping my coffee and relishing the scalding heat as it brought me back down to earth. I let out a long sigh.

"How's your gran doing, anyway?" Ady asked. "Is she home yet?"

"Yeah. She's… She's okay. A bit frightened. Doctor White stopped round yesterday and he seems to think she got off easy."

"That's not really what I'd say to somebody who got hit by a car." Ady frowned. "But as long as she's got you to look after her I'm sure she'll be okay. You should make some time for her, stop this running around and focus on that for a while." He smiled.

I thought of Bella and Grace and all the coincidences with Olive and the guilt hit me again. I *should* be at home with Gran right now. But I couldn't do both.

"That's what Doctor White said." I sighed. "It's just hard to balance everything. I'm used to working – and that being the priority. You know? It's a different pace here. You've heard me complain about being bored often enough. And I can't be unemployed for ever."

Ady nodded. "Well, it *is* lucky that your gran wasn't seriously injured and that you're around to look after her. I hope they catch the guy. In the meantime, give me a yell if you fancy helping out with the vigil or anything like that. Jake and I could use all the help we can get."

33

31 May 2001

OLIVE WOKE WITH A grumbling pain in her stomach. Her lower back ached too, and she lay for a moment trying to locate the source of the pain. She reached down tentatively, her fingers probing the tender skin of her abdomen. Her eyes were crusty with sleep but she could see from the grey light that it was just after dawn, a time she had grown to love over the last year. It was a peaceful time. It wasn't the quietness, although she did remember that from before the room, how the day would start still and quiet and get livelier as the birds began to sing.

Now it didn't matter about noise, because she couldn't hear much of anything outside anyway. Not even with the new sensitivity in her ears. It was more that the light itself was calming, its greyness washing the pain out of the world.

But this morning she felt only pain. She rolled onto her side, bringing her knees into her chest. That helped a little bit, but the pain was so intense that she had to screw her eyes shut.

What was causing it? She tried to scroll back through what she'd eaten. Perhaps Sandman was right when he harped on at her to keep her dishes clean. And herself. She'd been lazy recently, let the dirt build up under her nails between Sandman's health checks. She knew better than to test him, but she'd reasoned that she didn't need to bother the rest of the time. It wasn't like she was going to catch a cold.

She thought, with some mirth, back to the early days. With Mickey. She'd been cleaner, then. Course, she couldn't tell Sandman that. When Mickey was sharing the room she was very careful to keep her hands clean, to keep herself scrubbed in the tin bath. She could laugh.

She did laugh, forced it out. It made her stomach feel tense and unhappy. She unrolled herself from the bed, thinking maybe a bath would help. The griping, stomach-clenching pain was unlike any she had felt before. She dragged herself from the bed, doubled over and breathing hard.

As she turned back to turn the sheet up, she saw the red. A smear of it, across the mattress. She glanced down, seeing it had also stained the insides of her thighs, just below her T-shirt. It was drying brown, streaks running across her skin.

Panic started to bubble inside her, a hot overwhelming feeling that she hadn't felt in a long time. But she moved methodically over to the tap and started to run the hot water, ready to fill the bath.

As she watched the water swirl into a jug she focused her thoughts. Tried to make her heart slow down.

It wasn't fear because she didn't know what was happening. She wasn't stupid. She remembered when it had happened to Cassie, how her big sister had freaked out until Mum could calm her down. Mum had explained it then.

And Cassie had re-explained it to Olive later.

She knew what it meant. She was thirteen years old, just like Cassie had been. Olive had been waiting for it for a while. But it was a thought she'd kept in the back of her mind, along with thoughts about her family. She didn't take these thoughts out for inspection very often any more because they made her upset, or scared, and she had learnt early on that it didn't help. She had to focus on the here and now, what book she was reading, the newspaper Sandman had brought her most recently…

But now she couldn't ignore it. The blood was staring at her, and she felt more at the tops of her thighs as she slowly filled the bath.

Her first period.

She was a woman now. Those were his words, not hers. She'd clocked fairly early that the health checks were all part of it – whether he realised it or not. Sandman was inspecting her, like you might pick up an orange in a supermarket to check its ripeness.

We'll be a proper family one day.

Sandman's words echoed inside her head along with the steady thrumming of the water as she poured it into the bath. When it was full, she started to strip automatically, creating a neat pile with her soiled T-shirt and pants. She climbed into the water slowly, examining her stomach. It still looked the same. Not like a baby would one day fit in there. The aching had eased some, but she still felt vulnerable. Bruised somehow.

Nobody had told her it would be like this.

Normal people didn't get scared. Or if they did, they got

less scared when they understood. But Olive understood, and that only made things worse. She was a woman now.

There was nothing to stop him.

Could she hide it? She eyed the bloodied clothes and bed sheets, panic giving way to despair. She couldn't hide anything from him. She'd need new sheets, new clothes, sanitary towels. Her whole body felt scooped out.

She remembered the day the TV had broken. Wished she could have saved one of the pieces of glass. Maybe she could convince him to let her go if she stabbed him with one. But there was nothing in here remotely dangerous. The despair grew and grew in her stomach like a lump of black tar, making her shudder with emptiness.

She washed her face before the water could get dirty, and then let her tears fall unhindered. She wished Cassie was here now. She'd probably know what to do. And if she didn't, at least Olive wouldn't be on her own. Olive could be brave if she wasn't alone.

She was just so tired. Tired of being tired. And out of ideas.

34

"EVERYBODY IN TOWN SELLS the same six designs, Marion," I said that afternoon. I'd been to every shop in the Circle and a few in the streets around it, determined to prove what I already knew. "Bella could have got it from Darren Walker, I guess, since he sells all that vintage stuff, but you said you only found the newer designs in his van, right?"

"Cassie, that's – that's really interesting," Marion said. She sounded breathless. "But this is important."

"I was just trying to prove—"

"*Cassie*," Marion cut me off. "It's Walker. We're going to have to let him go."

"What?" I felt a wave of dizziness. "What do you mean? I thought you said that he was – that Fox wanted to… I thought you had fingerprints in his van. And her blazer. And what about *Olive*?"

"Bella was a regular customer. At this shop in his van. We've got witnesses, video."

"What about the blazer? Was it hers?" I demanded.

"He said she left it in his van. The woman he works with

confirmed it. He's – talking to him is a bloody nightmare… It's like trying to get blood out of a stone." Marion huffed in annoyance but I could tell that it was a front. "Anyway, his mum told Fox that Walker always got on better with younger kids except for one or two older friends. He had a little brother who moved away to Australia or somewhere. And that's when he started to do the boot sale."

"She could just be saying that…" I said weakly. "He could still be hiding something."

"We've had forensics going over the whole inside of that van, and aside from the fingerprints on the door they've got nothing. No DNA, hairs, trace. Just those prints right in the door where he hangs the clothes he's got to sell. Which anybody could have touched."

"Did you ask Bella's mum about the boot sale again?" I pushed.

"Yes, Miss Ace Reporter, of course I bloody did." Marion paused. I heard footsteps and then the same swuffing door as before. She was outside now. "Sorry. I'm being a bitch. I'm just knackered. And I shouldn't even be telling you any of this stuff. We're not telling the papers—"

"Marion, I haven't written a word in days. I wanted this to work – wanted it to be a job. But I can't do it. It's not about that any more." I glanced at my laptop, the text document still open, the cursor still blinking.

"I know," Marion said. "I'm sorry."

"Mrs Kaluza still won't answer my calls." I rubbed my hands over my face. I had so many questions and I was sick of feeling like I wasn't doing anything useful.

"She doesn't want to talk to anybody outside of the police," Marion said. "Especially not the press. I think she's feeling a lot of pressure, and a few people have written some – uh – less than supportive things about the family not being 'English'. I don't think it's just you she's avoiding."

I didn't have to try hard to imagine how it felt to be hounded by the press. I had spent years going to press conferences and interviewing families, feeling more exhausted every time, remembering my own mother's stress when the phone calls wouldn't stop, the gaunt way she looked after only a couple of weeks of the relentless harassment in the name of the "news". The closed curtains, the whole house coiling in on itself, dusty and quiet and the constant feeling of being watched.

And then, one day, I walked outside and they were gone. I remembered the silence of the street; I could hear the birds, a distant lawnmower, could smell the early autumn breeze – and not a reporter in sight.

I ran inside, adrenaline buzzing in my veins.

"Mum! They're gone! Do you think they found something…?"

But Mum knew what it meant. She shook her head and just said, "No, Cassie. It means they've stopped waiting for her."

I shook myself back to Marion and our conversation, the old sadness rising inside me, along with the deep-rooted determination to be different. I never wanted to be one of those journalists – I wasn't just going to give up. Not without answers, not without the truth.

"Well, I wouldn't want to talk to me," I said with feeling. "What about Darren's past?" I asked. "I mean, with Olive."

"I don't know, Cassie. He hasn't got any priors or warnings or even a speeding ticket. He says he doesn't know anything about her but he's quiet and tense when we talk to him. It's like he's holding something back and I'm less and less convinced it's anything to do with Bella." She let herself trail off, and I heard the quiet rumble of a car somewhere far away driving off. "All I know is that he was in town at the time of the last eclipse. But so were loads of other people. That's what started all that mess with your dad."

"That wasn't the same," I muttered. "He was... with Carol. He just wasn't at home where he *said* he was. That was the problem."

"I know." Marion sighed and then was quiet for a moment. I could imagine her, standing outside the police building, savouring her cigarette break. I was grateful that she'd called me when she had so little time.

"You're cute when you're thinking," I said.

"You can't see me."

"I know. Doesn't change the truth though."

Marion laughed. "All right, smart-arse. Stop sucking up. Just be careful, okay?"

I felt my heart beating hard as I switched on the windscreen wipers. It had been years since I'd been to see my dad. Since I'd ventured onto his territory. I'd never been to his current house in Chesterfield, although he'd been in it for five years.

We usually met in public; restaurants, cinemas, sometimes at a shopping centre to do some brusque and cheerless Christmas shopping. He'd never even met Helen – hadn't even acknowledged how awkward I felt when I came out to him. It was better that way, though, easier when one of us could escape if things got uncomfortable.

It had been this way between us for a long time. I knew my dad loved me – of course he did. But after Olive, he found it harder to show. So did I. Our mutual blame-laying saw to that.

He moved out during the police investigation. After six months of hotel and sofa-surfing, he got his own place. Well, a place with Carol. I was almost glad. It meant I could hate him legitimately. Even if he hadn't hurt Olive – and I felt terrible about thinking that – he *had* hurt me. He'd left me. His new house, and girlfriend, were evidence of that.

Within a year I was seeing him only once every couple of months for a weekend of forced father-daughter bonding that only made us both angry. When I turned sixteen, I brought that down to only once a year at Christmas. It was easier that way.

I was seventeen when Mum died. I used to joke that she ended her life as soon as I was old enough to care for myself – but Henry made me realise that it wasn't a joke just because I laughed about it. And saying horrible things didn't make the pain go away. Even when she died I didn't turn to Dad, couldn't bring myself to cross the gap that yawned between us.

It was Gran who came to stay with me in our house. The day she turned up she brought an empty suitcase. Even now whenever I saw her making tea I thought of those hard days, when she'd rise at dawn to sort through more of Mum's things before I woke up – and then she'd bring me a cup of tea and kiss my forehead. Every morning without fail.

One morning, about two weeks after Mum was buried, Gran had sat on the edge of my bed with her tea, her face creased and her eyes distant. She seemed so solid in the grey-blue light, such a force of comfort that I didn't notice at first that she was crying.

"I want you to come back to Bishop's Green with me," she'd said. "Just for a little while. Until you start university. I want to take care of you. Grandad does too. Will you come with me?"

I realised then that she needed me to be there with her as much as I needed her. That she had lost her daughter. So I let her pack that empty suitcase for me because we were family and we needed each other.

That was why I had to help her now. I had to be there for her, struggle through the days where she wasn't the woman I remembered, because without her I wouldn't have made it. My dad didn't understand that need, that desperation. I recalled him suggesting we just put Gran in a home and I ground my teeth in frustration. I nearly turned the car around.

But I needed to see him. To ask the questions I'd been dancing around. I couldn't run away from it this time. I tapped nervously on the steering wheel as I made a left turn, the old satnav doing its best to get me down a one-way street until finally I pulled the car to a stop outside number nine Rose Crescent.

It was the sort of home I'd imagined he'd have. Big, neat. Large windows and red brick. This could have been my house.

My family. If everything hadn't happened the way it did.

I climbed out of the car, slamming the door shut with more force than necessary, hoping that he was home. If not I'd have to drive to the university and somehow that was worse. I walked slowly up the garden path to the front door. It was a nice front door, too, but I took great pleasure in the single scratch that ran right down the middle of it. I wondered what had caused it, and whether I could do some more damage without them noticing.

"Psycho," I muttered to myself.

I hadn't seen Carol since Grandad's funeral. She hadn't brought Hailey to that, and I realised guiltily that I wasn't interested in seeing either of them today, just as I hadn't been a few months ago. Hailey wasn't my sister in any more than name. I didn't need another sister – and she didn't need whatever I was.

It was Carol who opened the door now. I saw her smile go stiff as soon as she saw it was me, but she guided me through to the kitchen without a word.

My relationship with Carol had always been complicated; she had no intention of trying to be my mother and deep down I resented her for this. Part of me wanted what Hailey had but I could never bring myself to ask. I hadn't come to live with Dad when he offered. I had always avoided Hailey's birthday and family gatherings after she was born. I refused to participate in everything that reminded me of what I was missing.

"Hi Dad," I said as he came into the kitchen. His glasses rode low on his nose and his chin was smudged with graphite.

It looked like he'd been sketching again. I felt a rush of familiarity. I felt perilously close to tears.

"Cassie. What are you doing here?"

"I just… I wondered if we could talk. I wasn't sure you'd be home but…"

"Come on, I'll make tea."

Carol stood awkwardly in the doorway behind us, leaning against the doorjamb as though she couldn't allow herself to intrude on our conversation but couldn't drag herself away either. Dad filled the kettle and then plonked himself down at the table. I took a seat, my whole body tense with nerves.

"I could have just phoned you," I said, trying to make light of it. "But I realised I hadn't been here. Ever." It was a weak attempt to make him smile.

"No, I guess not." Dad shrugged. "You know I'll always have time for a cup of tea with my big girl."

We made small talk for a minute but my heart wasn't in it. A natural lull in the conversation made me cast a glance over my shoulder. Thankfully Carol had gone. I felt my body relax a little bit and I leaned back on the wooden kitchen chair.

"Dad, I came here to – to ask you some questions, actually."

Dad sighed but attempted a smile. "Figures. Go on, then."

"I wanted to ask about Olive." I took a deep breath. "I wanted to ask about… about the investigation. About what happened. I know you don't really want to talk about it because – of everything."

Cassie was meant to be watching her. I remembered his words. Only a few days later I caught him on the phone to Carol.

That was when Mum found out, and the police said it meant he had an alibi after all.

I had seen the phone, heard the feminine lilt of a voice at the other end, and thrown myself at him. My whole body flew into his. I grabbed the collar of his shirt and screamed. I was hot and shaking.

I wish you were gone instead of her! I hate you. This is your fault!

I pushed the memory down.

"You're the only person I can ask," I said now. "You're the only one left. So why didn't you ever tell me you knew Cordy Jones?"

Dad wouldn't meet my gaze. He hunched in on himself, elbows to his sides as he sat at the table. He looked almost afraid.

"I thought it would – make things worse," he said eventually. His voice was thick with emotion. "You already hated me. You were hostile and angry all the time. I didn't mean to keep secrets, but I didn't think you could…"

"Handle it."

The realisation hit me, and I recognised his fear for what it was. Not a fear for himself, but a fear for me. For my safety. He thought he was protecting me – just like I hadn't told Marion about the text messages. Because I wanted to keep digging, yes, but also because I wanted to keep her safe.

"Do you think Cordy took Olive?" I asked quietly.

Dad shook his head. "I don't know. You never know, do you? There was a lot of evidence but it was… I don't know. The papers made a massive deal out of it all, but the police never told us anything tangible. People – I think they wanted somebody to blame. For a while it was me. Then they fixed on him. Olive walked out of Chestnut Circle by herself – a couple of people remembered her leaving – so the police assumed Cordy followed her.

"I didn't know him very well. I only went to a few youth group events because of you and Olive. Your mum didn't want you going until I'd scouted it out. I think I went to one or two, right at the beginning, before you guys even started going. Just to make sure it was safe."

A wry look passed across his face.

"I guess that didn't work out so well, huh."

I pushed down the wave of pity that made my throat thick.

"Do you remember the people at the youth group?" I asked.

Dad shrugged. "Not especially, but a few of them were memorable. Some I only remember from afterwards, when we were all here in those weeks after she was taken. There were all sorts of vigils and things. It was… It was horrible." He paused. His voice was hoarse when he next spoke. "Why are you asking now?"

"Darren Walker. He's the current suspect in Bella Kaluza's disappearance. He was a member of the youth group the summer Olive was taken. I just wondered…"

Dad looked at me blankly.

"Older. Kind of dorky, skinny, dark hair—"

"The nervous kid? Dodgy teeth? Yeah, he went by Daz, then. He used to hang around the Circle a fair bit with a few other lads."

"Do you remember Darren well?"

"Not really. He was a bit – odd. Liked to play with the

younger kids. He was dead shaken up after… after the eclipse. After Olive was taken. I don't know why – I don't think he'd ever spent time with her. But he kicked off big time at one of the vigils, started yelling about how he'd never wanted to watch the eclipse anyway, how he wanted to stay inside – but somebody made him go.

"He made a right scene. But a lot of the kids were upset afterwards. I think that's normal. It was the first time they'd dealt with – well… bad things. I'm sure a lot of parents handled it poorly. Daz was really shaken, though. He got into a bit of a scuffle with somebody at the vigil and they had to get your grandad's GP to calm him down – the doctor was the only person he'd listen to. It was a bit of a mess. His dad had to drag him home before the police were called." Dad pursed his lips and shook his head.

"Doctor White?" I asked. I tried to imagine him striding into the fray. Dad nodded.

I thought of Darren's reluctance to talk to Marion. He'd freaked out when Olive was abducted; was his current silence on the topic the adult equivalent? If so, then what had there been to argue about at the time?

"And what about Cordy?" I asked. "What about him?"

"He seemed – like a regular guy. I'm sorry, sweetheart. I don't know any more than that."

My head felt too full, bouncing between thoughts so fast I felt dizzy. None of it made sense. There were too many threads and too many people to keep track of. Darren, by all accounts, was nervous. Tense. Like he was hiding something. But what? I focused on what Dad had told me. Darren probably *was* there that day. In the crowd. He was somebody Olive would have recognised, and he wasn't scary. Had he *seen* something?

I thought of the mood rings, and then Bella's fingerprints inside Darren's van, all my thoughts swirling into a pot of cloudy suspicion.

"What are you thinking?" Dad asked, a frown forming on his face.

"I don't know," I said quietly. "I guess I guess how you never know what people are really like, or what they're thinking. Even when you think you do."

"Cassie…" Dad leaned forward in his chair, worry creasing the skin at his eyes. "You need to be careful. Don't let this get out of control. Obsession isn't healthy."

"I know, Dad."

I didn't tell him about the text messages. About Gran. It wasn't in the past any more. I had brought it back into the *now*, and I was terrified. I hadn't received anything on my new phone but I was checking it compulsively, scared that any minute I'd receive another one – and this time he'd do more than just tell me to back off.

We lapsed into silence, thoughts stretching between us. Dad had relaxed a little bit but I could see I'd shaken him up. I wondered if he'd been expecting me to talk about Carol, about him being with her during the eclipse while my sister was stolen. It wasn't a crime to be an absent father but he *had* lied about it.

That was an old topic, though. One that I had exhausted

as a teenager. I didn't care if he felt guilty about it. It didn't matter any more.

And to show him, I did what I'd never thought I would manage to do. I smiled at him and said, "Do you think we could – all meet up some time? For lunch or something? I've not seen Hailey in ages. And Carol…"

I wasn't even sure if I meant it, but the look on Dad's face was worth it.

35

I MET HENRY AT his hotel. Typical he'd choose somewhere out of the way, frequented mostly by the kinds of tourists who didn't mind paying a little extra for the luxury of quick access to the Peaks. It had a spa, a lounge, a bar and a Michelin-starred restaurant.

We met just before six in the lounge, where my hot-mess self didn't stand out so much. We settled down with glasses of sparkling water that reminded me of the period I had tried to give up Diet Coke back in university. It left a sour taste on my tongue but I drank it anyway.

Henry sipped his water. "Business before pleasure," he said, pulling a few sheaves of paper from the pocket inside his jacket. He smoothed them out on the table and his characteristic scrawl greeted me. "Business," he gestured at the paper. "Pleasure." He pointed at me.

I groaned.

"I'm just saying, you keep postponing our dinner. I want the gossip. I reckon you've been seeing Marion more than you've admitted." He winked. I hid my face in my hands, ignoring the butterflies in my stomach as I thought about Marion's toner-and-coffee smell, the feeling of her hand on my knee or her shoulder pressed against my own.

"What did you find out about Darren Walker?" I prompted. He rolled his eyes.

"Boring lad, really. Left school at sixteen but he's never been in any real trouble. He's worked a bunch of jobs, but never for very long. Maybe the longest one he's had is this stall at the school. Looks like he buys his stuff cheap at larger car-boot sales, and then brings it to the school in his van to sell to the kids."

"So, you're saying he's just run-of-the-mill *I-hang-out-with-children* creepy, not prison-material creepy?"

"What I'm saying is, there's no proof that he's creepy at all – not on paper anyway."

"And? What about *off* paper?"

Henry's head was cocked to one side in that *I know something you don't know* way that I'd become familiar with when I'd worked with him. Not that he'd lorded it over me *at all*.

"Maybe the most interesting thing about him is that when his dad died – years ago now – he left him some money from a property sale."

"What sort of property?"

"Industrial. A warehouse, I think. Warehouses always *scream* bad guy."

"That's not funny, Heno."

"Sorry. Anyway, I can't find any evidence of the sale beyond the fact that it happened. Doesn't seem like I have the full picture. But he's sitting on a lot of money, by the looks of things. Not sure if it's relevant."

"I won't ask how you found this shit."

"Good."

"Marion says they've let him go," I said quietly. "But there's got to be more. Can you keep digging for me?"

Henry steepled his fingers and looked at me. "Speaking of Marion…"

"Oh for God's sake, Henry. What is it with you and her?"

Henry's face softened. "You know I'm only looking out for you, Cassie." He shrugged. "If I had a penny for every time you said her name over the years we worked together… Call me old-fashioned, but I know what love looks like."

"I don't love Marion," I said.

Even as I said it, I knew it was a lie. There had never been a bigger lie. There might have been a time when I'd even believed it, believed completely that Marion was nothing but a friend. A *source* I could use for my job. A remainder from my old life – from the life before Olive disappeared. Nothing more.

But I knew that wasn't true any more. If it ever had been. I still felt the same way about Marion Adams as I had when we were thirteen. The emails, texts, telephone calls over the years – they'd made her a part of my routine in a way that was removed, boring, stagnant even. But Marion wasn't any of those things.

She was safe. Seeing her always felt like coming home; she was beautiful and capable. I wanted her to be *mine*.

"Are you still with me?" Henry's voice snapped me back to the present.

"What?"

"I said I was going to ask you to come home – to London. To stay with me." He paused, watched as I flinched.

"That's not my home any more," I said. It was the truth. "Maybe I wanted that before I came back here. Wanted things to stay the same. But they can't. I've seen…" I couldn't put it into words. How I'd seen my future, what could be, in Marion's eyes when she laughed and in the curve of her neck and the mole on her chin… "I'm moving on."

"But you haven't moved on," he said. "I know you. Are you going to ask her on a date?"

I glanced from side to side, suddenly aware of how loud he was speaking. I was totally fine with being Out and Proud, as Henry called it, in London. But up here it felt different. Smaller. Closer. Less forgiving.

I remembered the way my mum had looked at me when I'd told her about Marion. This was years after that summer, a long time after Olive was gone – and I'd needed to tell somebody. That was the first time I really felt angry at Olive, because when she'd been taken I had lost my sister but I'd also lost Marion. Lost what could have been, whatever had been growing between us during the darkness of the eclipse.

I told Mum that Marion and I had been more than friends. Mum had been angry. Not just angry but livid. Then quiet. So quiet. I'd carried that with me for a long time, aware that my sexuality was still a big deal to some people. Henry had normalised that. He had supported me. He knew what it had taken to come back to this town, afraid that Marion wouldn't want to connect in an offline world.

Henry was right, though. I hadn't moved on. Smug bastard.

"I don't want to ask Marion on a date," I lied, pushing back the inevitable for another day. "It's not like that."

Henry shook his head. "But don't you want it to be?"

36

MARION OPENED THE DOOR with a glass of wine in her hand. *Three days gone.* She'd been working around the clock and I didn't blame her for needing to relax and get a solid night's sleep for once. I was grateful her evening plans included me at all.

"I didn't realise you'd be here so early," she said by way of greeting. "Figured you'd be with your gran."

"Her pain medication knocks her out. Doctor White prescribed some sleeping pills too. She'll sleep until morning now. I just have to make sure I don't get home too late. Anyway, I won't tackle you for a glass of wine, I'm not an animal."

"Shame." Marion smirked. "What time *is* it?"

"Half eight?"

I imagined what it was like for Marion. Her days a blur of false leads, sending teams out to re-canvas areas already searched. The weight of a missing girl on her shoulders. And all this circumstantial evidence pulling her in so many different directions. I was only making things worse, throwing information at her and hoping it might mean something when it didn't even mean anything to me.

I knew exactly what day it was. I was aware of every second that passed. But that didn't help anybody. Clock-watching wouldn't find Bella or bring her home.

Marion led me into the lounge and sat down on the sofa, grabbing a take-away menu.

"I thought we could have pizza," she said. "I haven't got any food in."

I nodded and let Marion choose the pizza. She looked exhausted, lines around her eyes and mouth that I was sure hadn't been there last week. She looked thin, too. I wondered if she'd found time to eat at all today.

I held my questions back until we were done eating. Marion cradled her wine glass. She swirled the ruby liquid round and round but didn't drink. When she realised what she was doing, she looked away.

"Sorry. I'll stop." A pause. "You make me nervous."

"That's what they all say."

Marion didn't dignify that with a response. "I'm exhausted," she said instead. She gulped a mouthful of wine and then put her glass back on the coffee table. "I haven't slept in – ages. I don't know. We've got officers re-canvassing the area around the school and around Bella Kaluza's home. They're searching off the main grid this time, in the fields and around the lake again. We've tried to expand the search, into Matlock and the Peaks, but there's a lot of empty space and there are only so many of us. Nothing's turned up yet. Tips are coming in, but so far it's all rubbish." Marion shook her head.

"I spoke to my dad about Darren Walker," I blurted.

Marion didn't say anything, but I saw that I had her attention.

"I went to his house because − I found this photograph from the youth group. The one Darren was a member of. I didn't know... There's a picture of my dad and Cordy Jones. D'you remember, he ran it? Apparently my dad helped out a few times but I don't remember *that*. He knew Darren."

"And?"

"And... don't you think it's weird how Darren's so afraid all the time? Of me, of you. Could he have been confident enough to lure Olive away? I don't know."

That was the truth of it. It wasn't that I couldn't imagine him hurting Bella, because anything was possible these days with phones and technology, the lure of the Insta-creep; what I couldn't get my head around was the idea of a much-younger Darren Walker somehow successfully getting Olive to go anywhere with him.

"I don't know." Marion shook her head. "If they're connected—" She stopped, catching my expression. "If they *are*, then you're right. Walker would have been, what, fifteen? And given his current conversational abilities I'm not sure he'd have known what to do or how to hide it."

"Exactly." I rubbed my hands over my face. "So where does that leave us?"

This was the most we'd spoken about Olive in years. We'd never talked about her. About the eclipse. About that day, and our kiss and how it had spiralled into something so hideous. Marion had tried to talk to me but I'd always shut her down, my anger and guilt so hot they were likely to incinerate anything they touched; I couldn't afford to let Marion get close.

But tonight I *needed* to talk about my sister, to air out her ghost for fear that this time it might be me that burned up from keeping it all bottled inside.

"I used to say Olive wouldn't have gone off with *anybody*. But now I don't know. We know she left Chestnut Circle by herself. Gran said somebody gave Olive that mood ring. As a gift. Somebody gave it to her − just like somebody gave it to Bella. How much did I really know about her? She could have gone with anybody. Olive wasn't stupid, but if somebody was nice to her or made her feel special..."

"Yeah," Marion murmured. She reached for her nearly empty glass again and fingered the stem with delicate hands. I had always admired Marion's hands, the long pianist's fingers and slender wrists. She always wore the nails plain, pink and natural, unlike my own bitten and painted ones.

"I wish I could remember more." I watched the wine move in Marion's glass and felt my heart flutter. "I just − you're all I can think about. It's always been the same."

Marion went pink. "The kiss," she whispered.

"I feel so guilty. You know I'd been telling her off? Before you came over to join us? She wouldn't stand still and she was driving me mad, so I got angry with her."

"That wasn't what made it happen," Marion said quickly, her defence weakened by unsteadiness of her voice.

"You don't know that," I said. "What if she wandered off because of what I said to her?"

How could I explain it to Marion? Olive's ghost, haunting

301

me all these years? She had dealt with what had happened by being her usual practical self. She studied. She became a police officer. She helped people.

"I might be able to help you remember more." Marion sucked in a deep breath and reached over. Her hand was warm on my knee and I felt a familiar tingle. "I do it sometimes with the people at work. It can help. If you replay the same moment over and over in your head, it might get distorted, or cut off. What if there's something inside your head that you've been – well, ignoring? What if you could prompt your brain, gently, into letting that image resurface?"

I started to shake my head but stopped myself. I had tried this once with Henry. Or something similar. It was when I first started dating Helen, my defences lowered by new love. I had been drunk – I had to be drunk before I'd do it – and nothing happened.

I didn't remember anything.

Marion was breathing faster now. I realised that this was something she had wanted to ask me for a while. Something she had held in. Her eyes were wild almost, the desire to *know* making her grip my knee hard.

I had been so selfish. In all the years it had never occurred to me to think about how Marion felt. How she blamed herself. How she blamed *me*.

Suddenly it all made sense. It wasn't my fault, what happened; it wasn't Marion's fault. It was *ours*. And Marion wanted to fix it as badly as I did.

"Okay, I said. "I'll do it."

* * *

Marion dimmed all of the lights and set up her phone balanced against a pillar candle in the centre of the coffee table. She had an app that made a flashing silver-white light. It moved from one side of the screen to the other on a black background, and subconsciously I found my eyes following it. Marion sat opposite me, perched on the edge of the pouffe that matched the armchair. She had her elbows planted firmly on her knees, her white shirt unbuttoned at the neck.

"I want you to follow the light with your eyes," she instructed.

"Like hypnotism?" I asked.

"No. Well, sort of. Shush." She leant further forward, her collarbones drawing my gaze. I realised she was smiling, a tired, drawn-looking smile, but a warm one anyway. I'd always loved that smile. Loved it more when I'd caused it. "Pay attention to the dots – or I'll have to take the damn shirt off."

"Is that a promise?"

"Don't be so vulgar." Another smile. "Now, try to relax. Don't move. Just breathe. I'm going to start with some obvious questions, questions we both know the answer to. And then I'm going to be a little more sensory, let you think a bit about stuff outside your brain – outside your repeated memories, that is."

"Okay."

"It was August. We were standing in the Circle. Outside the corner shop there was a shaded spot. You got there before me and you were with Olive. What time did you get there?"

"Around ten maybe," I said, letting myself remember. "It

was already getting dark anyway. Olive and I walked from Gran and Grandad's. We walked because Gran was getting her hair done and we wanted to watch the whole eclipse. She was fine with us going – said I was old enough to watch Olive. We'd read that it would take an hour to get totally dark, maybe more... You met us there. And I was glad you came."

"What did you do then? Before I got there?"

"We hung around a bit."

"Can you be more specific?"

I dragged back into the depths of my memory. I remembered the walk from Gran's house. Olive was chattering about astrology. Her current obsession was Mars, which somebody had told her was the planet associated with aggression and conflict.

"What's lust?" she'd asked. I felt my face get hot as I ignored her, frustration and nerves and the heat a deadly cocktail of irritation.

"Come on Olive," I snapped. "We're going to be late and then we'll miss it and we'll have to watch the stupid thing from this stupid road."

"We won't." Olive had shrugged in her careless way. She knew she was right. I was edgy, wanting to get a good spot. Secretly hoping I could stand somewhere I'd be able to see Marion when she arrived. Hoping she would see me. I'd been fascinated by Marion's walk, her legs, her body...

Olive kept on talking, oblivious to my discomfort. The air was dusty and hot, the kind of heat that made my mouth taste like rocks and salt. It felt like we were wading through treacle.

"We won't see it properly for a while anyway," Olive said. She was jingling some money in her fist, a couple of pounds in change that Gran had given her to spend. It was driving me insane.

When we got to Chestnut Circle people were already there. The air was getting colder all the time. Shadows grew longer, and it was like twilight in the middle of the day. Some shops were closed. Others were buzzing with business.

"What can you see?" Marion's voice brought me back to the room and I once again saw the flashing silver light moving before my eyes.

"Bollocks," I said.

"That seems like a strange thing to see." Marion laughed. "Sorry, was that my fault?"

"This isn't going anywhere. I'm just seeing… Before. That's what I always remember; before and after."

"Just follow the lights," Marion said. "Come on, we'll try again."

I made my eyes focus, tried to block out Marion's father's ornaments on the mantelpiece. I followed the lights as Marion instructed. Silver flashing dots, over and over and over, like a thousand shooting stars.

"What did you and Olive do when you got to the Circle?" Marion asked. "Did she want to stand somewhere in particular? Did she mention anybody, or talk to anybody?"

"No. We just wandered about a bit. We decided to stay outside the corner shop because it was the only place left to stand. People were coming and going but nobody was that far back from the stage near Earl's. We stood underneath the awning where it was cool.

"Olive insisted on climbing about. She found a crate or a box or something but she still couldn't see. She tried to drag me closer but her hands were sticky from spilled pop and I got mad at her and pushed her off. Everything was annoying. You know when you're so frustrated you can't stand it? Even the smells and sounds were driving me crazy. It smelled like…"

The heat was oppressive. It was the hottest it had been in weeks. Olive and I were in shorts. My T-shirt kept sticking to my back and I was getting worried about seeing Marion and her noticing the sweat patches under my arms. The air smelled like onions – somewhere, a van was selling hotdogs and burgers. And under it all, the persistent, sharp and tangy smell of… "Oranges."

"Oranges?" Marion asked. "Where was that coming from?"

"I don't know…" I shook my head, trying to draw on the memory, to make it real. This wasn't something I had thought about before. The smells. "I think… It might have been Olive."

The tang of orange was strong, though, as though Olive was peeling them right in front of me. And then Marion was there, walking out of the crowd with her head high, people parting to let her through. She had that power and I felt a thrill that she was headed straight for us.

Olive was kicking off because she wanted something taller to stand on. She twisted and twisted that mood ring on her finger like it was a worry doll. And I didn't care.

"I can't see." Olive pouted, her golden eyes narrowing at me. There was nothing to see except the sky and she could see that just fine.

"Olive, Gran said you're not meant to wander off."

And then Marion was at my side. The eclipse had started in earnest now and the sky was getting so dark that the hairs on my arms rose and I felt a cold breeze snaking up my back. But that had everything to do with Marion's lips on mine. That first kiss, stolen, and the scent of oranges still there but forgotten. And then…

"And then Olive was gone."

I reached up to wipe my face, realising that it was wet. Tears made my lips salty and they stung viciously. The memory of the frustration I'd felt had twisted and grown in my stomach, anger now fully-rooted there.

I slammed my hand down on the coffee table. Marion's phone fell over with a clatter and she jumped.

"It was because of us."

"Cassie—"

"No, Marion. I can't… I don't know where Olive went. Not because I can't remember, but because I *never knew*. I didn't even notice she'd gone!"

"Cassie, I'm sorry."

"You said we needed to watch her. I told you she would be fine. I wanted her to *go away* – and for a second, when she was gone, I was glad."

I grabbed my jacket and left the house, stalking into the darkness.

37

I DIDN'T GET INTO my car. I needed to walk, to get some air. I sucked in the damp evening, breathing so deeply my lungs were on fire. I marched with purpose so that nobody would dare stop me. But there wasn't anybody around anyway. I walked all the way to the Circle, my mind beating against itself as my thoughts piled up.

Keep an eye on her, Cassie. The words haunted me, following me like a spectre down the street. I walked faster, my arms pumping and my heart thudding, trying to outrun the feeling. As though any minute somebody might leap out and attack me, drag me screaming to the ground as they yelled IT WAS YOUR FAULT.

And suddenly I was by the fountain in the middle of the Circle. The sound of the water brought me back to the present and I realised how hot I was, how sweaty and out of breath. I stopped for a second, hands on my knees, the anger clouding my vision receding slowly. I sucked in several more deep breaths, and then looked up.

A light caught my gaze. Warm orange light, which I realised

was from the corner shop. I didn't know what time it was, didn't care really, but it must be gone nine. I could never remember what time the shop stayed open until. The Circle was empty except for me. Me and Ady. It must be lonely. I walked over to the shop, fists digging around in my pockets. But I avoided him as I stepped inside.

I stalked straight to the fridge section and grabbed two bottles of the cheapest wine with screw-tops. Marion couldn't expect me to do this without liquid courage. I needed it. No, I deserved it, didn't I? Something to blunt the sharp edges?

I stalked to the counter as though I had something to prove. Maybe I did. Ady scanned the first of the bottles with none of his usual chattiness, and I thought again of our conversation about the mood rings, how it had been bothering me ever since.

"*The mermaid.*"

I hadn't realised I had spoken aloud until Ady stopped scanning and I realised he was staring at me, his expression the picture of confusion. I felt a swoop of adrenaline deep in my gut.

"You said you have different designs of rings now," I said, falling over myself to get the words out. "What did you mean? How did you know that Olive's ring was different from them?"

My heart was in my mouth, which was dry as sandpaper and just as unwieldy. But Ady just shrugged unaware of the hysteria bubbling inside me that threatened to burst out at any moment.

"You asked about a mermaid. We haven't had those ones in years. I'm – sorry. Are you okay?"

I let out a bark of hysterical laughter, unable to control myself. I wanted the ground to swallow me whole.

"Sorry," I said. "Oh my God. I must have sounded crazy. I just… I don't know. I'm latching onto things. We were doing this memory thing and I got so wrapped up in it…"

Ady didn't echo my laugh, but a bemused look flitted across his features as he scanned the remaining bottle of booze.

"Are you sure you need to buy any more of this?" he asked.

"Oh, I'm not drunk. Just hysterical. Don't mind me."

I could still feel the fire in my memory of that summer day in 1999. The unrelenting, angry heat. And the smell of oranges – now that I had smelled them once, they wouldn't go away. Tinged with the alcohol scent of the hand sanitiser that sat on the till. I was going insane, I thought. That was the only thing that made sense. I was going insane and I was taking Marion with me.

The memory of that summer day expanded, ever more haunting. I apologised to Ady again, grabbed the two bottles and left the shop.

Outside, the air had cooled considerably and I was no longer warm from the walk. One of the street lamps was out and another flickering ominously. I shivered.

It was getting to me. I knew it was, but what had happened in there with Ady… I felt like a fool. The way I'd spoken to him, and to Doctor White. This was getting to be a habit.

I cut across the Circle and sat on the edge of the fountain, the stone foundation digging into my heels through my shoes as I pressed them against the wall. I put one bottle on the ground next to my feet, and opened the other one eagerly. I stared at the bottle, felt the reassuring weight of it in my hand. There was nobody here, and given the fact that half the town was probably still out searching for Bella Kaluza I didn't think I was likely to be disturbed.

That's what you should be doing, said the little voice inside my head. *You should be out there. You should be helping, instead of accusing every bloke in town of kidnapping little girls.*

I stared at the bottle for another moment. Imagined the taste of the cheap wine, imagined the warm feeling in my gut. My fingers clenched hard against the cool glass, and I realised I was trembling. I thought of what Doctor White had said to me when he'd visited. That Gran was lucky not to have been more hurt. It hadn't sounded like a threat at the time but now, here, in the dark with the cold wind at my back, I was embarrassed to realise I was afraid.

What on earth did I think I was doing? I couldn't play at this. It was Marion's job, not mine. And, I realised, if nothing else, I was just making it harder for her.

I stared into the pools of lamplight across from the fountain. I had been so focused on trying to find out what happened to my sister I hadn't considered that Marion was going out of her way to follow my leads as well as her own, watching my back as I offended witness after informant after friend. Was I endangering Bella by wasting precious police time? If anything happened to her, I wasn't sure I would be able to forgive myself.

I put the bottle down next to the other one by my feet, suddenly tired.

"Cassie?"

I hadn't even heard the car. I craned my neck, seeing a figure silhouetted by the headlights of a dark vehicle. I knew it was Marion, knew by the slope of her shoulders. The sight of her made my blood rush inside my ears. I saw the bottles on the ground, saw them for what they were: a crutch. An easy way out of a shitty situation, just like it had always been. Marion's expression was warm as she approached, worry in her eyes, and I realised my breathing was finally normal again.

"I'm okay," I said. "I'm just taking a second. Panic attacks, wine... It seemed like a good idea at the time, but I'm having second thoughts about it."

"Good," Marion said, picking up one of the bottles and frowning at it. "I thought you had better taste in wine than that."

38

MARION SAT NEXT TO me on the sofa, her body pressed against mine. She cupped a mug of hot tea, blowing steam as we watched the fire that she'd lit. It cast the room in an orange glow, exaggerating everything. Marion's features seemed to stretch as she leaned over to place her drink on the coffee table.

"I'm such a shit," I said.

"No, you're not."

"I can't believe I stormed out on you like that, and I basically yelled at Ady too."

"It's okay, Cassie. I'm proud of you. I know I don't always say that, but I know how hard it is for you. I should never have made you do that – go through those memories. I knew it was going to be painful for you, but I didn't think enough about it. I should have let somebody else do it because me being there probably made you feel…"

"I hated you." I stared at her. "I actually thought that. I thought that I hated you."

Marion's face fell. "You… do?"

"No. It's just… I was angry. About then. And about now.

About you and Fox, too, I think. And then I stormed off and took it out on Ady."

"I only slept with Matthew once." Marion turned to me and took my hand. "I – I'm not saying it because I owe you anything. I'm just clearing the air. I want you to know that it happened, and that it didn't mean anything."

"I didn't…"

"Come on. We're both adults here."

I didn't want to imagine Marion with him. But the tone of her voice made it clear that, whether it meant anything or not, it was over. And I felt a weight lift off my shoulders, a weight I hadn't even realised I'd been carrying. I wondered if that was why Fox had been so horrid to me – because he knew what I meant to Marion. And what Marion meant to me.

The thought of her talking to him about me made me perversely happy.

We lapsed into silence. Despite the events of the night, it was a comfortable silence. It felt like we'd reached some sort of truce, admitted that there had been a problem between us, and now we could set it all aside.

Marion shifted, the vest she'd changed into pulled low on her chest. This time I didn't avert my gaze. Instead I thought back to that summer. How Marion was the only one I had eyes for. How I'd snuck away from Olive and Gran at every opportunity, happy to be sitting in the cool, damp air of the woods with her.

We'd cycled to the Triplet Stones with a picnic, spent hours lounging by the lake when we were meant to be at Marion's house. Her dad had been at work and Gran had been busy making plaster of Paris dinosaur moulds with Olive… Those days hadn't been long enough. I could almost taste the dusty air, smell the cut grass and the wet mossy kiss of the earth beneath our bare legs.

"Do you ever wish we hadn't…?" I stopped, unsure what I was asking.

"Kissed? Fallen in love? Been so wicked cool?"

"Yes."

"No." Marion nudged me gently. "Maybe once. But not now."

"What happened to us?" I asked.

"We grew up," she said quietly. "Realised that we couldn't fix what happened."

"Can't we?"

I turned my body against hers. She was still the most beautiful woman I had ever known – in every way. Marion was vibrant, somehow. She understood me better than anybody else. I realised now that this was because nobody else had shared the same darkness, the same guilt that we had.

But the darkness didn't own Marion. She had a light deep inside her, a storm lantern. A quiet sort of confidence. She had been there when I had needed her, even if only at the other end of a phone. She was the only one I'd trusted enough to call when I'd found my mother's body. The light grey and watery, my vision blurred with hot, salty tears, I'd staggered out of the room and fumbled for the phone. I didn't call Dad. Or Gran. After the police the first person I called was Marion.

"Do you ever think about Olive?" I asked.

"All the time. I often wonder what she'd be doing now. Whether she'd be anything like you. I have this image of her in a lab coat somewhere."

I felt a lump forming in my throat and I found it difficult to breathe. I'd had the same thoughts. I'd wanted to talk to Gran about them over the years but never could – even before she started to forget things.

"Oh, Cassie."

Marion wiped my tears, then leaned in and put her arms around me. She smelled like fabric softener. Her perfume was soft and musky and I breathed it in. I let her hold me, her body firm against mine. I shuffled closer, trying to rein in the tears.

"I…"

"It's okay," she whispered.

She lifted my chin with one hand, making our eyes meet. She was smiling, the kind of smile that made her whole face light up. Not with joy, but with a sort of happiness that came from our contact. Marion leaned in and pressed her lips to mine. The feeling inside me grew and the world exploded in colour.

It was the same feeling I remembered, only sixteen years bigger. Nobody had ever made my heart thud and my limbs shake with the same excitement as Marion. I drank her in, pulled her closer and wrapped her inside the blanket.

"Marion…"

"Shh."

She let her kisses travel from my lips down to my throat. I shivered at her touch, some core deep inside me vibrating. The years stretched behind us, a lifetime of love that we had never admitted. A lifetime of shared guilt and sadness and frustration.

Now, somehow, it felt different. How had that happened? I marvelled at it as I ran my fingers along her jaw and traced the outline of her collarbones. I wanted to be consumed, to let her kiss it all away. Leave everything else a distant memory.

"I'm sorry," Marion whispered. Her lips were so close to my ear that her voice made me shiver. I held her tight.

"What for?"

"For not believing you. For treating you like you were… crazy. You're *not*. I should have had faith in you."

"Yes," I said with a small smile. "You should have. But I know you're trying."

Marion shrugged. "I should have been more helpful."

I pushed down the guilt at the way I'd spoken to Ady, to Doctor White, to my father. Bella's disappearance was making me lose my mind but I couldn't blame it for all of my faults.

"I can probably forgive you," I said, turning my mind away from the hot feeling in my stomach, "if you let me kiss you again."

Her thumb massaged circular patterns on my palm as she stared into my eyes. Her lips moved without her saying anything, and I leaned in to kiss them closed. I was enveloped in softness, lost in her arms.

"I can help with your gran, Cassie," she whispered. "I can. I know you're having anxiety attacks again. I know you're trying to deal with them, but I don't think cheap wine is the best way—"

"I don't need help—"

"I *want* to help you. I know you think alcohol is better than sleeping pills, but neither of them are going to solve the problem. I can help."

"I know," I said. I ran my thumb over her collarbone, up underneath her chin. Her cheeks were flushed and her eyes grew bright and glassy at my touch. "I'm sorry. I'm trying to let you." I thought about the threatening text messages again. How I should have told Marion about them before Gran got hurt. I vowed to try harder from now on, to let her help me, to stop trying to do everything on my own.

Marion kissed me again, her hand at my back. Her kisses grew deeper, more searching. I let her fingers and her mouth trace the length of me, closed my eyes and lay back. Opened myself to her. She reached the little O tattooed on the inside of my elbow and let her mouth linger there, her breath hot on my skin. She didn't have to ask what it meant; she knew, as I'd known from the minute I walked into her house why she had image after image of elephants. For memory. For Olive.

I let Marion's body mould to mine, wrapped my fingers in her hair and pulled her into me.

We were still − after all this time − a perfect fit.

I woke with Marion's head on my bare chest. The fire had begun to die and the room was dim with the glowing embers. The light from the street lamp outside cast faint shadows through a crack in the curtain, and Marion's hair spilled all around her head like a pool of dark water. I brushed it back from her brow with tender fingers. She opened her eyes, shifting slightly so she could look up at me.

"How are you feeling?" she asked, concern making her voice husky.

"Like I scored big."

It was a joke, and yet it wasn't. I felt drained, my whole body suddenly emptied of the weight I had been carrying around for days now. Weeks. Longer, even. I had carried this weight since before Bella, before Grace. Perhaps since Grandad died and I came back here. Perhaps longer still. Perhaps it was a weight I'd carried every day since Olive disappeared. I realised that everything I had been doing to avoid Marion and Bishop's Green had all been for nothing.

I couldn't leave this town behind, just like I couldn't leave her. All this running and I'd somehow come full circle. Another circle. Back to the start – where we could try again.

"You remember, before Grandad's funeral, when you emailed me and told me I should take Gran out of town?" My voice was quiet and it cracked.

Marion tensed, her body pressed against the length of mine. I stroked her head, though, and she relaxed again.

"Were you afraid? Of what would happen if I came back here? That I'd ruin everything like I always do?"

Marion didn't say anything right away, and then she let out a long sigh.

"I was afraid," she admitted. "But not because of you. It was because… I've spent a long time trying to get people to like me. I'm respected. I have a good job, and people around town are – they're good to me. I was worried about what would happen if…"

"If I blew things for you with Detective Fox," I finished.

"No. I don't mean it like that. *That* was all a farce anyway. He's pissy because I called the whole thing off. But it was just… comfortable. For a while. It made me feel like I fit in for once. I figured I could do the marriage and kids thing. Just be like everybody else."

"I get it."

Marion swallowed again. "I also worried that I would lose you," she added. It was so quiet I thought I hadn't heard her right.

"What do you mean?"

"I was afraid that… if you were here, well, I thought… we wouldn't get past it. I mean, we haven't done a very good job, have we? There's so much – so much in the past. I was afraid of the painful memories. Of the thought that we'd been hanging onto each other when we'd be better off letting go."

"That's not true."

I could hear Marion's breathing grow irregular. I was sure she was trying to say something, but I didn't want to pressure her so I lay silently. I stared up at the dark ceiling, and then I turned my head so I could watch the dying fire.

"Cassie…" Marion's voice was quiet. It sounded like she was speaking from a room away. "When Olive was taken, I thought it was our fault. I've always thought it was our fault. And I know you've felt the same. But what if wasn't?"

"What do you mean?"

"Victims blame themselves for this kind of thing – I've seen it enough. I've been haunted by that moment all my life, but what if it wasn't anything to do with us? We assumed it was because we weren't watching her. But... there were loads of kids there that day. He could have chosen any of them, lured them away from the party."

I swallowed.

"What I'm saying is, I don't think it was coincidence. Or bad luck. I don't think it was because we weren't paying attention. At least, not *just* because of that. You said that you didn't know Olive as well as you thought — but you knew she was acting differently.

"What if the eclipse is the key to all of this? It was... *symbolic*. It was meant to be a fresh start — for all of us. It's also repetition and things coming full circle. You said it yourself, there are a lot of similarities between Bella and Olive. Divorcing parents, complicated home life. The mood ring before the eclipse. Bella looks sort of similar to Olive. They're both bookish children who like the company of grown-ups..."

I wanted to stop her. To stop the words that were pouring out of her in a sort of fevered frenzy. But I couldn't bring myself to do it.

"What if this, now, is about *repeating* it?" she said. "What if whoever took Olive is recreating it? It would explain Olive's ring turning up. Total solar eclipses — people get really superstitious. Even though it wasn't total everywhere, it was in the media a lot. Very visible. It could be a compulsion."

My heart started to drum loudly. I sat upright, scooting backwards on the sofa and trying to hold the blanket over my chest. Marion had managed to put it into words – this feeling I'd had, right since the beginning.

Marion scrambled over me and off the sofa, the suddenness of it making me jump. She was on her feet, completely naked, before I could say anything else. She grabbed her vest top and pants and started to get dressed.

"Wait," I said. "What's happening?"

"I want to show you something," she said. "Come on. I never showed you before, but I have to now. I won't be able to sleep until I do."

Baffled, I slid off the sofa and pulled my own clothes on quickly. Marion didn't bother to dress fully. She gestured that I should follow her, and she went out of the lounge and up the stairs.

"What on earth has got into you?" I asked.

"Look, I started to do this when my dad died. He left a lot of stuff lying around from when he was with the police. So I gathered it all up. At first it was just… a sort of morbid curiosity. I felt guilty and it was a good way to feel like I was doing something about that. But now…"

We came to a stop at the top of the stairs outside the room I knew had been Marion's father's. She pushed the door open wide and turned the light on.

I couldn't control my surprise.

The whole room was covered in bits of paper. She'd got rid of the bed, and in its place was a desk. I remembered what this room looked like only a little from years ago, but this was not what I'd been expecting.

"Are those…?"

"They're his case notes," Marion said. "He kept a load of stuff that I'm sure he shouldn't have, notes that he photocopied or hand-wrote." She turned to me, her eyes wide with what I assumed was pride. But when I stepped into the room I realised that actually it wasn't pride. Couldn't have been pride. It was something more like fascination. And fear.

"Marion," I said quietly. "This is all Olive."

"I know. I *know*. I've been through everything a hundred times. I've read over and over the stuff and it just – it just feels like it wasn't… it wasn't right. Not – not botched. But just…

"Because – because you guys were from out of town I think… I mean the case – Dad focused on…" She stopped and averted her gaze, as though she was trying to gain control of her words. "In most cases of abuse, it's close to home."

"It was your dad? Who went after mine?"

"No," she said quickly. "Not like that. I don't think he meant for it to get so out of hand. But by the time they moved onto Cordy Jones it was late in the day. And they never had hard evidence but most people in town were already convinced so…"

"So he let it go."

I wrapped my arms around my chest, suddenly chilly.

Marion took a deep breath. I stepped closer to her, wanting to touch her, to reassure myself that this was real. But I couldn't bring myself to do it. All around me were pictures of Olive. Pictures I didn't recognise, or pictures I'd never thought I'd see again. News articles, handwritten accounts of interviews, even a photograph from her birthday that year. Post-it notes, too, in different handwriting.

"Did he do this?"

"No," Marion said. "I told you. I put it up."

"No, I mean did he... did he keep it all because he felt like he'd not done enough?" I turned to her. Her shoulders sagged, and suddenly the energy went out of her.

"I don't know," she said. "Both Olive and Bella were taken because they were alone but I think it was more than just chance. Dad had witnesses who thought they saw Olive leave the Circle. She wandered away from the crowd, and that was why nobody saw anything more. Yet there were loads of children alone that day – and only Olive was taken. Same goes for Bella. Loads of the kids were late to school because of the eclipse – dawdling in, that sort of thing. But he took Bella. Why?"

Marion might be right, but that meant something I didn't want to think about. That if I'd been there – for Bella *and* Olive – if somebody had asked the right questions, then maybe they could have been saved.

What was it about these girls that had made him choose them? They were both smart, both friendly. Both older than their years. I felt a sickness settle inside me as I realised something.

He wanted what my gran had called "old-fashioned" children, ones who got on better with adults. From broken homes. Both Olive and Bella would likely have appreciated the affection of an older man – a father-figure.

I noticed one of the pieces of paper out of the corner of my eye. Then another. Photocopies of lined sheets filled with childish scrawl. My eyes prickled with tears. I stepped closer, saw the little doodles in the corner of the page, saw my own name. These were pages from the diary Olive had kept; the diary I had never been able to find.

I leaned in and read the page in silence. It referenced Bishop's Green. I saw the words *eclipse* and *Cassie* and *Chestnut Circle*. *Excited*. Nothing about a man, nothing about a ring. But here, on this piece of paper, was a tiny part of my sister.

"Do you want to stay here for a while?" Marion asked suddenly. She moved closer and placed her hand on my lower back, unaware of the storm raging inside of me. I leaned into her touch, relishing the pressure of her arms around my stomach as she held me close. "Or do you want to go back to your house. To bed? With me?"

I turned in Marion's arms, wrenching myself away from the ghost of my sister. For once I needed to put Marion first. I reached up, ran my fingers along the curve of her jaw, watched as her throat bobbed. Her raven hair was mussed, her blue eyes somehow both sad and mischievous.

"Bed," I said hoarsely. "Take me to bed."

39

30 August 2002

HE'D MISSED SOMETHING.

Finally, he'd missed something. For a second she was jubilant, until she realised what that meant. Realised the hardness inside of her. And then the jubilance faded to sickness.

She held the scrap of newspaper between her thumb and forefinger, tilting it towards the dim summer evening light. She'd spent the day finishing off the book Sandman had given her the night before. It was a dog-eared copy of *Harry Potter*. The fourth one. It was her favourite so far, and the biggest, and for ten blissful hours she'd been in another world. Another place.

Then she'd turned to the newspaper. A copy of the *Bishop's Green Chronicle*. She liked to read the news, but she often felt unhappy afterwards. There was so much going on in the world – and a lot of it wasn't very good. Today wasn't much better.

There was a story partway through that must have been an update, although Olive hadn't seen the earlier article. The bodies of two girls found in Suffolk by walkers.

Olive felt tears welling hot inside her eyelids. She couldn't believe Sandman would let her see that by accident. After all, he must have edited her previous newspapers. They'd been found over a week ago.

She felt a worm of panic eat into her, but sucked it down. She knew Sandman better than that. It probably wasn't a warning. Perhaps he was getting careless. She flicked through the rest of the paper, trying to ignore the faces of those two girls, their red football shirts blinking out at her. She'd smudged the pages with her tears and her fingers felt tacky with newsprint.

She reached the back half of the paper – the part she normally skipped on her first read through and saved for much later, when she was desperate between books. But something caught her eye.

And here was the real kicker. The thing that proved this wasn't calculated. Proved that Sandman had missed something. The name that leapt out of the births and deaths page was one she recognised.

Peter Warren.

Olive's father.

For a second her stomach lurched, but then she realised she was on the births. *Births*. Her eyes scanned the tiny paragraph, her tongue heavy and dry in her mouth. She wasn't sure whether to laugh or cry.

University Lecturer Peter Warren and his wife Carol welcome their daughter Hailey. Born: August 28, 2002. Weighing in at six and a half pounds. Welcome to the world, Hailey!

There was a picture of a balloon, and inside it was a baby's face. Scrunched up and raw from the traumatic experience of birth. Olive felt her head spin, and she had to close her eyes.

Dad. Wife Carol. Carol wasn't her mum's name. Where was Cassie? Where was Mum? Olive wanted to be sick. She knew her parents were unhappy. She'd known this long before she'd been able to understand what that meant. And logically over the years she'd wondered what might have happened after she was gone.

But this…?

It was so sudden. So unexpected. Olive felt a surge of rage. She grabbed the newspaper in both hands, balled up the dense pages and started to throw them. Stopped. Changed her mind and started to rip them up. The glorious *scrunch* as the paper tore made her feel white-hot.

She screamed.

Her voice was foreign to her ears. Even more foreign than the usual songs and stories. She was used to her meek self, not this one. But the fury burnt hot and bright and then died.

Moments later Olive was on the floor, surrounded by hundreds of tiny scraps of paper. Her whole body ached from the exertion, and she panted for a moment while her heartbeat returned to normal. Ink stained her fingers, her palms all smudged. She saw half the picture of the two murdered girls, and her hatred turned sour, sadness curdling there in her belly.

So Dad had remarried. They'd split up, finally. She guessed it was probably a good thing. Good for Cassie. Maybe Mum would find somebody else. Maybe this Carol woman was who he'd been with all those times when he wasn't at work. Olive wondered if anybody else knew about that, about the trysts and the secret meetings that weren't meetings. She'd known for ages, had known since she'd tried calling his office only to be told he was taking 'family time'.

Probably everybody knew now. Maybe finally Cassie would be able to see it.

Olive pushed down the residual spark of anger, thinking of those poor murdered girls. They were younger than her. They had had worse things than divorcing parents to worry about. Than a man who brought them books and chocolates and kept them clothed and fed. By force of habit, Olive grabbed her favourite book off her bookshelf, hugged it close, and started the familiar list in her head:

I'm glad I'm warm. I'm glad I'm dry. I'm glad I'm healthy. At least I have books. At least I have paper. At least he doesn't come every day.

In her mouth, she felt the words she could no longer think. *At least he doesn't hurt me. At least I'm not alone.*

At least, she thought, *I'm alive.*

But what did that mean?

40

Tuesday, 24 March 2015

I WOKE IN MY bed before Marion's alarm. The curtains were thin and let in a watery sort of light that spilled over the dark hair gloriously coiled on the pillow next to my head. I breathed in Marion's familiar scent, barely resisting the urge to trail my finger down the creamy skin of her arm, flung carelessly across my chest. The sight of her in my bed was warming, and Marion's suggestion – not mine – that she spend the night here instead of at her house because of my gran made me love her even more.

Her breathing was soft and steady. I marvelled at it, a warmth buzzing through me even as I felt the worry start to gnaw again. This wasn't the old worry, the kind that crept in whenever Marion and I went days without speaking – that she had no time for me any more. No, this was more primal. Fear, even. No more of the anonymous text messages had come, no more threats, but I couldn't shake the thought that this wasn't safe. That being around me *wasn't safe*.

Perhaps, I told myself, Gran's accident was just that – an accident. The messages could have been from anybody. A journalist. Grace's stepfather... They'd stopped once Bella was taken. Maybe they hadn't been threats at all. Marion hadn't told me if they'd found out who had sent them, but perhaps they weren't worth their time.

Marion was safe here. Wasn't she?

The alarm on her phone sent a shrill panic coursing through my veins before I figured out what the noise was. Marion yawned and stretched and smiled at me with cat-like warmth and my happiness unfurled a little more, pushing back the dark worry that bit further.

I sat with her at the kitchen table while she drank two cups of black coffee. I was still jumpy when her phone rang as she was buttering a slice of toast. She left the toast on the counter, still steaming in the dawn light. She made some muffled sounds, using the interruption of the call to shove her feet into her boots.

When she hung up her expression was one I hadn't seen before.

"Everything okay?" I asked, nerves making my tongue dull.

"That was Matthew," she said. "He had a voicemail from Darren Walker late last night. Said he sounded a bit drunk. Apparently Walker wants to talk to you. Won't talk to anybody else."

I felt a flutter of something. Hope? Panic?

"When?"

"Today. Soon." She shook her head in disbelief.

"And Fox is okay with that?" I asked. "After everything?"

"No," she said. "But what choice do we have? Take him back in for questioning and he'll clam up. Let him talk to you

– maybe you can shake something loose. Get him to come to us. It might be nothing."

"But you don't think so?" I asked.

"No. The guy's not smart enough to play the press, Cassie. If he wants to talk to you, he has something to say."

I massaged the back of my hand, unable to process it. A little voice trilled in my ear: *It might be about Olive. He knows something.* I shook it off, shoving the hope down hard. But why else would he want to talk to *me*?

"What should I do?"

"Go and see him," Marion said firmly. "But I'm going to get somebody to go with you. Might not be able to until lunchtime but he said he'll be home today. Talk to him and pray he's got something for us. I'll call you when I can about an officer to come with you. And then you must let me know the minute you've spoken to him."

Once she'd gone, I sat for a minute. Maybe this was it. The missing puzzle piece. Maybe Darren knew something about Bella. Or *Olive*.

Gran slept heavily and I didn't wake her until Marion had gone. The effect of an uninterrupted night was miraculous – when I poked my head through the door she was smiling in her sleep. I brought her a cup of tea and then made breakfast so she could take more of her painkillers. I helped her to get washed and dressed, all the while waiting for Marion's go-ahead for the meeting with Walker. Gran seemed brighter this morning.

More comfortable. I tried to distract myself by being the best granddaughter I could be.

"What are you going to do today?" I asked. "Would you like me to find you something to watch?"

Gran scrunched up her nose. "I'll probably read that book," she said. "I'm really struggling to get into it. I thought I might go for a walk later—"

"Please don't do that," I said, trying to sound cheerful but dreading the thought of her wandering about alone. "Not without me or the nurse. How about we go for one around the block? Just you and me together."

Until last year Gran had taken a walk every day without fail. It was her routine. Once Grandad died she'd stopped but I was aching to bring some sense of order back into her life. Once this was all over…

"Yes, I think I'd like to go now," Gran said with a smile. "Walk off my breakfast. I'm getting a little chubby."

She rubbed her non-existent belly absently, and I realised again just how skinny she was getting. I knew it tended to go either way with dementia: either you ate more because you forgot you'd eaten, or you'd eat less because you thought you already had. I wished Gran was the former. Or that I was around more to enforce a better meal routine.

No, I *would* be around more. Once this was over. When Bella was home…

"We'll just go for a little walk," I said in what I hoped was a firm voice. "I think you could do with resting a bit. If you do too much you might hurt yourself."

"I won't do any such thing." Gran glanced down at her arm and noticed the sling. "Bulky thing, this. It's getting in the way."

"That's okay," I said. "You won't have to wear it for ever."

After we returned from our walk, which had been slow and surprisingly enjoyable in the brisk breeze, the nurse arrived. I'd arranged for a few hours a day over the next few days, despite the cost, so I could have some peace of mind. It didn't do much to calm me though; I was skittish, my whole body aching with thrumming tension even as I left both of them settling down to a game of trivia from Gran's youth.

In my car I turned the radio on, listening for any mention of Bella's name, but there was no new information. Still, it was a distraction from thinking about Darren Walker and our meeting later. Marion hadn't called yet and the thought was driving me crazy.

The radio droned on. The suspect had been released; police informed reporters that he was just a witness; searches were continuing along Rosewood Avenue and up through Chestnut Circle. Blah, blah. All things I already knew. I tried to ignore the tense feeling making my whole body tight as I pulled up outside Ady's shop, but still it took me several minutes to drag myself out of the car.

Inside, Ady was at his post as usual, his gaze glued to his phone. I thought that it was funny that he spent so much time staring at his when he wouldn't let his daughter have one.

"Hey…" I began. "Uh, I just wanted to say I'm sorry I was a – a bit strange with you last night."

I stood by the counter, pretending to browse the array of chocolate bars. Ady shrugged.

"It's okay. People have bad days." He smiled.

"Yeah." I massaged the back of my neck. "I just have more than most. It's all just getting to me a bit. What with Gran, and trying to pick up the writing again, and that missing girl…"

The bit about the writing was a lie. It wasn't the idea of a job that made me feel so sick – but I didn't want to tell Ady my theories about Olive and Bella.

Ady nodded sympathetically. "You're working too hard. You need to stop writing and focus on what's important. I was like that after my wife died because it was so unexpected.

"You learn to find pleasure in the little things. The stolen minutes of 'me' time. I had Tilly as a baby, which was hard, of course. But you find distractions." This was the most Ady had ever said about his wife. Tilly was his whole life now, and he protected her.

"You do seem much better this morning," he said then. "Cheerful, even. It's nice."

I thought of Marion, of last night in bed with her. The butterflies in my stomach tripled. Then I thought of my interview with Darren Walker. I couldn't contain the hope that we were finally getting somewhere.

"Yeah, I'm feeling pretty good today actually."

"Can I get you a coffee?"

I smiled and nodded. Then, with Marion's courage buzzing

in my veins, I decided to ask the question I'd wanted to ask for a while.

"Do you remember the day my sister disappeared?" The coffee machine sputtered away. "You probably didn't know us well back then."

"I remember it okay." Ady shrugged. "Your grandad used to bring you in quite a bit, so I knew who you were. He always donated when we had fundraisers for the homeless kids, did charity bakes and stuff with me – he let you guys put the pennies in that tub I kept on the counter. The eclipse was something else, though. It was so busy."

"I think Olive came in here," I said. "Do you remember if she spoke to anybody, or if anybody was hanging around?"

Ady thought about this, his brow crinkling. "I don't think so," he said. "I don't know. I don't even remember seeing her."

"Oh. I thought she did."

"She might have," Ady said. "But if she did, I don't think she bought anything. I'm sure I'd have remembered – after what happened. I'm sorry, Cassie. I wish I could help more."

Nodding, I said, "I'd better get off anyway. Thanks. And sorry again for being a dick."

Ady's smile was warm and I was grateful. He was right, I needed to appreciate things more.

"Any time," he said.

Outside the shop I stopped for a second, breathing in the spring air. It was warming up, the sky a universal pale grey threatening rain. I was just starting to relax, feel the buzz of the caffeine kick in, when Jake Howden rounded the corner.

He was dressed in a pale grey suit and a blue shirt that was open at the throat. He gave me a smile, teeth flashing. I rolled my shoulders, half expecting a confrontation after the chat I'd had with his wife.

"Earl's has better coffee," he said by way of greeting, gesturing at the nearly empty cup in my hand. "But sometimes I drop in here if I've not got time to wait for the good stuff."

I let out a bark of startled laughter. Whatever I was expecting him to say, it hadn't been that.

"I don't think Earl's coffee is that much better," I said. I checked my watch. It was just after half nine. "Shouldn't you be at school already?"

"My first class today isn't until second period. Perks of being part-time." Jake's smile turned brittle. "Why? Are you keeping an eye on me, Miss Warren?"

"Do I need to?" I asked. Jake shook his head, his jaw clenching. "Anyway, you were the one following me," I pointed out. "I'm always here."

It was Jake's turn to laugh. "I had noticed," he said drily. "I only live over there." He pointed to one of the long residential streets that stretched off the Circle. I thought, idly, how close it all was – how easy it would be for anybody to have stopped Bella on her way to school, to offer her a lift…

"That's lovely," I muttered, unsure why he wanted me to care.

"It's called polite conversation," Howden said as if reading my mind, a smile on his lips. "Anyway, perhaps I'll see you Thursday – no doubt Ady mentioned the vigil. We're taking a leaf out of Doctor White's book. He did the ones for your sister, didn't he? You should come along, anyway."

Stunned, I watched Howden's back as he pushed open the door to Ady's and stepped inside. His mention of Olive had thrown me. Had he meant to hurt me or was he simply careless? Was this payback because I'd talked to his wife? I thought of the way she had jumped to the conclusion that I thought her husband had something to do with Bella's disappearance. The question was, did he?

41

BY MIDDAY, I COULDN'T wait any longer for Marion to call about sending somebody to Walker's house with me. I'd been home, checked on Gran and the nurse, and tried calling Bella's mother again. What if Walker got cold feet about talking to me? What if a police escort spooked him and he refused to open up? I didn't want to go against Marion's wishes but something wasn't right and I couldn't just hang around. We were running out of time.

I pulled up to Darren Walker's house just after twelve, my stomach twisting with anticipation as I noticed that his van was parked out front. The house was a semi-detached bungalow at the end of a cul-de-sac in an area I had never been to before.

The street was quiet. Suddenly I was nervous. Perhaps I should have waited for Marion's officer after all. I pulled my phone out with a sweaty hand, although I wasn't sure what I was going to do with it.

"Mr Walker?" As I got to the house I rapped my knuckles against the white PVC-coated door. The glass was frosted, but inside looked dark.

"Darren? It's Cassie Warren. You wanted to talk to me?"

I glanced around, checking for neighbours, but the house next door looked pretty empty. No cars on the driveway and a garden that looked in need of a good trim.

I knocked on the door again. Nothing.

"Mr Walker, if you changed your mind and you don't want to talk to me that's fine, but you need to tell me."

I stepped back, gazing at the bungalow. The curtains weren't drawn, but there was something eerily vacant about the whole place.

This wasn't right.

I gripped my phone tightly. If Darren had been home overnight, with the news broadcasting his release from police custody, all bets were off. I remembered Cordy Jones, what his wife had said about people being angry when he was let go.

My blood began to hum, adrenaline pulsing. I tried the front door handle. It dipped smoothly and the door swung inwards. I hesitated on the doorstep, bouncing on the balls of my feet. I should just call Marion, leave this to her. But what if he was hurt?

Yeah and what if he's not? What if this was what he wanted all along? What if he *sent those text messages and this is all part of his plan to get payback?* Payback for what? I halted my thoughts right there. Payback for what? He wouldn't have called Fox if he wanted to hurt me.

"Pull it together, Cassie."

I stepped over the threshold with my hands hovering down by my sides, Marion's number open and ready to go. As much as

I wanted to tell myself that everything was fine, I couldn't do it.

The front door opened onto a small entryway, bedrooms branching off to the left and the right. Both empty except for an array of dreamcatchers strung up in the windows and above the beds, their colourful feathers the brightest things in the house. The rooms were obsessively tidy, as though he'd gone round and tucked away everything that might remind him of himself. There was a lounge, a bathroom – empty as well.

Then, at the end, what must be the kitchen.

"Mr Walker?" I called again.

My voice was muffled by the carpet, a ghostly sort of quiet. There was a glass door that looked like it had been cleaned recently, the glass still lined with smear marks where somebody had used the wrong cleaning product.

The door was closed, and as I reached the end of the hall I peered through it.

"Oh my God."

I rushed into the room, slamming the door wide and hurrying over to the kitchen table. A chair lay upended on the floor where it had been kicked over. And there was Darren, inches off the ground.

On the table, a piece of paper lay under a teacup. Scrawled handwriting made my whole body ache – with sadness or guilt I didn't know. I couldn't bring myself to read it.

I stumbled, my knees colliding hard with the laminate flooring. I pressed my palms against it hard, trying to breathe. Failing.

Not again.

Kneeling on all fours, my eyes closed, all I could see was her. My mother. The kitchen cold because she'd opened all of the windows, the table laid for Sunday dinner. Her shoes – I'd fixed on them – the ones she never wore. Heels. Polished to a high shine. The ones she'd let me borrow for my seventeenth birthday months earlier. She was wearing her smartest dress, the one with the lace hem. Green. Her favourite colour. Her hands were white.

Her face was purple-blue. I'd screamed, tried to, but the sound was stuck inside my mouth. I couldn't even get her down. I couldn't move from the floor. Must have sat there for an hour before I had the sense to find a telephone. The police – and then Marion and Gran. I never even thought to call my dad.

Now, I gulped several deep breaths, the air burning my throat. Keeping my eyes closed, I made myself breathe for a few minutes. In, and out. *Easy*. When the wave of nausea finally dissipated I dragged myself back onto my feet and took in the scene. There was nobody else in the house; just the two of us.

Or rather, just the one of us.

42

"COME ON, I'LL DRIVE you home. You don't need to see any more of this." Marion's expression was softened by her worry, but she was using the business-like voice I knew to be an attempt at distancing herself from me while she was at work.

"You can't go home yet." Detective Fox appeared behind her, running a hand through his short black hair. His jacket, I noticed, was a little loose, his trousers buckled beyond the worn section on his belt.

He looked at me, but I saw no evidence of the maliciousness from a few days ago. I wondered if Marion had spoken to him. Or if exhaustion had worn away his spite.

"Nobody's taken my statement," I reminded Marion. I gave Fox a small nod, trying to telegraph that I'd be as much help as I could be. But in truth I had nothing to tell him that I hadn't already told Marion when she arrived, screaming onto the driveway with sirens and a couple of uniformed officers. Later came a whole other crew, ambulance techs and crime-scene people, all of whom gave me a wide berth.

And bystanders, too. Word got out fast, and within half an

hour the road was filled with people. Journalists, nosy people I recognised from around town. Somebody mouthed the word *suicide* and I felt my whole body contract. I spotted Earl from the café and his little spaniel – I'd not realised they lived around here – chatting with a little old lady stooped over a cane. Didn't these people have anything better to do?

As we stood at the edge of the driveway, Marion hovered close. I was disorientated, like the world had slowed down tenfold. I could feel the heat of her skin as she pressed her hand to my lower back. I wanted nothing more than to fold myself into her arms, but I held steady.

"What on earth did you think you were doing?" she asked. "For God's sake Cassie, I told you not to go alone for a reason." She shook her head. I couldn't blame her for being mad. "Are you okay?" she added then. No doubt she was thinking about Mum, too.

"Why would he kill himself?" I asked. "He said last night that he wanted to talk to me. He said…"

"Sometimes it's to ensure somebody finds them." Marion said this as kindly as she could, but still I felt the horror worm deep inside of me.

"Why me?" I looked at Marion, whose face was pale and gaunt.

"I don't know."

Fox finished a hushed conversation with one of the paramedics and then headed back over to Marion and me.

"I'll drive Cassie to the station to take her statement if you want to stay here and sort this lot out?" he said.

Marion flashed me a look but I didn't have the energy to protest. Once she was gone, Fox walked me to his car and opened the passenger door. I slid inside, suddenly grateful to be off my jelly legs. I clenched my teeth to stop them chattering and held my hands balled into tight fists.

I hardly noticed as Fox got into the car next to me and turned the ignition. When we didn't move, I glanced over at him. He was staring at me questioningly, one hand on the steering wheel and one on the gear stick. His brown eyes were intense.

I felt the questions burbling beneath my skin, each vying to be the first.

"Was he the person who took Bella?" I blurted.

"There's no evidence that Walker had anybody captive in his house." Fox spoke in a cool, practical tone, apparently content to put aside any issues between the two of us for now.

"Then why did he kill himself?" I said. "There has to be some reason. He must have felt guilty about *something*." I ran my hand through my messy hair, gripping the strands tightly just so I could feel the prickle on my scalp.

"When he rang me last night he was drunk," Fox said. "I think he'd come out of the pub. I could hear people milling around." Fox twisted further in his seat, his eyebrows raised.

"Why is that… Are you saying that you don't think he did it? That somebody else…?"

My brain went into overdrive. Anybody could have heard him on the phone, telling Fox that he wanted to talk. Anybody could have known that he was about to crack. I felt sick.

"I'm not saying anything," Fox said. "I'm certainly not

telling a reporter, off the record, that I think something else is going on here."

He held my gaze. My brain whirred and whirred and I didn't like where my thoughts were taking me. I didn't want to tell Fox that I wasn't even sure I wanted to be a reporter any more.

"Why are you telling me this?" I asked.

Fox sighed, massaging the bridge of his nose. He wasn't going to answer me.

Finally he said, "Marion… She's too good for you."

I felt my stomach drop, but he wasn't finished.

"But you know what? This morning, when she came into work… I haven't seen her like that before. Not ever. She was – the *energy*. I know you did that. So this is me trying to man up. Okay?"

He scowled. We were never going to be friends, but maybe this was good enough. I gave him a quick nod.

"What about the suicide note?" I asked.

"It's not a note. It's just my phone number and your name."

"He knew something," I said. "He definitely knew something."

"Cassie. He wanted to tell *you*. I know you and Marion had been talking about the past. Walker felt like he needed to talk to you for a reason."

My thoughts ground to a halt. If I'd been here an hour earlier, maybe he would still be alive. Maybe I could have done something.

"Maybe it was about Olive," I whispered. "And somebody killed him for it."

* * *

At the station, Fox made me a coffee before sitting me down in the same interrogation room as a couple of days ago. We walked through my morning, slowly. Every time I closed my eyes I saw Darren – or my mother. Hot, sticky guilt made me sick. Actually sick, this time. I didn't even have the energy to apologise when I bolted for the bathroom.

This was my fault. I'd pointed the finger at Darren, he'd tried to talk to me, and now he was dead.

I kept thinking about the note. Not the one he'd left but the one I'd seen years earlier. My brain was stuck in a loop, remembering my mother and the way she had left me.

Cassie, I'm sorry. I tried. It's long overdue. Just let me go and you'll be better off. Nothing works any more, nothing makes the pain stop. This will do it. Mum.

It hadn't made the pain stop. At least, not for me.

By the time I got back to my house it was mid-afternoon. I felt exhausted and shaky, too much caffeine and not enough food making my stomach queasy. I let myself into the house as quietly as I could, in case Gran was napping.

The lounge was empty. Gran's knitting lay in a confused mass of yarn on the arm of one sofa, and her book lay on another. Silently I slipped my shoes off and padded up the stairs. She was in her bedroom, curled up on her side with her bad arm cradled by pillows. I let out a small sigh. I

347

needed a minute before I could face anybody else.

As I stepped back into the hallway my phone let out a plaintive buzz. I went into the bathroom before pulling it out.

you've been hard to find.

My palms grew slick. I gripped the phone hard and tried to breathe slowly. I didn't have my contacts saved on this phone, I reasoned. It could be anybody. But even before the second message came, I knew it wasn't. I knew.

aren't you glad you kept digging around in the dirt? look what you've done. now he's DEAD and it's all YOUR FAULT.

I automatically tried to delete the message before I stopped myself, my hands shaking. My belly clenched, even though I hadn't eaten anything since throwing up at the police station. Bile stung the back of my throat.

It was him. If I wasn't sure before, now I knew.

Who are you? I texted back. *What do you want?*

i told you to leave it alone. back off. last chance.

Or what? I wrote.

No response. I waited for long, hot seconds. Sick and shivering like I had the flu. I hit dial, the number flashing, different from the one I'd told Henry to check.

I didn't know what would happen if somebody answered. But of course they didn't. I was about to throw my phone out of the bathroom window when it started to buzz again. Insistent this time. A call.

My whole body clenched. I swallowed hard, sweat under my arms.

"Hello?"

"She lives! At long last you pick up the bloody phone."

Relief flooded through me at the sound of Henry's familiar voice. I felt salty tears prickle the back of my throat but I held them back.

"Hi," I said. "Now isn't a good time."

"Typical. That's just the kind of reaction I'd expect after I go to all this trouble to find valuable information for you."

I was still trying to calm my breathing, my heart thudding an uneven rhythm.

"Heno," I warned. "That's not funny."

"Sorry. Look, I was just calling about that Walker guy you asked me about—"

"You're too late," I said.

"What? Why?"

"He's dead."

There was a humming quiet as Henry digested this. I wanted him to leave me alone to process it myself, even contemplated putting the phone down, but I didn't do it. Then I realised he'd asked a question.

"What?" I said.

"Foul play?"

"Heno, can we just leave it? We're not helping."

"Well I'm only asking because there was something that was bothering me a bit after we last spoke. That warehouse that Walker's dad sold – Walker only got a small amount of the money. The rest went somewhere else. Walker's had years doing minimum-wage jobs and accruing credit-card debt. It's like the money just disappeared."

"That's weird. Who bought the warehouse?" I asked despite myself.

"I don't know." Henry was tapping his phone again. *Tap-tap, tap-tap-tap.* "I can't find out that easily. But the timing is dodgy, Cass. It looks like it was probably sold six months or so before your sister was abducted. The dad died not long after – heart attack, so if he was involved with anything weird then he isn't now."

"Shit." I let out a long breath. Could this have anything to do with what Walker wanted to tell me? Could whoever bought the warehouse from his father be the person who took Olive – who took Bella? It seemed like a stretch, but it would explain Walker's nervousness, his fear. "Henry, can you find out who he sold it to?"

"It was cash, darling. Hard to trace."

"I know, but can you *try*?" My voice cracked and I swallowed hard. "Sorry. I mean, it might be nothing, or it might be everything. But Walker wanted to talk to me before he died. I need to find out why."

"What are you going to do?"

"I'm going back to where it all started."

43

THERE WERE CHILDREN PLAYING together by the fountain in Chestnut Circle as I came into the centre of town, a couple of mums watching them carefully. I'd left my car at home and was walking briskly, my eyes drawn into the window of every shop selling crystals or magical jewellery. The sun had come out again and was warming the cool afternoon so that I was sweaty as I powered on up the slight hill into the Circle. It was a good feeling, distracting from the horror of the day.

I looked at the face of every child I came across. Most of them were skittish, holding the arms of their parents or friends as though the woman in the black hoodie was dangerous. But then, I supposed, they didn't know that I wasn't. At this point, even I didn't know that for sure. Everybody I'd come into contact with in the last week and a half seemed to have got into some sort of trouble. I saw Darren Walker's distorted features behind my eyelids, the panic and fear, and forced the image away.

I paused for a second at the entrance to the Circle. I'd traced our steps, as best I could remember, from that day in

August sixteen years ago. I tried to recall the image Marion had helped me to generate the previous evening during our meditation. The eclipse as it cooled the air, the darkness that was so mysterious, cloaking everything in a fine mesh of magic. Olive, antsy and frustrated – me, distant and distracted. I examined the Circle from the far side, where I could see Ady's shop and the fountain, along with the spot where the awning had been on Ady's corner.

The awning wasn't there any more, but the street corner still looked the same. Where the striped overhang had curled around the corner into the alley down the side, there was still a pole jutting out of the wall. Now it looked lonely.

There was a small table out there in the alley along with a couple of plastic chairs where people could sit while they ate ice cream looking at the fountain. These hadn't been there back then, and I tried not to think what things might have been like if Olive could have just climbed on top of one of them to fulfil her desire to see better. Maybe she wouldn't have wandered away.

"Why didn't I just listen to you?" I asked as I walked, my voice bringing my thoughts back to the present. I shook my head.

As I approached the shop, I saw a figure standing just outside. A young blonde girl with her legs akimbo as she lifted something from the floor – a pair of paper glasses. As I got closer I recognised her as Ady's daughter.

"Hi," I said, a little breathless.

"Hello." She stepped back cautiously, scuffing her leather school shoes against the tarmac. Her skirt was too long, made for somebody two or three years older, and she plucked at it awkwardly, as though she'd been caught in a lie. "My dad's inside, if you want him. He's working all the time at the moment. I was just trying to see if these make things go 3D. I'm not allowed away from the shop but it's only round the corner—"

"Oh," I said. "No, that's okay. I was just—"

Just what? Just walking the route I'd walked with my sister sixteen years ago on the day she was kidnapped? I was just... what?

"I have to go," Tilly said. "I'll be in trouble. Dad hates when he can't see me. Especially now. He'll freak out."

"No, wait." I held both hands up to show her that I meant no harm. I was surprised when she stopped in her tracks. That didn't usually work. "Listen, you go to the same school as Bella Kaluza, right?" I gestured at her uniform, which was the same as those worn by Bella and Grace and their friends. It hadn't occurred to me before that the girls were probably the same age.

Tilly tilted her head suspiciously, her big circular glasses slipping down her nose. "Why?"

"I just wondered if you know Bella. The girl who's missing."

"Yeah, my dad – he won't talk about her. Like, *at all*. It's really upsetting him. But I watched some stuff on the news last night and this morning. You know, when he wasn't there. Mette – my babysitter – didn't stop me. Anyway, I'm not a *baby*."

"No, you're not," I said, although I thought she was very much a baby. She smiled. "Do you know Bella then?" I asked.

"Not very well. We don't have any classes together. Our

forms are like, opposite. But she seems nice."

"Nice, like friendly?"

"More like… cool. You know? Like, she doesn't take orders from anybody. Even though we're the bottom of the school and the big kids tease us, Bella doesn't care. I always see her talking to the teachers, but she doesn't do it like a teacher's pet. She's not doing it for marks or grades. She's… just grown up. That's all. I think she hangs out with her mum a lot and has lunch with Mr Howden sometimes.

"I met her in the doctor's office once. We have the same doctor. She was even cool then and she had the reddest nose you've ever seen. Dad said it's bad breeding to let your kids get that poorly."

Tilly wrinkled her nose and examined the eclipse glasses. She stopped talking but her expression was expectant, as though she had more to say.

"What do you think?" I pressed.

"I don't know." Tilly shrugged. "She comes into the shop most mornings by herself. Her friends all live in those big houses up near the school but she lives down here like us. She always buys the same thing – in the shop, I mean. So she's not that grown-up, I guess. And I know she doesn't drink coffee. She wears her hair in pigtails sometimes, too."

"What does she buy?" I asked.

"Orange juice – the kind that comes in a box with a straw. Same thing every day." Tilly sniffed, as though this might have been funny if Bella wasn't missing. "Dad won't let me drink those ones because he says they're all sugar. He hardly lets me have anything fun. He says bad food made my mum sick…

"But Bella drinks them every day and she's fine. Sometimes I see her walking with her friends when Mette drives me up to school. Sometimes I see her in here, if Dad drops me off instead."

"You sometimes come in here in the morning before school then?" I asked. I wondered if she had seen Bella the morning of the eclipse. Perhaps she had seen which direction Bella had gone when she left the Circle.

Tilly shrugged. "I used to all the time. Lately Dad won't let me. Says I need to stay home where it's safer. He leaves home pretty early so I'm glad. It means I can spend longer in bed before Mette makes me get up." She smiled, a cheeky smile that made dimples in her cheeks.

"Did you see Bella the morning she went missing?" I asked.

"Nope." Tilly shook her head. "Dad dropped me off at school early because there were gonna be teachers around. He didn't want me to miss any of the eclipse and he won't let me walk to school even though it's not far. *Everybody* was watching the eclipse, though. It was a big deal.

"Dad says in other places they don't care as much as we do. But Bishop's Green is cool like that, isn't it? Everything's sort of magic if you think about it. My history teacher was telling us all about the history of eclipses, about how they're even in the Bible. He said they're like ancient magic. We talked about it a lot. He knows a lot about that stuff.

"Anyway, you know the whole thing took like *two hours*. Dad says it's bad luck to miss the beginning. Did you know that during the last eclipse there was this big party? But that was during the school holidays and it was years and years ago."

Now she was talking the kid wouldn't shut up.

"What about Bella?" I pressed. "Did your dad say if he saw her? If she was acting weirdly or anybody was with her?"

"He didn't say, but I think he feels bad that he doesn't know what happened."

Inside, Ady was unpacking a crate of juice. He stopped when he saw my face.

"What's up?" he asked.

"Bella," I said, the word coming out like a squeak. "She comes in here every day. Did you tell the police?"

"I – no. I didn't think it was – I didn't…" He faltered, a look of sadness passing over his face. "They didn't ask me."

"Did she come in on Friday morning?" I pressed.

Ady dropped the crate and headed towards the till, where there was a little screen for the CCTV.

"Maybe?" he said. "I don't know. I didn't even think anything of it – she always…" His face was ashen. He fiddled with a box and the screen flickered. I didn't wait for him to ask, I simply stepped around the back of the till and stood next to him.

"Can't you remember?" I asked.

Ady shook his head, mute.

"Ady—"

"All the days are the same," he muttered. He wiped at the stubble on his chin. "I feel awful. I don't know…"

He was moving through footage on a tape or a recording,

now. I watched as the time stamp morphed, precious minutes passing in fuzzy monochrome.

"There," I said.

Ady hit play. Bella had walked into the shop. She headed for the drinks cabinet to the side of the till, rooting for one at the back.

"She always does that," Ady said, and his voice was full of emotion. As though he was thinking the same thing I was. How easy it would be for somebody to learn her routine and follow her. For somebody to lure her.

Ady wasn't at the counter in the recording. Bella glanced around. Waited a second. And then left a pile of change on the till.

Ady, beside me now, let out a breath of what might have been relief.

"I didn't think," he said softly. "I couldn't remember. I didn't think I had. I had a delivery I was unpacking. That might have been the day I spilled the rice…"

In the recording, Bella glanced up suddenly. Looked towards the door, where the CCTV cut off. Somebody had distracted her. Her lips moved in recognition. She grabbed her juice box and hurried to the door. And then she was gone.

"The police need a copy of that recording," I said. My voice shook so badly I wasn't sure Ady heard me. But he nodded.

44

"WE'LL GET SOMEBODY ON the CCTV immediately," Marion said. She leaned against the wall outside the police station, her arms folded across her chest and her buttons straining as she stretched. "It sounds like Bella knew the person who approached – maybe it was the person who took her."

I stood with my back to the car park, shivering a little in the cold wind. It was getting dark now. Cars were parked in all the spaces, but most of them weren't cops. Marion had told me about all of the people who'd been camping out at the station since Bella disappeared. The thought that I'd been one of them not long ago filled me with a strange mixture of longing and disgust.

I lit my cigarette. So much for quitting, but smoking did have some benefits; Marion was very close to me, her head bent low, and when she moved closer I felt safer.

"I wish we knew who it was," I murmured. "I wish we could find her."

"I know." Marion sighed. "Anyway, we've confirmed that Walker's body was moved post-mortem. He died in the early hours of the morning." She met my gaze.

"He was dead – all that time?" I asked. "And hanged *after* he was dead?" I didn't like to admit the relief that tinged the sickness in my stomach; I couldn't have helped him. I didn't even know he wanted to talk to me until after he was dead.

"Looks like it." Marion pulled back and I shivered again. I still felt awful. *look what you've done.* I'd shown Marion the latest texts but they still got under my skin. They were apparently having no luck tracing the number, which didn't make me feel any better. "Ligature marks around his neck were consistent with the width of the rope, but Fox said that the position was all wrong. He was strangled before he was strung up."

"Shit," I said.

A shadow crossed Marion's face, and she turned away, gazing out into the car park. "Whoever did it knew enough to try to hide what had happened, although they were too late. And there's little trace, no DNA."

"Why didn't they just leave him where he died?" I asked.

"He wasn't killed in the house. There was some dust on Walker's jeans, but his house was spotless. No signs of a struggle either. It seems likely that he was killed elsewhere and then taken home. And there were no defence wounds."

"No defence wounds," I said hollowly. "So he probably knew the killer?"

Marion chewed on her lip. "That seems likely."

"Just like Bella probably knew who took her." We smoked for a minute in silence. Then I said, "It's got to be somebody who she wouldn't have been afraid of seeing out there on a school

359

day. Somebody she was expecting, maybe? Or somebody who had reason to be nearby?"

My thoughts went back to Howden outside the shop. *I only live over there.*

"Perhaps an authority figure for her," Marion said thoughtfully. "Children – they trust certain groups more than others. Doctors, teachers, parents. People they see a lot."

I rubbed the goosebumps on my arms. It could be that easy. Somebody she knew, a face she recognised. An offer of a lift to school. I'd thought this before but now I was more convinced this was something like what had happened.

"I'm going to go through that footage again," Marion said. "I'll see you later."

Then she leaned in to kiss my cheek. Right here, right outside work, careless of who might see her. Her breath was warm. I allowed myself a small smile.

At home I made sure that Gran ate dinner – and managed to force some food into my own stomach, too. Then I headed to the bar at Henry's hotel. Bella had been gone almost five days. Over a hundred hours since the eclipse. *A hundred and eight hours, but who's counting?*

I sat down with a thump, all my energy draining out of me.

"You look knackered," Henry said.

I rolled my eyes.

"Thanks. So what did you find out about the warehouse situation?"

"It's all a bit of guesswork, but it looks like it was sold to a—" Henry shifted his glass of whiskey to the side and my mouth watered. "Neil White. Fifty-two years—"

"Not *Doctor* White?" The room seemed to shrink. Suddenly the dark walls felt close and claustrophobic instead of cosy. I unzipped my hoodie. "*My* Doctor White?"

"Unless there's more than one at the practice near the Circle."

My ears were ringing. I felt like I might pass out. I reached blindly for Henry's glass and took a swig. He watched with an inscrutable look.

"What on earth does a doctor need with a warehouse, Heno?"

"I'm sure there are lots of legitimate reasons," Henry said, but he didn't look convinced. I wasn't thinking of the legitimate reasons; I was thinking of the smell of oranges from that summer, how it had lingered in his office. I thought about his bowl of trinkets. I pictured the mermaid ring. The sleeping pills that made Gran pliant; that could make a child pliant too.

"Cassie, are you okay? You look unwell."

I sucked in a breath. Thought of the way he'd spoken to me after Gran's accident. As though it had been my fault. And of his concern for Bella, how she wouldn't have had any reason to be afraid of him.

"*Cassie.*"

"I'm okay," I said faintly. My heart hammered. I thought I might be sick. "Talk to me."

Henry watched me with hawk eyes but obliged. "Uh, it looks like he's been paying electricity on it but not loads. I spoke to Walker's mother. A close friend of the family convinced Walker Senior to sell because he desperately needed money and they arranged it sort of like an off-the-record loan. Apparently Mrs Walker didn't like the idea of selling it in the first place, especially not to a doctor because what on earth could he want it for?"

"Could that be what Darren wanted to tell me?" I said, more to myself than to Henry. "That he thought his dad sold the warehouse to – the man who…"

I was shaking. "I need to go," I said. "I need… I need to make sure – Gran..."

Doctor White. *Doctor White.*

45

THE BRUISES WERE COMING out, now. Their purpleness was livid almost. As though her skin couldn't believe what she'd let him do. Olive inspected the injuries in the wan light of the afternoon. A wet day, rain pattered against the glass where it dripped from the roof. She wished, not for the first time, that she could smell the air.

The bruises were about two inches across. One on each thigh, on the inside so she had to sit with them slightly apart today. It was her own fault, really. She should have known better than to protest after he'd fought with his wife. That was when he was most volatile, and Olive knew that better than anybody.

Absently she wondered what his wife thought of him. Whether that woman knew where he was going when he left to see the girl he held captive. One evening a week for nearly four years and she hadn't become suspicious? Maybe that's why they were fighting more recently. Maybe she suspected something was up but couldn't quite put her meek little finger on it. Sandman said his wife knew about Olive, but she didn't believe it. Couldn't believe that somebody would let her suffer like this.

Olive had only seen her once – way back before Sandman took her. She was beautiful in that sort of storybook way: midnight hair, snowy skin, so thin and frail a sharp wind could knock her over. Artistic, Olive had thought back then. Now she definitely thought the woman might be stupid.

When had Olive become so callous? So mean? Probably it was always that way. She couldn't be brave so she got angry. Olive was used to the anger, now. She nursed it like a cold stone in the middle of her belly. After all, teenagers were prone to anger. She still remembered Cassie's fits of rage. Cassie – for ever thirteen in Olive's mind – was almost an adult now. Olive had seen an article Cassie had written for the *Chronicle* last summer, had been impressed with how grown up her sister had sounded.

She wondered if she'd sound as grown up. Probably not, since her entire world was formed only by the books she read and the bad news she couldn't help but devour. Sandman said it gave her a sort of *graveness* that made her seem older. Olive figured that was just an excuse for him to act the way he did.

As she pressed experimentally against one of the bruises, she relished the pain that blossomed in her leg. It kept her anchored. More and more lately she'd been avoiding reading anything at all, just sitting on her bed like she had done those first days. Staring at walls. She was tired of drawing, tired of writing. She wished he'd never broken the TV.

She still had a newspaper from three days ago, which she brushed with one hand idly as she poked at the bruises with her other. She was putting it off, but it was inevitable. Eventually she'd become so bored that she had to read it.

She might as well start now. The bulk of the stuff in there would probably be the same old small-town rubbish. Garden shows, prize winners, empty buildings set alight (that had happened two weeks ago and Olive had been embarrassed to realise it was the most interested she'd been in the news in weeks). The list went on.

She made herself a tepid cup of tea in the microwave, wondering idly for the hundredth time whether she could keep enough water boiling that she could throw it at Sandman when he came to see her next. It really was an idle thought. She'd never do it. She knew that the room – wherever she was – was inside some sort of secure facility. He'd told her as much, though what he wouldn't say. It would do no good to just hurt him. If he survived something like that, Olive knew she'd have no chance. And if he didn't survive she might never get out anyway.

So she took the tea back to the bed and opened the paper. These days she started with the obituaries. Morbid, perhaps, but that way she got to the better stuff last. Then the births, then the people selling cats and dogs.

Then the news.

And then she wished she'd not waited three days. She wished she'd not made her tea first, or gone through the obituaries before the news.

It couldn't be true.

Olive felt the familiar tightening of her chest, the dizziness that she associated with panic attacks ever since she'd read a book where a character had one. She tried to count to ten in her head. *One, two, three…* But the words stared up at her and she couldn't do it.

Mother of missing girl found dead in suspected suicide.

The words rattled inside her skull as though she'd spoken them aloud. Maybe she had. She felt sick, her whole body suddenly heavy. Her heart fluttered and she realised she was gripping the paper.

Suicide.

Her mum was dead.

She didn't know if she could bear to read the whole article – but she also knew she couldn't bear not to. The photograph at the top of the page showed a house. Not their childhood home but a smaller one. A bungalow. Olive couldn't tell how big it was, or where it was, but she knew without knowing why that this was her mum's house. There was just something about it.

The article focused on Olive more than her mum. Olive saw her own picture staring up at her, and realised with horror that this was the first time she'd seen herself in the newspaper. Sandman had shielded her all the other times. But when he'd brought this paper, he'd said something that didn't make sense – not until now.

"I hope this makes you appreciate your life here," he'd said. Straight-faced, too. And then he'd turned off the lights and climbed into bed with her, and that was that.

Now his words rang loudly. He knew she'd see this. He knew her mum was dead. He knew… And he'd let her see it anyway.

Olive was surprised to feel anger. Towards her mother, some, towards Dad and his new bit on the side. Even towards Cassie, although she knew that was stupid. But mostly she was angry at Sandman. For letting her see this. Wasn't he supposed to protect her? That was what he always said.

She remembered him saying it on the day that it all started. That day when he'd given her the mood ring as a gift while Cassie waited for her. That was back when she had thought he was kind. When she trusted him.

"Circles protect you," he'd said conspiratorially. "Did you know that? Symbolically, circles are pretty neat. A circle of salt is said to ward off evil; a circle of silver – this ring – will help you. Spiritually proven."

Funny to think that, even then, she could have avoided what happened. If it hadn't been for Mum hurting her arm that time. If he hadn't noticed. If she hadn't stopped to listen to another theory about circles, about solar eclipses, over a free slice of clementine… If she hadn't made herself known to him, he might never have come back for her.

After all he'd said about her innocence, how could he do this to her now?

There was a line in the article – right there. Right near the picture of Olive's face. It mentioned a "local man who has now helped to arrange vigils for both mother and daughter". She shivered. Was it him? Sandman? But it wasn't *him*. It would be his other self, the one in town who nobody was afraid of. Despair threatened to swallow her.

Olive felt the tears on her cheeks, and she pressed the newspaper to her face. Felt the slightly tacky surface against her skin. Inhaled the familiar smells of newsprint and the faint trace of her own soap.

She searched for the anger again. Anger made her feel better. She thought about Dad and his new family.

Mum was the last thing. The final part of her life that was still there, still unchanged. When Olive felt brave enough to think about her family, she knew her mum would be the same – the same stubborn, beautiful woman that she had always been.

And now she was gone.

Mechanically, Olive let the newspaper drop to the bed and rescued her tea from spilling. She took a sip. Now there was nobody else. Just Cassie. But Cassie, to her, was still a kid. Just a kid.

Two kids didn't make a family.

46

HOT PANIC COURSED THROUGH me as I careened back into town. Gran was at home alone, no nurse or watcher this late, and I was suddenly seized by her vulnerability. I had thought she'd be okay for an hour, settled with a jigsaw and the radio. A man like Doctor White... I remembered the look on Gran's face when he'd visited the house. She would trust him.

I felt stupid but I was afraid. Properly scared. I tried Marion's phone on Bluetooth but got three rounds of answerphone. I didn't have anybody else – so I called my father.

He heard the panic in my voice and for once he didn't shy away.

"I'll be at yours in half an hour," he said.

The house was quiet when I arrived. I pushed down the worry, the nausea, and let myself in. But Gran was there. She was fine. Of course, he wouldn't waste his time on me when he could be with Bella. I bolted to the upstairs toilet and spent five minutes over the bowl trying not to hurl.

When Dad turned up it was clear that I'd caught him working late. It was almost eight and he was still dressed in smart trousers and one of his many dark-brown jackets. It was the first time he'd been to the house since the funeral, and I could see he was awkward as he stepped into the lounge, but he tried to hide it.

"Want a cuppa?" he asked.

I couldn't hold it in. "Dad. No. I don't know. God. *Doctor White*. Do you know him? Do you – is he…"

"Whoa, Cass. What's got into you?" He guided me into the kitchen. He sat me at the table while he made tea and then got me to explain. I couldn't get my words out fast enough.

"The *warehouse*," I said again. Dad's face was slack with confusion. "Darren Walker's dad sold it to Doctor White. Doctor White – people trust him. And now Walker's dead. I didn't… Marion won't answer her phone. I'm freaking out."

"Cassie, take a deep breath. I don't understand. We've known the doctor for – for years. Since you were a kid. He's a nice guy."

"What does he need a warehouse for, then?" I asked, trying to keep my voice down, aware of Gran in the next room.

Dad ran a hand through his hair. "His wife was an artist or something – I think she used the space for that? I vaguely remember your mother going to some exhibit that she put on there. I remember your grandad telling me about it. He knew her from one of his art classes. Got it off a patient – Walker's dad, I guess – super cheap because he wanted a quick sale."

I hadn't realised that Dad was holding my hand on the table. I came to myself slowly, like blood returning to my limbs, and withdrew my arm. Now I was calmer I could see with an icy sort of detachment how terrified I was.

"Quick sale?" I asked.

"Yeah. Something about pressure from somebody who was close to the family. Like a loan." Dad's eyes were steely. "Cassie, take a breath. You look like you're about to keel over. Listen, I'm gonna go and get you some of those Bach remedy drops – the calming ones. I have some in my car. You stay there."

I hardly noticed him leaving. The panic had made my senses dull. I barely even registered when my phone started to buzz; I only answered it in the hope that it would be Marion telling me I was wrong. I didn't know what to do. Didn't even know where to start.

But it wasn't Marion. It was Henry.

He didn't wait for me to say anything, just launched straight in with, "Cassie, I think I figured out where some of the money went. From the warehouse sale."

I didn't think I could take any more. "Where?"

"The family friend's name is Adrian—"

Adrian. I felt my blood run cold. Ady?

"*Jacobs?* I didn't realise they were friends." I wondered if he knew about Darren's death.

"Yeah. I don't have a lot of information about him. Just that his wife's a recluse—"

"Was," I corrected. "His wife died when their daughter was a baby."

"Right. Well there's a lot out there about him but a whole lot less about her. Quite the charity man, isn't he?"

I thought of the vigils. Of the searches. My brain was going in circles. The same searches attended by Doctor White. Jake Howden.

"So, the money – what happened to it?" I wasn't sure I wanted to know the answer. I needed my dad to come back. I needed—

"He used it to buy a small storage unit for his shop. Number eleven. Eleven…" Henry mused. "I'm seeing that number everywhere. Bella, Olive…"

In the Bible, I knew from my childhood reading, the number eleven meant disorder, chaos and judgement. Judgement of whom? The eclipse, the ages of the children… It was like history was repeating itself. And I was just as stupid and powerless now as I was then.

I didn't know what to say. I didn't know what to believe any more.

Dad came back into the room with a little spray bottle in his hand. "Henry, I'll call you back," I said. I put the phone down, numb with new fear. "Dad, what do you know about Ady?"

"Corner-shop Ady?" he asked. "We were friendly enough back in the day. He was always a nice man. Did a lot for charity. Your mum went to the same school as him – Arboretum Secondary. I think he was a few years ahead. Actually, Kathy was friends with the lady that he married – Annabelle somebody."

"What was she like?" I asked. "Annabelle, I mean."

"Eh…" Dad shrugged. "Quiet. Very awkward. Skinny as a rake. She reminded me of a bird, all nerves and twitches. She and your mum were close until Annabelle started dating Ady. She got a bit distant after that. But Ady… He really brought her out of her shell – at least for a little while. Although he was very protective."

"What happened?"

"I don't know. She just… She was always sort of a hermit, but then I think she got sick. Looked like some sort of digestive thing. She was always skinny but she got really bad. She looked *gaunt*. She started wearing these really weird clothes, really childish, and covering her mouth when she spoke. And then she stopped coming out completely. We all thought it was some sort of eating disorder. I heard she overdosed in the end, though I don't know how true that is. Rumours, you know."

I let this information sink in, an image of an emaciated waif, Edgar Allan Poe-style, coming to mind. But what did Ady and Darren have to do with Olive? With Bella?

"You need to be careful, Cass. You can't let your life be defined by this – by the tragedy of losing Olive. If you do, you'll lose yourself – that beautiful, brave part of you that cares for people."

"I don't know what else to do," I said softly. "I need to find her. I need—"

"Did you hear he had a baby?" Gran's voice floated from the dining room. I followed the sound. She was on her feet, holding my Olive Diary between both hands – but she didn't seem to know what it was. She hadn't opened it yet.

I felt my heart stutter.

"Oh, Gran," I said, moving so I could take the book from her but she held it close to her chest. She looked between me and Dad, a brief moment of lucidity making her eyes clear.

"She had a baby but we didn't even know she was pregnant," Gran said firmly, holding tightly onto the diary as I tried to pry it from her hands. "She got thinner and thinner. Like she was trying to disappear. And then she died."

Silence fell. Gran let go of the diary as I pulled again and it tumbled to the floor. I dropped to my knees, eager to gather the bits up before Dad could see them. But it was too late. He knelt down too, and picked up a photo of Olive that had fallen from the cover.

"This is a nice one," he said. His jaw worked as though he was trying to figure out what to say next. Whether to reprimand me, or what. In the end, he settled for a sad smile and a memory. "You always hated when she stole your things. I remember the god-awful fights."

He handed the photo to me and got to his feet.

"Listen, I'm gonna pop off. It was nice to see you – both. But I need to get home. Carol and Hailey..." He trailed off. "If you're okay now...?"

I nodded, distracted.

Because I'd just noticed the hair clip. The one in the shape of an owl, sort of brass-coloured. A cold sweat broke out right down my spine.

I'd seen it recently.

I drove to Marion's house at top speed. I gripped the spare key she had given me like a lifeline, but once inside I didn't turn on the lamps in her hallway or the lounge, feeling that this was almost too intimate. Instead I turned on the harsh ceiling lights that cast long shadows. I made the stairs two at a time, stumbling straight into Marion's makeshift incident room to find it as chaotic as it had been last night.

I knelt on the floor among the papers, interviews and photos, maps of police searches. I didn't even know what I was looking for. I tried Marion's phone again, got nothing.

I found my own statement among the sheaves of paper. And Marion's. Written up in Ben Adams' looping, jerky cursive, I saw my own words. *I just looked away for a minute... I wasn't paying attention... Gran told me to keep an eye on her.*

And then, I saw it. Ady. Ady who had been part of each step of the recent investigation, who had helped look for Grace and Bella and probably Olive, too. I'd seen him on the news, outside the school, his curly hair familiar and nearly invisible. I remembered what he'd told me, how he hadn't remembered seeing Olive or had anything useful to tell the police. If the police never spoke to him then why was his name written here?

I readjusted my glasses as they slipped and bent lower over the paper, squinting my eyes to read Detective Adams' writing better. Next to the typed script of a run-down of patrons in Chestnut Circle, I noticed a pencil note in the margins.

Witness remembered seeing Olive Warren that morning. Couldn't pinpoint precise time. She bought a can of Coke and left. Nothing suspicious about her behaviour, or about behaviour of any other patrons present at the time.

There was the pattern. Not a doctor but a shopkeeper. *The centre of the Circle.* A friendly face Olive and Bella wouldn't be afraid of. Ady with his mysterious dead wife who dressed younger than she was and disappeared off the face of the earth; the storage unit he'd bought with Darren Walker's money. The can of Coke he didn't remember selling. The eclipse. A circle, a do-over, a symbolic fresh start he'd been talking about to his daughter ever since...

Ady.

47

I LEFT MARION ANOTHER voicemail as I screamed into Chestnut Circle, my car bumper scraping over the pavement as I pulled up. I thought about calling Fox, too, but what if I was just going round in circles again? A few hours ago I'd been convinced our doctor was guilty.

I didn't bother with my jacket, or even locking the car as I climbed out. As I reached the doors I realised that something wasn't right. The light was too weak. Only the security lights were on.

Closed.

I went up to the shop, tried the door. Jiggled the handle. I glanced at my watch. It was just after nine. I was too late to talk to him. I could never remember whether the shop shut at nine or ten. Last night must have been a fluke. I was kicking myself, panic making my movements jerky.

"You just missed him. The night-time girl is on holiday."

A voice made me jump and I snapped to attention. An elderly man stood just a couple of feet away with a walking stick propping him upright.

"Rachel normally shuts at ten but he said he's been running it himself this week on account of her holiday."

"What?" I asked, my brain trying to catch up.

"The shop. Normally it closes at ten but the lady who works the lates is on holiday. I guess he nipped off early tonight. He's got a young daughter, so he's probably looking after her. I've noticed he's opened up later the last couple of days too. Can't blame him, really."

The man let out a wet rattling cough.

I felt my face paling as my heartbeat skipped erratically. I remembered what Tilly had said earlier, about how her dad wouldn't let her come to the shop with him before school any more. How he'd been leaving home to get to the shop *earlier* in the morning, not later, and yet I'd seen him opening at closer to 10 a.m. A hot wave of fear rolled over me.

Back in the car I fumbled for my phone. Nothing from Marion.

I knew where he lived, just a few streets away from Gran. I'd seen him pulling up once or twice, shopping bags in the back of his car and Tilly helping him to unload. I pictured the house, which was small but nice enough. Well maintained, even in the winter, with fresh paint on the wooden window frames and neatly trimmed window boxes.

It had always struck me as a pleasant thing, how organised he seemed. How hard he worked to keep his daughter safe. Now as I pulled up, I was struck by another feeling. Wasn't it weird how perfect everything appeared? How nice his house was, how orderly? There wasn't a broken plant stem or dirty smudge on a window in sight. It was too clean, too perfect. Just like his shop.

Almost like somebody hiding something.

I leapt out of my car with the motor still running. The lights were on in the downstairs windows, but the curtains were all drawn. I pushed my way through the garden gate and was banging on the door in seconds, making the lucky horseshoe above rattle loudly.

But when the door swung open I couldn't make myself speak. This was Ady I was talking about. I knew him, didn't I? Tilly stood in the doorway, her hair a mess and chocolate smudged on her upper lip. She wiped at it with her index finger and tried not to look confused.

"Oh, hello. I thought you might be my dad being silly."

"He isn't home?" I tried to keep the alarm out of my voice, but I failed miserably. Tilly glanced just behind her, stepped back a little.

"Uh, no. He's at work. He said he wouldn't be very late tonight."

"He's not th—" I stopped myself. "He's not here?"

"No." Tilly's frown deepened and she stepped further inside her house. "Um, hang on." She craned her neck back. "Mette? Can you come here please?"

There was a pause and then I heard the shuffling footsteps of a woman in slippers. She appeared at the door, grey hair pinned back at the neck and glasses hanging on a chain against the buttons of her blue cardigan.

"Who are you?" she asked in accented English.

379

"My name is— It really doesn't matter who I am. Where is he?"

The woman folded her arms across her chest and frowned at me.

"I'm Cassie," I said. "Cassie Warren. I know Ady. I'm… looking for him."

"He is at work," Mette said. She waved her hand dismissively. "Open late."

"No he isn't. He isn't there. I've just been there." I hadn't intended to say this in front of Tilly, but I couldn't help it. She looked at me with alarm, and then glanced up at Mette who made another hand gesture.

"Well, he is on his way home then," she said. "He will be here soon. He has been working late these last two weeks. Tilly, you go inside now. Finish your homework. Or else your father will not be happy again."

Tilly was instantly cowed. She disappeared without another word.

"I need to find him," I said, desperation making me sound crazy.

"Well, I cannot help you."

Then she closed the door in my face. I ran back to my car, my skin prickling with fear. There was only one place left to try.

48

1 May 2003

IT WASN'T TRUE. IT couldn't be. There was nothing she'd ever wanted less than this. And yet there it was. And all the other things started to make sense. Although deep down Olive had known for a little while.

She sat on the bed with her hands between her knees, knowing that eventually she'd have to call him back into the room. He was just outside – had stepped out for that, at least. But the display of courtesy wouldn't extend to going away and never coming back.

Olive felt the sickness roiling, the usual feeling of being trapped replaced by this feeling of being at sea, awash with feelings and a nausea she couldn't fight. She swallowed hard, and made a squeaking noise that was meant to be a word.

He heard her. Came inside, locked the door in one fluid motion. Her hands were shaking so she pushed them together harder with her knees. He met her gaze.

"Well?"

She nodded towards the little table in the centre of the room. She had sat at it that morning to paint Cassie – what she remembered of Cassie. Every time she drew her sister she was sure the picture got further and further away from the truth. But this time she had been relatively pleased with the outcome; while looking not much like her sister, the face was realistic and she was pleased with the shape of the nose – something she had struggled with before.

But now on the table there were no paintings and paintbrushes. No food. Just an empty mug and, next to it, a little white stick. She watched as Sandman gravitated towards it, picking it up despite his rules about hygiene and where the stick had just been.

He let out a crowing sound. She was sure it was delight, but the sound chilled her right through. She realised – in that moment – that this was worse. That she was more afraid than she had ever been before.

This… This feeling was like somebody had thrown her full force off a thirty-storey building. The world had suddenly dropped out beneath her.

And he was smiling. She thought he was, at least. She could hardly see through the blur.

"A family," he said, very quietly. He cradled the stick in his hands as though he already had the baby. Olive felt the sickness rise in her again, but this time she made no effort to control it. Come on then, she thought. Come out. All over the bloody carpet. He'd love that.

But once again, her body betrayed her. She couldn't make the vomit come up because she wanted to. Couldn't push it down either. So it sat, rumbling inside her, along with the beast he had created.

"A proper family," he repeated.

"What about your wife?"

Anger made Olive brave. Braver than she'd been in a long time. The way he held that stick was a mistake on his part. She knew his wife couldn't have children – or wouldn't, perhaps. Olive still didn't know how much Annabelle knew about her husband, whether she saw the monster that hid beneath his normal-seeming skin. Maybe that's why she'd never given him what he wanted and popped out a couple of innocent kids. Or maybe, just maybe, Sandman was the one making Annabelle sick. She wouldn't put it past him.

Olive knew then that Sandman wouldn't hurt *her*. Not now she had what he wanted. And the anger was there, inside her, bubbling out. She saw that she had been given a bargaining chip. Or at the very least she had something she hadn't had before.

"Is she out of the picture now? Your wife? What're you gonna do? Tell her you found a baby on the street? Tell her I'm just some cousin who can't take care of a child? Or are you just gonna beat her up and put her in a box too?"

Olive was breathless, but she saw that Sandman was more surprised than angry. As if he had never contemplated this part of the equation.

"Of course not." He shook his head. "Nothing like that."

"Well, what then?" Hope fluttered beneath the anger, but she pushed it down. "You'll just let me out of here, will you? What about doctors and things?"

"You don't need any. It's a contained facility. You're safe

here. You're not exposed to anything. It's safer in here than outside."

"I can't do it on my own."

"Of course you can. Women have been bearing children since the dawn of the human race! It's not like you can't take care of yourself." He gestured around wildly, and she realised just how crazy he was.

Crazier than she'd thought. More naïve.

Stupid, she thought. *I was stupid to think he'd let me leave.*

"You're just going to leave me here? What about—"

"I don't think now is the time to discuss it. Don't worry your pretty little head. I'll sort it out. There are ways to sort these things out." Sandman cut her off and his expression changed. He was growing angry. Olive reined in the urge to scream at him.

"It's still early days," he added. "I don't want you to upset yourself. I'd hate for anything to happen."

He looked at her belly. There was nothing there yet. Not that she could see. Especially nothing that he could see. He was making a point. There wasn't a baby yet. Nothing to protect, yet. Not really − not for him.

Olive wrapped one hand over her stomach almost instinctively. Not out of love, but out of a deep, almost painful desire to protect the one asset she had. The one thing she had that he didn't.

Sandman took that as a sign that he'd done his job. He smiled again, taking the little white stick with him as he left. She knew he'd probably return in a couple of days with flowers. Probably vitamins. Doing all the stuff he thought a good dad should do.

Olive waited until the door clicked shut and the sounds of his steps retreated before she stood. Stretched. Fetched her makeshift journal out from under the bed. And she started to write. She would write it all down, as best she could. Her handwriting wasn't great – had never really progressed past her eleven-year-old scrawl – but it would do.

She didn't worry about how long it would take. This, and the drawings, would be enough. To plan, to work things out. After all, time was the one thing she did have. And bravery didn't come overnight.

49

WHEN MARION FINALLY RANG I was driving. "Thank God, Marion." The words flooded out of my mouth. "I've been trying to call you—"

"We had a sighting. It was a bust. What's this about you knowing who took Bella?" Marion asked. I heard the worry in her voice. The panic. But also the excitement.

"It's Ady, Marion." I swore, a gulping sob strangling my words. "It's Ady. I know it."

"But—"

"I think he built up a relationship with her. Friendly. Gave her the mood ring – just like he gave it to Olive. She's there every day. He had the opportunity. She knew him. There was nobody else was in the shop. She bought her usual drink. Not even a can but one of those cartons. You could easily inject all sorts into one of those—"

"Cassie, I don't understand. You *know* Ady, don't you?"

"Yes, I know him. He's always been nice to me. But there's so much I didn't know. Stuff about his wife – she died suddenly. My dad told me he'd heard she overdosed. All the pieces fit. He has a storage unit." I wanted so desperately to be wrong. Like I had been about Doctor White. About Darren Walker. But I knew that I hadn't really been wrong about them; they were all wrapped up in this somehow, whether they knew it or not.

"Cassie…"

"He lied," I said. "About seeing Olive, about Bella. He knew them both. He knew Olive. And she… she wouldn't have been afraid of him."

"Cassie, you're driving." Marion sounded afraid. "What are you going to do?"

"I told you," I said. "I got the address from Henry. I'm going to bring Bella home." I ended the call before she could stop me.

It was the eclipse. The *eclipse* had started it all. As I drove, I knew this. Knew that the feeling in my gut was right, that I had been right all along. Somebody had told me once that in Hindu mythology eclipses were believed to be caused by serpent demons sucking away the light that gives life. Sucking away life…

That was exactly what Ady was doing. Taking girls during the darkness, using a time meant for new beginnings to start his own fresh game.

I felt used and dirty, remembering the times we had spent together at various charity events over the last two months; he was always eager to help, to buy me coffee, to volunteer late, even to close up shop early to get to venues in time to set up.

I thought about Darren Walker. Darren had known Ady for

years. His family had provided Ady with the money to buy his storage unit. Now I understood why he'd clammed up when Marion had asked him about Olive's mood ring; why he had wanted to talk to me. Because he'd learned something.

He was going to tell me what he knew – that his friend had abducted and held two little girls in a storage unit less than five miles from where Olive was last seen. That he was afraid.

And that's why Ady had killed him.

50

I DROVE AT CLOSE to seventy down the small country lanes, avoiding the centre of town and the traffic as rain started to pour from the heavens. I flicked on the windscreen wipers but was forced to slow down seconds later. I cursed under my breath, and then louder. I had never been to Ady's storage unit before but it was easy to find.

As the rain slammed against my windscreen, I peered through the glass into the darkness. Ady's unit was in an old industrial estate just on the other side of town. It was only small, with perhaps twelve or so squat units and office buildings in the area around a turn-circle, and I'd heard that most of the businesses that used the units did so as overflow for less urgent or bulk stock. It was quiet during the day and deserted at night.

I headed towards the gates of the industrial estate at full pelt, and had to slam on my brakes when I saw that they were shut. If they were locked, I was fucked. I parked half on the road, leaving my headlights on so I could see what I was doing. There was a large padlock on the middle of the gates. And it was very locked – with a combination and everything. Only the unit owners must have had access.

"Fuck!" I slammed my hand against the metal bars of the gate, which were already dripping with the heavy rain.

I immediately started to look around for something I could climb on. A box, a crate, anything. Eventually, I gave up. There was nothing. The rain poured into my eyes and streaked my glasses, sticking my hair to my forehead as the water dripped down my neck and back. I got back into my car, the windows steaming almost immediately. And then I had an idea.

Carefully, I inched the car forward. I pulled right up to the gate. Right up, inching closer and closer, until the front bumper touched. There was a metal clink, a thud, and then I put the handbrake on and got out of the car.

It was difficult, given the rain and the slick surface of my car's bonnet, but I managed to haul myself up onto it. I swung one leg over the arched top of the gate, feeling the water seep through the thigh of my jeans. Then I hauled my other leg over, and in a fluid motion I threw myself down onto the other side.

I landed hard, a shooting pain jarring my knees. My legs were soaking now, my shoes not waterproof and my socks soaking up the rain. I squelched onwards, realising too late that I'd left my car lights on with the key in the ignition. But I didn't stop. Instead I started to jog. I counted until I hit number 11. The industrial units all faced inwards around the turn-circle. I looked for Ady's van but couldn't see it.

I considered for a second: how stupid was I?

I headed straight for it.

There was no sign out front, and it was just an ordinary

grey brick building. It was weathered, not so well cared for as Ady's home, but it blended in perfectly with the buildings around it. Fear made my movements jerky but I didn't stop.

The door itself looked like solid metal. On the far side I noticed a roller shutter, but it was closed. I tried the door. It was locked. The roller shutter too.

"Goddammit."

Did I really think that Ady was this evil? To have stolen a child? Two children? The same man who'd plied me with many a cup of free coffee. Who had at one point been my only friend in town?

A shiver of pure anger flowed through me and I realised that was exactly what I thought. So I scooted around to the side of the building, and found a window. It was small, perhaps only for a toilet or a smaller storage room. It was nothing more than a small pane of single-glazed glass. This time I didn't stop to consider whether what I was doing was stupid. I thought about what had happened at Darren Walker's house when I hadn't waited for help. My phone had been vibrating since I'd hung up on Marion but I hadn't dared to read the texts in case she convinced me to go home.

Now I made myself look. A stream of messages.

where are you?

Cassie what are you doing?

Cassie CALL ME NOW

I typed up the address and hit send. Just in case. I still didn't really believe that this was happening.

Then I grabbed a rock.

The window gave with a satisfying smash. I listened intently, waiting for something to happen. But if anybody was here, if anybody had heard me, they didn't do anything about it. I waited for another ten seconds. Twenty. And then I used the sleeve of my hoodie over the rock to break out the rest of the glass.

I poked my head through the window into the dark space. It took a second for my eyes to adjust to the dimness, but I could just make out a toilet below, and a sink on the right. I hauled myself through. The door on the far wall was unlocked, and I took a second to catch my breath and wipe the rain from my glasses before I pulled it open.

It led onto a corridor that looked like it ran the full length of the unit. I found a light switch. Overhead the bulbs flickered and I saw that the walls were plain breeze blocks with no personalised touches. I noticed too late that my wet footsteps were visible on the unfinished concrete floor, which was clean except for white powdery dust.

Concrete. I remembered the dust they'd found on Darren Walker's jeans. Was this where he had died? My whole body was shivering, no longer with the cold.

I headed deeper into the building. The place seemed empty, but I couldn't shake the feeling that someone was following me. Sound seemed to echo but I heard nothing of the outside world. Even the falling rain was muted.

The corridor led to a T at the end. To the right there was a small kitchen, almost a cupboard. The left was a closed door. It was locked.

Three locks.

I stared at the door with a mixture of fear and disgust. The top lock was just a bolt drawn across the door. I slid this across, and the bolt moved smoothly with a quiet *snick*, as though it had been recently oiled. The other two were trickier. Far too heavy-duty for an empty storage unit.

A small voice in the corner of my mind said *Wait for Marion* but I brushed it off. Pushed it back. There wasn't time.

A flash of inspiration struck, and I ran back to the kitchen. There was no stove, but there was a small fire extinguisher still strapped to the wall, a relic from when this building was more than a ghost. I grabbed it, feeling relief at its weight.

I hauled the thing over, hoping the door was made of wood and not something stronger. If it was metal – I didn't know what I'd do. I counted to three inside my head, each time my heart skipping and nausea roiling in my stomach. I bit my lip, tasting iron, and focused. One… Two… Three.

I slammed the fire extinguisher into the door. The sound reverberated inside my skull and I winced. Then I did it again. Hurled it with all of my strength. After four or five strong blows, the first combination lock popped off, half of it falling to the floor with a clatter. I didn't stop to look around, just kept on smashing at the second lock until my arms were screaming with the effort and my legs were wobbling violently in protest.

I took one deep breath, then pushed the door.

It swung into darkness, opening away from me. I hesitated. The passage led not into another room, but onto a staircase. Dark enough that I could only see a few smudgy shadows that filtered from the lights in the corridor. I waited for my arms to stop hurting quite so badly, although I was still holding the extinguisher in a vice-like grip, unable to put it down. I groped for a light switch but couldn't find one.

The staircase was warmer than the corridor, as though something had been keeping all of the heat cooped up in here. My hoodie was sodden from the rain, but I didn't want to waste time in taking it off. I blew out a long breath and started the descent into the dimness. I kept one elbow against the wall as I walked down, terrified that I might slip and fall. The stairs were uneven, felt like they'd been hollowed out of dirt rather than made from bricks.

When I reached the bottom, there was another door. This one was locked too, twice, but one was just a bolt, and the other a standard cylinder lock – the kind Marion had once taught me to pick, out in the dusty warmth of her dad's garden shed.

I stopped, another wave of paralysing fear taking me by surprise as I dug out my phone. What if Marion hadn't received my text? I should have just told her. I hoped she would figure it out. I checked my phone, noticing that my signal was down at zero bars, and I shivered again. I couldn't face the thought of smashing this lock – wasn't sure I could manage it. So I held my phone in my mouth for light and finally put the extinguisher down, setting about picking the lock with a hair grip from my pocket. Sometimes it was handy being a girl.

Sweat beaded on my lip and along my spine. I had the phone gripped precariously between my teeth and the light shook. Every thud of my heartbeat in my ears made me tense up. My hands shook with the effort and something that had once been easy became almost impossible.

Finally the lock made a clicking sound, and then there was a hollow thud from the other side. A scuffling noise. I slid my phone into the pocket of my jeans and then pushed gently at the door. I left the extinguisher on the floor just inside the room, my arms like jelly at the thought of carrying it for any longer and my heart beating so loud inside my head that I could barely think. A basement room. A fucking basement room—

The door opened and I stopped mid-thought.

I felt nausea rise in my throat and I swallowed hard.

The room was perhaps as big as my living room at home, but in it were crammed enough things for a whole life. A fridge on one side, a microwave on the counter. Against the other wall was a tin bath, low and shiny, and behind a short wall there was a toilet. All around there were pictures. Drawings and paintings. They started off childish, green trees and horses, the paper curling with age, some torn and taped back together. The newer ones were more sophisticated. I was shaking as I took it in. These told the story of a life. A captive life. I felt my knees buckle as the breath whooshed out of me.

One of the later ones… My own face stared back out at me. Cheeks still teenage soft, eyes exactly the right shade of golden brown, hair curly and wild. My face. Painstakingly captured by my little sister.

I fought back a sob. Tore my eyes away.

On the right, there was a window, small enough that I hadn't noticed it from the outside of the building. It would have been floor-height, hard to see in the dark. Yellow lamp-light filtered through it from outside, but it was weak and created as many shadows as it illuminated. But there, underneath the window, there was a bed.

A single bed, almost like a cot. It had raised sides that made it look closed-in. Hand-made. And in the bed there was a figure.

"Olive?" I whispered.

The girl dragged herself upright, her eyes wide and glittering with fear.

"No," she said, her voice tiny and hoarse. "I'm Bella." She stopped, frozen and her mouth yawned into a panicked 'o'.

"Where is she?"

Bella's eyes were dry but raw with unshed tears. I knew what she was going to say before the words came out, the world going black so that all I could see was that drawing on the wall. My face...

It was true, then.

"I think she's dead."

51

MY HEART STUTTERED IN my chest but I forced myself to stand still instead of giving in to the wave of sadness inside me.

The kid didn't move. She was dirty, her face streaked with grime and tears. Her hair was matted, her cheeks too pink. She looked feverish, glassy-eyed, her knees pulled to her chest.

Then I noticed what she was wearing. For days I had been picturing this little girl in her school uniform like the last time I had seen her, but her dress was an old-fashioned plaid pinafore. The shirt underneath was white, decorated with broderie anglaise. I felt sick. It was like the sort of thing Olive and I had worn as young children in the nineties – the kind of outfit Olive had hated.

Seeing Bella dressed like this now I started to understand what had happened here. Like Marion had feared, this was like a recreation of something, some image or fantasy. Bella had fitted the bill. I could see it even more in the flesh, the curve of her jaw, the point of her nose – she looked like my sister.

"Did he hurt you?" I asked, trying not to inject a note of urgency in my voice. Bella didn't need to panic. We just needed to get up and walk out. Before he came back.

"He didn't – he said he would wait for me to get older, like he did with…" Bella was holding back tears. I could see it in the way her teeth were clenched, her whole face trembling with the effort of keeping the tears in.

"We can leave now," I said. "Do you remember me? I came here to take you home."

Bella yelped as I made a move towards her. "I should have known," she blurted. "I should have known when his daughter wasn't there. When he said he'd drive me to school. I should have…" She rubbed her face. "What if he *sees us?*"

"He won't," I said. "I promise. I'll take care of you. The police are on their way. Come with me and we can leave—"

"He'll hurt me."

She started to rock, burying her face in her knees. I took the opportunity to approach her, just wanting to touch her, to make sure she was real. She didn't pull away from me but she started to sob, great wracking sobs that pulled through her entire body, making her tremble.

"Bella, Bella," I said. I would have picked her up and carried her but I didn't have the strength. "Please, sweetie, come on let's go."

Bella snapped her head back, staring at me with tears still caught on her eyelashes.

"Don't you hear it?" she asked.

"Hear what?"

"He's here. He's here early. He doesn't know I can hear him but I haven't been drinking the water."

As she said this, I heard them. Footsteps. But it was too late. He was already here. Quickly, I grabbed hold of Bella's arm.

"When I tell you to run, you run. You hear me? There's an open window in the toilet upstairs—"

Before I had the chance to finish, he was there. The smell of oranges and hand sanitiser was overwhelming, as though he'd just come inside after a snack.

"I told you to back off."

For a second, a wave of what might have been relief washed over me. It couldn't be Ady. This man was bigger, stronger, more terrifying. He was built differently, wasn't he? He was darker and altogether more evil. But with a flick of his wrist at the wall he illuminated the room and the space was flooded by a screaming halogen brightness. I had to blink, and hope was replaced by the familiar sense of despair.

It *was* him. He just wasn't the man I knew. The man I'd called my friend. This wasn't the same man who ran charity races, who asked about my gran and doted on his daughter.

Gran. *At least he slowed down.* Her confusion that the driver had come at her slowly… The hit and run. I realised with a jolt that it *was* Ady. His comment afterwards wasn't just neighbourly reassurance. *It* is *lucky that your gran wasn't seriously injured.* That was for me. A message. Just like *back off.* A reminder that things could be worse if I didn't stop digging.

"You," I spat. I positioned myself between him and Bella, wishing I could reach the fire extinguisher. But Ady wasn't armed, except with his weight and height, and I wondered if I could take him by surprise.

"I could say the same thing myself." Ady paused where he was, taking in the scene. Bella sobbed behind me, her face once again buried. He tilted his head to the side, a predatory look taking over his face. "I always knew there was a rotten core in you. I knew you'd cause us a problem."

"What did you do with her?" I tried to keep my eyes focused on his face, the antiseptic clementine scent assaulting my nose. "Where *is* she?"

He started to smile, the quiet man I knew being replaced by the monster. I fought the panic that threatened to cut off the oxygen to my brain. Tried very hard to breathe. I had no phone signal, no weapon, and he was much bigger than me…

He ignored my question.

"Funny you timed it so well. The girl should be asleep by now." He tilted his head further, staring me down. "But I knew it was only a matter of time until you showed up. You just don't know when to quit."

"I know what you are," I spat, pointed at Olive's drawings. At Bella. "I know what you've done."

"Oh, do you? You know *everything*?"

Olive. I didn't know what he had done with Olive…

"I know everything I need to know," I said. Both of us saw it for the lie it was. I didn't know the one thing that mattered. But I kept going. "The police are on their way."

His body weight shifted backwards, and I realised that I had been wrong before. He was armed. He moved his right arm and I saw the length of a small kitchen knife glitter in the light. He'd seen my car – he'd known I was here, and he'd come prepared. And he didn't care that I'd mentioned the police – maybe he didn't believe me.

I fought against the urge that rose deep within me to lunge at him, to throw everything I had at him. All I had to do, I thought, was wait. Marion was coming.

But what if she wasn't? What if she hadn't got my message? What if…?

All the time my brain whirred Ady stood there, watching. Bella shifted on the bed. I heard the springs creak beneath her. Ady's focus snapped to her, his expression changing again.

"Don't you move," he said.

"I won't let you hurt her." I raised my chin higher.

"I would *never* hurt her. She's better off here where it's *safe*."

"Safe?"

I flicked my eyes from side to side, searching desperately for something to protect myself. No weapons in the kitchen. Nothing I could use in self-defence.

"Don't do anything stupid." Ady's voice brought my attention right back to his face. He pulled the knife in front of him, brandishing it so that the blade reflected the light.

I stepped backwards, one arm behind me. Bella reached out to take it, her clammy hand gripping mine. She was trembling. Or I was.

"You're disgusting," I said. "I thought you were a good person."

"I *am* a good person." Ady raised his eyebrows, genuine confusion crossing his face. "I saved them."

"*Saved* them?" I tried to force a laugh, but all that came out was a croak. "Is that what you think?"

"I saved them from the world." Ady shook his head. "I love my girls. I care for them. The world hasn't cared for them, not even the people who were supposed to look after them. To love them most. Look at Bella, here. She was a disaster waiting to happen! So beautiful and clever, but never nurtured. Nobody saw her gift, not like I did. She needs to be cared for. I wasn't going to let it happen – skimpy outfits and belly rings and boys. Jesus, she's a *child*—"

"A child who needs to be with her mother!"

"Mother? Did you *see* her press conference? It was a shambles. I was horrified. What kind of mother lets her child go to school in dirty clothes? What kind of mother puts her divorce before her *child's welfare*—"

"What gives you the right to make that decision? What gives you the right to decide what makes a good mother?"

"You wouldn't understand," Ady snapped. "Yours was broken too. You're broken, just like her. Weak-willed. You drink and you fight and you still think that you can take the moral high ground? That you're a good person? Well you *aren't*. I've seen you with that police friend of yours." He sneered. "I saw that in you from the beginning. It's disgusting. I saw your father with his fancy woman. He didn't care about you, about your rottenness. I saw what your mother did to your sister. Such a beautiful girl, and she *bruised* her."

Suddenly I couldn't control myself. I lunged at him, hands outstretched as though I could claw his eyes out. He batted me away with ease, knocking me to the floor with a swift kick to my knee. The pain was white-hot and angry; it shot through my leg fast enough that my vision blurred. My glasses skittered across the floor. Bella cried out and scuttled back so that she was pressed right into the corner of the bed, sobs echoing in the small space.

Ady turned on her, his face livid.

"And you—"

"Don't touch her!"

Ady looked at me, sat on the floor clutching my leg, and he shook his head.

"You just don't understand, do you?" he said sadly. "*I would never hurt her*. I love her. Like I loved Olive. The universe brought them to me – both of them. I've been *gifted*, two fresh starts, two eclipses. I gave them a better life! It was meant to be."

These words were aimed right at my heart, and I felt them like a thousand knives pressed to my skin. I wanted to scream and shout at him, throw myself at him again, but I knew I had to stay calm. Keep him talking long enough. *Marion, where are you?*

"How could you have loved her?" I said, my voice barely loud enough to be audible. But his face hardened and I knew that he had heard me. "You took her from me."

"I told you, I kept her safe," he said. His jaw was tense, his arms loose and limber by his sides. If I could get the knife, I'd stand a chance. "She was a good girl. Beautiful. She was clever, too. Read like nobody I've ever known. Books and magazines and everything. And she was always so polite."

"You hu—"

"I never meant to hurt her!" he shouted. Raw emotion punctuated his words. "I never meant for any of that. It was an accident. It never would have happened if she hadn't made me do it."

"What, like your wife? Was that an accident, too?"

"That was different," Ady said. I could see that I was right, though. His expression clouded and his grip on the knife tightened. "Annabelle was weak – she didn't understand. She didn't *understand* me. Not like I thought she did when I married her.

"She wasn't like Olive. By fourteen your sister was more mature, more graceful, more *everything* than Annabelle." His face screwed up in disgust. "When I told Annabelle about Olive she couldn't handle it. She knew she was too weak to handle the life I was giving her. So she took the pills I gave her."

"You killed her," I said.

"I told her not to take them unless she wanted an end. I told her they would make her ill. I gave her a chance to become a mother, I gave her a baby for us to look after. A family. I *warned* her. But, in the end, she didn't want to live. Like your mother. Weak, both of them."

I ignored the pain at his mention of my mum and ploughed on.

"And Darren? Did you warn him too?"

I thought of the texts Ady had sent me. How he'd tried to get me to stop digging after I mentioned I was looking into Olive's disappearance. He had known it would come to this.

"Darren couldn't leave it alone. He's been picking over all this money crap for years, going on and on about how I needed to pay him and his mum back because it was a 'loan'. His dad *gave* me that money. He was my friend. And Daz should have just let it lie. But no, he had to ask questions. And when your bloody police friend asked him about Olive's ring – the idiot recognised it. I knew I shouldn't have taken it from Olive after all. He confronted me. Said he was going to tell unless I paid him back. He should have kept his damn mouth shut, but he was just like Cordy."

"Cordy…?"

Ady rolled his eyes. "For God's sake. Considering you're supposed to be clever. Yes, Cordy. Idiot figured it out. Everybody thought it was him – I'd have been happy to let them. But he tried to blackmail me into giving him an alibi and he got crazy. So I had to get rid of him. It was easier back then."

My ears were ringing.

"You killed them… Just like you killed Olive. You destroyed her. You destroyed us. You took away my childhood. My mother. My *family*."

I clenched my shaking hands and fought the tears. *Come on, Marion…*

"Olive could have lived to a hundred if she hadn't got ideas from those books of hers. If she hadn't thought that outside was better. It isn't."

Olive was dead, then. All these years, and I'd been searching for a ghost.

She'd been here the whole time. This close to us, the whole time. Was she still here when Mum died? When I was living only streets away? A howling furnace of anger threatened to engulf me. It would be so easy to give in…

But, Bella.

"Where is my sister?" I demanded.

Ady shook his head. "You think I'll tell you? Just like that? Why should I? You need to leave. Get out—"

"I won't leave without Bella."

"You *will*."

Ady was on me before I knew what was happening. I saw the flash of the knife before I felt it against my throat. The metal was cold, the point so sharp that when it caught my skin I sucked in an involuntary gasp.

Bella screamed.

"Don't hurt her! Don't hurt her!"

"You think you're so clever," Ady hissed, his face pressed right against mine. "But you don't know anything. It was fate; it was my duty. While you spent your life getting wasted and defiling yourself with your women and God only knows what else, I was waiting for a sign. And this was *right*. Nowhere else have I ever seen a more perfect alignment of nature and time. The eclipse, the darkness, it was all meant to be. The Fates even gave me Grace – the perfect misdirection so I could act quickly. It was so *pure*."

I tried to pull away but Ady held me firmly. The metal bit into the soft skin of my throat.

"I loved her," he said again, punctuating each word with another glob of spittle. "Everything I did was *right*."

I bucked my arm up underneath his elbow. He was surprised and the knife jumped away. I took advantage and brought my head forward in a swift motion and felt it connect with his nose. There was a satisfying crunch and then I gagged as black spots flooded my vision. I heard Ady screaming, anger and pain all rolled into one. I stumbled to my feet. Ady was on his knees, hands cupping his nose and the knife forgotten on the floor.

I threw myself at it just as Ady started to get up. Bella jumped up, her hands going to her face in alarm. I looked at her, made sure our eyes locked, and I mouthed one word.

Run.

52

EXHAUSTION MADE HER THOUGHTS sluggish, but she watched the baby's sleeping face in the wicker basket he'd brought her. A Moses basket, she thought it was called. Wasn't sure. Wasn't sure about anything much.

She was sure about one thing, though. And that was the timing. It had to be soon. While he was still enamoured. While they still had a chance. The moment she had seen her daughter's face, Olive had understood that all her planning had been useless.

She'd taken for granted her ability to leave the child. But this little girl was as much a part of Olive as she was of *him*, and her face looked so much like Olive's own – at least as far as she remembered it – that the plans were wrong, now. She couldn't leave her behind when she went.

That made things simpler, Olive thought. But also more dangerous. Tonight he would come, as usual, and bring the supplies. He'd said he would bring her more nappies – neither of them had anticipated how many a new baby could get through.

She knew that the bag of nappies would be big. He'd buy

them in bulk so it was less risky, so he could make fewer trips. Getting them through the door – that was the hard part. Olive knew she had to wait until the right moment, and then she could probably make it out.

But probably wasn't good enough.

She knew she had to try and conserve her strength. But already the baby was a poor sleeper. Colicky. That's what the book had said – the one he'd bought her. *What to Expect...* Olive would bet that whoever wrote that book had had no idea where it would end up. Or what to expect. Not really.

Olive finished her orange juice and counted inside her head. It had been two days since he'd been here last. That meant tonight, definitely. He wouldn't go any longer. He hadn't gone more than two days at a time since the baby had been born. But she didn't want to think about him.

She focused instead on her daughter's face. Her *daughter*. Just the thought made her squirm – but in a good way. She felt her daughter's heavy warmth even when she wasn't carrying her, felt it like an absence. She could smell that baby scent on her, of milk and talcum powder and love.

Olive reached out and pulled her sketchpad towards her, seeing a mirror of her daughter's sleeping face. She used a shading motion with white pastel to catch the shininess of her baby nose, of her moist little mouth as she pursed it.

Tonight was the night. Olive wasn't sure about anything except that. Her daughter couldn't spend her life in this room. Not like Olive had. She wouldn't let her. Staring at the same walls every day, never smelling the outside, never feeling rain or seeing real sunshine. Olive glanced down at the pallor of her skin, the faint bruises on her knees and arms. She bruised so easily these days.

Her hair was long. Really long. She'd asked for scissors to cut it, but Sandman hadn't allowed it. Too dangerous. Now it was ratty and reached below her waist. She hated it. No child of hers would endure the things that she had had to bear. She had spent nine months thinking of the beast inside of her – not realising that she would love her so much.

Olive finished the sketch with a flourish, and then scrambled for a dark pen to sign it. The baby's name she'd chosen even before she knew she was having a girl. If she'd been a boy she would have been called Arthur, after the boy who nobody believed could pull a sword from a stone. Instead she was Matilda, like the Roald Dahl girl. The little girl who nobody loved.

Except somebody did love her. Miss Honey, for starters. Matilda was the little girl who could make magic happen. And Olive marvelled now at how true this was. Her little hands had had the power to overthrow months of planning.

Olive eyed the letter she had written earlier in the day. Her writing was terrible, but she had hardly been able to see through the fog of tiredness and tears. She grabbed it, folded it in half. And again. There was a loose brick beneath the bed, pried away from the rest only to reveal a metal lining. That was a year ago, that particular failure, but its presence still stung.

The letter was a precaution. Against failure? Olive didn't know. She knew that by writing it she had explained herself. To God, if to nobody else.

But what if nobody ever found it? What if *he* did? For a moment she stood, indecisive. Then, in a swift movement she stuck it to the back of her sketch instead. Better to be found and destroyed than left mouldering in this prison for ever.

Task complete, she leaned over and scooped the baby into her arms. She stirred but didn't wake, settling against her mother's chest. It was the most natural thing in the world.

As she held her, rocking gently, Olive considered bravery. How she had spent so many years feeling like she wasn't brave enough. But it wasn't a lack of bravery, she realised now. It was the same way she had felt when she had lost Mickey – it was a lack of hope. Alone, the risk hadn't been worth taking. But with somebody else…

That's when it became about bravery. The decision to leave. To not let him have her. Olive knew now that the risk of staying was bigger. More certain. She couldn't risk him hurting his daughter as he had hurt her. He hadn't meant to. Or at least, that's what he told himself.

But Olive wouldn't risk it again.

Back on the bed, Olive felt under the pillow, gripping the paintbrush for security. She'd sharpened it to a point, intending to simply stab him and run. He'd save the baby instead of hurting her, she was sure of it.

Now… She fingered the edge, catching her skin on its wooden tip. Would it be enough? Olive didn't know. But she knew she needed to try. Anything was better than this. She hoped her family would be proud of her. She hoped she would get to see her sister again once she was outside.

She was ready.

Then, she heard it. His feet on the stairs. The thumping of her heart almost drowned out the turn of the second lock. She jumped to her feet, hovering by the door.

It was now or never.

53

THE TASTE OF IRON was the first thing I noticed. Followed by the extreme nausea and the smell. God, the smell. It was like metal. It took valuable seconds to realise it was blood. My blood? My vision was blurry, and I tried to move. My right arm was bleeding. I hadn't noticed that he'd cut me but now the pain was like a razor against my skin.

I looked around, completely dazed. Then it came back to me. The room, Ady, Bella. Olive... I rolled onto my side on the cold concrete floor and vomited. This made the pounding in my head worse, but at least the smell of copper wasn't around my face any more. I dragged in two deep breaths, coughing, and then I felt a pressure against my back.

Startled, I tried to scrabble away. But my arm was throbbing and my whole body felt battered. I didn't make it very far before Ady's face swam over mine. He grabbed my shoulders and hauled me upright as I screamed. The pain shot through my arm.

"I don't know what you're hoping to achieve," Ady started, "by letting the girl escape."

"She'll be long gone by now," I said.

"Not likely." Ady brushed me off as though I'd just asked him whether he thought the rain would last overnight. He shrugged. "There's no way out of the gates even if she makes it out of the building. She'll be back when she gets cold and wet. But honestly, after this charade I'm not sure I want her. I was so sure she was right for me."

I wanted to try and reach for my phone, but then I remembered the lack of signal. *Marion, I need you...*

But I didn't have time to wait. There was Ady – and there was me. That was it. I had to get myself out of this.

"If you loved Olive so much," I said, hoping I could buy myself some time, "why did she get hurt? Was it like Darren?"

Ady's eyes flashed black, the monster inside him coiling, ready to strike.

"He freaked when the police asked him about the ring. He figured out it was Olive's. I should have hidden it better but I liked to look at it, kept it at home and he saw it. He knew I gave it to both of them." Ady laughed. "The police assumed he'd sold it to Bella, didn't they? Idiot thought he could just come clean and tell you everything and it would all go away. He thought he wouldn't get into trouble if he told you."

I noticed that Ady was holding the knife in his hand again, the same knife as before. Only now it had blood on it. In his other hand he held a roll of duct tape. I felt a shiver of fear rush through me but I refused to baulk.

He ripped a piece of tape off, and I was embarrassed by the sob that escaped my throat.

"I just want to know what you did," I cried. "Please. If

you're going to kill me anyway, please tell me what happened. Why Olive? Why her?"

"I already told you," Ady said. He grabbed the tape and cut it with one smooth slice of the knife. "She needed somebody to care for her. A proper family. Mother, father, child. That's why we created one."

Olive had a child. I tried to process this.

"But then why…"

"Why did she die?"

Again the words hit me hard, as Ady knew they would. Hearing it spoken aloud like that, it was the worst pain in the world. I prayed that Bella had found the open window. I hoped she could get out of the estate, maybe through the bars of the gate. She was a skinny kid. She might fit. She…

"She tried to take my family away." Ady said it so simply, without any guilt. Sadness, perhaps. No guilt. "My daughter was all I had in the world… Olive was happy here, you know. For a long time."

"Happy?" I let out a bark of laughter that turned into pain. "She was a prisoner. You took everything away from her."

"I suppose she just got the sickness," Ady continued, ignoring me. He cut off more tape. "All adults get it eventually. You already had it, didn't you, when Olive came to me? It's a sickness that just inhabits people. I've seen it so many times. A loss of innocence. It's just infects everything. I thought in here she would be all right. In the end I suppose nobody avoids it."

"What do you mean?" I asked. I realised that the salty taste in my mouth was tears, and I swallowed hard. "What sickness?"

"She grew up," Ady said. He peeled the tape back and forth between his hands, the knife balanced carefully between his thumb and forefinger. The tape made a crackling noise as he passed it from palm to palm, the stickiness slowly wearing away. I supposed he thought he was being caring, doing that before sticking it on my face. I felt the nausea rise again.

"You made her grow up."

Ady narrowed his eyes. "She loved me," he said. "I waited until she was ready, until she was old enough. Until she could decide. And I would do the same thing with this one – do it all exactly the same."

He said this proudly, his eyes sparkling with the memory of it. I couldn't hold in the wail that shook through me. Images of Olive's sweet face marred by Ady's words.

"*You're* the sickness. You raped my sister and you'd do the same thing again."

"NO!"

My head rang as Ady slapped me. My teeth chattered together at the impact and stars shot across my vision.

"It wasn't like that. I didn't make love to her just because I wanted to. It was more than that. It was passion, it had *meaning*. It was all part of something bigger. The plan we had – for the future. Now I've had enough of your questions." He grabbed the tape and pressed it against my mouth. The bloody iron taste intensified and I had to fight to breathe through my nose, which was clogged and sore. "I don't have to explain myself to you," he said. "Ever. Olive was a beautiful young woman. When she died, I mourned her. But I couldn't just let her leave, not after everything we'd been through. I didn't mean to kill her, just slow her down, but the stairs and she was holding the b——"

I didn't need to hear the rest. The pieces clicked into place.

I lost it. I didn't care about my arm, the pain in my leg now dulled to an intense ache. I hurled myself off the floor with more strength than I thought possible, adrenaline fizzing inside me and pushing me further, faster, harder.

I threw myself at him, my whole weight directed right at his chest. I caught him off balance, and together we went to the floor.

With my good arm I ripped the tape off my face as Ady struggled beneath me. He threw me off with little effort, but he was winded. I could see that in his face. *The knife.* Where was it? I glanced around wildly, my heart in my throat.

Under the bed. I dove for it, my right arm useless as I grappled for it. Ady launched after me, grabbing hold of my leg. He started to pull. I had a firm hold on the blade and it cut into my fingers. I kicked once. Hard. Caught Ady in the upper thigh, close enough to his crotch that he doubled and scuttled backwards. When I came upright I had the blade in my left hand. I was ready to do it. Ready to swing.

I caught sight of Olive's pictures, and I felt a familiar thrum inside my chest. A familiar call. *Find me.* I lowered the blade. If I hurt him he might never tell me where she was. What he had done with her body.

Then I caught sight of her, a figure darting from one side of the door to the other. Bella. For a second I thought she'd made it unseen. Then his head swivelled, his nostrils flaring. He was already moving.

"No!" I shouted. "Bella, run! Go outside and scream!"

Bella tried to run back towards the stairs but Ady was faster. He grabbed her foot and started to pull. I darted after him. He had hold of Bella's ankle, and I heard a thud as she hit the floor. He yanked harder, pulling her back into the room. I clawed at his back, wrestled the knife against his skin. It pierced clothing, but I misjudged and didn't get skin. He didn't stop.

"Please!" Bella cried. "You're hurting me!"

She tried to kick him off, but Ady aimed a blow to her face. I felt the slap rather than heard it, and I pulled my arm back hard. I swung the knife again. Ady howled but only increased his grip on Bella.

In that split second I realised that I had to do it. I threw myself at the fire extinguisher, right there by the door. Holding it in my good hand, I hefted it high. Ady was holding Bella down, his arm across her throat. Her eyes were wet with tears.

"Last chance," I said quickly. "Let her go."

But Ady stared right into my face, and I saw him press down harder.

"You won't do it," he said. "If you do – Olive will be gone for ever. You'll never find her."

I closed my eyes. Heard Bella's raspy breathing, my own heartbeat in my ears. *I'm sorry, Olive*, I thought. And then I swung the fire extinguisher at his head.

Ady crumpled with a sickening thud. Bella was frozen, trapped under his weight. I leapt forward, pushing and pulling his body with my good arm until she managed to wriggle out. I took a moment, ignoring the spreading pool of scarlet on the floor.

His lips were moving. Bubbles at his mouth. He was trying to speak. I shoved Bella behind me.

"Matilda knows."

"Knows what?" I demanded. I knelt on the cold floor, blood pooling around my knees. "What does she know?"

But it was no good. He was dead.

Bella was panting and crying and I could smell ammonia as I pulled her to me, wrapped her in my arms. She sobbed, heavy, uncontrolled tears. I felt my own eyes burn in response.

"You're her sister," Bella whispered, then. "Aren't you? She was in here. Before me."

She looked up at me, her golden-brown eyes glistening and tears still hanging on her lashes. I couldn't trust myself to speak, but I nodded.

After a moment, I pulled back. Looked around. Not at Ady's body, still on the ground, but at the walls. The paintings. Bella didn't move, her eyes fixed firmly on her captor's body. I pulled the nearest picture off the wall. There was something taped to the back of it, making the paper bulky. I held it close to my heart.

With one final glance around this room – this prison – I grabbed hold of Bella's shoulders and steered her out. And then, finally, I heard the police sirens.

Marion's face was the first I saw. She was there with a whole team. Bella and I fell towards her, and Fox reached us just as she did. I let her wrap her arms around me, pulling me tight.

Bella hung onto my wrist, and together we let ourselves be helped out of the building.

"Where is he?" Marion demanded. "Cassie, where is he? Is he here? What happened to you? I saw your car – and then the broken window and I... Your arm. You're bleeding—"

"He's in the basement," I said. "I don't know – we managed to stop him. I just..." I glanced at Bella, who still clung onto me. "I hit him with the fire extinguisher," I said.

Marion turned and gave instructions to Fox, who gathered several men. They headed for the back of the building. Marion ushered Bella ahead of us, and guided me with a hand firmly at the base of my back. Outside there was a mob of cars, bright blue lights flashing. Marion pulled us towards a waiting ambulance. Bella was lifted inside, but she kept her eyes firmly on me.

"You brought the cavalry," I said to Marion.

Her face was a mess of confusion and anger and frustration and a whole host of other emotions I couldn't read. But instead of speaking, she crushed her lips against mine.

"I'm so glad you're okay."

I gasped at the pain in my head but I didn't want to pull away. Our foreheads touched, breath mingling in the cool evening air. I clung to Marion's arms, my knees threatening to buckle.

"When you didn't answer your phone I freaked out," she whispered, blinking tears away. "What happened?"

"It was him," I said. "All of it. Gran's accident, Darren Walker, his own wife. Bella... *Olive.*"

"Is she..."

420

"She's dead." The words were hollow. "He wouldn't tell me where. There are drawings in there. Paintings. They start pretty young, and go right up – right up to… I don't know. Her teens, I guess. There's one of me in there. I left it…" I burst into tears, unable to get the words out.

"Shhh." Marion pulled me against her, careful of my arm, and stroked my head gently. It hurt, but the motion was still soothing, and I let her hold me for a minute. Tears stained the front of her shirt, and I couldn't breathe. I pulled back.

Behind us there was a commotion. Another ambulance had arrived, and now paramedics were coming back out of the building with a stretcher. One of the paramedics came to check my arm, cleaning it and wrapping it in white gauze.

When he was done Marion tried to guide me away from the stretcher again, pulling at my shirt that was sticky with blood and sweat, but I didn't budge. I watched with a hard expression as the stretcher was placed on a gurney. A sheet was pulled up over Ady's face. I felt nothing but a stony coldness at his death.

I still clutched the drawing in my hands. I lifted it up, watched as Marion absorbed it all, the lines and shapes and the soft etch of shading smudged in a fingerprint. My hand was shaking so badly; I wanted Marion to take the drawing from me, to tell me I was imagining things. For once, I was dying to be the crazy one.

But Marion knew.

"Tilly is hers," I whispered. "Olive died trying to escape once she had her. He took the baby and raised her and she's the same age – that Olive was when he took her. I think he needed to do it again, because *she* reminded him of Olive. That's why he dresses – *dressed* her like she was younger. Why he keeps his daughter like a baby. He needed another one – for the eclipse. So he took Bella instead." My voice was hoarse with tears. Another onslaught rocked me.

Marion said nothing, just held me to her chest as I convulsed and allowed the last shred of strength to shatter.

"Tilly Jacobs is Olive's daughter."

54

Thursday, 26 March 2015

I CLUTCHED OLIVE'S DRAWING, and the sheet of paper that went with it, in my good hand as Marion came around to open the car door for me. Watery grey light spilled over the world, but the rain had cleared. The morning was fresh and cool, and the air tickled the wetness on my cheeks. Marion's face came into view as she ducked down to take my hand.

"Do you think you'll be okay?" she asked. Then she paused. As I climbed out of the car, her face became a mask of embarrassment and sorrow. "Sorry, I didn't mean—"

"It's all right," I said quietly. The paper in my hand fluttered as a gust of wind rippled through the spring leaves. The rustling sound made me shiver, and I gripped the sheets tighter. These were just photocopies – the real ones I'd had to leave behind as *evidence* – but I didn't want to lose them. They were the last thing I had of her.

"Come on, I'll walk you inside."

In the lounge, I found that there was already a police officer present. Or was she a medic? I couldn't tell any more, my brain was so dazed by the events of the last day and the previous night. Whoever she was, she was sitting with my gran and two cups of tea, and they were discussing a movie that as far as I knew Gran had never seen. But Gran was animated, waving her uninjured arm as she talked about the actress who had played the lead – the woman smiling and nodding away.

I blinked hard as Dad came out of the kitchen. He was wearing baggy jeans and a sweatshirt, his face drawn with worry. When he saw me his face lit up and he rushed across the room, enveloping me in a hug.

"Oh, Cassie. Oh, sweetheart."

I relaxed into the embrace, feeling his solid chest and the bristles of his beard against my forehead as he held me tight. With a lurch of something like excitement, I realised that this was the first hug we'd shared in years. Even when he'd visited in the hospital yesterday there had been an awkwardness, as though everything was still sinking in.

"I'm… I'm proud of you." He gestured at Gran. "We both are."

That's when Gran noticed me. I smiled at her and the official-looking woman sat with her. Gran's eyes sparked with something like recognition. She took in my bandaged arm, my borrowed clothes, my mussed hair.

"Oh, Cassie," she whispered. "My Cassie. What happened to you?"

She climbed to her feet and tottered over. Our bandaged arms matching like for like, we made a funny pair. A soaring in my chest accompanied the disbelieving smile on my face. She knew me. She loved me. She was my gran.

"I got into a fight," I said to her. "I won."

Gran reached out, hooked a finger under my chin. She lifted it so that we were eye-to-eye and smiled.

"That's my girl."

"I did it," I said then, tears closing my throat so that the words were like tar. "I found out what happened to her."

Gran's expression shifted rapidly; hope, fear, and then, finally, relief.

"She's gone. But so is he."

Gran opened her arms wide and pulled me to her chest. She smelled of tea and home and lavender powder and I breathed the smell in deeply. When she stepped back, I could tell that the moment had passed, but it was enough.

Marion left Gran with Dad and led me into the kitchen. It was warm, bathed in yellow light from the ceiling lamp and I collapsed at the small table. The grey tint of the light that fell through the window was making me feel washed out, and the warmth inside made me want to sleep for a year. I looked around as though this wasn't my house, these weren't my things. Everything was strange, too vivid, too real.

So I laid out Olive's drawing on the table, smoothed out the page. The sleeping face of a baby greeted me, drawn in pencil and shaded with tones of umber. She looked like Olive. And I knew in my heart what Olive had felt when she'd drawn this. Trapped. In love – *real love*. You could see it in the lines, in the curve of the baby's nose, her tiny rosebud lips…

I blinked at Marion with bleary eyes when she handed me a cup of tea, and I felt the burning sensation in my hand as I held onto it for a second too long.

"The liaison officer will be here for a little while," Marion said kindly. "Just while I'm at work. I have some stuff I need to sort out. Paperwork from Walker's post-mortem. Then I'll come over." She sat down at the table and reached for my hand. "We will get through this, Cassie. It might not seem like it, but we did good. Okay? We did *great*. Bella is home, she's with her mother. Because of you that little girl can be happy again."

"I get the feeling that he—"

"Don't think about it, Cassie," Marion instructed me firmly. "You did what you had to do."

We sat in silence for a minute, each lost in thought. Dad came into the kitchen, his eyes filled with tears.

"What about the girl?" he asked. Somebody had told him, then, while I was in the hospital. I hadn't been with-it enough. "What about my granddaughter?"

My granddaughter. Such primal possessiveness. My heart swelled with surprising pride. He would make a good grandfather.

"Social services will take Tilly." Marion's tone was cautious, and I could tell that she was trying to gauge my reaction. She watched my expression as I fought back the same anger I could see mirrored in Dad's eyes.

"So, what, she'll go into care?" I swore.

"For now."

I pushed the tea away and looked directly into Marion's face so she could see how serious I was.

"Marion, I don't want that for her. She needs to know. She has a family—"

"Cassie," Marion said, so softly it was like a sigh. "Mr Warren. Both of you need to give it time. This is going to be hard for her. The kid lost her father. We need to work out what's best for her."

I thought of Ady, thought of the way he had made Tilly dress, the way he had lied to her for her whole life. Then I remembered the man I'd thought I'd known – the man he may have been with her. Marion was right. We needed to give it time.

Dad folded his arms but he didn't argue.

"I'm here, Cass." Marion leaned into me, wrapped an arm around my shoulder. I let the heavy warmth sink all the way through me before I nodded.

"I'll stay with you for as long as you want," she said. "Don't worry about your gran, or letting your journalist friend know what's happened. I'll help you. And when you're ready we can start any paperwork for Tilly – but for now, she's better off somewhere settled."

She didn't seem embarrassed, didn't even seem to notice my dad as she pressed her lips firmly to mine. I held her tightly, soaking up the warmth of the kitchen, the smells of toast and tea and *home*. I knew I wouldn't sleep without dreams, probably wouldn't ever again, but I thought of Bella's face, a mask of triumphant shock, when she realised Ady couldn't hurt her any more. And I felt a bit better.

"Promise you'll let me help you," Marion said.

"I will."

55

April 2016

"HEY." MARION'S CAR PULLED alongside the kerb and I got in. The air was scented with her favourite perfume mixed with coffee that came from two cups in the holders at the front.

"Hey yourself," I said.

"How did the therapy go?" I watched her jaw angle as she checked for traffic before pulling out. I smiled.

"It was okay. Better, actually. We're talking coping mechanisms. Apparently alcohol and sleeping pills *still* don't count."

"Good." Marion reached over to pat my hand. Her touch was warm. I tried to relax, knowing that if I got tense what I had to do next would be harder. Marion continued to make small talk, but I could tell she was as nervous as I was. "How's your gran holding up?"

"She's doing okay, too. Now we've got a decent nursing situation. That baby doll we got her has gone down well; she rocks it and feeds it and everything. It's sort of given her focus."

"Not a bad idea from Jake, then? I can't believe you actually took his unsolicited advice." Marion snorted. "What was it you called him when you first met him? *God's gift?*"

"I distinctly remember that was all *you*," I said. "Anyway, turns out he's not a bad person. Just a little bit conceited. And more than a little damn nosy. But Gran likes his bake sales, so I think it's unavoidable.

"Between him and the carer we're doing okay, though. I'm not sure how long I'll be able to afford Anne – the bits and pieces I've been doing for Henry are fine, but it's not steady enough again yet. Doctor White says it's probably for the best anyway."

I still felt the embers of embarrassment when I thought of my panicked belief he could have been responsible for what happened to Olive and Bella.

"Relax, Cass," Marion said, snapping me out of my thoughts. "It'll take time to get back into the swing of things. You can't expect everything to come together all at once."

When we pulled up, it was outside a large red-brick house with lights on in all the windows. I clenched my hands, and then made sure to occupy them by grabbing the coffee Marion had got me. I sipped it nervously.

"Are you ready?" Marion asked.

"I… I don't know. It's such a big thing. For her, I mean. The papers… I'm scared she'll change her mind. That she won't want me. I killed her father, Marion. One day she's going to want to have a proper conversation about that. Or she'll ask me about Olive, or about the woman she *thought* was her mother, how he killed her… She might ask me for my take on it. What will I say? How on earth will I handle that?"

The questions rose and rose in me and I started to panic. It had already taken so long to get here, so much time and energy and trust. What if I scared her off again? I didn't want her to return to the wary child she had been in those first months after everything.

Marion twisted in her seat, and then reached up to stroke my face. She pulled my chin up and planted a small kiss on my lips, halting my thoughts in their tracks.

"Stop," she said. "I'll be here with you. I'm not going anywhere. It's okay to be nervous. This is a big deal. But I promise you that if you want me – I'm here."

"I do want you," I said. "I love you. I'm still scared though, Marion. What if—"

"Stop, Cass." Marion kissed me again, this time harder. I let myself melt into her touch, felt her hand pull me closer. Her kiss was gentle yet demanding and I yielded to it.

When she pulled back the air was cold where her mouth had been. I reached up to touch my lips, marvelling at the tingling warmth that rushed through me.

"Look, there's your dad."

Marion pointed. Up ahead I saw Dad's car pull up. He climbed out, one hand shielding his eyes from the early April sun. Marion and I clambered out of the car as well, and tense hugs were exchanged.

"Are you nervous?" Dad asked. He gestured to the papers in my hands. Official, and not so official. The start of a new beginning. I gripped them tighter and shrugged.

"Excited," I said.

I let Marion lead us up the garden path, but it was me that knocked at the door. There was a clatter of movement inside, and then the door swung back. I was greeted by two bright, golden eyes and a big smile. Her hair was longer than when I last saw her, almost down to her shoulders now. And a chocolate brown like Olive's had been – her natural colour, unlike the blonde Ady had insisted she keep hers.

"Cassie," she said. "You're late."

She turned, spied my dad just behind me, and then grinned. Her eyes looked brighter without the glasses, too. It turned out she didn't need them. Another of Ady's insistences. She'd told me last year that he used to drill her about how important it was to blend in, to become invisible. I wasn't surprised that she seemed like a different kid now, after a year with foster carers. A year to become herself.

"Grandad," Tilly said.

This word sounded foreign in her mouth, but she seemed to like the sound of it. She mouthed it again, and then wrinkled her nose.

"That's a bit weird. I just wanted to try it. Not sure about it yet."

Dad held out his hand, a bewildered look on his face. One full of nostalgia and disbelief that this was real. Tilly was real and she was ours and she had just called him grandad for the first time.

There were so many things I wanted to say. There were things I wanted to tell her every time I saw her. I wanted to tell her that she looked, in this light, just like her mother.

I wanted to tell her that I was sorry, that I hadn't meant for Ady to die. But I knew that I had to slow down. So instead I massaged the tattoo on the inside of my arm, a gentle reminder that it wasn't going anywhere. And I let her drag Dad by the hand into the lounge of the foster house, Marion and me not far behind.

Once we were settled, I reached out to her, unfolding the pieces of paper from my pocket as I did so.

"I've got some things for you. These are the papers we're going to fill in later, when you come home with me. It'll kick-start everything, if you still want it to."

I waited. Gauging her reaction. At the smile that extended across her face, a shy smile I hadn't seen before, I felt a wave of relief wash over me. She wasn't dreading it, wasn't waiting for a way to tell me she didn't want to come home with me.

"The next two are gifts," I said. "From your mother."

Tilly took the drawing first, her eyes misting as she saw the shape of her own face, her own nose. I watched her trace the curve of her lips, and the soft outline of her baby face. And then she opened the second piece of paper, and I could just see the loops of barely familiar handwriting through the photocopy, although I knew what it said – had read it so many times over the last year that I had committed it to memory.

Tilly read it slowly – and then she started to cry.

"Oh, sweetie." I glanced from Dad to her. "Grandad told me something once. He said, 'Don't be defined by tragedy.' He didn't want me to be sad all of the time, to let that change who I was. He was a bit right, but he was also wrong. If I'd done what he suggested I might never have found you. It's okay to be sad sometimes." She watched me carefully. I pointed at the letter in her hands, the one we had found taped to the back of Olive's last painting.

"I found you because I never gave up. I came back to Bishop's Green, even though it was sad, and I tried again. Do you want to try again with me?"

She sniffled. And then nodded.

"Can we go now?" she said, glancing between the three of us. "I mean… to your home?"

Hope soared in my chest like a bird. I pulled Tilly into a tight hug, wrapped both of my arms around her and breathed in her shampoo-sweet hair.

"Yes," I whispered. "Let's go home."

"And then…" Tilly tucked a piece of hair behind her ear. "Then I want to show you where I think my mother – my real mother – is buried."

56

MY BABY, MATILDA,

I've tried to write this letter before, but it comes out all garbled. Time is running out though so this will have to be the last one. I'm tired, it's been a long few days, and I'm sorry. If the words come out wrong, I hope you'll forgive me. But I also hope you never have to read this.

All I ever wanted was the best for you. I don't know if you'll ever see this, but if you do it will probably be in bad times – and for that I'm sorry, too. If you're reading this, then I'm sorry that we didn't make it. You and me. All I wanted was to keep you safe. I knew that it would be up to me to save you. I don't know why I'm writing this really… By the time you read it, you'll be old, and you might not remember me at all.

The truth is, I'm afraid. I used to think that I knew what fear was, but I didn't. The moment I saw your face for the first time – I was afraid. Not just for myself but for you, too. A mother's love is strong and I learnt what it was to be afraid for somebody else.

I used to think that my own mother was weak, you know.

She used to shout at us, at my sister and me. Cassie didn't care, or it felt like that, but I hated it. But now I know why she shouted. She shouted because she was afraid. That's what motherhood is. Fear and love in equal parts.

I still marvel at you. Your face is perfect. You have ten fingers, ten toes, and I think you look a lot like me. Even if you hadn't been perfect, I would love you anyway. Another truth: I don't know what to do. I just know that we can't stay here. I can't let you live the life that I have lived. The darkness, the cold. The loneliness. He is dangerous. Really, truly dangerous. I realised that the moment he hurt his wife instead of letting us go free. I don't want that world for you, hiding just to stay safe.

I often wonder if my family is out there, somewhere. I have thought long and hard about whether I should just keep going as I have been. Keeping my head down, so that neither of us want for anything. Tonight I realised that in not wanting, we are still wanting. We want for fresh air and freedom, if not blankets and food. And although we would be safe in here – as safe as we can be – I can't let it continue. I have lived lives through books, but they aren't real lives. They're mirrors. Tonight the mirror is reflecting so much more than this room, and I'm going crazy.

In another life, I would have named you something like Sophie, or Hannah. Those were my favourite names once. But you are a Matilda, like the little girl in a book who was so different and special – and who never let anybody take those gifts from her. I hope that you can believe me when I tell you that I love you with all of my heart. No matter what happens tonight, this letter is proof of that. I feel better knowing that somehow, somewhere, there is proof.

Matilda, no matter what happens, remember this: you are not alone.

With endless love,

~~Olive~~ Mum

ACKNOWLEDGEMENTS

FIRST NOVELS ARE OFTEN a long time in the making and *After the Eclipse* is no different. I have been telling stories for as long as I can remember and having my words in the hands of readers means more to me than I can express. Thank you to all of you, I hope you have enjoyed reading this novel as much as I enjoyed writing it.

This book would not have been possible without the support of my amazing agent Diana Beaumont. Thank you for having faith in Cassie, for helping her to find a place in the world, and for your continued warmth and knowledge. Thanks also to Sandra Sawicka for putting up with my foreign rights questions and tax-related freak-outs!

Huge thanks to the Titan team for helping me shape Cassie's story into one I am proud to share, especially Miranda for taking a chance on me and Cath for the incredible insight along the way. Thanks to Joanna, Sam, Lydia and Philly, and to Julia Lloyd for her stunning cover designs.

I've had some fabulous teachers and supporters over the years, including Karen Sherwin, Gareth Summers, Rosemary

Archer, and Chris Bigsby. The decision to study on the City Crime/Thriller MA was one of the best I ever made and I want to thank Claire McGowan, William Ryan and Jane Casey for their feedback and advice – I know I am a stronger writer for every piece. Much love to all of my classmates, but especially to my cracking #SauvLife crew. Chris, Jenny and Lizzie you guys mean the world to me and I know that in you I have truly found my people. Also the fabulous Crime Kissers: Vallery, Finn, Litty and Liz. I'm so grateful for your persistent help and feedback and for you putting up with my awkward work schedules. Vallery, thank you so much for trusting that I wasn't going to murder you in your sleep and for giving a poor student a place to crash every week. Show this to your mum and maybe she'll finally believe how harmless I am!

I have made some of the best friends during my writing journey, but a big shout out to the Derbyshire Doomsbury writers: Roz Watkins, Jo Jakeman, Sophie Draper and Louise Trevatt. You guys keep me sane! I cherish our Friday evenings and all of the work we definitely do during them.

Thanks to all of my early readers and friends and to everybody who has been part of my life, especially: Jordanna Rowan, Paul Cockburn, Lee Hulme and the Notts NaNo group, Ginny Larkin-Thorsen, Becky Clarke, Natalie Beale, Isabel Muller, Vanessa Chainey, and Alex Doughty. Allison Hargett, this is a reminder that I love you For Good and I am incredibly grateful for our friendship. Much love to everybody at Waterstones Derby who has supported me but most of all Callie, my bookseller bestie, life would not be the same without you and I'm so happy I get to work with somebody who makes me laugh (#Trashfire).

I know a lot of people think their family is the best but I know mine is. Tom, you are the best sounding-board and friend I could ever ask for. Thank you for cat-juggling, for dog-wrestling, for snack-fetching and for believing me every time (okay, some times) that I said we would go to the gym again soon. Thank you, too, for being selfless and patient and helping me out without warning.

Sian, thank you for your patience during my edits and for putting up with my writer brain. I appreciate every kind word and smile. I hope you enjoy reading the finished product!

Mum, Dad and Steve, thank you all for your continued love and support and for always encouraging me to be myself and follow my dreams. Truly I could not have done any of this without you. Alisha, you are the best little sister anybody could ask for. Thank you for always being there for me, even after I told you about my vampire twins story idea when we were kids. I love you to infinity. I know you don't read books but you'd better read this one! Finally, to Star, Magic, Zeus, Xena, Juno, Shadow and Jet – I would be endlessly more productive if I didn't spend accidental hours snuggling you furry monsters and I wouldn't change a thing.

ABOUT THE AUTHOR

FRAN DORRICOTT is a bookseller and author. She studied creative writing at the University of East Anglia, and she received a distinction for her MA in Creative Writing from City University London. Her day job in a bookshop is secretly just a way for her to fuel her ridiculous book-buying addiction. The opportunity to draw inspiration from the many wonderful and wacky customer requests is also a plus.

THE BELOVEDS
MAUREEN LINDLEY

Oh, to be a Beloved—one of those lucky people for whom nothing ever goes wrong. Everything falls into their laps without effort: happiness, beauty, good fortune, allure.

Betty Stash is not a Beloved—but her younger sister, the delightful Gloria, is. She's the one with the golden curls, sunny disposition and captivating smile, the one whose best friend used to be Betty's, the one whose husband *should* have been Betty's. And then, to everyone's surprise, Gloria inherits the family home—a vast, gorgeous pile of ancient stone, imposing timbers, and lush gardens—that was never meant to be hers.

Losing what Betty considers her rightful inheritance is the final indignity. As she single-mindedly pursues her plan to see the estate returned to her in all its glory, her determined and increasingly unhinged behaviour—aided by poisonous mushrooms, talking walls, and a phantom dog—escalates to the point of no return. *The Beloveds* will have you wondering if there's a length to which an envious sister won't go.

"Keeps the tension humming all the way to a deliciously satisfying finale"
Publishers Weekly

TITANBOOKS.COM

A BREATH AFTER DROWNING
ALICE BLANCHARD

Sixteen years ago, Kate Wolfe's young sister Savannah was brutally murdered. Forced to live with the guilt of how her own selfishness put Savannah in harm's way, Kate was at least comforted by the knowledge that the man responsible was behind bars. But when she meets a retired detective who is certain that Kate's sister was only one of many victims of a serial killer, Kate must face the possibility that Savannah's murderer walks free.

Unearthing disturbing family secrets in her search for the truth, Kate becomes sure that she has discovered the depraved mind responsible for so much death. But as she hunts for a killer, a killer is hunting her...

"A spectacular, gripping, psychological thriller
not to be missed"
**Lisa Lutz, *New York Times* bestselling author
of *The Passenger***

IN HER BONES
KATE MORETTI

Fifteen years ago, Lilith Wade was arrested for the brutal murder of six women. After a death row conviction and media frenzy, her thirty-year-old daughter Edie is a recovering alcoholic with a deadend city job, just trying to survive out of the spotlight.

Edie also has a disturbing secret: a growing obsession with the families of Lilith's victims. She's desperate to discover how they've managed—or failed—to move on, and whether they've fared better than her. She's been careful to keep her distance, until the day one of them is found murdered and she quickly becomes the prime suspect. Edie remembers nothing of the night of the death, and must get to the truth before the police—or the real killer—find her.

"The perfect read. Spine-chillingly good"
The Sun* on *The Blackbird Season

For more fantastic fiction, author events, exclusive
excerpts, competitions, limited editions and more

VISIT OUR WEBSITE
titanbooks.com

LIKE US ON FACEBOOK
facebook.com/titanbooks

FOLLOW US ON TWITTER
@TitanBooks

EMAIL US
readerfeedback@titanemail.com